T0367517

THE
TOWER

JOE DELTA

THE TOWER

iUniverse books may be ordered through booksellers or by contacting:

iUniverse
1663 Liberty Drive
Bloomington, IN 47403
www.iuniverse.com
1-800-Authors (1-800-288-4677)

ISBN: 978-1-4917-8536-2 (sc)
ISBN: 978-1-4917-8537-9 (e)

Library of Congress Control Number: 2016900884

Print information available on the last page.

iUniverse rev. date: 03/24/2016

"You have been weighed in the balance and found wanting."

OLD TESTAMENT, Jehovah's fatal judgment
against the king of Babylon.

THE THRONE OF JUDGMENT

Nine year old Corey Brecken stood motionless before his grandfather's easy chair throne of judgment. His towhead was bowed and his eyes were lowered to the Persian carpet covering the floor of the cavernous living room of his stately Victorian grandparents' tropical, yet chilly, Palm Beach estate. Strict and standing grandparental orders decreed that our little boy in a big jam should wait and worry in silence while Grandpa Joe, tsar above tsars and judge above judges, readied himself to pass sentence on his dancing daughter's minuscule problem child.

Our frightened little boy's body was in -- or "on," the islanders insist on saying -- Palm Beach in his grandparents' austere habitation a block from the Atlantic Ocean. But his spirit was sunk down, down, down below the mighty ocean's rolling waves, In sub oceanic limbo he was imprisoned in a world of doubt and fear deeper than the deepest of the cold, black craters at the bottom of an endless, freezing sea.

He was on the carpet and meant to worry and wonder what his fate might be, for, in his elders' eyes he had sinned. Corey waited, his head humbly bowed, while old Grandpa Joe calmly sharpened the headsman's ax.

While their charge fidgeted and stewed Grandpapa Joe and Grandmamma Carlotta dispassionately discussed the crimes of their only living daughter's "little mistake." They ignored his presence and talked the matter over as if he were not there. His respected elders regarded his current behavior as that of a white rat in a mad experiment in socio-genetic engineering, a rat who had failed to perform to optimum. Obviously, it was, in their view, an experiment which had gone catastrophically awry.

"They talk about me like I'm not even here!" Corey thought, burning with resentment, his cheeks red with the shame of being the topic of a conversation he was specifically forbidden to enter.

His forebears' Victorian dictum?

"Children should be seen and not heard."

His grandfather, prosecutor, judge and jury was winding up his dark summation, his preamble to a brat-fry. The old man's repressed anger showed through a mock-complacent mask of cool disinterest:

"Rock Dinker's giving me HAIL COLUMBIA down at The Bath and Tennis Club!" ranted he, "He says this juvenile delinquent of yours beat up his son.

"But he hasn't stopped there. No, it's not just HIS son, he's been practicing his criminal rough-stuff on most of those poor little rich boys at Coconut Row Elementary."

Terrible in his wrath, Corey's all-powerful grandparent paused for a tense moment to reflect upon the senior Dinker's wealth, connections, business and property holdings and inescapable influence on this island escape for the filthy-rich, and the island where the elder Breckens' had chosen to retire.

The terrible highland chief focused his attention on his trembling quarry, this naughty little boy. Grandpa's severe black eye was the eye of an eagle on the hunt. In the triumphant moment of the kill, he swooped down upon his helpless prey:

"Do you recall that day last year when I had occasion to call you down for disobedience, young Corey; and that YOU actually had the crust to say to ME, 'I don't care'?"

"Yes, sir," choked a frightened boy, his apprehension building.

"I told you then what happened to I-Don't-Care, did I not, grandson?"

"Yes, sir," gasped Corey, the thunder of his own heartbeat deafening him.

"And what did happen to him?" demanded his irate grandparent.

"I-Don't-Care went to the gallows, gran' pa."

"That is correct, grandson."

The blood was coursing madly through the youngster's head like a raging hurricane, "Oh, God in heaven, are they really gonna hang me for beatin' up that snotty little Dinker brat 'n' makin' his big-shot old man mad?"

"I cannot deny that this poor little soul is sadly lacking in so many of the good and upright qualities we had hoped to instill in him, Joe," sermonized Corey's grandmamma, with just the proper mix of grandparental concern and self-righteous piety, "I fear this errant boy has surely been weighed in the balance and found wanting."

The old girl paused for half a moment to allow the dramatic effect to kick in, then she emoted for The Academy Award:

"Oh, where have I failed our pretty little charge, Joe?"

"Don't fret, Lottie," grandpa comforted her, "No one could ever say any of this is your doing."

His eagle eye fixed pitilessly upon his towheaded little embarrassment. Aflame with repressed rage, the highland chief's black eyes, burned with his naked desire for this bad little boy's blood. The old man's thin, cruel lips curved upward into a grin of awful resolution, for Grand Judge Joe was now ready to pass sentence at his big brat-fry:

"This boy is one of those delinquents the criminologists of the present day refer to as 'incorrigible.' (In our day we would have said he was a bad seed.)

"Young Corey is obviously a repeat offender who should be locked up in the state reform school with the other rough-cut little scofflaws who've misbehaved similarly.

"Corey is too wild a colt. He cannot be gentled at home as you have tried to do, Lottie. No, this boy must be broken to the whip. But, because he is our sole living daughter's only child, I shall be lenient enough to send him away to military school for discipline. He will not only be broken to the whip but it will be done by war hardened veteran army officers, fresh from The War.

"Oh, yes, my dear Lottie, he is going to military school. There this disagreeable little business will be taken care of for us professionally, dispassionately, thoroughly and without a single scintilla of mercy.

3

"The blessing here is that Corey's rowdiness casts no stain on our family's honor and our good name remains intact."

"Thank your grandfather very humbly for breaking you the respectable way, little Corey," his doting grandmamma instructed her tiny transportation-bound convict.

She was angry with and disappointed in her darling little favorite, and she could not pass up this chance to rub a little salt in his wounds:

"My heavens, Corey, God knows we've given you a good name, a fine home and provided lavishly for you. And I am just at a loss to know why you are so ungrateful to us, your only family."

"This is for your own good, young Corey," smiled Grandpa Joe, winking merrily at his panting kill as he leant forward to pinch the shamefaced kid's freckled cheek, "Military school will make a man of you, grandson dear, so make the best of it."

"Thank you, sir." choked their thoroughly chastened miniature miscreant.

Grandmamma captured the condemned boy, swept him outdoors and deposited him on the big rattan couch on the huge front porch.

"Someday, Bill," she tried to convince him, "You will thank your kindly old grandpa for the lenience he has showered upon your undeserving head this fine day. He has given you a chance to redeem yourself in his eyes, young man -- and that is very important to anyone in this family, young man."

The faintest hint of a silver lining was peeping through the looming thunderhead of denied and repressed grand-maternal passion, for Gra 'ma could not be so terribly mad at him if she called him "Bill." Bill was her pet name for him.

Corey had always been the apple of his pet-loving old Gra' ma's eye, albeit today he knew he could not hope to escape exile. In the Brecken clan disobedient pets were doomed to suffer in the very severest of obedience schools imaginable. The fearful reality of his future unknown trials did frighten him, for those trials must soon be inflicted on his own tender, living flesh by big, strong, scary men. Worse, the punishment was to be visited upon him in an unknown venue, a someplace far from home.

Oh, yes, my dear, little Corey was to be forged into steel and galvanized into manhood at age nine. And this feat must be accomplished in a white hot crucible far from home. He must be beaten, broken and proven miles and miles away from the only home he had ever known.

His loving grandparents had adopted him for being cute. Now they were casting him into the outer darkness for being inconvenient.

The dark abyss, a stark and unknown venue of raw abuse, gaped hungrily before little Corey. He knew the fearful denizens of the academy must be hungry and eager to devour the tender flesh of any and all affluent bad little boys cruel Fate might send their way.

Corey realized from his earthly judges' blather that he was, now and forever, sequestered away from any hope of forgiveness. No, Corey Brecken must sit, silently outside to await his destiny. No piteous array of abject apologies, no legion of demeaning petitions for mercy, no ocean of salt tears from his repentant eyes, no amount of heartfelt of supplications could soften those cold Victorian hearts. Nothing in this world would ever move the highland chief to reverse his stern fiat. Nothing might persuade grandpa to forgive his erring tot. His iron grandparents were bound to pursue their severe perception of duty, for little Corey existed only at sufferance in their austere, thoroughly nineteenth century world.

"Where is MY world," mourned our half-pint hero, deserted and bound for some unspecified house of pain.

Forsaken and alone, a heartbroken little boy did what he could never let his grim judges see him do -- he gave way to his grief.

The tears of this little boy's insufferable pain, attendant upon his protectors' abandonment of him, flowed freely down his red-hot cheeks:

"Why can't I ever say anything?

"They, they 're always scolding me, they, they're ALWAYS talking about me like I'm not, not even there, not, not even a person, not even human, just, just a, a thing!

"Now, now they're kicking me out for, for jus' havin' a little fun at th' playground, jus,' jus' for beatin' up a bunch o' snotty little kids -- that needed it!"

Corey Brecken was painstakingly shut out and rejected by the only people who had ever loved him. His maternal grandparents were the only parents he had ever known or been allowed to know.

It was true that, in their own peculiar way, they loved him, they just didn't love him enough to let him be a rowdy little scamp inclined to make waves for his grand papa at The Almighty Bath And Tennis Club.

But what had brought all this about?

If he had been allowed to defend himself the boy might have explained that he was in trouble for picking on his schoolmates because he had swallowed their whole "strict disciplinarian" package, hook. line and sinker. His youthful exuberance in prosecuting severe discipline on his schoolmates had started the whole mess.

When his saucy classmates had baited him in the schoolyard, he instantly applied his own version of "severe discipline" with a physical and violent vengeance.

He was a sturdy third grader and none of his classmates could match his prowess in the Coconut Row Elementary School playground lists.

Our aggrieved little bully would grip the wrists of all contending offenders who had dared challenge him, swing his hapless, helpless tormentors around and around his head until their balance was a brokenhearted memory.

Then our grade school angel of vengeance dashed them down, Antaeus-like, on the hard and unforgiving earth, but they were not Antaeus and returning to Mother Hera did not revivify them.

To top off their humiliation, Corey pinned them, made them eat sand and galled them with sandspurs. And this he did to redeem the honor of the Brecken Clan from the gibes and insults of haranguing brats.

Now our freckle-faced Captain Blood was marked for transport because he had defended the honor of those he loved.

And now he was cast out by the very family whose honor he defended. He had fought for the old Breckens only to see them turn their oh-so-respectable cold shoulders against him because children were not heard in doughty old Queen Victoria's court. No the influential Rock Dinker's loud and baleful complaints were all that his grandpa had heard, and grandpa's word was law.

A carefree Grandpa Joe flew blithely back up north to D. C. to fleece some more legislative suckers by acting as their jovial panderer so his clients would be able to blackmail them into voting his big-coal-and-natural-gas-robber-baron-bosses' way. It's been an eon or two since Old Joe's heyday, but the Washington lobbyist's slick shell game hasn't changed. His well heeled bosses had already spread black lung disease to workers and miners all over West Virginia and western Pennsylvania.

As long as Old Joe was able to sucker enough senators and "representatives" into voting the bosses' way, that's the way things always were and that's the way they always will be.

Such was the gift of these "respectable gentlemen," the mine owners, to the working poor who struggle doggedly on, paycheck-to-paycheck, beneath their heels, beneath their notice and beneath their contempt to make the owners richer.

Oh, yes, my dear, Grandpa Joe was a real-life All-American success story.

The old boy was especially pleased today to have been able to discharge his grim duty all over his grandson's bowed head.

"Serves him right," reflected the resentful man, "That dirty commie trumpet player's blue-eyed little brat, that spoiled baby our crazy daughter had the gall to pup into the world, that holy terror my crazy Lottie 's so gone on!"

Even better, he was going back to work to escape his demanding, overbearing, always angry wife, "The Mad Carlotta," and that was always a relief.

Grandmamma Carlotta was left alone once again with her precious baby, Bill, and that was just the way she liked it.

Now she would have enough time to sell the little scrapper on the unbelievable, patently outlandish, absolutely ridiculous and impossible proposition that his future life of exile and ceaseless corporal punishment at the calloused hands of tough, hard-muscled reserve officers fresh from the rigors of World War II was to bring him social advancement and be edifying as well. Well, the family didn't call her Hard Sell Lottie for nothing: "Remember Harold Burner and his big, fat wife, Pegeen, Bill?" laughed Gra' ma, delivering one of her "severe discipline" milk-and-cookie treats to her "Bill."

Her apprehensive pet smiled and risked a hug, "No, Gra' ma."

"Oh, Corey," smiled she, snuggling him close to her heart, completely caught up in her sentimental remembrances of things long past, "That dull witted Harold was your dopey little mother's first husband!"

Gra' ma was a great one for whimsical reminiscences, notably those in which she came off as brilliant and everyone else were mindless boobies.

"What a mess that Harold was!" laughed she, "Your ditzy mom, that silly little goose, just had to marry the big dummy 'because he was such a good dancer!'

"That was all that mattered to her at the moment, and the moment was all that mattered to my flighty little modern, Glencora.

"Oh, but she had such pretty, curly auburn hair, Bill! I just HAD to love her!

"Well, poor old Grandpa had to take her intended in hand and prepare the dull-witted ape for business. Harold wanted to be an accountant, Bill, my love, but the big dope kept failing the c. p. a. exams.

"Grandpa finally ended up sending him to Georgetown to learn his trade and THEN he failed three or four more times before he finally clicked. Wouldn't you just know it?

"Well, our dancing daughter fell out of love with the big, dumb brute as fast as she'd fallen in when he had no more time for dancing because grandpa was keeping him busy making a living in the real world. Harold The Dancing Bear could no longer chase around night clubbing the way Glencora wanted to. You know her, Bill!"

But Corey didn't know his mother. The elders were careful to keep their wild child playgirl as far away from her infant son as they were able, and the affluent are always able.

They had money and they used it to bribe both his mother and Frank (her trumpet-playing second husband, Corey's father) to stay just as far away from Palm Beach, Carlotta and Corey as they could manage to take themselves on the considerable bribe money provided by the old folks. The elders had always found bribery to be a phenomenally effective tool for keeping poor relations out of their aristocratic hair.

Gra' ma warmed to her subject:

"Your flighty mamma always had a legion of no good lounge lizards and playboys loafing around her apartment. Those dregs were always willing to escort her around to the nightclubs, and she would go!

"Our dancing daughter tripped the light fantastic right straight down The Primrose Path with those shiftless modernists until even that dopey Harold caught on to her! The institution of marriage means nothing to these fast and loose modern types, they, they're just nothing but hoodlums and ner' do wells, my Bill!

"Well, grandpa came to come to her rescue again and got her a fast divorce.

"Between you and me, I thank God you're not Harold Burner's child, old Bill!

"It's bad enough to be the progeny of a two-bit-commie-trumpet-player, but at least Frank's not stupid like Harold!

"I guess it's just lucky you came along when our little chippie had the bad judgment to get in with a lousy commie!"

The Mad Carlotta had assiduously held private love-hate seminars for her pet grandson ever since Corey had been a babe in arms. She would gather her Bill up on her knee, ply him with sweet treats and instruct him as to the only one he must love, and the others he must hate.

Her treatise was simplicity itself:

Everyone other than grandma and Corey was either is a thief and plotter with designs on the family fortune, or an idiot to be exploited. Only grandma was to be trusted, so only grandma must be loved.

In her bedside parables from his babyhood his mother, her friends, her husbands, poorer relations and every stranger in existence were invariably depicted as villains and halfwits who were up to no good.

Only Gra' ma was good, only Gra' ma was wise, noble, kind and just. Obviously, only Gra' ma was worthy of her beloved little Bill's love and admiration for the simple reason that all others were fools, connivers or boobies, unfit barbarians poised somewhere in the darkness of the cold outside to invade and rob Corey and Gra'ma.

"Your parents, my silly little trollop of a daughter and her scheming commie trumpet player gigolo, are unfit parents, Bill. You should thank your lucky stars that grandpa and I loved you enough to adopt you and bring you into our own home.

"Why, those two little nothings would probably have raised you in the slums!

"Your father came from the slums of Pittsburgh and they'd probably have dragged y' right back there to suffer with them in abject poverty.

"Yes, you came from two downright bad apples, Bill. It'll be a tough go for me t' turn you into a real Brecken, but you're a pretty baby and I love you. I mean to work hard and subject you to severe discipline. Only by being hard on you will I be able to turn you into a fine young gentleman, one the whole world 'll look up to and admire."

The old basket case really did love him in her twisted, self interested way. She usually "disciplined him severely" with milk and cookies rather than drills and blows. In general Corey was spoiled rotten and had it made. But there were lessons he must learn as well. The hardest of those was that when The Mad Carlotta actually was angry with him her punishing hand was heavy, swift and merciless.

Now demand the impossible of Bill, Hard Sell Lottie. It's what you do:

"Now, don't breathe a word of what I've told you to Harold and his Pegeen when they get here for God's sake, Bill!

"Those two 're coming up to visit for a week, Grandpa's orders!

"At the end of that week, they will take you up north to The Tower Military Academy in the Great Smoky Mountains of Tennessee.

"Your generous grandpapa is sending you to the finest military academy in the United States and, therefore, in all the world. You have every reason to be thankful to him, Bill, and you must be more than proud of your new school. It has the most brilliant reputation for boosting a schoolboy's discipline and grade-point average imaginable!

"Oh, how happy and grateful you must be to us for giving you this golden opportunity to redeem yourself, young man!"

At last the old girl came back down from the stratosphere of her Hard Sell Lottie propaganda to see that back here on earth to look down and actually see its effect on her little boy. Back on earth she noted the expression of naked terror in her grandson's teary eyes.

The old girl was quick to cuddle her difficult darling close to her bosom and smile, "Come on, Bill, laugh and the world laughs with you! ... Sure, it'll be strange at first, but it'll all come out just fine in the wash, I promise!"

Corey smiled hesitantly and hugged her back. Hers was the only love he had ever known in his life, and he was inured to and in need of it.

The old folks' doormat/c. p. a., his mammoth second wife and their annoying, smelly little wirehaired terrier arrived the next day.

Predictably, both of Grandpa Joe's employees were cringing toadies. The edgy couple, nervous in the boss's shadow, were eternally babbling about what a great honor their Big Boss Joe was showering on them in inviting them to his posh Palm Beach estate. They waxed poetic about what a signal privilege it was for them to be escorting the boss's precious little grandson into his military school exile.

The august lady of the house placed them in the master bedroom, Old Man Joe's sanctum sanctorum during his infrequent sojourns to Palm Beach.

"If this aint livin,' what is?" cooed the gratified couple with charmingly bumptious innocence.

They felt amply rewarded in their master's raja yoga for the tedious work boon he demanded, that they spirit the his little embarrassment away to a far off mountain fastness to be relentlessly disciplined.

For a while the guests were treated to dinners at The Colony, canasta and cocktails, and everything was going smoothly. But too soon the honeymoon came to an abrupt end. The explosion occurred when the naive Harold was impolitic enough to get too relaxed:

"So-ho, young Corey," blurted out the notorious booby, "You were too wild and wooly to be gentled and they're sending you to military school to be broken to the whip, eh?"

Poor Corey felt like a subhuman "thing" all over again.

A heavy anchor of deep shame sank him to the bottom of that same cold, black sea of melancholia in which he drowned before grandpa's terrible throne of judgment.

Gra' ma's boy hung his head and made the only reply he could, "Yes, sir."

Down, down, down from the topmost peak of Olympus screamed a kill-bent mother eagle, set to evict this brash intruder from her nest, to tear him apart and cast the threat down from her endangered nestling. Corey's aroused Gra' ma circled celeritously downward from her dizzying aristocratic stratosphere to grip the offending churl in her iron talons. The Mad Carlotta loved both her own toy tyke and her rigid class distinctions, and loved them to distraction.

"You have forgotten yourself, sir!!!" Gra' ma gutted Harold with a blinding lightning bolt from her cold, grey eyes, "That boy is a Brecken, Mister Burner, and you will do yourself a distinct service to remember who and what in this hard, cruel world you are. Who, pray tell, are you to mock my poor little grandson in his present fallen state?"

"Well, gee, I don' know, Lot," struggled her pinioned victim, pale beneath the baleful stare of a willful old woman who had the power to have him fired on the spot, "But, that, that's just what Boss Joe told me, an' I, I'm real s-sorry if I said th' wrong thing -"

"You, Mister Burner, will do yourself a great favor in addressing me as Missus Brecken for the duration of your visit with us! That will doubtless remind you not to ridicule a poor, heartbroken little child, a child whom it is my duty to nurture, to perfect from the bad jokes of any such a brainless, unfeeling, unthinking boor as yourself!

"This is both a pivotal and an extremely painful juncture in my poor little fellow's development.

"That our Corey must learn a hard lesson at a military academy dedicated to the very harshest of discipline has been established. A road to that end has been mapped out and explained to him by his devoted grandparents. That is enough of a cross for him to have to bear without being subjected to the your scorn, your uncouth ruffian's groans from the gallery and your disrespect toward a member of my family.

"Now, for that very reason, you shall apologize instanter for your gross offence. You will beg both our pardons and apologize most humbly, before you ever dare to address me with such a familiar sobriquet as 'Lot' from this moment until such an apology is delivered.

"My Christian name is Carlotta, it is not Lot, Mister Burner. But that does not concern you because I must now insist that you address me in no such familiar terms:

"I am Missus Brecken to you until I have forgiven your insufferable insult to my poor, defenseless little boy. And let me assure you, my fine sir, you shall apologize to us very humbly before you are forgiven!"

"Yes, ma'am," gasped her terrified subaltern, scared to death and at the point of tears, "I am really very, very sorry for my bad judgment, Missus and Master Brecken. I, I guess I j-just got carried away and forgot myself because of our v-very informal and pleasant visit here.

"Do please forgive me, y-young master and, and, and ma-madam."

Harold could not see the humor in his apology, but Gra'ma and Corey were enjoying it to such a degree that they were barely able to suppress a smile.

"Very well, Harold," the grand dame in the driver's seat smiled a thin lipped smile of triumphant condescension, "But in my first letter to Corey I am going to ask him how you two used him on the way up to the academy, and I do not want to hear about any more fun that you've had at his expense."

"Yes, ma'am," whimpered her whipped dog accountant.

All of the adults involved here were hardboiled business types who knew just how hard and cruel is the world we live in for the simple reason that that is the way the bosses have made it.

The Burners agreed wholeheartedly with their boss that there was a modicum of wry black humor in packing willful Lottie's spoiled brat off to an out of state military school to be pushed around, bossed and whipped by spit-and-polish thugs.

Even so, had they known what a vortex of extreme abuse the condemned boy was heading into they should have realized this was no laughing matter. They must obey the all-powerful Joe because abject obsequiousness sure beats an unemployment line.

They knew only that they were taking a bad little boy away from home to be corrected, but they had no way of knowing what sort of web of temptation, unbridled passion, black intrigue and savagery to which they were escorting him.

Corey was headed into a vortex of pleasure, pain, madness and chaos at "the finest military school in the United States, and therefore in all the world." Had they but known his granddad's minions would have found no occasion for jocundity in their chore.

Little Corey Brecken was bound for transportation into the cold, dark night of The Tower Military Academy, and that would turn out to be a shameful thing.

ALONE AND AT THE
MERCY OF STRANGERS

Victorian "Morality" had crept like a virus into every corner of the English speaking world, mega-phonically projected, touted and imposed on all its nations by the incessant trumpeting of the brazen British press propaganda machine of the nineteenth century. Its hidebound dogma and unforgiving priggishness infected the denizens of that devious age with the diseases of widespread toadying and insincerity.

Said denizens quickly gave birth to a second generation of sneaks and phonies, the sons and daughters of the Victorian Age. And these, the spawn of an epoch of falsehood and hypocrisy, grew into some of the most hellish, two faced sadists and pederasts ever to wound and break the hearts of humanity, children first, of course. Through the tear-stained eyes of one harried little nine-to-ten-year old, we will have the privilege of becoming closely acquainted with some of these same amoral and unrepentant criminals and predators.

On the appointed day and at the appointed hour Corey and the Burners said goodbye to Gra' ma and Palm Beach and Harold's old, reliable station wagon ventured northward into the Old South.

Once the travelers were out of Florida, little Corey was delighted to find himself surrounded by the enchanting Joel Chandler Harris's UNCLE REMUS idyll of The Brers Rabbit, Fox and Bear.

Our edgy for various reasons interstate motorists drove through seemingly endless cotton fields, stretching away and away and away into the distance for miles and miles. They trekked ever northward through those vast stretches of real estate on which corn and cotton were being picked by colorful and humble negro sharecroppers and field hands tricked out in multicolored bandanas and huge straw hats (the year was 1948).

To further delight our reviving boy's virgin eyes, there were numerous intact antebellum "ole masah's" plantation mansions. Albeit many of these majestic structures was sadly run-down and in immediate need of the paint and plaster plastic surgery which never came.

There were many quaint little towns along the way where the travelers stopped to eat and rest. Every one of these tiny burgs came equipped with its own modest town square, replete with a stone statue of one General Jubilation T. Cornpone defender of The Confederacy or another.

The only difference between these colorful Deep South scenes and a GONE WITH THE WIND Hollywood film set was that these 20th Century Johnny Reb communities came equipped with both electric lighting and at least one local movie theatre -- sometimes even two!

This simple, rustic ambience was just what our boy needed to bring him out of his tropical funk.

All of these wonderful to a nine year old boy's eyes sights, coupled with the first hints of the life-giving cooler and drier air wending down from the Great Smoky Mountains, jogged young Sir Corey's romantic imagination and buoyed up his flagging spirits, even in the face of his imminent adversity.

"Maybe this isn't gonna be so bad after all?" hoped our revivified young scamp, for the renewed hope that something fresh and different was about to come into his life had awakened in his high young heart.

Something wonderful, life's dearest treasure will be yours, Corey, but it will be followed by an avalanche of unimaginably unspeakable cruelty.

"It will be just the thing for you, my boy," harmonized the Old Joe party line spouting Burners, "This is bound to make a man of you, little Corey!"

The subject of how such a tadpole was going to be magically transformed into a grown man between the ages of nine and ten simply by means of military school enrollment, regular class attendance and frequent beatings had never come up for discussion.

Our wayfarers motored ever northward through and out of the seemingly endless, steaming and unhealthy Florida swamps.

At length they emerged into the bracing, pre-global-warming climate of the Great Smoky Mountains, a place which was destined to be Cadet Corey's new home.

The blessing of cooler, drier air brought with them the heady ether of high adventure for him. Adventure was a flower that had from infancy always found fertile ground in this youngster's romantic imagination -- and adventure was to be his.

Up and down and all around those high mountain roads chugged the Burners' old reliable station wagon. Over the topsy-turvy highland terrain, and through the spectacularly flamboyant foliage of an ineffably beautiful Smoky Mountains Fall they ascended.

Harold and his heavily upholstered lady wife were as much fun as they were able to be, hobbled as they were by the lowering specter of The Mad Carlotta and the extreme discomfort they felt as to the contents of young Cadet Corey's first letter home. They had reason to hate and fear every Brecken, for they quailed and quaked beneath the terrible Old Joe's and the fickle Mad Carlotta's whims of iron.

The poor old Burners must be syrupy-sweet to their Big Boss's brat's-idea-of-a-brat. A bad report might wing its way back and sour the hard cases who directed their lives to turn Joe and Lottie against them. Due to that vital consideration the Burners were quite gooey in the boss brat's presence.

Our travelers three reached their goal when they drove into the not-so-thriving little community of Honeysuckle, Tennessee. It was here that The Tower Military Academy stood ominously a scant mile from the center of town.

It was a little past suppertime, so Harold treated his crew to a fine dinner at the burg's most presumptuous eatery. That modest bistro was, of course, located directly across the town square from the municipality's very own statue of that very popular and heroic savior of the ante bellum status quo, General Jubilation T. Cornpone.

Darkness was overtaking the three wayfarers by the time they pulled up abreast of the academy's far-flung campus grounds.

Corey was barely able to make out the disposition of the academy's far flung topography. But our curious schoolboy strained his sharp young eyes so to do:

The highway they traveled was colorfully lined with old Tennessee Williams stories' live oaks covered with ghostly hoar moss.

There was no tower here, only three low, two-to-four storied barracks buildings. These comprised the academy's junior school campus. All of those barracks had been laid out close to that part of The Tower's rangy property which bordered the highway.

To spark a young boy's romantic notions, obsolete field pieces were proudly displayed at several points along the campus's streets.

The sound of distant bugles and the sight of smartly uniformed little boy cadets of Corey's age hurrying off to "afternoon school" whetted our young romantic's voracious appetite for exploration and an invigorating plunge into a treasure trove of high adventure which promised to be found here.

"That's for me!" Corey exclaimed.

The Boy Who Must Morph Into A Prefabricated Man Any Instant Now was daydreaming, right on cue, of his future brilliant army career.

A huge reception hall into which the travelers were escorted on their arrival there was located in MacAdam Hall, The Tower Military Academy junior school's central headquarters which also housed the academy's premier cadet barracks. The spacious and impressive reception hall shone resplendently in all its alabaster glory to dazzle the weary, wide eyed pilgrims as they were admitted.

Three two-legged travelers (and their smelly little four-legged friend) were shown directly into a gleaming reception structure by a resplendently festooned seven-foot-tall cadet captain. This lanky lad wore a shako which was topped by a high plume, accoutrements which made him appear even taller than he actually was.

All six of the visitors' eyes went saucer-wide with admiration at the barbaric splendor of the gigantic kid's regalia. Little Corey gaped covetously at the tall boy's kit. Our boy couldn't wait to get his own dress uniform -- which he imagined must include the shining officer's high-plumed shako and long, immaculately burnished cavalry saber like those of the imposing young cadet captain.

The towering Pentagon poster boy took particular care to icily ignore the star-struck runt longing so enviously to be kitted out in exactly the same proud regalia. Instead of acknowledging the sprat's admiration, he quietly and politely requested that the newcomers be seated in any of the several deep, soft, burnished leather sofas dotting the radiant anteroom.

Here they must wait while he fetched the housemother of McAdam Hall to officially welcome them to the academy.

The travelers waited and soon a diminutive, white-haired-professional-old-school-society-dowager, right down to her long, black satin gown, high-ruffled collar which sported a cameo, of course, appeared at the top of a high spiral staircase above them. Again, of course, she wore the inevitable gold framed spectacles-on-a-fine-gold-chain.

As the white haired grand dame glided languidly down the stairway she made the most of her excessively theatrical entrance. She swept gracefully down the highly polished stairway into the anteroom. This personage was the very picture of a modern Clytemnestra, as she wafted majestically into the lives of these recently arrived insignificant mortals she obviously deemed unworthy of notice.

"Welcome to The Tower Military Academy, Mister and Missus Burner," drawled she, "And my special valediction to our brave new little Cadet Brecken!

"May I offer you the very warmest of greetings, my dears?

19

"I must do so both on my own behalf and that of our junior school commandant, Major Donnybrook. It is with some regret that I am constrained to inform you that the major is sadly unable to be present this evening to welcome you in person. I assure you that it was his fondest wish so to do; but, unfortunately, the major is occupied with serious family business at present.

Do be assured, my dears, that only the most pressing of family business could keep our headmaster from us this evening. It must be said of our esteemed commandant that he is a tirelessly devoted family man. Family is ever his first consideration, and, otherwise, he would have been delighted to greet all of you, our honored guests, to the academy; and to welcome our latest novitiate into our proud junior school cadet corps with as much pride and heartfelt pleasure as do I. Ah, yes, the commander would have loved to welcome our precious new cadet into the school's ranks but, sadly, it was not to be. However, I dare say Cadet Brecken will meet his commander soon enough.

"I am Miss Crop, the house mother of Mc- Adam Hall, and it is my privilege to bid you welcome to the academy and to express my sincerest concern for the comfort and wellbeing of you all."

"My thanks, Miss Crop, we are all quite well," replied the easily overwhelmed Harold, trying and failing to keep up with the old girl's honey-dripping, aristocratic front, "We would just love to have met the major, ma'am; but unfortunately we are called back to Palm Beach on business:

"We must return there without delay to make our report to the boy's grandparents."

"By all means, dear sir," condescended the lofty matron, "Business before pleasure, to be sure."

Harold gripped Corey's little shoulders nervously and Old-Joe-party-lined him in farewell:

"Goodbye, Corey-boy.

"Uh, be a man! ... This is the very best thing for you, so, so try to learn from this new experience, young man!"

"Goodbye, sir, and thank you for bringing me -" Corey began, but the effusive Pegeen turned on the water works and clutched the boy to her mile-high-fathom-deep-bosom. The new cadet disappeared into a mountain of flaccid flesh, where he nearly smothered.

"Thank you, ma'am, and, and goodbye," the suffocating brat managed to gasp.

Then a little boy's traveling companions were gone, his home was gone, his Gra' ma, her "severe discipline," her sweet treats and her nighttime stories, all these things were gone now. All of the things and all of the people that had made up his life and his home were now to be but fleeting visions of the past. Everything the little boy had ever known was vanished from the face of the earth, and he instantly realized he was all alone now.

As if by some black sorcery all of the familiar things and persons The Tower's newest cadet had ever known in his life were no more.

A new reality decreed that, frightened, small and vulnerable, Corey Brecken stood so lowly, so alone at the mercy of complete strangers in this cool, formal, miles from home, terrifying place, this strange and forbidding locus.

Miss Crop dropped her genteel antebellum dowager act the split second she saw that Corey's traveling companions were out of earshot. Immediately, the false mask of beneficence was gone. Celeritously the homey old welcoming spinster replaced the false face with the true. Sadly for the new boy, hers was the harsh and penetrating glare of a relentless bird of prey. The old woman drew her thin, cruel lips tersely up into the contemptuous sneer of rejection which truly expressed her feelings (or lack of any such an affected luxury) for this miniscule annoyance, this tidbit of vulnerable flesh thrown to her merciless thrall by his fed-up forebears.

Miss Crop regarded this and every new "goober" destined to be meticulously mangled in the unfeeling gears of The Tower's ever-churning meat grinder with undisguised malice.

"Cadet Beasterling is the senior boy in command of your barrack-room here at McAdam, BRECKEN. He has complete charge of you. You will obey his every command, or else, insignificant wretch that you are!" this suddenly fierce hag snarled sharply at her long-faced, sad-eyed little quarry.

Then evoking an even fiercer voice which was thrice as commanding as the one with which she had just frozen little Corey to the very marrow of his bones, to bawl:

"Beasterling!!!"

"Yes, 'm!" came a distant answer somewhere in the dark upstairs.

"Come down here to me at once, you lazy cur!" spat the erstwhile ersatz welcoming gentlewoman, "You know my name is the very same as the instrument of discipline I choose to use on you shiftless dogs, you idle hound!

"If you don't want a good thrashing from my riding crop you'd better jump to it and bring your worthless hide down here!"

"Y-yes, 'm, at, at yore service, ma 'am!" shouted a lanky boy just coming into view, his long legs racing downstairs for dear life.

Beasterling was just as tall as the brilliantly festooned cadet captain who had greeted the travelers earlier, but this current daddy longlegs was modestly attired in regulation junior school cobalt-blue fatigue uniform.

Both of Corey's heartwarming new companions regarded the junior academy's most junior cadet with a most baleful stare of pronounced revulsion.

"Cadet Brecken," Miss Crop glared at her newly arrived, thoroughly despised new little piece of meat, "this is the senior cadet in charge of your barracks. His name is Cadet Beasterling:

"You will follow all of Cadet Beasterling's instructions to the letter, you bad little boy, for, should you fail so to do he will punish you; and may God have mercy on your soul, BRECKEN, for Beasterling will have none on your body:

"You and every inch of your disgusting little, cutie-pie body are our property now, boy!" hissed that heartless old sham spitefully, "Your loving grandparents have sent us your sweet, darling little body to dance a lively measure to our marshal tunes. If it is slow to perform it will suffer some terribly heavy and extremely painful consequences!

"Cadet Beasterling, this benighted little creature is yours from now on:

"You are to teach it the terrible consequences of being such a bad little whelp that it had to be sent to us. Make it clear that its being so bad is what has delivered it up to us. Teach it that it is now to feel the pain we shall inflict upon it to correct its wicked ways at our extreme little obedience school.

"Issue it its linen, teach it a proper respect for its betters, and make sure that it learns a right reverent respect for our tight bed policy here at McAdam Hall, senior boy,

"McAdam must set a high standard for both the lesser halls."

"Yes, 'm," the tall boy acknowledged his taskmistress's instruction.

Then the tall boy turned to Corey to sneer:

"Come on wif me, y' dumb li' l' goob!"

Corey made the mistake of pausing just long enough to thank his new housemother politely:

"Thank you for your courtesy, and good night, Miss Crop," he ventured timidly as he followed the big boy up that darkened stairway to he knew not where or what. He was burdened with considerable discomfort and apprehension.

"Good night, you insignificant cur," hissed a matronly dowager turned rusty iron maiden, staring daggers through and through the open heart of this latest little annoyance.

"She aint studyin' you, y' dumb li' l' goob!" was Cadet Beasterling's stern admonition as he gave the novice a rough shove toward the stairway, "Now git yore honkers up them stairs 'fore y' aggravate 'er 'n' she puts 'er ridin' crop whar you aint a-gonna want it!"

"Yes, sir!" his junior responded respectfully.

" 'N' don' chew never try t' taffy me up like that neither, Brecken!

"You are one dumb li' l' goober, boy.

"Why, I bet chew don't even know whut a goober is, do y'?"

"I think it's a peanut, isn't it, sir?"

" 'I' think it's a peanut, huh?" the big boy propelled the small one toward the linen closet with another hard jab, "Well, hyar's yore first lesson in army talk, son:

"You aint no 'I' no more, you are 'the cadet'!

"Th' cadet thinks this, th' cadet says that. Get it?

"You aint 'I' no more, Brecken, you are th' cadet, 'n' that's th' onliest way yore gonna refer t' yourself frum here on out!"

"Yes, sir!" the new goober regurgitated, "From now on the cadet is not 'I' nor 'me' ... From now on the cadet is the cadet; and the cadet thanks the senior cadet for settin' th' cadet straight, sir!"

"Din' I jus,' gawdamn it, tell you not t' try t' taffy me up, dumb goober Brecken?" bawled the big boy petulantly, "You better damn well start payin' attention, son!

"I know when you simple li' l' rookie saps 're tryin' t' green me, so YOU better jus' watch it!"

Corey thought it wise to change the subject before Beastrling got worked up enough to punch him:

"But, sir, isn't a goober a peanut?"

"'Tha' 's jus' one thing 'goober' means, y' dope!" the lanky bully smirked, puffed up at being smart enough to know the goober secret, "But here at Th' Tower a goober is a junior school cadet, or any po' li' l' s. o. b. who's dumb enough 'n' green enough t' be junior t' ever-body else -- an,' rookie, that's you!

"You shore got a lot t' larn aroun' hyah, Ka-det Brecken!!!"

"Yes, sir," said the junior boy, remembering Gra' ma's strict orders to fit into his new surroundings, always to defer to anyone in authority and never to cause trouble.

The old boy issued the newcomer his linens, and Corey followed him up into the darkness of the barrack room. The room was dimmed and all the little cadets here were meant to be asleep when Beasterling poked Corey over to his bunk to spread it up:

"Now, you jus' watch 'n' I'll show y' how t' make a bed up nice 'n' tight, li' l' bo," instructed the head boy, "Now, I'm only gonna show y' how t' do this onct.

"If I order y' t' do it up again tomorrah 'n' ye git it wrong I'm a-gonna punish you bah givin' y' a bunch o' de-merits!"

"Oh, that's okay, sir," smiled Corey confidently, "M' Gra' ma already showed me how t' make a bed up properly (with th' military hospital corners 'n' all).

"She makes me make m' own bed down there, so I know how."

There was a ripple of muffled mirth all around the two. But the giggles were not muted enough to suit Cadet Beasterling as they tittered softly all around our hospital corner protagonists.

The terrible bull of the woods thundered, "Do I hyah a bunch o' dumb bunnies who want 'o be standin' off a million de-merits in study hall instead o' goin' to town this Saturday?

"All o' you gawdamn dummies dern well better git shut up, stay shut up, 'n' git th' hell t' sleep right gawdamn it now!

"Reveille comes early aroun' here, ka-dets, 'n' you better damn well be bah them blamed racks 'n' at attention at 'o' six hun' ed hours when it blows, or else!"

The silence which followed these pungent remarks -- commentary which Corey did not understand at all -- was immediate and complete.

"An' you better KEEP shut up, too!" added the big noise, "I mean business!"

Beasterling turned once again to his littlest cadet, "Okay, short-round, since yore so hot t' trot, le' s see yore stuff."

The short-round did know his stuff in the tight rack department. Corey made short work of tucking his bunk up smartly.

"Well, well, if that don' beat all!" approved the barracks room bossy boots in deceptively friendly tones, "That job aint half bad, ka-det; 'n' you-all might jus' make a fair-t'-middlin' li' l' ol' goober 'round hyar after all, son -"

Then he tore the sheets off the bed furiously and threw them violently right into little mister fair-to-middlin' 's astonished baby face.

"Now y' can just do it all over again!

"Then git yore dumb rookie ass to bed, ka-det wise-ass!!!"

There was a second ripple of suppressed laughter from the "sleeping" boys around them in the darkness as Corey obeyed.

The bull of the woods let this one go.

He was tired too and they all had to get some sleep if they were to face the reveille call, and they must.

Grandiose grandmamma had given her husband's little embarrassment his thoroughly impossible instructions for his good conduct in exile:

"You must be friendly toward all of your schoolmates; you must obey to all those in authority at the academy; and you must be clever enough to impress your new officers and masters."

This was to be the proof of young Corey's good behavior and he knew the old girl was adamant. All of those specifications he must meet before he might ever hope to come home.

But Corey was apprehensive. He was at a loss to know how to proceed within demanding regimen of this strange new home.

Having no other road maps or guideposts at hand he must somehow pick up his cues from the other boys. Everything here was foreign to him and his troubled mind could never find peace. There was no way of knowing what might happen next in this frightening Tower.

Little Corey was all alone and at the mercy of strangers totally disinclined toward mercy, and no one knew it better than he.

But for now he was far too road-weary not to fall instantly asleep no matter what his worries might be.

Reveille blew promptly at six to fulfill the yard bull's prophecy.

Grandmamma had given her bullying little rakehell explicit instructions to avoid his beloved and eternal fights which had ultimately sent him into this unsettling exile from her signature hot-and-cold-running affections.

Here in this Spartan venue, he must atone for his past sins of bullying his schoolmates by the strict avoidance of those, his favorite sins. He must obey authority to the letter and get along with all of his fellow cadets. Most difficult of all, he must not throw them down, sit on them and pour sand in their faces as had been his wont at home.

If her pet Cub Tartar ever hoped to return to the iffy affections of his Iron Patroness he must follow those instructions verbatim.

This was his chance. He was determined to take it and run with it and, to that end, he interacted docilely with all his fellows. Corey was even friendly toward the overbearing charge cadet who had the power to punish him and all of the rest of his barrack room brothers. That was a challenging task indeed for our scrappy born brawler.

The McAdam Hall cadets were comprised of a heterogeneous medley of divergent characters:

The barracks room comedian was engaging and humorous. To his sorrow he was forever joking within earshot of either Miss Crop or Cadet Beasterling. As an immediate consequence of his error of poor timing he was frequently marched off to the major's office where he abandoned comedy to howl a tragic aria at the business end of his esteemed commandant's winnowing razor strop.

A majority of the boys were yes men willing to play the military school game by its own strange rules. They knew they had been bad, were sent here to pay for it, and were resigned to comply with all the academy's rules and commands. By so doing they aspired to be allowed to come home one day.

These little soldiers were the obedient and compliant flock of sheep their old folks had instructed them to be. And, of course, this was the group to which our half-pint hero's Tyrant Gra' ma had commanded her wayward offspring to attach himself.

There were malcontents in residence here as well. Said soreheads were forever complaining about anything and everything connected with the academy.

The resident bad boys' role model was "The Demerit Queen," Cadet Peebles by name. Peebles was the idol of all junior school rebels, an incorrigible runaway. He ran away habitually, and with surprising frequency, only to be brought back to the academy by the highway patrol or the local Honeysuckle police. Each time he was returned the runaway was beaten black and blue by the commandant.

Afterwards he was condemned to walk the bull pen. (The bull pen is a small, cement piece of real estate right outside the junior school commandant's office.)

Peebles, and all recaptured runaways, and they were always recaptured, were condemned to walk endlessly around and around the bull pen at attention all day long wearing a pack and carrying a parade field toy rifle. The only breaks in this colossally wasteful of time and effort routine were classroom attendance, meals and repose after taps.

Then there were the know-it-alls. Everyone has had the misfortune of encountering more than his fair share of know-it-alls in life. They are the boys who know everything and anything right up until the pesky facts invariably emerge and disprove their fallacious hypotheses. The less said of the know-it-alls the better, and the less attention one pays them in life the better off he will be. Little Corey Brecken was stupid enough to be exiled to The Tower, but he'd never been so stupid as to congregate with the know-it-alls.

Under stern and particular grandparental orders to befriend every single person in every single one of these wildly divergent cliques, Corey was constrained to comply. He was specifically forbidden to join a gang, by order of the supreme order giver of the universe. But our half-pint hero must grin, hold his nose, stick out his mitt and do his duty for Gra' ma and country in the camaraderie department -- and he did.

The bugle ordered everyone up and out at precisely 0600 the very next morning, just as the boss cadet of the barracks had promised. And it did so without fail each and every morning for the duration of Corey's military school life.

He arose to meet and interact -- albeit docilely -- with all his fellow "goobers" he was under orders to befriend.

Military school cadets do everything together and in smart close order drill formation. Bathing, brushing teeth, combing hair, going to chow, attending morning formation, close-order drill and classes were all done together, uniformly and to an interestingly distinct variety of bugle calls.

From dawn to dark, The Tower's junior school cadets did it all simultaneously, and with a smart martial air -- lest the major's razor strop await them. This drill team ballet was choreographed entirely, and eternally, by the bugle's clarion call to action, regimentation, order and uniformity.

After dusk the bugle called all sub-standard pupils enrolled at the school to "afternoon school." (Afternoon school was actually a misnomer because that assiduously tutored, scrupulously disciplined equivalent of a civilian "study hall" is conducted in the early evening hours and not in the afternoon.)

Misnomer notwithstanding, the application of that heaven-sent, assiduous tutoring proved miraculously effective in the case of one Cadet Brecken. Our boy's former scholarly weed patch, blossomed and unfurled into glorious bloom under the academy duty officers' instruction.

Soon our eager little cadet's grade-point-average skyrocketed out of the garbage dump and into academic excellence.

BENEATH THE AEGIS

Corey Brecken conformed to all of the drills, rules and regulations of this strange new pied á terre, but with one unacceptable exception:

He refused to eat.

He did not attend the junior school's voluminous and icily formal dining hall. He had deferred ever since the night of his arrival.

It was not a hunger strike per se, only an all-compelling longing for what had been and was no more, a hopeless yearning for his lost hearth and home. His cold and difficult exile weighed heavily on him and he was beginning to see this barren, inescapable desert stretching endlessly away before him as unendurable. The Tower Military Academy was certainly no place for this brokenhearted little transport. Only after he had begun this foolish fast did Corey realize that, if his health failed due to a lack of sustenance, he might well be sent home to heal.

Now, with that goal in his stubborn little head, our own little jackass was ready to stick to his guns at all costs.

He was beginning to feel the ill effects of his ruinous choice. He often had to run to the bath to cough up the green, bitter, disgusting mouthfuls of bile attendant upon his foolish choice.

Now he had begun to feel his native strength, his youthful resilience, at first slowly, then more and more rapidly, draining from his failing young body.

He was too honest to fake an illness and too proud to complain, but he was determined to see his bad decision through.

He was certain that soon his condition would worsen, for Nature was already revenging herself upon his stubborn recalcitrance. She must soon fell him.

However long it took, whatever he must suffer to attain his goal, even his frostbitten grandparents must ultimately be driven to relent. After all he had gone through to get back home, even they must be persuaded to forgive their prodigal and welcome him back to their chilly subtropical mansion.

It was a long shot, but Corey was determined; and his painful path toward collapse and resurrection proved as bitter as the insufferable bile which daily burnt up his stomach lining and must be regularly regurgitated.

Major Donnybrook's plan A:
Operation gentle the skittish little colt.

A response from The Tower's rigid military power structure was forthcoming on the bright afternoon of the fourth day of Cadet Brecken's foolhardy fast.

The premier hard truth of our unforgiving and scrupulously demanding animal natures is that a growing boy desperately needs sustenance to thrive and survive. But here one little cadet was depriving himself of food and suffering as a consequence. An expeditious intervention must be prosecuted at once for the good of the cadet in question, the academy and its headmaster. An even harder fact of life at a military academy was that the junior school's Top Brass had been informed of this little hardhead's recalcitrance and was advancing upon his position post haste.

In The Tower's venue The Brass's action was to be immediate, swift and decisive:

"ATTENTION!!!!" was called in the barrack room this bright afternoon, for attention to our half-pint hero's problem had blown airily into the barracks with the force and speed of a cyclone. Tremble and obey, all ye guilty little cadets on hunger strikes, for attention was called and attention to Corey's problem was here in the terrifying form of his Headmaster Almighty:

"ATTENTION!!!!"

The call alerted every cadet in McAdam Hall to the descent of the king of the gods from his high mountain into their humble presence. Every boy there present snapped to and stood tall before his rack like good little toy soldiers.

The all powerful, wise and wonderful commandant swept into their lives like a hurricane, attended by two miniscule cherubs in civilian dress.

Erect and austere, Major Lynwood Donnybrook was the apotheosis of marshal perfection, the very personification of an outstanding military leader. He was tricked out in a splendidly tailored uniform, his broad chest ablaze with an impressive array of combat decorations won in World War II.

Their commander's picture perfect regalia was capped handsomely by the aquiline featured, square-jawed visage of a commanding officer whose flashing eye could burn a hole right through to an academy cadet's soul, especially the one who's been burning bile-holes to his own stomach. This man among men could look through a boy to penetrate his every secret. As this resplendent duplicate of General McArthur stepped energetically up to a small, querulous and insignificant Cadet Brecken the frightened little boy quaked with fear.

Corey saluted his headmaster, the man who held the power of life and death over the entire cadet corps in his brawny hands.

An exhilarating albeit terribly uncomfortable mixture of admiration and dread cascaded through the highly emotional makeup of an impressionable child. The boy regarded the man with a mixture of hero worship and terror, for this all-powerful, all-punishing, completely overpowering authority figure had cast an ominous shadow over him.

The Almighty King of Olympus not only returned our boy's salute but condescended to offer Corey his big, strong hand in friendship:

"I am Major Donnybrook, headmaster and commandant of our academy's junior school, Cadet Brecken."

"How do you do, sir?" our querulous cadet made an heroic effort to stammer.

"Very well, sir," said the academy's topmost Top Brass with an amused smile.

As they shook hands Corey's terror abated somewhat -- but not much.

The major presented his two tiny companions, "May I present my young son, Lynnwood Junior, and his sister, my younger daughter, Antoinette?"

Scrapper Corey was refined enough to address the two little rug-rats politely, "How do you do, Master and Mistress Donnybrook?"

"Tee-he," was their giggled response.

"Cadet, I have heard some disturbing reports, reports that you have not eaten since your arrival here," intoned the major seriously while his intense eyes burned a hole through little Corey's cowed orbs to plumb the depths of our scared kid's guilty little soul, "Furthermore, I have never seen you in the dining hall, son.

"You aren't sick are you, Mac?"

"N-no, sir!" our cadet on the hot seat labored to lie.

"You have been with us for nearly a week, son. Have you never eaten in all that time?"

"No, sir," Corey murmured sheepishly.

The look of concern darkening the brow of the master of his fate made Corey ashamed of his truculence and fearful of possible punishment.

The only way he was able to keep looking directly into the great man's frightening eyes, rather than down at his shoes, was that he knew it was expected of him.

At the very least the major liked him well enough to give him a nickname, "Mac." Corey had no idea why the commandant called him that. He surmised it must have been because they were both of Scots extraction.

"You're a growing boy, Mac," the major pursued him, bent upon securing this mixed up little boy's persuasion to sounder judgment, "Starvation is a dangerous game for one so young as you and I am concerned for your health.

"I hope you understand I cannot tolerate this sort of thing to continue, Cadet Brecken!"

Corey was forced to concur with his overpowering commander, "YES, SIR!!!!"

"Now, Mac, I'm your friend, and I want you to attend me when I tell you that we have a strenuous regimen here at the academy. The cadet who does not have the good sense to eat, drink and exercise regularly must fall prey to illness and fall short of the mark. When he does become ill we will have to send him to the infirmary. You don't want that, do you, son?"

Little Corey knew he was in enough hot water already and must have the good sense to reply, "NO, SIR!!!!"

Our innocent little waif had no idea what an "infirmary" was at that time -- but it sure sounded scary.

"Why don't you come down to the dining hall with us right now, Mac. We'll all eat together at my table and you'll feel a whole lot better than you have all week."

"Th-the cadet is, is sure the major is right, and the cadet is, is sure that y-you do him great honor, sir

"Th-the the c-cadet is v-very grateful to the major f-for his generous invitation, b-but he, he just can't, not, not now, not today!" stumbled our thoroughly cowed, but frightfully stubborn little dope.

"Tee-he," giggled the commander's over-privileged elves. They were comfortably amused to see how their pushover daddy scared the hell out of all these shaky-legged "big boys," especially this one.

"Well, son," said the major shaking little Corey's hand in departure, "It's an open invitation; and I will visit you again soon to renew the offer because I am sincerely concerned for your wellbeing.

"When I return I hope for all our sakes you will see good sense and change your mind."

"Y-YES, SIR!!!" responded Cadet Corey with as much enthusiasm as he could muster.

"We must go now," said his commandant.

Corey saluted the major, the major saluted him, and that was that -- for the present.

"Tee-he!" was heard once more.

"ATTENTION!!!" rang out as the major and his tots marched briskly off.

Corey's bunkmates were befuddled and horrified:

"YOU said 'no' to HIM?" inquired the group of small pale faces ringing him with awe, "Brecken, where'd you ever get th' BALLS t' do that?"

But Brecken could not answer that. He was too busy wondering the same thing. He might certainly have met with swift and fiery punishment on the spot for refusing the mighty Zeus Alastor's demand.

In departure the commandant reflected on his little problem. This brief skirmish was of no consequence, for, at The Tower, Major Lynnwood Donnybrook would always have his way.

But the great man would never have felt justified in just beating an obviously weakened and depleted nine year old to force him to eat. That could only have worsened the situation.

No, The Colossus of The Tower must study his field of battle carefully and dispassionately. Then he was sure to settle on and employ a more refined tactic.

Plan B:
Prick the skittish little colt.

Early the next morning Corey was crossing the quad in a big hurry to get to his first class, but this was a class he would never attend.

He was blindsided by a flying tackle that sent his books and pencils skyrocketing upward and knocked him sprawling on the cold, hard ground.

His attacker was one Cadet Basin, the junior school's bugler and, parenthetically, a big, fat bully.

The fat boy swept his victim unceremoniously to his feet and, holding his dazed victim up face to face, Cadet Basin pummeled our hero's face and body with a hard-fisted barrage of punishing blows. The fat boy hammered away at his shocked mark's face and head, the face and head of a boy who had been specifically forbidden to fight back.

But in this case our half-pint champion felt justified in repulsing an unprovoked and cowardly sneak attacker.

Corey tried his best to fight back expecting an easy victory over this pudgy softy. But starvation had taken its toll, and Corey's pathetically weak attempt at resistance availed him not. The mighty avenger of The Coconut Row Elementary School playground was too starved out and rundown to put up any kind of fight.

As a consequence of his starve-your-way-home fast, our hero took a merciless beating at the hands of this contemptible softy, a fat clown he could have made hash out of in his heyday.

But this was not his day.

Sitting atop his hapless quarry, Basin flailed away at Brecken's unprotected face and head, loudly declaring:

"If there's anything I hate most in th' whole gawdamn world it's a gutless, homesick, mama's-boy crybaby!

"Got that, Brecken?

"You're nothin,' y' gutless, homesick li' l' crybaby, a nothin'!!!"

Having delivered the message, the fat boy rose, kicked his vanquished mark in fond farewell, and further insulted him by scattering his books and notes all over the quad.

In time Corey was able to stand up on two very shaky pins. Dazed, bloodied and beaten, he was a shamefaced monument to defeat.

"Beaten!" his mind cried out in an outburst of ineffectual rage.

He gathered up his books in pain-wracked silence and hobbled back to the barracks to wash up. He realized that no cadet could attend a Tower class in his present state of shambles. No, he must wash up, put on a clean uniform and present a smart appearance to his teachers. If he did not, he risked a thorough whipping from an adult officer and a tidal wave of demerits on top of the beating he had already taken.

"Beaten, and by that fat pice o' shite, Basin!

"Beaten like a dog by a dog!

"Well, so much for starvation! ... Now I'm gonna eat to get m' strength back up t' snuff, I'm gonna stomp that ugly-ass Basin's fat duff into a blob o' bloody pulp an' then I'm gonna make that fat-son-of-a-bitch eat dirt 'n' cry like a baby!"

As of this moment Gra' ma, Grandpa, Rock Dinker et al could go fly a kite.

Corey's mammoth pride had kicked in and our schoolyard brawler was ready for reentry into a little boy's world. The disgrace of this encounter had steeled him for survival, for the only way boy might survive in this world must be by fighting and winning.

Our half-pint hero had come again unto himself. Here and now, he was resolved that Corey Brecken should be the toughest little scrapper out there.

Rock Dinker, Palm Beach and The Bath and Tennis Club cut no ice up here. The academy was beyond even that plush congregation of reprobates' jurisdiction. Now bad boy Corey was going to eat, get fit and kick ass as he saw fit. From this shame-sullied, body-bloodied day forward he must and should win.

But now he must go directly back to McAdam to clean up and change. He would never be accepted into an academy classroom in his present state.

Corey was in the bathroom busily washing his bruised and blooded face -- and wincing at the painful shock of a rough cold washrag scraping against open cuts. But attention was called and he had to scamper desperately to the head of his of his bunk to be in his correct place.

Major Donnybrook, every little cadet's dynamic superhero, swept into the barrack-room at top speed.

But this time the mighty Zeus did not descend from his lofty throne into the lives of his mortal cadets alone, nor was he attended by those tiny runny noses who'd laughed at Corey on the occasion of his commandant's earlier sortie into his barrack room.

This time the commandant was attended by the most magnificent creature our boy had ever seen:

A vision of grace and beauty glided gracefully into his life close beside the commandant. This superb apparition took Corey's breath away. Her glossy curls and flashing eyes entranced our cadet as one fairer than Aphrodite approached the tiny mortal, so compellingly lovely was she.

Was this an optical illusion, he wondered, a mirage, a chimera or was this a living, breathing love goddess descending to brighten his poor life from her alabaster habitation on Olympus?

Given Corey's weakened condition she might well have been a vision occasioned by his euphoria attendant upon his truculent fast. Was she paradise in human form, or was he having an hallucination?

The pretty young lady on the all powerful headmaster's arm made our Corey's heart leap sky-high in her presence. Never before had our dumb-struck, wide-eyed little bantam encountered a girl whose presence had so moved him.

This young beauty was by far comelier, better dressed, more carefully groomed than any of the high-born, strutting peacock, embryonic heiresses with whom he had attended Coconut Row Elementary.

Our ardent swain was so overawed in the presence of such perfection that all he could scrape together in the competency department was to remember to salute the major.

"G-good morning, sir!"

"Good morning, Mac," the commandant smiled easily.

The headmaster pretended not to notice the deplorable state of his wounded little student warrior post his disgraceful rout on the quad. But the man noted with approval the damage inflicted on this tough little nut by Cadet Basin's enthusiastically executed assignment to bring Cadet Brecken back into line with academy policy -- and back into a boy's world.

And the major's eye was the eye of an expert in this particular field of operation.

"I'd like to introduce you to my eldest daughter, Mac," smiled his beloved headmaster, "Cadet Brecken, may I present Miss Leto Donnybrook?"

"YES, SIR!!!!!"

"Leto, this is Cadet Corey Brecken.

"I have invited him to sit with our family at meals. I'm sure you will approve, my dear."

"I, I am-am most, most, uh, very, very d-deeply honored, M-miss, Miss Donnybrook!" Corey stammered out a clumsy salutation to the breathtaking love goddess before him. Our boy was both elated and terrified -- and so he should have been.

"I sure do, Daddy!" smiled Leto in answer to her father's query, for she was a self-possessed young lady of the world, at ease in every social situation.

"Hi, Cadet Brecken," she sparkled -- managing not to laugh in her admirer's roughed-up face, or his obvious confusion, for she liked this face, "You're a cute kid, even when you're all beat up, dear boy."

As their hands touched boy and girl tingled to the electric shock of an immediate and inexplicable recognition of the familiar. The magnetic presence of something inescapable, something intimate, something that was about to change everything mysteriously bound them.

At this charming, this compelling first touch, ever so gentle yet so dynamically charged, the two were riveted to the spot as one. A mighty torrent of electrifying emotion at once edified and united them with the source of life's primal power to draw our two new lovers closer than close.

Our captivating young beauty's warmer than warm welcome for her strange, yet somehow familiar, schoolboy had captured her heart. She loved the same scrappy little tyke her beloved Daddy had opted to take under his wing even as he loved her. Cadet Brecken had gone down for the third time to drown happily in depths of Leto's dreamily compelling, magnetically kaleidoscopic eyes and he was ecstatic.

"You'll eat for me, won't y,' Mac?" she breathed in his ear.

"I'll do anything for YOU!" he blurted out enthusiastically.

The two Donnybrooks smiled knowingly.

"I'd better clean this beat-up li' l' soldier up for chow before we go down there, huh, Daddy?" chirruped the girl merrily, "He sure looks like he's been run through th' mill, huh?"

"Right y' are, kiddo," her dad responded, "I have to get down there right away to open the ceremonies before I'm missed.

"You clean Mac up, and then I expect you two to get right down there on the double. See you down there, kids."

"Right, Daddy!" piped the devastatingly delicious Leto.

"YES, SIR!!!" saluted the reanimated Corey.

The major returned the cadet's salutation a happy man. The junior school's Top Brass was always a new man in the presence of his favorite girl. The years dropped away from the academy's dreaded hatchet-face when he was with his best beloved little girl.

The great man exited, pleased with the success of his Plan B, and even better pleased that the plan's victory over Corey's stubbornness had been driven by his keen insight into the motivational psychology of a proud little nine year old.

"Mac's going to be okay now," his spit-and-polish boss reflected, "The humiliation of that beating has awakened him up to the efficacy of strife. Now my plucky little thug is ready to fight back.

"Leto's a good girl and Mac's a good boy, so let 'em have a little candy."

Corey and Leto were all alone with one another for the very first time in their lives as she led him into the bath to wash him.

All the other cadets had already raced hungrily downstairs to eat.

Boy and girl stood, bathed in the filmy mists of intoxication and mystery only young lovers can ever know.

"What d' they call y' back home, kiddo?" queried our pretty young miss.

"C-cadet Brecken, miss!" fumbled our breathless schoolboy.

"No, dopey!" she corrected him, "What d' your folks call y'?

"C' m' on, boyfriend, don't y' be scared o' ME. Daddy's th' one 'n' only scary Donnybrook, 'n' I'm not even one little bit like Daddy!

"And, by the way, C-cadet Brecken, miss, if we're gonna be best friends -- 'n' Daddy wants us to be best friends -- I am not some snooty ol' Miss Donnybrook to you, dear boy, I am jus' plan Leto, y' cute li' l' dope, LETO, got it?"

"Plain?" gasped her enraptured dope, "F-forgive me for contradicting you, Leto, but th' only plain you could ever be is just plain beautiful!"

He was in heaven when he saw her smile and blush to acknowledge his compliment.

"Th-they jus' call me Corey back home," he volunteered.

"Well, Daddy calls y' Mac, so that's what I'll call y,' too," she purred, "I like your attitude already, Mac, 'n' I like you, but right now, cadet, YOU are a MESS. I got 'o get you cleaned up before we can go down 'n' eat in the stuffy ol' big-deal dining hall, so you jus' march yourself right up t' that sink, my li' l' soldier-boy.

"Li' l' ol' Mama Leto's gonna scrub her baby nice 'n' shiny clean!"

"YES, MA'AM!!!" deferred her beau.

Boy and girl gazed deeply into one another's longing eyes as their passion awakened. The two children were eager to enter the unfurling blooms of life's sweetest, most secret garden. A new day, a magic day was dawning for them because they were kids, and kids believe in magic.

Now Corey was able to shake off the shackles of rejection with which his coldhearted elders had formerly weighed him down in the darkness of his recent past. Now his elders' frozen world was miles away from their chattel, for they had wished it so and exiled him. But here in this stark locus of duress Gra' ma's pet was fortunate to have found a vibrant and playful new mistress. With his lucky introduction to the intriguing Leto, he found himself reborn into a new world ablaze with hope and promise.

Was our beat-up little castoff truly to be so rewarded here in his lonely life of exile?

Yes, regeneration was to be his.

A prepossessing and generous guardian angel had descended from her high place in the pantheon of The Tower's most elite. She had come into his deserted life to favor her darling schoolboy on this, the luckiest day of his life. Today boy and girl have drunk deeply of the cup of Eros and the immortal beauty dormant in our blissful innocents has brought them joy.

Meanwhile, back on earth our industrious Leto busily scrubbed the dirt out of her scruffy Mac's sore, tender and throbbing wounds.

While she did so, she was looking him over -- all over -- and she liked what she was seeing. Already attracted to him, she painstakingly examined the new boy on campus and concluded that he had something that was just right for her. Yes, Leto decided, Corey's got that indescribable something for which she had been searching all along. The other schoolboys of the junior school cadet corps lacked magic. That was what she was looking for, and that was what Mac had.

The girl he loved loved him, and that has been the most potent magic since the beginning of time.

After her close inspection of Mac Miss Leto Donnybrook decided to mold the little boy she had chosen for her love into the man of her dreams, the perfect man as girlfriends have done since this old world began. A nine year old perfect man would surely be a hat trick.

Leto was two years Mac's senior, and already a woman. But for this strong willed little beauty that was less than a trifle. Her loving heart had accepted him and she had burst into flame. Her proud, free spirit was instantly awakened to the intoxicating secret that this lucky little boy must be hers and bring her happiness.

His powerful electricity made all of her senses tingle with sensual delight. She was happy beneath the spell of his commanding, brightly shining, sky blue Viking's eyes. Those eyes seemed to dare her to leave the safe harbor of convention and sail away on an endless sea of passion.

Corey knew nothing of romance. Adoration had never roused him until today. He had never experienced anything akin to physical love. But on this enraptured day of rapture, this day he recognized her as his love, Leto's alluring eyes had called out to him and he must answer. Today he stood ready to join her and walk with her into the uncharted, mysterious garden of love into which she called him. He was inexorably drawn into the beautiful dream in those kaleidoscopic eyes. He now realized he must adventure with this beautiful girl into the hidden mysteries awaiting them there. Together they must and will fly blindly into the vortex of life's most compelling adventure. At first touch Corey and Leto knew it, for it was an intoxicating touch, a touch that kindled in them an all-consuming thirst for a life together.

But it was and is a hard fact of life that the laws of society did then and do now proscribe minors from falling in love.

Hard facts meant nothing to our little heroes. All the societal taboos down through the ages were but smoke in the wind to our adventurous golden brats. Their nine and twelve year old worldly wisdom had been quick to assure the kids that the grownups who wrote such stuffy laws were just trying to spoil their fun. In their young lives they'd both found that grownups could never to be trusted when it came to fun.

No, our two beautiful underage lovers were ready to enter into their own forbidden love without written permission from their parents, or even a hall pass. They knew full well they could never hope for acceptance from the grownups, but they were lost in the concupiscence of their strong love bond. With or without adult supervision, they were committed and no power in heaven or earth could part these loving hearts.

Back to earth and in the workaday world our busy little Leto scrubbed away at her brave little Mac's sore face, hands, arms and chest and got them cleaner than clean as our lovers stood at the bathroom sink of his deserted barracks.

Leto's brisk and thorough scrubbing hurt him, but Mac knew he was her hero and must live up to it. Never could he allow himself the luxury of showing even the slightest hint of weakness in her presence. Ergo, her underage he man did not grimace but remained stoically impassive in the face of the pain. He'd received superhuman strength through the nearness of her hypnotic female charm.

After she had scrubbed him clean, he was glad that he had played the role of the hero. Leto, the materialization of his wildest dreams, put her arms around him and reward her brave little soldier with a long kiss to culminate her labor of love. And Mistress Leto Donnybrook's kiss was no tepid peck-on-the-cheek. No tentative brush from a grade school teacher for her dear little student's assignment well done. No, Mac's Miss Preteen Love Goddess came down into her excited admirer's mouth with all the hot, sweet energy of the untamed passion of her own hot arousal. His dream girl pressed her soft, sweet smelling and supple body close against his in the most intimate of all embraces he had ever experienced in his young life. And it was a breathtaking dream come true love goddess so favoring the nine year old man of her dreams. Leto burned her red hot brand deeply into his delighted and bewildered lips.

Hers was a big screen, flaming Hollywood romance full body contact kiss to end all kisses.

Young Corey was on fire with excitement, ignited by his first taste of Leto's heavenly ambrosia, but he was also made painfully aware of a frighteningly inexplicable, exponentially growing phenomenon awakening in his pants. His strong young body's inevitable response to the unexpected, commandingly moving and overwhelmingly potent nearness of this most desirable of all females in his ken immediately filled him with confused dismay. While our Corey was only a little boy of nine, he had often experienced those mysterious and frightening dreams that are prone to roil and disturb a boy's sleep. He had often had such feverish nightmares and they had thrown him out of bed and into a state of wakefulness and perplexity.

Now the unexpected appearance of this nocturnal dilemma at this inopportune moment filled him with the fear that his lady love might flee him, horrified by appearance of this persistent unwanted guest. He realized the brash intruder would subside in time, but Leto was here now and so was his disastrously erect embarrassment.

Why did this have to happen right in the middle of his Olympian goddess's first torrid and honey-sweet kiss?

But Corey had no clue as to why.

Reared in a strict Victorian household where sex was discouraged as an improper topic of conversation, he knew nothing of what might cause the stirrings of the flesh. Any allusion to such disturbingly intimate processes in the field of human physiology were strictly forbidden in his grandparents' august presence.

Corey quickly tried to hide his "shame." But this particular form of shame was far too prominent and much too hard to conceal.

It was lucky for her inexperienced Mac that his worldly and lively young Leto was no Victorian. No, his exciting and aroused new girlfriend spoke right up to express her admiration for her perfect man on the sudden materialization of ths convincing new evidence of her favorite cadet's manly prowess.

"Wow, Mac, you Tarzan, me Jane!" she gushed lovingly, "I knew right off you 'n' me were gonna click, but never as great as this!"

Corey was greatly relieved when he saw that his wide-eyed enchantress's interest was piqued when she purred her support and encouragement of his arousal.

"But we got 'o t' talk about your big soldier some other time, my cute li' l' soldier," she cautioned him hurriedly, "Daddy wants us down there on th' double ... We're already late, so we better get a move on, cadet super stud!"

"You got it, Leto!" he concurred.

"Thanks for noticing, Mac," she smiled, pleased with him -- and even more pleased with herself, "You got it, too, and in spades!"

Leto took his arm and they floated downstairs high above all the aches, pains and cares of The Tower. Buoyed aloft on the rare ether of their blossoming romance, the infatuated duo clambered down and scurried into the great hall to take their places at the almighty commandant's table of honor. There our enchanted young lovers sat down side by side to their eminent mutual satisfaction.

"Look what I found, Daddy," the major's darling daughter crowed as she proudly presented her beaming conquest to the family, "Young Cadet Brecken has rejoined us in th' land o' th' living!

"Confidentially, I think all your starvin' li' l protégé needed was a little encouragement from his friends, huh, dad?"

The Tower's Zeus Alastor smiled benevolently down on our two happy children in love. He benevolently gave his favorite girl a wink of approbation, "I think y' may just be right there, dear girl."

The almighty headmaster's warm acceptance of his favorite kids' evident felicity hid a mortal danger. It was right in front of them but its dark malevolence was completely obscured from our golden brats' view. It coiled in darkness, eclipsed below the sunshine of the headmaster's brightly burning benevolence. Our golden brats failed to notice six angry eyes burning white hot with envy, resentment and a hell-driven thirst for vengeance, a revenge that screamed for the golden brats' fall from the major's grace -- and the end of their happiness.

Such was the burning gaze of Mrs. Donnybrook and her two younger children.

Long ago the lovely Leto had realized that her mother hated her because she envied her daughter's cushy place in their august lord and master's affections. But that had never been a matter of any consequence to the commandant's charming and self-absorbed favorite.

Daddy's girl just knew that she would forever be beautiful and clever enough always to neutralize her jealous mom and her impish cradle creep spies, for she'd never had the slightest difficulty doing so. She was and would be the commandants darling and he would forever be receptive to her wise counsel.

Her only problem now was that she must somehow acquaint her untutored Mac with the danger those three unhappy Donnybrooks posed to their favored positions. She must warn him of the lovers' need for extreme caution beneath the spiteful Medusa mom's cobra stare.

Three inveterate haters seethed and writhed like the serpents' nest they were. The three boiled with their hot resentment, engendered by our little heroes' obvious happiness. Such blatant evidence had awakened the dark Donnybrooks' overpowering drive to be avenged on the unsuspecting innocents:

Mrs. Donnybrook had been awakened to the realities of life, love and passion, and they had withered, embittered and crumpled her into a burnt black cinder of resentment. Leto had roused to the same realities and they had made her an accepting, warm and loving blessing for all -- except mom and the rug rats. Leto lived and lusted after love as strongly as her perverse mother existed and lusted for vengeance. And tonight the envious old snake was adamant in her murderous ambition to bring down our two high flying lovebirds at any cost.

"Oh, yes, my pretty little lost darlings," ruminated the malicious Mrs. Donnybrook, "In love are we, my dear, beaming junior Paris and Helen, my vibrant little Abelard and Heloise.

"Well, well, my dears, have your fun now because obviously you have forgotten how those little fools were punished for their idiotic indiscretions. And I am going to make sure that you end up just as they did, my dears:

"First I shall punish the boy."

"You know Daddy 'n' th' rug rats already, Mac," Leto began her introductions.

"Hi, kids," Corey smiled, politely acknowledging the toddlers.

But those partisan elves only giggled and pointed at Corey and Leto as if they were a peculiarly freakish pair of sideshow oddities.

"Do not call your younger brother and sister derogatory names, MISS!" hissed an unnatural mother aroused.

"Okay, ma," Leto dismissed and ignored her.

"So much for THEM," scoffed the younger siblings' high and mighty big sis, dismissing the cobra and her diapered spy apparatus from the of the face of earth with a jaunty wave.

"This is my mother, Missus Donnybrook," continued our lively young mistress of ceremonies.

"I am privileged, ma' am," smiled young Cadet Brecken graciously.

But Corey instinctively feared this gaunt, intense woman, although he had no idea why.

Mrs. Donnybrook's huge, coal black eyes seared into him with undisguised malice. Hers was the calculating stare of a venomous serpent bent upon hypnotizing, debilitating and devouring its prey.

"How do you do, Cadet Brecken?" glowered the major's lady, alive with hostility. Mrs. Donnybrook regarded all her husband's disgusting cadets as so many dirty ragamuffins, but she saw this Cadet Brecken as a particularly distasteful annoyance -- one she must dispatch with alacrity:

This unnatural creature had watched Leto and her Mac bounce happily into the dining hall without a care in the world. This insane reptile had observed with great interest the evidence that this blue eyed scamp was somehow bringing joy to that pretty little girl she had resented above all other humans on earth from her innocent child's hour of birth.

And now, for the sin of happiness, Mrs. Donnybrook had determined to punish both children just as painfully as she was able.

Miraculously, Corey'd survived the introductions and the meal began.

With the formalities out of the way everyone settled down to a more or less peaceful, and eminently toothsome, repast.

When everyone else had entered into their customary dinnertime diversions, Mac's irrepressible Leto addressed this query to her lover boy in a whisper, "Y' know any jokes, Mac?"

"Why did th' moron -"

"No, Mac, those musty ol' moron jokes 're strictly out," she braced him, but softly, for neither their esteemed elders nor her gorgon-mom's cradle creep spies must ever know the confidences our ardent young lovers must share in secret between them, "I mean DIRTY jokes!"

A horrified little cadet in the presence of his all punishing chief shot a distracted glance in the direction of the two all-powerful adults seated, directly, and precariously, across the table.

But his giggling girlfriend was quick to reassure him (albeit in a whisper):

"Aw, don't be scared o' THEM, lover boy.

"They jus' always talk about their own grownup stuff. They live someplace way up above us in their own grownup stratosphere. Believe you me, kid, they never give even a thought t' what us little do-dos 're doin' down here on earth.

"Don't you worry, my special li' l' baby, Mac. You're all mine, 'n' you're gonna be safe down here on earth with me 'cause li' l' ol' Mama Leto's gonna take good care o' you, 'n; she's never ever gonna let her pretty baby fall.

"Th' only problem we have is we jus' gotta be extra special careful that th' rug rats don' ever hear a word we say, 'cause my mom hates me, she sees I like you, so she hates you, too, 'n' they are gonna spy on us 'n' report back to 'er!"

With extreme caution, forewarned of the cobra's spite and the duplicity of her conniving spies, our half-pint hero hit his lovely starlet with a couple of Dagwood and Blondie cracks he'd heard from some of the madder wags back home at Coconut Row Elementary School. And he topped off his off color comedy with the old reliable Chinese detective wheeze.

This naughty material was a lot better received by his rapt little girl audience of one.

"That's th' stuff, lover boy!" she applauded his efforts, "Now we're cookin' with gas!"

The supper went well.

The commandant, his perfect little best beloved and his newly appointed little protégé -- or the only three people at the table who were able to love -- retired satisfied and complacent. This was peculiarly true of her Mac and his Leto, for they retired excited by the prospect of meeting here the very next morning at breakfast.

Let us not speak of those odd three protagonists not so richly blessed. At that time those schemers were creatures of very little merit and even less consequence.

SAVAGED BY THE BEAST

Mistress Leto Donnybrook was the picture perfect young lady. Her stylish and expensive mode of dress, her refined manners and her pronounced personal magnetism had distinguished her far above the norm. Corey's girl preferred the earthy demotic to the more formal mode of address employed in that upper middle class society into which our vibrant little heroes had had the questionable good fortunate to be born. Her modernist attitude may have been due to the fact that she had been unceremoniously wrenched into life's fast lane by a strong and heartless sexual predator. Only a year before she met her loving and reverent Mac the muscular, self-important and sociopath captain of the senior school's football team always seemed a dashing and aristocratic companion in the innocent eyes of Major Donnybrook's little girl until the evening he had raped her. That criminal had robbed our screaming and inflectionally resisting little heroine of her virginity. It had been our seemingly carefree and footloose Leto's hard lot to have been yanked prematurely into the estate of womanhood by the brutish act of an uncaring brute.

When Leto and Corey met they fell in love, and that love was real for both our heroes. But the pair was scarcely evenly matched. While our boy's love goddess was a strikingly beautiful and intoxicatingly attractive girl child, she was also a woman.

Even our exalted headmaster, a man who adored his first born, even the immortal all-father of The Tower's Junior Academy, even the haughty commander in chief of all he surveyed had been powerless to avenge his darling's rape.

That criminal assault against his best beloved's honor had been prosecuted by the highly connected son of a senator.

That vastly influential and scurrilously immoral politico had used money, power and his extraterrestrial connections to gloss the matter over. The predator's dad had threatened and paid off the injured girl's parents, various expensive but easily bribed Tennessee judges and the press to keep his own personal American tragedy his very own privatized dirty little secret.

At the tender age of twelve Leto Donnybrook was an astonishingly beautiful and irresistible woman of the world. It was no wonder Corey had found her so and fallen directly in love. Our blossoming young heroine had awakened with juvenile exuberance to the female imperative to seek out the consolation of a male companion, and she loved Mac.

To the lovely Leto's credit she'd early seen in herself the ever blossoming, unfurling flower to be admired, adored, savored and loved. She's opted to enjoy her womanhood rather than to hide from it. Unlike her mother she had never been tempted to deny herself life's joy, to evade its beauty nor to ignore her intimate desires. Never disposed to hide her abundant gifts away, Leto Donnybrook was a brave and adventurous young woman inclined to reach out for life rather than hide from it away and become a burnt-out cinder of her mom's description.

After meeting her gallant Mac our petite heroine's fertile imagination cried out:

"Oh, mama, we're gonna be as hot an item in th' romance department as THE GYPSY AND THE LITTLE MINISTER OF THE AULD LICHT KIRK!"

And the first bloom of their taboo romance, was born into the chilly clime of her Mac's grand mamma's finest military academy in all the world. Their resilient young love at once sent forth its deep roots to stubbornly grow and prosper even in this cold and thorny wasteland. Even in the nuclear winter of The Tower Military Academy the golden brats' forbidden love blossomed and grew right at the severe commandant's rigid and formal dinner table beneath the watchful and disapproving Medusa-glare of the coiled to strike Mrs. Donnybrook and her watching and listening spies.

But the flowering of the young romantics' love's first shoot must perforce be kept safely beyond the ken of all in attendance on that beautiful evening in the big, boundless, drafty and glittering confines of the de rigueur dining hall

Only the two blessed souls of our golden brats must ever know the unspeakable joy of this, this most incredibly joyous day of all. Only his pretty Leto and her ardent Mac were privileged to dive into the deep, dark pool of Fate and find their bliss, now and forever. On this very first day of their love her Mac and his Leto were grateful and so happy to be able drink of the sweetest of all cups, for it was their very own chalice of the purest and most intoxicating joy a kindly angel had brought to their eager grasp to raise up their battered spirits and wet the lips of two lost children desperately thirsting for love.

Our happy lovers' toast to life and love rang out silently deep within the fastness of their minds, as it must. Had they declared their taboo relationship publicly, they would have alerted everyone. And then a cold and repressed world would have hurled a legion of enemies, envious of what our heroes had found, and that cohort would have rent the lovers limb from limb.

No, their forbidden love must be pledged in our beautiful underage outlaw lovers' mute toast:

"To the present!"

Outlaw love can live only in the present, and for the sake of safety it must dwell in secret.

Had it but known the adult world would cry out:

"Love at The Tower Military Academy?"
"Preposterous!"
"However could such a thing be?"

But it could and it had, and what an earthshaking, game-changing miracle it had been for one small and friendless little boy.

Morning's reveille had stirred Rooky Brecken, Miss Crop's bad little whelp, bully boy Beasterling's dumb li' l goober to yet one more sad and colorless day of rejection and neglect.

But evening's taps blew for Mac, the headmaster's protégé (and his darling Leto's brand new toy cadet).

Our boy was privileged. He had been elevated to a glorious new life in the intriguing company of the commander in chief and his high born favorite child, Mistress Leto Donnybrook. His grandparents' disgraced and discarded castaway, the loneliest, most despised exile in an entire military academy full of just such puerile throwaways had begun a new and promising life this fine day. The impossible was suddenly transmuted into the law of The Tower by the Grace of God and the loving mercy of Major Donnybrook and his Leto. Orders from the academy's Top Brass had decreed our formerly tarnished beyond recognition toy soldier should be gloriously reborn. Cadet Brecken was no longer to be the object of anyone's scorn, for he was the major's protégé and his Leto's prize. The high and mighty Donnybrook Clan, the epitome of the elect, had adopted this pathetic little stray.

Now this poor boy (yes, I said poor, for Cadet Corey Brecken had always been poor, be it "ON" or off Palm Beach) was blessed with this most generous outpouring of affection he had ever known in all the days of his life. It had poured down over him from the highest peak of Donnybrook Mountain to comfort him and enfold him in the loving arms of the only two Donnybrooks able to love.

It would seem our little lost boy must be safe now beneath the Aegis of his almighty commander. Thenceforth their Mac was privileged to sit with the academy's headmaster -- AND LETO!

The kindly major even took enough fatherly interest in Corey's academic advancement to make sure that the boy went out for two sports each semester to improve his sense of sport and tone the muscles of his developing physique.

Corey regarded this patronage as just like having a real father. Our boy had never been allowed even to meet his real dad by order of The Mad Carlotta.

The major had shown him favor and his Princess Leto had elevated him high above all other junior school cadets by making him welcome in the loving garden of her generous heart.

What could go wrong?

The major's cold, hard lady was dangerously psychotic. The cobra was coiled to do whatever wrong she might against our lovers by any means at her disposal -- preferably the very foulest. The demons inside her deranged and tumultuous head were eternally screaming that she had too long eked out a lonely and barren existence beneath the major's enormous shadow.

This mean, small minded creature had long labored under the delusion that she'd been dwarfed and neglected in the shadow of Major Donnybrook, that monument to martial rectitude. In her mind she'd been deserted by him for that flirty little tart, Leto. In her insanely jealous eyes the birth of Leto had somehow robbed her of her husband's affection. In the cobra's mad imaginings the flashy young Leto had taken center stage to monopolize her husband's affections from her on the very first day of the poor girl's life.

Mrs. Donnybrook's twisted mind was a raging bonfire of hatred and envy even before Corey Brecken had appeared at the table. Then along came this just too adorable little whippet to further estrange her man's attentions away from her, to torment her, to annoy and incite her. And that had kicked her mad fantasy into overdrive:

The Donnybrook Deepfreeze saw that, though she had given the major a perfectly good son of his own to foster, the headmaster had bypassed him to pick Brecken, Brecken, BRECKEN to be his protégé?

Brecken, Brecken, BRECKEN must pay, pay, PAY for that insult!

Mrs. Deepfreeze Donnybrook had watched those two damnably annoying golden brats' advances and good fortune from the cold, deserted sidelines. She hated them more and more with the passing of each day. She nursed an ever growing litany of complaints against the commandant's sickeningly winsome, beloved daughter and his maddeningly charming protégé.

"That conniving little outcast has stolen my idiot husband's love away from his own son just as my scheming little movie star daughter stole all his love from me!" this lost soul cried out to, Eris, her dark pagan goddess of discord for redress from the blacker than black night of her stygian netherworld, "Punish him!

"Punish ALL three of them, Eris!"

She had felt her wicked prayers answered at the major's board on the night of Corey's introduction and admission into the family, and she had declared with renewed confidence:

"I shall punish the boy first."

But lovable old Mrs. Donnybrook's premier hatred was even less to her credit. It was one the wretch had nurtured for twelve long years. And this was one grudge against her fairest daughter for which she was damned for eternity, for it was the loathing this unsalvageable wreck hoarded up against her own daughter. It had so long festered in her unforgiving heart that it was now the cornerstone of this unpardonably warped dross's existence. This unspeakable monster's obsession was that she was meant to destroy her first born:

"Oh, yes, my dear, it is Leto who must pay for taking everything away from ME, Leto must pay dearly, LETO has forfeited her life for being so cute, so fetching, so endearing as to get all of my commander in chief's love."

Mrs. Donnybrook's fiendish thrust to see that just-too-perfect Leto and Mac cast into the freezing night of outer darkness must be sated at all costs.

Mac and Leto were in constant danger. The Tower's madwoman was full of tricks and snares to catch them up, capture and humiliate them. And to that end this senior psycho had indoctrinated her youngest to hate and snoop relentlessly on the great man's favorites. Like their obsessed mom the intrepid infants were bent upon their elder sister's downfall.

From the golden brats' rosy perspective nothing could go wrong as long as they were scrupulously careful around mom and the cradle creeps.

Our beautiful children believed no power in heaven, on earth or in hell was strong enough to sunder the bond of their perfect love. In the bright sunshine of their perfect present our littlest exile was an exile no more and his breathtaking girl was no longer a victim. In the misty enchantment of their love's magic our half-pint hero was at last regenerated by the love of his new, all powerful, kind and loving friends. The major's little princess and our lucky young cadet were privileged to soar high above the evil machinations of The Tower's frighteningly malevolent legion of schemers, for a time.

Skyward the lovers sailed, blithely coasting along in that jet-stream of enchantment woven by Leto's compelling and magic orbs.

Our happy little golden brats dirty joked their way through breakfast, dinner and supper each and every day.

But meticulous care must be exercised for safety's sake:

One memorable evening Leto's giggles of delight reached her doting Daddy's ears, and the king of the gods made inquiry, "What is it that you two children are enjoying so, my dear?"

(It was a lucky thing that Daddy Donnybrook had addressed his query to the astute Leto because Corey was completely dumbfounded at that moment. His master's query threw our hero into a state of blind panic.)

Luckily for our dirty jokers, our panicky little booby's lady love adroitly saved the day without a moment's hesitation by being far better versed in this sneaky old world's art of dissembling than her rough and tumble boyfriend:

"Oh, daddy!" beamed she, "Mac has just turned out t' be the most interesting and amusing dining companion ever!"

"How so, my dear?" wondered the author and finisher of the children's fates.

"Why, dad, he has just told me the funniest joke ever:

"It's a joke about a moron who threw his alarm clock out of the window because he wanted to see time fly!"

"What's so funny about THAT, YOUNG LADY?" spat the black cobra vehemently, "You know very well I have specifically forbidden you from making fun of those poor souls less fortunate than yourselves -- morons are included, MISS. "

But her doting dad chose to ignore his killjoy scold's rebuke (as was his wont). He dismissed the matter amicably, "Why, that is most amusing, children; carry on, kids.

"The children don't mean to reflect upon the disadvantaged, my dear," the academy's jovial chief patiently explained to his exacerbated mate, "Loosen up, they're just a couple of nice kids trying to have a little fun."

The table of honor's master's voice had spoken and everyone at the major's table (however reluctantly in three dark cases) picked up their cue from their lord and master to join in the subdued ripple of polite laughter.

Corey was now convinced that -- notwithstanding the ever present threats and vicissitudes which daily dogged every boy enrolled at The Tower Military Academy -- this was just the place for him. Here he had met his charming Leto and here they were and would always be the king and queen of the universe. Sure, it was a cold and painful world outside the comfortable sphere of their magic love cloud. But, with such strong allies as the commandant and his little princess in his corner, Corey felt he must finally be able to weather the most devastating of The Tower's Arctic blasts.

With his breathtaking Leto by his side he must surely be proof against the most insidious of contrivances of that frigid cobra and her nursery spies, any and all conspirators and the naked brutality of the toughest hard-bitten martinets here. Our boy firmly believed he had the sand to digest anything that the strongest, most determined enemy might muster up to throw at him. Our resilient Cadet Brecken now had the unconquerable talisman of his own true lady's love, and the protection of the almighty Zeus's Aegis.

The kindness, interest and hardy sustenance of his two Donnybrook patrons' love had lifted him so far from the low of his starvation slump that one short week after his humiliation at that skulking sneak-attacker's hands, a Corey renewed caught and beat the offending churl. Brecken proceeded to make Basin eat dirt from that very same spot where the fat oaf had disgraced him when Leto's boyfriend was just another displaced and dispirited waif.

May our little outcast and his gentle lady, the healing victim of a brutal rape, have their share of happiness in this glorious present of their love's creation. Heaven knows such divine consolation had been denied them all their lives.

Be joyful your now, little Leto, for the forces of evil toil tirelessly here.

Even now a conspiracy had been planned to deliver your darling boy into the horny grip of this heartless academy's strongest, most brutal and sadistic monster:

"I shall punish the boy first."

And Leto's preteen gallant was to be bound over to an avowed and dedicated devotee to the art of torture the academy called Heeler Hall, but all cadets called Heeler Hell.

At the same time two carefree golden brats' rosiest dreams of love enlivened and delighted them, the most dedicated and deadly of their enemies had surrounded and captured Leto's Mac, and the academy's deviants meant to have their psychotic way with him.

Let us leave our happy young lovebirds floating high above all such mundane considerations on the clouds of their concupiscence to turn our saddened eyes to the major's office for this stark and disheartening revelation. It is here that we shall learn just what shocking surprises The Tower's dark forces have concocted and set in motion to vex our valiant half-pint hero:

A salvo of pain was being muzzle-loaded into a puritanical, withered and thoroughly embittered old hag's blunderbusses and aimed directly between Cadet Brecken's unsuspecting eyes.

Those malevolent powers of the junior school's hierarchy, the housemothers, has met in secret to hatch a plot which was to be spearheaded today by that wizened old phony, Miss Crop.

Corey's hostile and malicious housemother presided directly over his destiny at the time and she was about to crush him. That same shriveled and hardhearted harridan who had put a frightened, unceremoniously dumped on her doorstep, little novice in his place his first night at the academy was detailed to kick off the unholy festivities.

Old lady Crop was angry with our Corey because she had never been able to reach into his heart of hearts to wound it with the scolds and threats of her barbed tongue. This disturbingly happy little boy was beyond her reach, for he lay blissfully in the soft sanctuary of his loving Princess Leto's lap. And, as if that were not aggravating enough, Brecken had also found succor and safety beneath the Aegis of Commandant Daddy's favor. Ergo, Crop was itching to hurt our little hero.

The three gorgon-housemothers of The Tower's junior academy had put their snake-heads together and figured out a way to accomplish the task:

Now, at that time the major, Corey and all the other little cadets on campus had comfortably lulled themselves into a false sense of security by accepting the fiction that the commandant was actually running the show at The Tower. But they had forgotten to recon The Grey Sisters into the equation. Three Grey Sisters, three misanthropic old harpies, three disgruntled crones, or all three housemothers of the junior school, were about to have their cruel and destructive way with our charming Leto's beloved.

But the three gorgons were not content to take out their hard core spite on young Cadet Brecken alone. No, Miss Crop had two other innocent little heads in her crosshairs this day.

Crop had her instructions from the same black eyed Deepfreeze who sat across from Corey and hated him with all the gall in her black heart at every meal of their lives. Crop's orders that she must also throw two additional victims under the juggernaut had emanated from that monster. The Grey Sisters and their Black Witch boss sought to create the illusion of objectivity to avert suspicion in the major of what was actually afoot, vengeance against Leto and her lover. But in pursuit of their vile cause The Grey Sisters were set to employ their most debilitating and destructive weapons, their array of guile and intransigence, to take command of their commanding officer.

Old lady Crop struck the first blow against our Corey and his two unfortunate house brothers under the gun on the very day our hero's health returned and he celebrated the occasion by beating up the churlish bugler boy who had earlier insulted and disgraced him. On that same day the conniving old snake who held Corey's fate in her gnarly hands sat in conference with our heroic Major Donnybrook, the boy's most powerful ally.

What could she possibly have said to Corey's esteemed mentor to poison the all powerful Zeus's mind against his foster son that could make him punish his beloved protégé?

"I do not propose to wet-nurse every whining little crybaby that comes simpering down the pike, my dear sir," was Miss Crop's emphatic ultimatum.

"Nor should you, dear lady," the mighty lion of the junior school concurred good humouredly, puzzled as to what the loony old bat might mean.

But the Mighty Lion of The Tower should have been on his guard that fateful day, for a lion was just another variety of pussycat viewed through the beady eyes of a cold blooded viper of Miss Crop's stripe.

"What is it that distresses you, dear Miss Crop, and what can I do to assist you?" the lion inquired of the snake.

"The so-called 'normal' brats quartered here at McAdam Hall are difficult enough to put up with, major.

"Lord knows I do my best. But I have to draw the line when it comes to that homesick puke, that blubbering crybaby, that poor, poor tragic little Prince Hamlet, that blue eyed, sulking little mooncalf, that, that BRECKEN! ... And while we're at it, McAdam could very well do without a gloomy, fault-finding malcontent the likes of Crabtree, AND that hopeless little refugee from his mammy's teat, Little Milan."

"Are you indeed forced to draw the line against these three poor little souls, ma'am?" our almighty lion smiled with some amusement at this scheming old nag's ardor -- and her considerable impudence.

"I do indeed, sir!" evoked the deadly old adder in an outburst of vehement ire, "Those three undisciplined little misfits don't deserve to be here with us, for ours is the model dormitory and a shining example for the whole school to admire and emulate!"

"Well, if they don't belong here, where in this world do they belong, my dear lady?"

The major was amazed at the main force of her passion against three small and unoffending children.

"Well, sir, WE are too grown up for the likes of THEM here at McAdam," the viper coiled to strike, "Now, Booker Hall is reserved for only our most incorrigible delinquents, those tough cuthroats dumped on us by completely exasperated parents to keep 'em out o' reformatories. Those hardened young criminals foisted off on us by the parents who've given up on 'em might just make life a little bit too raggedy for the three wet milksops I mean to unload TODAY."

Crop mulled her choices over aloud. She was careful to feign a modicum of concern for the welfare of the boys she was about to drive into the shambles. The old fraud pretended to study the problem of where to put the unwanted boys dispassionately. But all the time the slippery old hypocrite knew precisely where she had been directed to send these three lost souls. "Therefore, it is my considered opinion that these three slipshod young basket cases will fit right in with Miss Bite's teddy-bear-hugging, thumb-sucking, half-baked, bed-wetting mental defectives in Heeler Hall."

"Don't you think you're being just a little a bit too hard on those boys, ma'am?" protested her pussycat boss.

He knew Miss Bite, the fury driven pervert who presided over the hall in question. And the commander knew her to be the worst, cruelest and most unforgivably sadistic housemother employed by the academy, as did everyone else. The concerned headmaster was loathe to fling three more innocent cadets into the living hell of a deranged torturer's fiery inferno.

"Miss Bite is very hard on her cadets," he argued in his boys' defense, "As we both know the boys at Heeler have been sent there because, well, because they are special cases.

"You must allow, Miss Crop, that none of the cadets you've mentioned have ever wet the bed, nor has any one of them refused to surrender a teddy bear as one of Miss Bite's more difficult cases has most vociferously done.

"Miss Crop, I see no harm the cadets you suggest for transfer are doing here, nor do I know of any problems they've caused," reasoned the headmaster, "Can you not find the kindness in your heart to keep them with us?"

"NO, major, I cannot, nor will I ever consent to keep any one of these three substandard CULLS here for ONE more day, sir!" averred a spiteful old woman possessed of no heart to call upon for mercy, "I tell you plainly, Miss Bite and Heeler Hall are exactly what those three little ingrates have got coming to them after all the trouble they've put me through!"

"I do wish that you would reconsider," suggested the viper's pussycat boss.

But it was becoming more and more obvious that Corey's undefeated war hero and staunch defender was about to lose this one.

"I will NOT, sir!!!" howled the intractable harridan forcefully.

"Well, if you actually believe this to be in the best interests of all concerned -"

"By all means, sir!" the old termagant rejoiced at the headmaster's capitulation to her satanically unjust terms.

Her victory over the three targeted innocents was assured. Exiled from their own homes, they must now face a new expulsion from one of the cushier halls into the dreaded darkness of that place every junior cadet at The Tower knew as Heeler Hell.

"Oh, yes, dear sir, send those three little wrist-wringing weak sisters directly to Miss Bite, if you will please do me that kindness. I'm sure SHE'LL show 'em a nice warm reception over there!"

Miss Crop thought her little joke was hilarious, but the major still had enough fire in his eye to sober the old viper up and staunch her cruel laughter before it escaped her lips.

"Then it shall be so, miss," buckled Corey Brecken's truest friend, kindest patron and the best beloved foster dad this lost child had ever known.

Now three little lost and friendless boys must face the crushing bulk and sharp claws and fangs of a ponderous and poisonous behemoth, and the academy's worst deviant and predator.

But Miss Bite already had her orders to seek out one boy of their number.

"My thanks, dear major!" smiled the triumphant snake, "Miss Bite 'll give those little crybabies something to cry about!"

Please be kind enough?

Had this pitiless old asp the temerity to invoke the headmaster's kindness when she had never even wondered what the meaning of that unfamiliar word might be?

Cadet Brecken was no longer safe beneath mighty Zeus's impregnable Aegis, for his almighty patron was never safe from the nagging tongues of his ghastly wife and her Grey Sister cohorts.

"Well, at least she said 'sir,'" reflected the great man as he hastened out of his office to attend to the school's more pleasant business, i. e. anything else in the whole wide world.

No headmaster wants to deal with animus amongst his senior staff.

To shut those harpies and gorgons up, he had dispatched three innocent boys to be billeted at Heeler and deserted to face the unforgiving talons and fangs of the most deranged, the most unfit, deviate at the finest military academy in all the world. Their commandant had sent three tiny innocents to suffocate in the iron grip of the very worst housemother in an academy comprised of three of just such homey and heartwarming creatures: "ALEA IACTA EST!"

"CADET MILAN REPORTING AS ORDERED, MA'AM!!!"

"CADET CRABTREE REPORTING AS ORDERED, MA'AM!!!!"

"CADET BRECKEN REPORTING AS ORDERED, MA'AM!!!"

"That's th' one!" Miss Bite reflected in triumph as she regarded Corey. The housemother from hell was highly excited, but the old deviate must never betray her secret dark intent to her terrified gamin, "Oh, yes, my dear, that's him alright."

Three tiny, extremely apprehensive cadets saluted their ponderous, obscenely obese and dangerously psychotic new housemother on the grim occasion of reporting for their new billeting assignments at Heeler, Hall Of The Damned.

As per their revered commandant's orders they'd marched here directly after bolting down an antsy evening meal. Their fate had been relayed to them by The Top Brass before chow and the boys had stewed over their slavish fate over supper (Corey was just a bit more relaxed than his brothers at supper because his ravishing palliative, the charming Leto, had been present to comfort and cheer him in his impending plight).

But now, looking up into the hate-narrowed eyes of such a formidable giant even as she sat leering down at him from the forbidding Bald Mountain of her comfy easy chair, his courage failed him.

The housemother of Heeler Hall, known to every cadet as the hall of lost souls, regarded the new boys trembling before her with both smug satisfaction and bad intent. The Beast had picked right up on her unfortunate new arrivals' pronounced dismay with eminent satisfaction. This amorphous anomaly was ready to take her time, for she realized that eventually she would crush each and every one of them.

But tonight the golem salivated and burned with her dark obsession. She hungered to press on to the exciting feast of those delicious agonies she was poised to inflict on the naked, living flesh of one boy, Brecken, Brecken, BRECKEN. Bite was set to release her accustomed plethora of the most extreme abuses imaginable against each and every one of them; but Brecken and only he was designated to accommodate her nightmarish appetites this particularly peculiar evening.

Bite's fiendishly deviant, satanically perverted appetites were the paramount drivers in this abandoned leviathan's perverse and obscene existence, and she meant to sate all of them tonight.

The most hated and feared of all of the three hard-bitten housemothers competing for title of The Tower's prima hard core sadist was to be their taskmistress now and all three cadets trembled in the knowledge of it, and her horrible presence. Miss Bite's new boys all realized that being sent to her had been a shameful demotion. They had been condemned to a new exile, and this one was assured deep in the bowels of perdition:

This perverse and sickly old leviathan's reputation for her notorious and excessive cruelty was old news in every quarter of the academy. The extremity and calumny of her criminal acts of abuse, habitually practiced upon her luckless charges had reached every gossip mill in every quarter of the school, and their blather had made her beastly excesses legend. There was not one junior school cadet who hadn't heard the chilling horror stories of the delight Miss Bite invariably derived from the overboard punishments she daily visited upon every one of her boys.

And now three condemned boys were hers to quake with horror beneath the torturer's baleful gaze while this monstrously vile abuser of helpless children grimaced victoriously down upon them.

Miss Bite eyed these brand new tasty tidbits with all the pleasure of a skulking scavenger within the sight and scent of its cornered and helpless quarry.

The monster's new boys knew all about her ghastly excesses, and all three shook beneath the ominous shadow of a cadet-crushing machine of destruction.

This huge, amorphous glob of negativity regarded her trembling conscripts with undisguised contempt.

Her nose wrinkled and her normally narrowed and squinting eyes narrowed as she searched for, then singled out one boy.

The one boy Miss Crop had been directed to hurt by the headmaster's lady, the never charming and ever harming Mrs. Donnybrook had been easy to spot.

Bite must punish Brecken first. She must tantalize him with a brutality far more severe than she had ever employed on all those before him to make them cry.

Miss Crop's instructions were to send Brecken to Bite for special attention, special treatment, and the special torture she knew only her old crony had sufficient twisted motivation to adequately deliver.

"Oh, yes, my dear Miss Bite, I dispatch this sugar-sweet little imp to you:

"Prosecute the just vendetta of your one and only friend and avenge my spite, my dear and faithful friend," the wrathful and unnatural mother of Corey's lovely Leto whispered venomously into Miss Bite's obedient ear.

And now the vigilant Miss Bite had searched for and found out her friend's one special boy. She'd singled him out when she had reviewed the three brightly scrubbed little faces of the cadets who stood at stiff (and apprehensive) attention in her fearsome presence.

Cadet Brecken and none other was to be her very own little chew toy on this most exhilarating night of his initiation into the realm of pain. Brecken alone must fuel The Horror of Heeler Hall's peculiarly extreme, perverse and altogether nasty pleasures tonight.

"Oh, yes, my dear," the towering behemoth reflected, her high expectations of ghoulish fun mixed with the calm of complacency, "He shall not escape. He shall amuse me.

"I'm a-fixin' to make this crawling cur scream his lungs out for me.

"He's a-gonna scream jus' lak a little girl!"

His bright blond hair and sparkling blue eyes had at once betrayed Corey into the callous hands of this grotesque and implacable enemy.

The gentle and considerate Miss Bite always named any and every cadet doomed to feel the heat of her heavy hand:

"You filthy hound."

Such was the name she assigned to all her boys.

But now her dearest friend, the one constant entity that had been her companion from the time of their damnation at the very beginning of this world, has whispered these delicious and empowering words into the ear of this merciless engine of instant reciprocity, "This accursed hound I give you to fuel your especially depraved sinfully and delicious amusements, my dear. You must tantalize Cadet Brecken with the most exquisite twists and turns of your very own favorite sport, the torment of small children.

"I give you leave to inflict the very vilest of your furious punishments upon this worthless delinquent's naughty little hide.

"Punish him with my heartiest blessings, dear girl, for this fearful little wretch, this unspeakable little cur, this mongrel filthier than any of the unclean hounds we both hate together is infinitely more deserving of your most thrilling tortures and diverting amusements than any. He merits none but your harshest floggings and the most scornful and blasphemous of your curses!

"Oh, yes, my dear, Brecken The Lover is worse than all the rest, Brecken The Bold must be harried and winnowed down, down, down into nothingness through our collusion. Oh, yes, my dear, Brecken must be flayed alive, Brecken, Brecken, BRECKEN must be broken, broken, BROKEN!!!

"He insults me by pleasuring my frisky little tramp, that disgustingly pretty whore, Leto:

"Oh, Hecate, how I hate that bewitching girl -- and how I hate that horrible, horrible boy for making her smile, for making her laugh!

"I, I just know those two filthy little sinners are laughing at ME!

"Oh, I KNOW those two little no goods, those smarmy little brats, are up to something decidedly nasty, my dear; but my spies, Lin and Annie, have not yet been able to discover the mischief they're up to -- as yet.

"Make that sexy little blue eyed culprit scream for me ... Whip him, my dear, whip him, whip him, WHIP HIM!!!!"

And now, for his unpardonable sins of pleasing Leto and angering Mrs. Donnybrook, old lady Bite has both her sacrifice and her heartless commission to punish this young child's flesh beyond human endurance.

The Beast of Heeler Hall had determined that this especially filthy hound shall suffer a fiery furnace ten thousand times ten thousand fold hotter than any of the other poor little souls she has taken perverse pleasure in punishing before him this very night. Yes, the redoubtable Miss Bite was adamant that Brecken and Brecken alone must perform an abandoned whip dance for her entertainment tonight.

Bite must be quick to dispatch the other two microscopic pests given into her care, and then she should hasten to prosecute her favorite obsession, tonight's grizzly cabaret:

"Crabtree, you get your grousing li' l' tail into that there bedroom where you'll bunk with McNichol and Curley:

"One of 'em's a fairy boy and th' other one's th' basket case teddy hugger.

"Lots o' luck with those two, ye carpin' little sorehead!"

That overflowing vat of blubber was amply rewarded to note the abject terror in the eyes of her new boys as she led them through her hall and bossed them. It fed into the spirit of ill will she'd always harbored against all of the hardy and rambunctious children her work forced her to countenance.

"YES, MA'AM!!!" cried a frightened Cadet Crabtree as he jumped to it.

"Brecken and Milan, you two filthy hounds come to th' end o' this here hall with me." glowered the gruesome housemistress.

"YES, MA'AM!!!!" the last two among her condemned boys harmonized tremulously.

They followed the dragon in mortal dread of what unknown insults she might practice on them.

Heeler Hall was not arranged in the same manner as McAdam and Booker halls had been. Those two august erections both contained large common barrack rooms with long lines of bunks meant to accommodate scores of cadets in one barracks. But Heeler Hall was more of an afterthought. Heeler was simply the second story above the junior academy's elementary school classrooms.

The hall of the damned was comprised of four individual bedrooms, all of which might accommodate from four to six cadets in upper and lower bunk beds.

Our last boys followed the lumbering saurian blob down the hallway to a four bunk bedroom at the rear of the building.

A fat little cadet already abed there quickly leapt up and stood to, shivering with dread beneath the stygian darkness of Miss Bite's threatening shadow.

"This is Cadet McMoon, boys," grimaced the boss hag with a sneer of pronounced disgust, "McMoon's the biggest, fattest crybaby at Heeler Hall, aint y', boy?"

"YES, MA'AM!!!" he wailed in horror.

"Say hello, McMoon!" she spat out an order.

"H, how do you do, Miss Bite?" the flustered fat boy bawled in dismay.

The lethal leviathan caught Cadet McMoon in the midriff with a hard right hand, a punch that lifted her victim off his feet on impact.

That vicious old coward's blow doubled the poor soul up in agony and made him cry out piteously.

The Beast took careful note of the effect of her assault and grinned with undisguised pleasure. His darling housemother gave a thin-lipped smirk of approbation at the boys' new roommate's distress.

Then she softly corrected him, "Not to ME, y' stupid li' l' hound, say hello to your new roommates."

"Y-yes, 'm!" the poor soul wheezed through his tears. "H-hi, guys."

"Hi, McM-" Corey began to greet the injured lad.

"SHUT UP, FOOL!!!" bellowed his new housemother.

Miss Bite slapped her new chew-toy, so hard across the mouth the blow drove him across the room to career off the opposite wall.

Our dazed hero could taste the blood in his mouth and his ears rang. He was alive with the pain and shock of her unprovoked insult.

"I've got no time or patience fir th' likes of YOU, blue eyes," she growled angrily.

Then she turned to the academy's youngest cadet to bark:

"YOU, Little Milan, you just get yourself into that bed. It's way past your bedtime, y' puny little runt!"

"YES, MA' AM!!!!"

And the academy's extremely frightened littlest cadet rushed in a mad panic to make up the lower bunk across from McMoon's, undress and jump in it before the monster hit him as well.

Hurt, disgusted and petrified with terror Corey hastened to follow suit.

But he was not to be so lucky as the others because his dear old housemother had her own plans for him:

Bite The Avenger had eliminated the other little pests from today's contingent. And now this special little piece of meat, her Deepfreeze pal's heavily punished disciplinary problem, was to be his executioner/ housemother's especially toothsome little chew-toy de jour. Oh, yes, my dear, the frisky little star of tonight's diabolically deviant shower room floor show was to be Brecken, Brecken, BRECKEN. Brecken alone must be stripped naked to delight her bleary eyes. Brecken and only Brecken must be flayed alive on this lovely, lovely night of his trial and torment -- and her delight.

Miss Bite, legendary deviant and torturer extraordinaire was ready to play.

Corey's kindly old housemother opened this evenings' festivities on the spot.

The Beast of Heeler Hall grasped the dazed and shocked nine year old, pinned his arms to his sides with a lunatic's strength. The leviathan squeezed his arms tightly against his torso to constrict his lungs. The behemoth slowly applied added pressure until her satanically powerful grip drew his silent tears.

The snarling, sweating behemoth held her prisoner high above the concrete floor. She got herself off by slapping her helpless and imprisoned treat's upturned face until it flushed blood red.

Hard, harder and HARDER, again, again, again and again her thorny paws belabored her struggling quarry's upturned face.

Poor Corey hung there aghast, suspended in mid air and suffering The Beast's repeated insults. His heart failed him as he became more and more aware that his slavish fate had decreed that he must be savaged by The Horror of Heeler Hall. His deep duress must satisfy the bloodlust of two diseased gorgons bent on the vengeance fired satisfaction of their villainous and prurient pleasures.

Brecken's undoing was a delicate repast The Beast felt called upon to evoke from his torment. Slowly and deliberately she must bring him to a thundering crescendo of agony the better to savor her vice. She should be sated through her victory over him and gratified by the punishments she should inflict upon her little captive's pain-wracked body.

Oh, yes, my dear, this was The Beast's idea of a festive evening's gala enchantment.

"I've heard ALL about you, my darling, darling little BLONDIE!" his torturer cackled, merrily gloating to see her quarry so disgraced and so aware of it.

A satanic leer lit her hideous features as she regarded her tasty little chew-toy.

"'Oh, yes, my dear, dear little BLONDIE, I've heard all about YOU, my darlin' little 'CADET BRECKEN REPORTING AS ORDERED, MA'AM!!!'

"YOU FILTHY DOG, YOU, YOU DIRTY SCUM!!!!," she cursed and mocked him as she squeezed the life out of him, raked her big, thorny claw across his face and laughed at his misery, "I know you all right:

"You're th' lovely Leto's pretty li' l' boyfriend, AINT YE, huh, AINT YE, LOVER BOY???!!!!"

Suspended in midair and imprisoned in the her awful grip, in great pain and gasping hard for every breath of air, our brave Corey was completely in this gigantic pervert's power. But even in his awful extremity he refused to answer any inquiry made concerning his holy love for his darling Leto.

"How dare this ignorant, low born hag pronounce her name in derision?" he wondered, twisting in the air and in intolerable pain.

"Won't talk t' me, huh, my stubborn little yellow bird?

"Well, I'm a-gonna make ye DANCE and SCREAM like a little girl fir ME, lover boy:

"You STRIP NAKED 'n' git yore FILTHY-DIRTY HAUNCHES into that there shower room, ye disgusting little mongrel!

"And mind ye turn that shower up just as HOT as ye kin get it ... I want that water PIPING HOT!!!!

"HEAR WHUT I SAY, YOU HEAR ME, BOY??!!!"

"Y-yesss-yes, M-MA'AM-MA'AM!!!!" he squirmed and labored for enough air to reply.

Corey didn't know he had ever got the wind to answer his tormenter because Bite had gripped and squeezed his overtaxed torso with such gargantuan force so long that he was unable to breathe.

It seemed to him hours had flown by while his dread enemy had held him up, writhing and suspended in midair.

But an executioner has no thought of showing the slightest pity to her prey. This insouciant torturer grinned and drooled in satanic glee as she continued the pressure on Corey's overtaxed torso and held him up on display and inspected him closely to note the damage she'd wrecked upon his body for her own perverse delight. She knew she was crushing him, she knew she was grinding away at his resistance, tantalizing him and constricting the wind from his laboring lungs, and she was happy.

But it was not so with our Corey. He writhed while his grinning tormenter held him up to perceive his pathetic dolor, delighted at the sight of his helplessness, his miniscule size, his agony and his evident shame.

That smirking old devil held Cadet Brecken aloft, terrified and writhing for her amusement. Leto's little beau, the boy who had awakened her love, was now The Beast's luckless captive. The sadistic golem was playing with him and dancing him aloft like her toy puppet.

He was hurt, dizzy and dazed behind her hard slaps and her demoniac constriction of his chest.

"Oh, yes, my dear, dear little toy, you are mine!" Satan's attendant anaconda declared triumphantly, "Leto's gone now, baby boy, and dear ol' Miss Bite's kissin' ye now."

The little boy's laboring lungs, fighting hard to get just enough air to survive as he struggled in the behemoth's vice-like grip, were exploding.

But now this monster in quasi human form whispered softly to him that this was not to be the worst of his troubles, "Oh, no my dear, this aint th' end o' play time -- it's only the beginning."

Now The Beast brought her horrible face up close to his. This notorious torturer of small children gloried in her absolute power over this friendless little boy as she noted that he was sickened by the malodorous blast wafting from her diseased mouth, her signature stench. It was the unmistakable odor of a corrupt, cell-rotting, flesh-eating disease that ate away at her rotten old guts that was emitted from her thin-lipped, hate-twisted mouth.

Pinned and helpless Corey was gagged with revulsion by the ghastly reek. It was as if some alien entity, a being even more diseased and corrupt than she, had taken up residence in her guts. Immeasurably more deadly and diseased than her own obsessive need for and hatred of the little boys she had imprisoned in the vice-grip of her powerful hands for the purpose of their torture, was the scent of some unknown and completely odious decay.

That unknown entity was a murderous and inescapable specter from which even the horrid housemother had no egress. Bite was its prisoner as her boys were hers. This unknown thing owned her and Bite could no more escape it than could Corey escape her, and The Unnamed Terror was slowly devouring and killing The Horror of Heeler Hall.

After what seemed to him a thousand years of suspended torment, Corey's torturer dumped her gamin unceremoniously onto the hard cement floor.

Now he must jump up, strip with dispatch and run into the shower room to obey a superior's order. Corey's mind was a hodgepodge of disoriented and unthinking confusion. He knew nothing would ever be the same again after this frightening shower room encounter.

But he must obey this disgusting thing because his intractable grandparents must receive nothing but good reports of his conduct if he was ever get back home.

He skinned out of his fatigues and underwear in record time and ran naked into the shower room to begin his bath.

He turned the water he turned up just as hot, hot, HOT as he could stand it.

Oh, yes, my dear, hot, hot water was The Beast's cardinal catalyst, the primary catalyst which had never failed to release the energy which ignites the carnival of Miss Bite's very own private and sadistically teaming and satisfying shower room floor shows.

The horrid Beast's steaming arena of a young child's torment was the otherworldly locus of a sadistic monster's rapture, and this magic evening Miss Bite was ready to play.

"So THIS is what that spoiled little piece of a Leto's idea of what a cutsie-pootsie little lover-boy ought 'o be, is it?

"Well, I don't see nothin' so special!"

Corey heard her mock him from the hallway just outside the shower as he soaped his rag and nervously began his bath.

He knew she was going to try her best to break him. He was mortally afraid of an enemy so monstrously huge and obviously deranged, but he was determined that he must never let this humongous pimple on the nose of humanity, this insult to the race of man, break him.

Even in the oppressive heat of his housemother's steaming shower room his blood ran cold to hear that hideous dragon's hiss from the anteroom:

"I'll soon make you PAY, Leto's li' -l' lover boy!

"Leto loves ye, huh?

"Oh, yes, dear, dear boy, 'n' th' major loves ye, too, do he?

"Well, well, WELL, yore a-gonna PAY me for all THAT, you, you filthy-dirty little WHELP!!!"

Yes, to sate her unworthy lusts this one boy must pay this deviant sport back ten thousand, thousand, thousand fold more than any other little boy has ever done:

"Brecken, Brecken, BRECKEN must be broken, broken, BROKEN!!!!" had been her crony's demand.

Her best friend and patroness had ordered it, and Bite was prepared to make Brecken pay. He should pay the gorgon for being young and fair, for she was old and ugly. He must pay, and he pay dearly for being healthy and full of life and hope, for she was aged, mortally diseased and totally without hope.

Frisky little Brecken must pay the joyless Bite for every little bit of joy he had ever felt (and with a Scot's grandmother around we know that couldn't have been much joy). But, whatever joy he'd had she must take it all away from him, for The Beast's only happiness lay in the torment and suffering of the helpless young children condemned to the dark, dank dungeon of her wicked netherworld. Above all else Brecken must pay for being the one thing The Beast had never in her misbegotten life been -- loved!

Corey Brecken has enjoyed love, and being loved was the one unforgivable transgression The Bite must never abide.

A saurian brute crept inside her dark, dank underworld to test the mettle of little Miss Leto's lover boy. She meant to try him, to put him through her own personal brand of hell. Oh, yes, my dear, his must be a hell hotter than any of the others had endured. This diseased and anomalous blob must burn him in a hell ten thousand, thousand, thousand times hotter than anyone had suffered before him.

Old lady Bite must welt him for the sake of her dearest friend, Mrs. Donnybrook. Harpies in tandem, Bite and Deepfreeze Donnybrook were hungry to make this impudent tiny golden brat sweat, and sweat blood. Corey Brecken must ache and burn and scream for being all of those vital, wondrously youthful and high-spirited things those two lackluster gorgons never were. But tonight sickness, infirmity, madness and envy were to feast voraciously on the vibrant flesh of this jumped-up little scapegrace sacrifice's summer health and childish beauty.

In the morbid, gloom-caste half world of a madwoman's steaming shower room, that self same twisted, subhuman caricature of a woman advanced slowly, ever so slowly, ever so silently. Bite was mesmerized and clothed in the eerie cloak of her own signature ambiance.

Here she would prosecute her dark revenge. She moved ever so quietly forward, intent on branding this annoying little major's pet, this favorite delinquent protégé, with a fiery thrashing, and one he would never forget.

Foremost, his deranged punisher must hear his screams. She must thrill to those outcries of outrage. For her they were the sweetest of all the music in all the world. She must hear his full throated supplications for the mercy she could never grant, for mercy did not exist in her world. The high pitched screams of a small male animal in torment were the sweetest -- the only -- balm ever to sate her black desires:

"I'll make you SCREAM LIKE A LITTLE GIRL, my pretty little Leto's pet cadet!"

Corey stood frozen with terror.

He knew she was coming for him. He knew there was no way out of a whipping for him.

This horribly misshapen anomaly's child prey waited in his guileless innocence upon his evil mistress's dark design while this twisted and disgusting child abuser stalked him gradually, deliberately, methodically anticipating the sensuous waves of stimulation that were to be hers when she heard his screams. The Beast was in the throes of a particularly familiar orgasmic joy, the same surge the old lowbrow had always felt in the rapt anticipation of the heartless prosecution of her signal vice.

The Beast was drooling ecstatically as she viewed a mental picture of her tasty little chew-toy's torture trial. Her perverse imagination previewed the delight she was to feel as this toothsome little miscreant writhed in a transport of pain for her vile diversion. She must brand his guilty hide. She would make him jump and cry out for expiation, and she must hear those sweet, sweet screams, the sounds for which she lived.

Oh, yes, my dear, this pretty, naughty little sinner owed you that and more.

The delicious outcries of all the boys she had harrowed in the past were ever the epitome of sexual gratification for The Bite. More beautiful, more deliciously exhilarating to this relentless soul in torment than the pleasing picture of her naked little children's outraged whip dance, a dance that had never failed to make her laugh aloud in an heartless paroxysm of joy. All of these victories were honey-sweet, yet they were always subordinate to the delicious howls for expiation she craved.

This evening she must prosecute the trial of her best friend's enemy to the fullest. Only a lost soul the like of Mrs. Donnybrook could ever have been so shameless as to declare a young boy her enemy.

It was meat and drink for this lost and depraved deviant to hear a child's unheeded protestations for mercy as he writhed in the trials she forced upon him in her torture pit. She was nearing orgasm in anticipation of the infernal cantata she was about to wring from the quivering lips of this evening's delectable child-tidbit. The glob's passion piqued her curiosity and spurred her bloodlust onward, ever onward to Corey's outrage -- and her transport.

The screams of her cadets toy soldiers were peculiar to Miss Bite's signature lunacy. Her infernal lust for them must be glutted this very night, and it would be so only when this boy's naked and convulsed flesh vessel had been pressed and driven so far that he must yield up his stentorian petitions to her. Bite must hear Brecken's piteous screams to sate her primary driver, her paramount obsession. Corey's cries of outrage were to have been the most delicious course in The Beast's impending engorgement of pain and degradation.

The pliant, yielding flesh of Bite's tiny, defenseless sex object awaited her pleasure in her arena of shame. He was hers to have and to hurt. Brecken, Brecken, BRECKEN was hers, ripe and sweet and waiting for punishment.

This amoral anomaly, this unchecked criminal, who lived only to satisfy her voracious appetites was stalking him in the darkness, and she was assured of having her fun with him.

Oh, yes, my dear Miss Bite, you shall have those vital supplications from the very soul of the major's little pet, his beloved and loving boy protégé. Your old pal, the high and mighty Mrs. Donnybrook, has thrown him to you to scream in the torture trial of your doleful arena of tears. Now he waits for you to throw him into the midst of your rabid rendition of fun and games:

Oh, yes, my dear, his screams shall be yours, or will they?

Her tenuous grasp on the rudiments of human physiology had given Miss Bite a marked advantage over the ignorant bullies (Basin for example) who only dip their toes into the bottomless whirlpool of her black art. Old Schoolmarm Bite was in this business to take all the suffering and shame she could from her little toy soldiers.

Tonight The Beast was going to make this randy little blue eyed scamp pay for being cute, for being blond -- and, worst of all, for being loved!

Hot water activates the subject's nerve endings, bringing enhanced sensitivity to surface of his skin to cause her subject greater pain. Bite knew it and she loved it.

The Beast's primary catalyst, hot, hot water has been employed, given ample time to take effect and now it was time for this cool and calculating reptilian predator to insinuate herself into her pit of pain. Now the slimy dragon crept silently into her steaming hot shower room to do him harm. It was time to practice her art and have her disgusting and deranged fun with him. She came creeping in to flay the soft, pink hide of Leto's fetching little golden brat, and she came to hear him scream, Corey's self-righteous housemother had come to beat his soft pink flesh black.

Had she not always entered this same steaming arena of tribulation to burn the fear of Eris into the distressed flesh of every one of her little toy soldiers?

Yes, she had.

Bite's weapon of choice was a narrow, flat sled board inscribed with the jaunty motto:

THE SILVER STREAK.

Had her criminal practice not won that sweet ambrosia, that nectar of the gods, that comely, lively reward for her eyes to see and for her ears hear?

It had.

Had it not always been so?

So had it invariably been for this deranged and misshapen dross, and so should it ever be until the ravages of the deadly cancer little Corey had scented in the midst of his shame and duress finally dragged her down to hell.

Above all, had those divine screams not been wrenched from the gasping lungs and trembling lips of her prey in the winnowing wake of THE SILVER STREAK'S damage?

And those outraged cries for mercy were the sweetest trophies of the chase for this pitiless and relentless monster.

Oh, yes, my dear, they were.

The Beast of Heeler was ugly, old and sick, ergo she made sure these comely, lively little bucks recompensed her for that bold affront.

In the insanely twisting avenues of her warped, pain distorted mind this was justice. If she must bear constant pain, why should they not?

Miss Bite had what was then the incurable carcinogenic blood disease, leukemia. It was leukemia that had engendered the sickening pang which had repulsed and sickened Corey when Miss Bite had held him up to her face -- and a kiss that gagged him.

Our hero scrubbed away briskly, hoping for the best, but knowing the worst was on its way. Corey busily washed up in the vain hope of getting out of there before his grim captor remembered him.

No such luck, Brecken, Brecken, BRECKEN.

Suddenly, a little boy's acute senses picked up on danger and sounded the alarm. His very essence, every fiber of this threatened little animal's being awakened to a mortal and proximal mortal peril right behind him.

"Oh, God!" gasped our naked sacrifice to his fearful enemy.

A mountain of malice, a leviathan of dread, a silent monster possessed of a black reservoir of incredible animal ferocity that could kill him, stood in ominous silence directly behind him.

Only seconds ago it had not been there. But suddenly a tower of evil had enveloped Corey in midnight darkness.

Without warning, Miss Bite's hot, hot, HOT shower room had gone ice cold, frozen in the icecap of horror.

The thing that hovered over him was so close he could hear her labored breathing. He was able to feel the threat in her lethal brute force shrouded inside the swirling clouds of low hanging vapor.

The thing standing over him was only a dark outline obscured by the dense clouds of rising steam. The menace's lowering presence had cast a shadow over the whole room. Its stygian darkness completely covered and obscured the trapped little boy. It had swallowed him up whole.

The silent monolith of malignant purpose spoke never a word even though a legion of starving demons were screaming from her huge, amorphous maw to be fed the pain, the disgrace and screams of the innocent.

This insuperable enemy of children had claimed her prey, eradicated him, for she had buried him in the catacomb beneath the shadow of her dark intent. This canopy of unspeakable evil engulfed her naked prey in preparation for her black feast. The evil hell hag had wrapped the boy up in the black thunderhead of her vile desire.

"That rotten stink!"

His senses sounded the alarm.

Corey's heart sank and his flesh crawled as he recognized his deadly enemy's halcyon reek.

The Dragon of Heeler Hall was here to claim her helpless toy cadet.

Hope fled him, for Corey realized he was about to be tried by the most infamous, notorious sadistic monster The Tower Military Academy had to offer.

Leto's little lover boy was surely lost, but our gutsy half-pint was a hero. And heroes don't run from danger, even a danger they can never hope to defeat. No, Corey must face his tormentor like the nine year old man all his elders wanted him to be.

He marshaled every scintilla of failing courage he had.

He wheeled sharply around and face his foe.

"Oh, God!" he gasped when he saw her in her fiendish delight. His blood ran cold at the sight of the misshapen mountain of malice and perversity that stood drooling down on him.

The deviant raised THE SILVER STREAK high above her head to strike the first blow.

The sight of her ghoulish visage, horribly distorted in its psychotic longing to possess and torture him, made the lost boy's mind cry out to his Creator for succor.

Deep in that reeking, steaming den of a child's monstrous abuser, glistening with her own sweat and the water from the shower, aimed her first strike. The night's lively entertainment began when Bite struck downward with all her power. The gorgon aimed directly at Corey's center. His loving housemother swung her weapon sharply down, aiming to cripple the darling Leto's prize.

"Meet MY little boyfriend, THE SILVER STREAK, Missy Leto's pretty little boyfriend, BLUE EYES!!!!" screamed the deranged hag in a spasm of wild delight.

Corey jumped sharply around to frustrate her.

As he wheeled he had to grab desperately to reach his shower's spigots in an all out effort to keep his balance in such a slippery venue. He was lucky and coordinated enough to hang on tight and avoid falling.

There was an almighty explosion.

A flaming lightning bolt of unbearable pain shot upward and outward throughout Corey's young body under siege.

The shock radiated from his bare backside outward.

The loud, hard blow telegraphed extreme pain all through his brutally assailed nervous system. A reverberating shock wave of unadulterated pain drove his child's acute sensibilities directly into the bowels of hell, and that was exactly where his grizzly old enemy wanted him to be.

A resounding crack of hardwood on wet, bare flesh ripped through the barracks. It was a sickeningly familiar sound, one that sent an immediate cold shiver through the being of every beaten and badgered little boy who'd been sent here to moan beneath the heavy yoke of The Beast.

Those living, breathing little trophies Miss Bite had heartlessly pinned like so many brightly colored living, suffering butterflies into her personal scrapbook of pain realized at once that one of their own was in the barrel with The Bite tonight.

And the poorest boy, the one presently under assault, thanked God the vicious old hell hag hadn't been quick enough to hit the target she'd specifically aimed to cripple, for his was the organ of Leto's fancy.

He was a tough one.

" Scream for me, boy, SCREAM!!!" howled the incensed old nut case, angry at his intransigence.

An instant epiphany had told Corey exactly what she wanted from her distressed chew toy de jour.

In the very hour of his fallible little body's defeat, that instantaneous spark of recognition struck our half-pint hero like lightning:

The trophy his lost and deranged enemy of children wanted most was that he scream his weak capitulation to her inner demons. A little boy's shamefaced surrender to her insuperable might and boundless girth was what she craved above all things.

If Corey had been smart he would have screamed instantly and fed her sickness. He might have yielded up his long and furious shrieks, the halcyon declarations of his surrender to his criminal tormentor, but heroes are not smart, they are brave. And Corey Brecken was his beloved Princess Leto's own hero.

He knew this diseased old monster lived to hear the impassioned wails from her pinioned butterfly's pain-wracked lips.

Well, that was just too bad for this bully and torturer. Corey The Hero wasn't playing ball with Bite The Beast.

From this very moment throughout the farthest reaches of infinity a little boy had resolved that this sinister enemy of every child on earth, this crawling serpent who made life hell for little boys would never hear him scream her whole life through.

Yes, he knew he was here at military school to be broken to the whip but never would he allow himself to be broken by this hated practitioner of pain.

A little boy burdened with every human weakness, under the duress of a hulking monster's most intense torture and enveloped in the urgent desperation of his childish extremity, sent up a feverishly urgent prayer from this seething inferno. In the darkest dark of this iniquitous temple to Satan's monster handmaiden and her demonic practices a child's prayer was heard by The Master of the universe.

God's enemies longed to hear one more suborned and defeated little mortal's cries, but that was never to be.

From this stinking arena of foul perversity a brave little innocent in desperate need has earnestly petitioned The Eternal Spirit to lend him the raw courage to bear what he must in steel-strong silence.

The torturer became angrier and poured on the pain.

The punishment grew ever harder and more brutal, but our insulted little hero held onto those spigots so tightly they galled his hands bloody.

He would never scream for her.

Miss Bite's blazing weapon rose and fell again and again and again. THE SILVER STREAK reddened, then blackened the white skin of our suffering little cadet's outraged back as The Beast punished Brecken, Brecken, BRECKEN mercilessly. The dragon blackened the boy's back from his shoulders to his knees.

The flagellation continued until Corey's posterior was nothing but one big bruise.

The countryside's crickets outside the hall ceased their chatter.

Cadets and crickets alike listened in amazement as all nature attended THE SILVER STREAK enraptured. Bite's awful flail filled the surrounding countryside with the strident noises of the behemoth's implacable scourging of Cadet Brecken, Brecken, BRECKEN.

THE STREAK branded our Hero Of The Shower Room and left wide, red welts in its scathing wake even as a little boy's super-sensitive nervous system suffered long in the flames of hell.

Miss Bite had dipped him deep in her blazing crucible of fire again and again and again.

A young boy's violently assaulted senses begged for release from this confirmed deviant's lashing sea of flaming lava while his heartless abuser punished her infuriatingly stubborn little brute with the might and main of a lunatic's all-out bombardment. But she could not make him cry out, for a merciful God had answered a frail little boy's plea and granted the child His Divine Fortitude.

Brecken was fortified with the almighty power to endure the virulent ferocity of a gigantic dragon's unfettered wrath. Brecken, Brecken, BRECKEN took an unholy beating but he was proof against the unbridled fury of an enraged Beast.

Corey Brecken held on, tenaciously refusing to cry. He would never satisfy his enemy's satanic desire though his writhing body suffered monumentally for the intransigence of his plucky spirit.

Infuriate, Miss Bite released her most destructive cyclone of abuse on the one boy she must break.

Not smart, but heroic, our boy remained mute. His silent, bitter tears mingled with the shower's cascading waterfall, but he would not yield.

"Why don't he scream?" whispered one of those wakeful and worried "sleeping" cadets at the hall to the next.

"Yeah!" wondered his bunkmate, "I hear th' STREAK, 'n' I hear th' dragon, but I don' hear HIM."

"I KNOW she's skinnin' 'im alive -- but he aint makin' a SOUND!" Little Milan gasped in wide-eyed wonder, coupled with reverent admiration at his roomie's "big balls."

Poor McMoon whimpered and hid his frightened face deep beneath his bedcovers. But it was no use, for the poor, cowardly fat boy lay frozen with fear beneath all the blankets he could find.

"What BALLS!" Curley allowed, "But 'e can't hold out on HER much longer.

"That ugly ol' gargoyle 'll break 'im tonight for sure."

"What a MAN! Oh, boys, he's my HERO!" sighed his roomie, the unusually graceful McNichol.

Meanwhile, in the shower room fray their cuddly old housemother's hard curses and harder blows continued long, loud and unabated through the night:

"How dare you report to Heeler Hall in such an UNMILITARY state of SQUALOR, you, you MANGY LITTLE CUR?!!!

"I'll soon TEACH you a thing 'r two, my darlin' little BLUE EYES, BLONDIE!!!!!"

She savaged his pain wracked body with all her power.

She continued to scourge an injured little boy's blackened flesh in an all out firestorm of aggression against this gutsy little hold out:

"HOWL FOR ME, YOU DIRTY LITTLE HOUND!!!

"SCREAM or I'll KILL you, Leto's precious, LOVER BOY, BLONDIE, BLUE-EYES!!!!

"Scream for ME, SCREAM, DO YOUHEAR ME?!!!!"

It was impossible for a little boy to resist this avalanche of persecution, but our Corey was given the power to do the impossible. He was impassive to his housemother's volcanic eruption of insult, but could our cheeky little rebel actually persevere against her?

"Unthinkable, my dear, whip him harder!" the dragon's absent patroness whispered.

"When will it end?" wondered her embattled victim, burning, writhing and throbbing in the shameful throes of his naked extremity, "Will she whip me to death?"

Shivering in their beds the remainder of Bite's petrified little victims wondered, "Aint she NEVER gonna STOP?"

But Bite's inferno went on and on.

Small and frail, Cadet Brecken had called forth and clothed himself in the terrible Aegis of Divine Providence. His prayer was answered and he was blessed with the Eternal's fortitude to resist the vicissitudes of the damned soul pursuing him. The Power which orders the universe has denied a stinking hag her victory over our more or less innocent little hero's unconquered spirit.

A loathsome hag from the deepest, darkest regions of hell was given temporary license to brand and outrage Corey's overtaxed body, and she had. But his spirit was still inviolate. It was his and only his. He'd persevered over a frightful pain engine, a Goliath that had battered his throbbing, burning person fanatically.

In the face of his defiance, a frustrated attacker's rage flared up and burned ten million fold. Bite whipped her tiny prey with the united fury of that legion of demons in her lost soul. Her rage was stoked by this scamp's defiance. This hated and feared leviathan's inability to force this one boy, the specific little cur pointed out by her mistress, to grovel at her feet and beg her for mercy had driven the horror to paroxysm.

This tiny insect's refusal to do her will spurred her on and on through her fog-shrouded, surrealistic half world to attack him in a blind frenzy. In her very own dark waterfall, in the morbid venue of her shower room torture chamber The Beast must triumph.

Oh, yes, my dear?

The dragon spewed her volcanic oceans of excruciating abuse over a cornered little animal's brightly shimmering, hopelessly squirming body. She cursed him ever more and more vehemently, driven by her mad obsession to break him. The Beast's insane possession to steal yet another young child's soul and force him to surrender to her slowly built into a deafening crescendo of lunatic fury.

Corey at length slumped down onto the shimmering concrete.

The monster's scalding blows had robbed him of the ability to stand up for more of this protracted and extreme battery. Our harrowed young hero's body was spent but he manfully refused to yield up that last scrap of himself he still owned:

Our brave little warrior clung desperately to his humanity. He refused to scream for this deadly enemy's pleasure. Sure, little Corey's body and soul had screamed for mercy deep inside his head, for no living child could hope to stand up to such a grotesque titan's excruciating tortures without tears. But his unheard shrieks of outrage were forever silenced, locked deep inside his psyche by The Power above all powers.

A seriously wounded boy's cries have been forever staunched down in the remote recesses of his soul.

The ravening monster beating him had driven him mad, but never would he give in and scream for her.

The Hero Of The Shower Room's visible and audible instrument remained supremely impassive throughout the insupportable torture trial.

Our savaged little cadet's throbbing, heavily distressed body had been incessantly begging his unconquerable spirit to surrender to his implacable enemy from the moment of her first slap across his shocked and bloodied mouth.

And, when Bite's punishing STREAK had risen and fallen again and again to thrash his raw, burning and convulsed flesh, his body had implored his spirit to give it up, but his spirit had remained unmoved.

The Hero Of The Shower Room had repeatedly asked himself the same question every cadet in Heeler Hall was asking, "Will it never end?"

An all out battle of wills was joined in Miss Bite's dark arena of shame. The withering fury of her silver flail made the Heeler Hall Horror's victim grip the metal spigots before him until his white bones shone through the pink flesh of his bleeding fingers. Corey's death-grip forced the blood from his palms to release its dark red stigmata into the torture chamber's waterfall.

The accelerated force and frequency of that stinking tyrant's strokes against his body now detonated such a panic in the brain of the madwoman's stubborn captive that he wondered if he could really prevail. Blind terror rolled ominously through Corey's wildly pulsating brain. A chilling fear that defeat at the hands of this unspeakable toad might be inevitable hit home. With exhaustion his resolve began to flicker low.

A little boy's tortured body -- naked, exhausted and in the clutches of a merciless all-powerful foe -- begged his unyielding spirit again and again to give up the screams of shame and surrender his poison-bloated foe demanded.

"Oh, Heaven!" his spirit begged in silent desperation.

But his fierce determination to resist the horror's dreaded victory was weakening with her every lash, reverberating through the countryside. And Corey's courage was drip, drip, dripping slowly away with every drop of Bite's hot, hot, HOT shower water as it cascaded over him and disappeared down the drain.

Little Corey Brecken's heart sank lower and lower, haunted by the ghastly vision of The Beast's sickening victory. The gorgon must win if the blows of her insupportable outrage continued to rain down on him, even for one more instant. Was he to lose the hard fought war after the torture trial he had braved so long?

No!

Finally, a harried little schoolboy's forever and ever of insupportable agony had ended as celeritously as it had begun.

The Horror of Heeler Hall had succumbed to her own fatal morbidity. The horrid hell hag's poor excuse for a body had broken down, overtaxed by the physical effort her project required. Miss Bite's corrupt, cancer-riddled body was unable to persist in her vile commission no longer. The monster was just plain worn out.

Corey's shocked senses had been dulled. His ringing ears were barely able to pick up the far off sound of a tyrant queen's huge carpet slippers scrape, scrape, scraping across the shower room floor in full retreat.

Out of the shower and into the hall they shuffled. Even a dragon must return to its slimy lair to rest after its fiery breath has failed to fry an unusually gutsy little knight. The one boy the dragon had sought, found and punished until they had both dropped had won.

At first he couldn't believe it.

The one boy's tear-dimmed eyes fought as hard as they were able to make out what had happened. With great difficulty he focused on his perfidious foe's putrid, ponderous bulk as it slithered into the distance.

The Beast had exited her dark, dank torture pit in full retreat. This unspeakable monster, the inescapable Pain Mountain shuffled away in her clumsy, lurching flight from those very same billowing fog clouds that had once brought her unclean spirit so much joy.

A huge, carnivorous dinosaur from the bowels of an infant earth's murky and long dead past has suffered her first defeat.

The Beast had been beaten and a tiny schoolboy had whipped her!

It had been a matter of pride to this scabby old monster to break him. Unfortunately for her, Brecken had more pride than Bite had ever dreamed. And a helpless child's heavenly Master had answered his prayer and come from beyond the beyond to save him.

Defeated and deflated, The Heeler Hall Horror had failed to wrench one scream from her embattled chew toy. Drained of all her deadly venom by this exhausting catharsis, that unspeakable saurian slithered out of her obscure arena of degradation, for she must return to her slimy lair to rest.

She had quenched her ghoulish bloodlust on the abject misery of yet another tiny innocent -- but this time she had lost.

In the smoldering wake of a gigantic and perverted devil's fury, a wounded little boy lay battered and abandoned, where his vile taskmistress had left him to rot.

Our savaged child wept silently in his loneliness and sorrow.

Only by Divine Providence's mercy was our hero still half alive.

After his outrageous scourging he trembled spasmodically in shock. His jangled nervous system made Corey's ravaged body jump and twitch, a consequence of his ruthless and insouciant abuser's infuriate firestorm of abuse. The Beast had rushed in to beat and curse him, but now our little toy soldier must somehow summon up enough courage to effect his own recovery -- alone and hurt.

A monster of perdition, huge in her boundless dimensions and arrogantly overconfident that her superior strength, weight and girth must quickly suborn one friendless little boy, had lost to that same despised little boy. How could a naked little child, stripped of family, home and comfort and delivered into the horny hands of cold, uncaring strangers ever beat The Horror of Heeler Hall?

Oh, but he has, my dear.

A cold blooded, prehistoric saurian has fled the scene of her crime. Now she's coiled up in the fastness of her lair to console herself with slumber-fading visions of a comely youngster's naked body dancing to her manic's measure.

But Bite was still able to make the victor shudder with fear when he heard her hiss her parting threat as she fell asleep, "It's not over for you, Blondie.

"Oh, no, dear little Leto's sweet blue eyed lover boy, not by a long shot!"

Corey's silent tears mingled with The Beast's hot water. Both trickled down the drain as our half-pint hero struggled manfully to come once more to himself.

For a long, long time he was only able to lie still on the shimmering shower room floor, crying silently as his enemy's hot water continued to patter against his prostrate form. Corey was pitifully weak and sore in body and in spirit.

The words of his faraway elders-and-betters, so comfortably and safely ensconced in their tropic paradise, echoed faintly through the corridors of a heartbroken child's memory, "This will make a man of you, grandson."

He imagined his grandparental judges must be quite pleased with themselves now. The wild young colt they had sent away to be broken to the whip was well on his way to that very respectable and highly genteel end.

But their end had been prosecuted with such vitriol, such hatred and such excessive force as to render this dish unpalatable, even to their austere tastes.

Half conscious, a battered and bruised Corey wondered how much more of this could take.

Nothing he had ever known or imagined, nothing he'd read in books or seen in movies could ever have begun to prepare him for this night's devastating avalanche. It's effects had laid him out like a corpse. Today a confirmed child abuser had buried him beneath a mountain of excruciating torment.

But he had persevered. The Beast's extreme practices might well have sickened the mad marquis himself, but Corey's nine year old manhood was still intact. His frail and battered body had been sickeningly ravaged, mauled and branded for the diversion of a depraved monster.

Brecken, Brecken, BRECKEN has suffered the unspeakably unjust punishments of an insane deviant. But he had won and The Beast could report nothing else to her Deepfreeze Boss.

Mrs. Donnybrook's spies were listening everywhere and a lie would never work.

Though victorious, Corey knew his future was not to be a bright one. His courage failed him as he remembered the dragon's parting promise:

"It's not over for you, blue eyes ... not by a long shot!"

Tonight's crushing eruption of agony and invective had been a prelude to an impending opus of outrage. No one knew better than he that The Beast's words foretold a greater evil.

"Oh, Curley, he's SUCH a MAN!

"Pretty -- oopsee -- I mean handsome, too!" giggled Cadet McNichol in an enthusiastic outburst of boyish-girlish passion.

And he was just one of Corey's dorm mate hero worshipers.

"Shut up, y' li' l' sis!" snapped his hardboiled roommate, hugging his teddy bear tighter (The dead butch Cadet Curley was unwilling to admit that he admired Corey's guts as much as his lacy roomie.), "What's a limp noodle like YOU know about a REAL man anyways?

"But Brecken's got BALLS, all right," the teddy hugger allowed deferentially.

Cadet McMoon was crying. Hidden deep beneath the warmth of his blankets the poor little coward lay frozen with fear.

"But now my hero's REALLY in for it!" worried McNichol.

Curley, concurred, "Man oh man, is he EVER!

"Well, better him than us, right, teddy bear?"

Completely drained, their tiny superhero never heard a single word of his cadet fan club's adulation. It was all and nearly more than he could do to stagger up on his wobbly pins. Holding on to the shower room walls for support, he battled for the strength to turn off the spigots and drag his battered, shuddering, ice-cold with shock body off to bed where he silently cried himself to sleep.

Corey's last thought before sleep released him was one of gratitude to his beloved Eternal Spirit for granting him his impossible victory over a bullying giant's heated and cowardly assault.

"God, please, please damn Miss Bite!" was Corey's parting supplication to The Deity.

The Deity knew Corey was just a boy and let that one go. Actually, it was too late to damn Miss Bite to hell, for that had already been taken care of long ago.

Whatever the morrow might bring (and no one knew better than our Heeler Hall cadets that it was not going to be anything good) the little lost boys thanked God their housemother's beatings and curses had at last abated for today.

Corey's blasphemous and squalid toad-enemy had hurt him grievously. But now the healing balm of lovely sleep had come to lift our outraged little lad high above the academy, and even higher above reality. He sailed skyward, over the heads of the frightening powers-that-be that loomed menacingly above our tiny goober's towhead.

In dreamland Corey was on top of the world. He was safe and sound in his own Technicolor kingdom, a place where his terrifying foes could not get at him. In the academy's dour world of reality his aching mind and body were still burning with the shame and outrage of being humiliated for a squalid old deviant's pleasure. But in his dream world he was a triumphant dragon slayer, and one whose dauntless spirit winged aloft, victorious over the forces of villainy and wickedness that had laid him low that day.

What glorious dreams were his when his unconquered spirit was free to fly directly into Corey's Leto Heaven.

Leto Heaven was a magical place where all her hero's wounds were miraculously healed. There two reunited and rejoicing young lovers were met in a happy embrace.

Corey and Leto held hands and ascended through the halls of alabaster splendor of the glorious Cinemascope Technicolor Olympian Dream Palace of their fancy.

Here Leto and Corey were free to play. Here they were ecstatic lovers, safe in their own impregnable stronghold to enjoy the bounty of their never ending youth and beauty.

In dreamland the happy golden brats adventured, lightly and curiously, into the notorious bedchamber of the highly adventurous and very lively Tsaritsa, Catherine the Great.

In that enlightened despot's glittering bedchamber Missus Donnybrook and Miss Bite had been turned into a pair of strident, eternally scolding magpies. Fortuitously, the carping magpies were locked up in a big iron cage where they could no longer injure little children. Oh, what a wonderful dream!

The cunning Leto quickly covered the birdcage with a big black shroud. And his girlfriend's prompt action immediately sent both magpies to sleep forever.

To celebrate young love's victory over witchery and envy, The Golden Brats climbed higher and higher into the mysteries of The Scarlet Empress's endless bed, stopping often to continue their impassioned embraces.

The Chinese detective of dirty joke fame appeared to report, "Corey play with she, Leto play with he, Missy Bite play with she, Missy Bite fall out of tree!"

The enraptured pair gazed longingly into one another's eyes, leant torridly forward into their big screen kiss and reveille sounded!

Corey was plagued by his mysterious curse of an irrepressible morning erection. It had made its appearance in dreamland. But, now that his dream was broken, it remained to confound him. Sure, Leto liked it, but could he ever dare to hope that anyone else in this frightful academy was in any way similar to Leto?

Corey, the grandson of two severely repressive Victorians, knew good and well he must hide this from such a judgmental punisher as Miss Bite.

He busied himself with his hospital corners to get his mind off his dreams.

SAGE ADVICE FROM A LOVED ONE

Reveille blew promptly at 0600, much too soon for one Cadet Brecken, on the early, early morn following his scandalously savage welcome to Heeler Hall.

Even so our hero was the first to bound out of his rack and make it up, tightly enough to bounce a quarter off its tense surface (just as soon as he could corral his prominent embarrassment).

As he put the finishing touches to his immaculate hospital corners Corey was made aware that he hadn't remembered to clothe his nakedness since he's been outraged. He was still just as he had been when his dear old housemother larruped him in the abominable fog of her torture chamber.

Now he was surprised to hear a long, low whistle out of Little Milan.

"What's wrong with you, Li' l' Milan?" Corey demanded of the school's only cadet junior to him, "What're y' doin' whistlin' at ME?"

"It's your BACK, Brecken!" the awestruck mite whispered, breathless with wonder, "Oh, my God, Brecken, I, I KNEW she was givin' it to y' BAD from all o' that noise she was makin,' but, but I never, ever thought one human bein' could do THAT to another person!"

"Like What?" wondered our battle scarred superhero.

McMoon, roused by his roomies voices, added his own whistle of adulation to Little Milan's.

"DAMN, Brecken!" gasped the fat boy, "Ol' lady Bite REALLY gave you a WHALING:

"Oh, God, Brecken, your whole back is BLACK!

"You, you're nothin' but one great big bruise from your shoulders to th' backs o' your knees!!!

"Ol' lady Bite, she, she WHIPPED you jus' like a SLAVE!!!!"

"Oh, well," smiled Corey, "We were all bad boys back home. And that's why our old folks sent us up here in th' first place:

"To get badness beat out of us."

"Not ME, I'M a good boy!" projected the terror-transfixed fat boy emphatically, "I, I don' NEVER need NO whippin' like THAT, no, not never, never, never ME!!!!"

Both of his friends smiled knowingly at poor old McMoon's ingenuousness.

Little Milan was the youngest cadet, but he wasn't the stupidest. And Milan and Brecken both knew that every cadet at The Tower had been sent here by exasperated forebears to grin and bare it for The Brass.

All three schoolboys rose and went about the business of preparing for the early morning formation, breakfast, drills, sports and classes of their day.

Cadet McMoon was extremely fearful and agitated in the presence of Corey's painful marks of distinction. The scared little fat boy was afraid of what might happen to his own thin skin. In the academy's eerie venue of ever present danger the fat boy instinctively recoiled from the stalking specter of physical abuse.

The frightening prospect of every cadet's harsh reality of mistreatment had been illustrated by last night's bold victim-yet-victor's stoical acceptance of his lot.

"I, I aint no BAD boy, not ME I tell you, not ME!" McMoon raved with all the vehemence of a card carrying coward, "I, I wasn't never a bad boy and I don' never-ever want a whippin' like THAT, no, no, not ME, not NEVER ME!!!"

Suddenly Little Milan's eyes got as wide and round as saucers. Frozen to the spot, too mortified to say a word, he pointed a silent trembling finger at the dark and deadly lurking shadow that hovered high above them just outside the doorway.

Our littlest cadet had been the first to spot the Horror of Heeler Hall standing mute and blotting out the sunlight filtering dreamily through a window behind her.

"SO, fat boy, yore ad-mirin' th' nice decorations I done give pretty-boy las' night, HUH?" hissed the skulking menace who had been listening in all along, "Well, well, WELL, IF you AINT down there in formation standin' TALL when assembly blows, that's just exactly th' kind o' beauty spots I'm a-gonna give ye, little Mister McSloppy!"

This festering boil, this rotting canker on the posterior of humanity had been spying on the three comrades. She had heard their every word from hiding, and how she hated little boys.

"Admiring pretty boy's fancy black butt, huh, moon pie?" raged the hideous saurian, "Well, well, WELL, if you don't git yoreself into that there formation on th' quad right quick, I'm a-gonna fix ye up with th' same kind o' burnin' welts I fired into that damn stubborn little fool's worthless hide las' night!

"Oh, yes, yes, YES, poor, poor li' l Blondie Brecken," she turned to last night's quarry, "You poor, misunderstood li' l angel! Did that mean ol' devil house ma mark up yore sweet li' l darlin' po-po las' night, BLONDIE?"

"The cadet has no complaints, MA'AM!!!"

"Savaged and still defiant!" she raged within, "Oh, how I hate that imp!"

"GIT into that dad-blame formation ON TH' DOUBLE, all you lazy, shiftless hounds, a-fore I give ye th' best whippin' ye ever got in yore lives, one I ain' ner gonna let ye firgit!"

The Nightmare had hid herself to spy out his friends' reaction to the revolting thing she'd done to Cadet Brecken. From concealment their malicious matron had peeped into the little boys' room to discover their thoughts.

Now the plague revealed herself to thunder her morning salutation at them.

Three frightened cadets -- along with every denizen of Heeler Hall -- jumped smartly to and prepared for the worst.

Poor McMoon almost fainted at the ghastly sight:

The fat boy would never have admitted it but he'd been to the shower room with The Beast and she'd broken him. His dreams of "good boy" clemency were only dreams, and McMoon had known shame beneath THE SILVER STREAK.

"YES, MA' AM!!!" the terrified trio piped in unison.

They rushed headlong into their closets to dress, wash, comb and dash out of doors and onto the quad for morning muster.

Heeler Hall boys were the most highly motivated cadets of all to get into formation fast, principally to escape their reeking, peeping, forever skulking Komodo dragon in charge. This morning they clambered down the stairs, desperate to elude her.

But there was one boy who was not nearly so lucky as his fellows:

Oh, no, my dear, Bite was laying in wait especially for her one boy. And the possessed deviant snatched Brecken up in her powerful claws when he did his best to dart past her.

The slavering monster sow lifted her pesky little headache up and squeezed his arms tightly against his body as she had last night.

Corey, held aloft by the tyrant, struggled and gasped with pain while the other boys rushed past them in horror.

The others counted themselves lucky to get downstairs and out of doors while the slavering behemoth busied herself with her new toy.

Now our cocky little mini-hero had been left alone to face the same ghoulish apparition that had terrified and menaced him through billowing clouds of steam in the worst night any cadet had ever been forced to countenance.

The Bite leered smugly down on her captive chew-toy to view his misery closely. She sickened him. The shocking threat of a repetition of Bite's personal brand of cowardly violence froze him stiff as her moribund breath reached out, touched and repulsed him. The same deathly reek that had sickened him in the fogbound shower made him gag and retch anew.

The Golem tightened her grip on him and drew him irresistibly closer and closer as she hissed her hatred directly into his fresh-scrubbed infantile face:

"You think you've WON, don't you, YOU pathetic little BUG?

"YOU win over ME?

"You've won nothing, NOTHING, you, you, you annoyin' li' l' SKEETER!!!!

"WHY?

"A-cause I'm STILL gonna hear ye scream, you, you insignificant little GNAT, Leto's pretty little CADET BLUE EYES?"

"Please, please, M-Miss-Miss Bite, Cadet Brecken re, requests per, permission to be ex -" her captive labored for enough breath to gasp.

"NO, BY THUNDER," the horror roared directly into his suffering face, "Cadet Brecken AINT excused!

"Cadet Brecken's a-gonna listen to its dear old housemother tells it WHY I'm gonna hear it SCREAM like a LITTLE GIRL:

"I've GOT you, you, you tiny flea. YOU are MINE, body-and-soul, and yore dear ol' housemother kin do jus' exactly anything she wants to you -- ANYTHING!

"I did just what I wanted to ye las' night, didn't I, BLONDIE, DIDN'T I?

"NOW what I'm a-gonna do is wait fir ye to slip up, 'n' tha's ALL I'm a-gonna do, Leto's sweet li' l' baby doll. And when you do, and you will, I'll send ye right straight to th' MAJOR.

"Oh, no, dear, dear brave little Cadet Blondie, pore ol' Miss Bite couldn't break ye las' night, but HE can!

"And, DEARIE ME, jus' as soon as you make your first teensy weensy little mistake, just the smallest misstep in the world, I am gonna turn you over to the MAJOR for THE BEST WHIPPIN' OF YORE LIFE!!!

"Oh, yes, my dear, believe you me, when th' MAJOR takes that razor strop down off 'is wall and uses it on yore filthy hide, you will RUE the day you EVER tried t' hold out on ME!!!!

"Yore gonna SCREAM, Blondie, 'n' yore gonna howl for ME, little dearie, all for me, Leto's darlin' little star cadet.

"And, while the major makes ye scream I'll settin' right here in mah comfy ol' arm chair listenin' 'n' laughin' at YOU!"

Miss Bite wheeled him sharply around, still forcing his arms into his bursting torso painfully to punish him for his defiance. She marched him into her parlor to give him a closer look at her easy chair, positioned hard by the window over the quad.

Then a vile abuser of helpless children released her caged bird.

The bird dropped to the floor. He was hurt but he quickly recovered his balance and ran for his life to find his place in ranks. He was fast enough to dive into formation just in time to elude The Brass's notice (A cadet not at attention and in place when the bugle call's last strains had faded into the wind was up for an immediate stropping).

Our hero shot out of the tyrant's talons and into the gloriously invigorating East Tennessee mountains' brisk Autumn air. Outside was a whole new world where Corey was free of the dragon's dungeon.

Revivified. he told himself he was millions of miles from the killing fog of kindly old Miss Bite's shower room torture chamber.

Outside the oppressive atmosphere of the hall of the damned, Corey was able to smile once more.

His boundless resilience, his youthful buoyancy must always triumph over a perverse old harridan's vengeful spite.

The adversities of The Tower's drill-a-day world vanished. All its freezing slights, its vociferous curses and its eternal brutal beatings were forgotten in his regeneration wrought in the open air. This was more especially true because Corey was able to look forward to the best feature of his now even more difficult than ever military school adventure:

"Leto for breakfast!

"Leto for dinner!

"Leto for suppertime!

"Leto is my sugar,

"And I love her all the time!" was the joyous song that Corey's rejuvenated heart sang happily standing in formation and answering roll call.

Our half-pint hero had been puzzled by something ever since his arrival at the academy. Corey could never figure out why the tall, lanky cadet platoon leaders made their reports to the towering cadet officer of the day, "Sir, first squad all present on the count of four."

"Sir, second squad all present on the count of four."

He'd never been unable to unravel this daunting conundrum in the loudly bawled thrice daily reports of his platoon leaders.

After that day's formation was dismissed, a curious goober asked, "Excuse me, geeb, but why d' all th' platoon leaders say 'all present on the count of four'?"

"Why, you dopey li' l' GOOB!" the senior boy guffawed boisterously at his benighted junior, "It's NOT 'on th' count of four,' it's, 'Sir, first squad all present OR ACCOUNTED FOR,' y' dumb bunny!"

"Thanks, geeb!" larked an enlightened Corey.

Our boy he made a mad dash for the dining hall and breakfast with the brightest star of the cosmos.

The "geeber," which means a cadet who has seniority over his goober rookies, went his way laughing at that innocent little goober's ignorance.

Corey stood at attention behind his chair at the major's table as did everyone else present in the big dining hall. All were waiting for the great man to appear.

At last the commandant entered, attention was called and the head man signaled to his boys to be seated.

"At ease!" was called and all cadets lowered their arms from the seated position of attention (ramrod straight with both arms folded Indian style and raised to an uncomfortable chest level).

Everyone in the junior academy was present with the exception of Mac's junior Miss America Donnybrook.

Pretty little Leto was the star of this show, and she knew it. And, being the star, she was at liberty to be fashionably late for everything. Being late makes a bigger ripple in the human pond, and here it drew everyone's attention to the leading lady, and the leading lady loved it.

Fashionably late then, the junior school's beauty queen appeared, slipped gracefully into the chair next to her Mac, and slyly gave his black and blue backside a fresh and friendly pinch.

But poor old Corey was much too sore to be pinched after what he'd been through last night. His waking nightmare with the charming Miss Bite had branded him painfully and left its fiery mark, a mark that made him jump.

Corey was ashamed of having been thrashed by that diseased old attacker. He didn't want to remember his scandalous night of naked humiliation at the hands of that deviant monstrosity. He desperately hated what he'd been forced to countenance. He wanted with all his heart to forget it, but here it was.

He tried to let the wince pass unnoticed, but his savvy young Leto knew too much about the ins and outs of academy life for her lover boy to hide anything from her.

"Oh-oh!" she giggled, "old lady Bite let y' have it last night -- huh, Mac?"

"I, I guess," he lowered his eyes and blushed red.

"And YOU tried t' be the big-shot movie star hero?" she pursued him, "You held out on her, huh, boyfriend?"

"I DID, too!" he bragged, proud of his his heroics, "Only, only now she's REALLY got it in for me:

"Now Bite wants t' send me to your Daddy. SHE couldn't break me an' she knows he can."

"You're my big, strong, brave superhero," she squeezed the prominent embarrassment Bite had failed to cripple to console her love, for now she must give him the hard news that heroism can be unwise, "Even though what y' did was BRAVE, it was also DUMB!"

His girlfriend did love him and she was just as concerned for her favorite cadet as he was devoted to her and warmed by her love.

"Look, kid," she lectured him, but kindly, gently, "I do NOT want you goading that sick old two ton horror movie monstrosity into damaging you.

"She can and WILL cripple you IF you keep tryin' t' be Errol Flynn keepin' secrets from th' Black Duke in some kind o' sword fight movie.

"This is how our life is here, Mac-boy:

"It's a tough life, but it's our life 'n' its REAL life, so you 'n' me got 'o help each other make it just as happy a life as we're able. I love you, my darling boy, and I'm gonna make it just as good for y' as I can. And, believe me, I can make life sweet-"

"You already have, my beautiful, beautiful Leto-" he broke in.

She stopped him, "But real life is NOT a movie, lover boy; and th' bruises that stinkin' ol' perv burned into your poor, poor back las' night are NOT greasepaint, now are they?"

"No, beautiful, they're real!"

"NOW, I know ol' lady Bite 'cause she's best friends with my stiff ol' corpse of a mom, Th' Deepfreeze.

"Those two ol' loonies 're always jabberin' on 'n' on about what they want 'n' what they don't want.

"I listen in sometimes, so I know what they want. And what that sick ol' sow, Bite wants is to hear lots o' naked little boys screamin' like girls when she's whippin' 'em:

"She LIVES for that stuff 'cause she's NUTS, and what she does NOT want is some stubborn li' l holdout who won't give it to 'er laughin' up his sleeve at 'er 'n' keeping' shut. THAT'S why you're in Dutch with 'er, dear boy.

"Now, Mac, I know you want 'o be brave, and I know you are brave, but y' can't get away with it at Heeler, not and stay healthy.

"Now, Mac, Daddy 'n' me jus' got you healthy, and we want you t' STAY that way (especially ME).

"I want YOU t' give that monster JUST EXACTLY what she wants, lover boy. YOU, my cute li' l favorite, are to scream like all get out when that ghastly ol' basket case even TOUCHES you -- jus' like all th' rest o' th' Heeler boys do. And you'd better do it before that big, fat blimp messes you up BAD. You were dumb t' make a blimp like that MAD at y' 'cause she CAN mess you up BAD, my best ever lover!

"YOU scream like a banshee for that ugly ol' perv, 'cause that's really all she wants out o' life.

"PLEASE, won't you do that for your best girl, Leto, my big, strong, brave Mac?"

"You KNOW good 'n' well that I'll do anything for you, my darling Leto, anything in this world!" he averred passionately, "But I'll only do it for you 'n' just for you, beautiful!"

"Smart boy!" she smiled a sunny smile of relief.

The joy he saw in her loving eyes sent her Mac into orbit.

"Now YOU listen t' ME, Mac:

"Bite, 'n' my deepfreeze mom both hate all men and despise ALL boys!"

His love goddess lowered her eyes and shuffled her feet uncomfortably.

Then she continued, "Here's exactly why mom told that cheesy old lady Crop t' send y' over t' Heeler so fast; 'n' it, it's kind o' my fault:

"Mom hates me. I'm Daddy's best girl 'n' she thinks I'm hoggin' all his love.

"Mom knows WE click, so now she HATES you too! Mom hates us, so she sure as heck does not want 'o see us havin' fun, but she knows like we do that we are going to have fun.

"Daddy won't let 'er punish ME, so, to punish us both, she ordered old ol' lady Crop to pack YOU off t' Bite's house of horrors for some real hard core corporal punishment. Everyone at The Tower knows how ol' lady Bite is, 'n' that she'll do stuff to a boy that 'd make a normal grownup throw up.

"Oh, my poor Mac, I just should never 'a' let mom see how much I love you.

"Please believe me, boyfriend, I, I'm so sorry I let it show. But, but I couldn't help it -- and SHE saw it!

"That, that mean ol' Deepfreeze bitch sees EVERYTHING, damn her!

"It, it's all my fault those hardhearted ol' devils 're doin' this to you. Because I love you they're usin' you to punish me. They, they're monsters! They only know how to hate and hurt. That's ALL they care about, they love it, they're good at it 'n' they know th' only way they can hurt me is to torture YOU!

"Oh, my darling boy, I didn' mean for HER to see my love, but she DID!

"Now th' only way I might be able to stop 'em is to stop loving you, and I'm NEVER-EVER gonna stop loving you, oh, my best boyfriend!

" 'Sides, it's too late:

"They've got our number, they've got us 'n' they're never-ever gonna stop torturing us, 'cause that's th' only way they're able t' get their jollies. They are so addicted to torturing little kids that now it's all they're living for.

"You 'n' me, WE live for our love, my best boyfriend. But all THEY live for is their HATE!

"But your li' l' Leto LOVES you. You are MINE, mister, and I'm never gonna let that great big tub o' guts kill MY baby!

"God only knows all ol' lady Bite 'd have t' do to kill y' is SIT on you!"

There was not much for our young lovers to laugh about, but they got a big kick out of that.

"Now, for me, AND to stay alive 'n' in one piece, you WILL cower and cringe like the coward we both know you're NOT.

"That way Bite 'll be satisfied 'n' let up on you some, got me, soldier-boy?"

"I'm proud to say I DO have you, lover girl!" he beamed right onto her big eyed wavelength. " 'N' don't worry, my love, I can take it."

She had been close to tears before he promised to do her will. But now that he had her smile shone like the morning sun over him.

"Goodie!" said she, "If Daddy, Th' Deepfreeze AND 'er little sneaks weren't here, I'd kiss y' so you'd KNOW you'd been kissed, lover boy!"

Our two golden brats beamed ecstatically on this crucial day of her revelation and his correction. They basked in the pastel euphoria of the misty dream clouds of their love's dawning. The lovers sat, entranced in the concupiscence of their ardent new love's blossoming courtship. At this point the smitten pair were content to dream sweet dreams of being together one happy day sometime in the near future.

Our golden kids were enjoying a pleasant sojourn into an exciting dream world of their love's future ecstatic fulfillment.

They were happy to be swaddled comfortably in this pink and rose stratospheric daydream. That period before all lovers seek -- and the lucky ones find -- what heavenly bliss lies in the maelstrom of overwhelming passion when love's sweet dreams materialize into an even sweeter reality. For the present her Mac and his Leto have found sublime happiness in just plain togetherness.

They'd found their bliss in the formal chill of The Tower's huge junior school dining hall, a place where watchful cadet officer/ monitors oversaw the entire hall to make sure all cadets adhered to the academy's painfully strict code of conduct.

Such larks as singing, loud talking, boisterous laughter and like fripperies were proscribed on pain of demerit.

Any infraction of The Tower Military Academy's rules and regulations was punishable by one or more demerits per offence. A demerit is a black mark against the cadet's record of proper military conduct. All demerits must be strictly accounted for before the offending cadet was allowed to walk to town to enjoy himself Saturday afternoons.

The offending cadet's debt was satisfied only when he had "stood off" each and every demerit accrued during the past week.

Standing off demerits was done at attention every Saturday in the afternoon school study hall. Demerits must be stood off in toto before a cadet was unleashed on an unsuspecting Honeysuckle for town liberty. This process was accomplished under the watchful eye of an adult duty officer;

Demerits were forgiven only after the offender had stood motionless at the position of attention for a period of five minutes per demerit. A large number of demerits meant more time at attention and less time in town. When all demerits had been stood off, the officer in charge dismissed the juvenile culprit, and then the chastened offender was free to go to town.

Standing off demerits meant nothing to our pretty little lovebirds on this, the day of their concupiscent rapture, but it would later be of concern to them.

Classes followed breakfast. Corey attended these with relish, for reading, history and grammar classes were the subjects for he had a particular affinity.

Drill ensued post studies and the cadets got plenty of fresh air and exercise by marching and marching and marching up and down and all around the quad.

After close order drill lunch and Leto again transformed Corey's world into a rainbow of earthly paradise.

Afternoon classes then ensued to round out the day. And this fine, fine day had gone by quite well for little Cadet Corey Brecken.

But each day differs.

The next day our happy boy was to find that the academy's darkest powers had been busy choreographing yet another schoolboy punch-up.

The big problem was to be that this fight's choreographer was not a friendly and benevolent commandant trying to convince a stubborn little shaver to eat for the preservation of his good health.

No such luck for our hard pressed hero.

This day's match was being concocted and promoted by the major's scheming Lady Deepreeze and the Dreaded Dragon of Heeler Hall:

Miss Bite had covertly instructed her own favorite boy, Cadet Bobby Biddle, to pick a fight with least favorite that she might have "just cause" to send Brecken, Brecken, BRECKEN to the headmaster's office for the razor stropping of her wildest dreams, and that of his disgrace and undoing.

Oh, yes, my dear, the wretch was longing to listen to the sounds of Brecken's sweet, sweet beating from her comfy easy chair. The Beast's cardinal dream of delight was to hear the music of that thorough basting that would crack the hard shelled little nut wide open and release his long awaited screams she coveted.

Right on cue, Biddle picked his fight with the dragon's mark:

The boys were directly below the diabolical old schemer's parlor window where she had a ringside seat to watch of the bout.

The querulous Cadet Biddle had heard of Brecken's prowess in the lists. Even so he must challenge the champ to fight. It was the last thing he wanted, but he had his orders and a beating from Brecken was preferable to a scourging from Bite.

Bold in his innocence, Brecken readily accepted. Our arrogant Achilles junior even allowed the trembling Biddle his choice of fighting modes as a condescending courtesy from the invincible warrior to his puny inferior.

Biddle picked fists because he knew Brecken was an unbeatable wrestler.

In full view of the wretched old sneak, Brecken split Biddle's lip, Biddle blackened Brecken's eye -- and The Beast sprung into action.

Armed with precisely the kind of trumped-up evidence she had sought from this setup, but fearful that her favorite might really get hurt if the slugfest continued, the conniving old creep roared at the half dozen or so cadets in attendance:

"You lazy hounds get yore worthless backsides down there and break them two fools up a-fore my pore Bobby Biddle gits hurt!

"Mind ye bring 'em BOTH up here to ME ... Don' never let that gawdamn Brecken git away:

"Bring Brecken up here, 'n' stand him right here in front o' ME fir JUDGMENT!

"If my Bobby gits ONE more mark off'n that brawlin' rowdy I'll BLISTER th' lot of ye BRIGHT RED 'n' turn ye BLACK AND BLUE. I do mean I'll baste EVER LAST ONE o' ye, 'n' baste ye RIGHT!"

Six terrified cadets leapt celeritously into action:

They broke up the fight, rescued Biddle and informed Brecken that he was to report immediately to his dear old housemother for the disposition of his case.

"You're in for it, Brecken!" they gasped in horror, "SHE set y' up for this, YOU fell for it and now she's GOT y'!"

"CADET BRECKEN REPORTING AS ORDERED, MA'AM!!!!"

Corey was livid as he reported to his frightening nemesis even as the other Heeler Hall boys heart's sang a joyful hymn of deliverance because they were not Brecken.

A grinning dragon lounged in her easy chair, towering over her little foe. The misanthrope was comfortable as she regarded her easily entrapped mark in her grim complacency. Bite leered down on him in the pleasurable anticipation of what she was about to do to him.

This morbidly obese glob of rotting protoplasm was ready to play cat and mouse with her hapless prey. The criminally abusive sneak basked in the glow of her easily won victory.

Her satisfaction upon seeing the jaws of her trap snap shut on her victim inundated her very essence with pleasure.

Now she had him!

The monster was satisfied that the dark deed had been engineered by her. She and she alone had trapped him. Her rapture was as hellish as it was complete in the knowledge that Brecken had been presented to her for her pleasure by means of her own vile duplicity.

Even sweeter to this sick curse than Brecken's delivery into her hands for more abuse was the comforting realization that her quarry was already bruised, whipped full of sores due to her own recent strong arm antics. Her very own prelude of savage flagellation on one boy's person the night before last was the agent that had softened him up for what was to come. At long, long last Brecken, Brecken, BRECKEN was to be broken, broken, BROKEN!

"I told pretty boy it's not over for him," reflected The Beast smugly, "Not by a long shot, dearie."

Corey was acutely and uncomfortably conscious of terror's cold hand strangling him. Corey knew he was going to be punished far beyond anything he might hope to endure. Brecken was to scream longer and louder than any other boy had screamed, and he was to do so this very day.

The horribly diseased old wretch who had planned this crime knew that the angry cuts and bruises she'd branded into Corey's naked back on their first dark encounter were far from being healed and The Horror of Heeler Hall was ecstatic.

She knew any further ravishment must perforce bring one boy to such an irresistible apex of insupportable pain that he was sure to scream for her.

And today there was to be no escape from the major for the major's own little pet protégé:

The major must punish any cadet with an adverse report from his housemother, the condemned tyke must scream and bear it and an ugly old hag was to hear it and love it.

The aggravating little brat was about to learn his revolting housemother's vengeance was as inescapable as it was hellish.

This time it was the major's turn, and the headmaster was just the man to break that intractable little colt like a china doll.

"I didn't penetrate your thick hide the other night, blue eyes," the petrified cadet's ghastly foe relished her victory, reeking in the fetid stench of her corruption, "Now it's your beloved headmaster's turn, your own loving patron's turn.

"Major Donnybrook WILL make you scream for me, BLONDIE; ye kin bank on that, ye blue eyed blondie-headed little FREAK!"

She clutched her chest in a paroxysm of joy occasioned by envisioning one boy's impending nightmare overwhelmed her,

"Oh, YES, my dear, dear boy, your beloved headmaster is going to make you howl like you aint NEVER howled in yore en-tire life.

"Why, that man 'll make you scream so loud I'll easy be able t' hear ye all the way up here in my nice comfy easy chair, "And, dearie me, when I hear that there screamin' -- like a little GIRL -- I'm gonna LAUGH, d' you hear me, ye DIRTY little DOG?

"But YOU aint a-gonna do NO laughin,' Blondie, a-cause yore gonna be havin' a real different kind o' time ... but it aint gonna be nowhere NEAR no good time!"

"YES, MA' AM!!!" barked Corey, trying to remain completely impassive in the face of the monster's thundering salvoes of verbal aggression.

He knew that he was far too hurt and bruised to take another such scorched earth whipping. And this time the punishment was sure to be much more severe.

But Corey would never let this hated hell hag see his anxiety. He knew he could never prevent his impending disaster, but he would never let The Beast know he cared. That would only enhance her pleasure, and he must never do that.

The only thing a junior school cadet in trouble was allowed to do in his extremity was to stand stoically at attention while the bloated anomaly presently in command of his destiny pleasured herself by mocking him.

His still tender back was the primary reason The Bite had staged this setup schoolboy set-to only a day and a half after she had blackened his still throbbing hide. A hard, amoral and calculating Beast knew how much he was still hurting. She had planned and timed her grizzly farce perfectly.

Now the wretch was enjoying a good old fashioned satanic gloat. The jowly dragon's flaccid bulk was quivering with laughter as she witnessed the triumph of hatred and envy over youth, beauty and love.

Bite gloried in the delicious anticipation of Brecken's downfall coupled with her joy at the ease of her hapless young dupe's entrapment and capture.

"YOU jus' stand rat there 'n' wait on me, fool," a mountain of malevolence instructed her diminutive prisoner.

The diseased old sow quickly penned a short note to the junior school's strong armed commander in chief.

After the lowering saurian had completed her missive she waved it vindictively in her terrified little chew-toy's impassive face, the face of a boy determined to hide the confusion of his rueful and disconsolate heart from Satan's handmaiden.

"Do you want me to tell you what my little note to your dear ol' friend, the major, says, baby-face?"

"IF YOU PLEASE, MA' AM!!!"

Heroes aren't smart, but they are brave.

"You want me to read it t' ye, don't you, you scrubby li' l CUR?" she prodded him comfortable in her victory, "All right, I'll read it to ye, but you'll just have to wait, my dearie

"Know why?

"A-cause YOU are not that important, you, you FILTHY little cockroach. I've got lots more important things on my mind than YOU:

"YOU come last, THEY come first."

Miss Bite had demoted her prey to last place limbo, though all present knew full well that she was dying to dispatch him to the commandant and hear him scream.

"Cadet McNichol, you will take Cadet Biddle into th' bathroom and clean up 'is injuries while I read this here puny, insignificant SKEETER its swatting orders."

"Come with me, honey," minced McNichol, his eyes wide with his fear and aversion of that cadet crushing dragon.

Curley's fancy roomie jumped to obey The Beast while Corey, his mind lost in a vortex of fright, awaited her pronouncement.

"Now then, Cadet Brecken, I might jus' be kind enough t' set aside some time, even fir a mangy little cur like YOU," smirked Bite playfully, "YOU can just stand there and listen t' ME while I read ye this here note from me to yore darlin' ol' headmaster -- that big, strong war hero who jus' LOVES you so much.

"But, o' course, this little note will be sure to put an end t' all that lovey-dovey pap!

"Yore about t' find out just how strong yore big, strong idol IS, my dear. Why, honey, yore a-gonna FEEL it in yore bones!"

A dramatic pause ensued while an accomplished sadist waited for her little victim's paroxysm of horror to build to its deafening crescendo.

Miss Bite took her sweet time.

No one knew better than she how excruciating were the ravages of psychological torture. Its application, so deliciously potent, was particularly rewarding to such an accomplished deviate.

The stinking hag had purposefully prolonged Brecken's agony. She was anxious to savor his pain. Breathless with fear, he must wait to hear the fearful pronouncement of his wretched denouncer.

At length the dragon spoke:

"You're a-gonna deliver this to your beloved hero, so I'll just read it to ye now. That way you'll have somethin' t' think about on your way over to yore big strong war hero idol."

"IF YOU WISH, MA'AM!!!"

Never would he let her see his discomfort.

The stinking hag leant forward to leer at her catch over her spectacles.

She studied him carefully in order to discover any hint that the torment she intended had touched and hurt him.

But our Corey was careful to maintain his outward calm.

The deathly stench of her putrid breath reached and sickened him. But he would cheerfully have died before he let her see it.

"Oh, yes, Blondie," dear old Miss Bite purred contentedly, "Your dear ol' housemother DOES wish it, my gallant young sir."

She studied his face intently in an all out effort to discover some ever so slight hint of emotion.

A single tear would have brought her to orgasm, but his face showed her only his hatred and contempt for her.

"This is your passport to hell, cadet cutie pie!" the bullying old wretch need not have said what he already knew, but she was satanically explicit, "THIS is the day I told ye about that morning, blue eyes, the day when you're gonna git t' whippin' o' yore life:

"My dear Major Donnybrook,

"I trust this note will find you and yours in the best of health.

"Dear sir, it pains me to have to relate that Cadet Brecken has been incorrigibly insubordinate, disobedient and downright rebellious since you sent him to us.

"Cadet Brecken has been nothing but a contentious and belligerent delinquent. He continually picks fights with my other cadets. Just today he has injured one of my best boys.

"I fear this wild animal needs a man's strong hand to enforce his correction. Therefore, I am forced to make this adverse report of flagrant misconduct and advise you that his unacceptable behavior leaves me no recourse other than to recommend the most severe corporal punishment.

"Please do oblige your faithful servant, my dear commandant, by beating this hardened little criminal until I can hear him scream like a little girl that I may be assured that his willful defiance has been broken at last.

"I thank you, sir, for resolving this distressing matter.

"Please allow me to tender my deepest respects to you and yours.

"Your faithful servant,

"Miss Bite."

"LIES!" stormed Corey's yet unbroken spirit buried deep beneath his unruffled exterior, "It's not enough for her to trick me 'n' set me up for a stroppin.'

"No, no, she's tryin' t' turn th' major against me!"

Corey longed to shout those words in her ugly face. He was mad enough to tear her prevaricating head off her massive, stooping shoulders and throw it all the way across the quad, through the Uncle Remus fences around the academy and out onto the highway. But he was a junior cadet at a highly respected military school and regulations permitted no such outbursts:

A junior academy cadet speaks only when given leave so to do by his superiors.

A murderous rage burned red hot in his heart, but the visible and audible Cadet Brecken stood motionless, mute and respectful beneath his housemother's withering stare.

Corey burned with shame and rage at the disgrace of being sent to his kindly patron to bear the academy's ultimate chastisement courtesy of an old snake's snares, lies and apocryphal missives.

Bite had lied about Brecken and addressed her lies to the most powerful and supportive patron in this little lost boy's world.

Clearly, The Beast had hoped to create a rift between the major and his protégé by means of guile and prevarications. Bite was trying to deprive Brecken of his patronage.

Cadet Brecken knew he'd been set up but it was not his place to speak. At the academy it was the cadet's duty to be silent and take his hiding for being stupid enough to fall victim to his tormentor's perfidy.

The major might possibly guess that her note was false, for he was well acquainted with both of the protagonists in this particularly immoral moral play, but how could Corey be sure of that?

It was not a cadet's place to rat out his housemother. But it was his housemother's place to rat out any cadet against whom she harbored up malice. Bite had licence to do so willfully and without respect for truthfulness, justice or fair play.

Here at The Tower a housemother's function was to lie about any boy she might single out for a stropping. A commandant's function was to strop the accused cadet's nethers black and blue until he screamed like a girl. A cadet's function was to submit, bow low to convention and sweat, sting and scream for the powers that be.

The Beast examined her tiny captive closely, but our boy in the barrel just stood at attention, as outwardly unconcerned as if none of this current nonsense had any effect on him whatsoever. Inwardly his blood was boiling, his guts were churning and all his being roiled in turmoil.

He wanted to kill the horror leering and drooling over him in his invisible cage. But that would have contravened Tower regulations. His powerlessness, his doleful lot made him want to cry like a baby.

But he would never cry for her!

Corey's attitude of defiant indifference might have bothered his darling housemother had her disarmingly cute little annoyance's slavish fate not been so neatly signed, sealed and delivered into her filthy paws.

But it was, and Brecken's ruthless tormentor was content only to smile a knowing smile and press her apocryphal missive into the poor soul's hand:

"Okay, blue-eyes, you made your bed when you defied ME.

"Now you're on your way to the major to learn just how uncomfortable a bed of fire can be:

"CADET BRECKEN:

"You are to deliver this note to the hand of your commanding officer, Major Donnybrook, AT ONCE!

"When ye git to the major's office you will salute his nibs and say, 'Cadet Brecken reporting as ordered, sir.'

"You will then await your beloved commandant's pleasure, you, you SICKENING, blond little BRUTE -- and what he does to you then will be MY pleasure!!!

"Is that understood?"

"YES, MA' AM!!!" her querulous mark barked stoically.

"Then go on 'n' take what's comin' to ye, BLONDIE!"

Miss Bite's whipping boy de jour about faced smartly to exit her web of convoluted infamy.

He made for the stairs determined to take his bitter medicine without a hint of remorse, or the slightest complaint.

He must tread the straight and narrow path along the edge of the quad to the major's office, a trail of tears for every cadet with such a note in his hand.

His mind was a forest fire:

"This is it!" his bursting heart told him, "They're finally gonna BREAK me.

"Well, Grandpa ought 'o be happy."

BROKEN TO THE WHIP

"Will he believe th' vicious ol' hag's lies?" Corey wondered, his brain whirling crazily down, down, down into a maelstrom of doubt and dread as he headed for the stairwell.

He could take a whipping. But never could he countenance the disgrace of being thrown out of the high perch of Major Donnybrooks' favor.

His companions lined the hallway by the stairwell to rally round their hard put comrade and superhero. They pressed eagerly forward to tender their advice on the etiquette of enduring, and hopefully surviving, his impending trial. Every boy present was sad to see him go out this way, for many had already known the shame and pain of the major's fiery strop inferno.

They all knew Corey had been set up; and they also knew very well that the dragon had set him up because she'd so miserably failed to break Cadet Brecken herself:

Bite had caught their friend in her black widow's web of falsehood and deceit and dispatched the little poor mutt to the commandant to face his excruciating moment of truth.

McMoon, hoarse voiced from screaming for The Beast's diversion this very day, was the first small, pale face to speak up.

"Run for it, Brecken!" gasped McMoon desperately, "I would!"

"Oh, Mac," Corey sighed wearily, "How many times 've I gotta tell y' that we've just gotta stand up 'n' take what's comin' to us 'cause that's why they sent us here?"

McMoon's advise was immediately followed by other superhero worshipers. Each of his fans spoke up admiringly:

"You got GUTS, kid!"

"You gotta have a gimmick, Brecken!" advised one, "Listen:

"Stick a notebook down your pants. He never notices; 'n' that's what I always do."

"Man oh man, don't try t' hold out on HIM, Corey-boy. HE might jus' KILL y'!"

"Oh, my brave, brave Corey!" gushed McNichol, touching his superhero's cheek softly, "You're just like Alan Ladd when that mean, old ship's captain whipped him in TWO YEARS BEFORE THE MAST ... What a MAN!"

"Aw, dry up, sissy-pants!" groused his tough guy roomie, "It's comin' to him, he knows he's gotta take it an' he knows it because he IS a man!

"But, look here, Brecks, don't try t' hold out on THIS guy!" cautioned a sagacious Curley, "NOBODY wants t' see y' get hurt THAT bad 'cept old lady Bite! ... SHE wants t' hear y' yell 'n' scream, 'n,' believe me, th' major's gonna make y' yowl, so be smart and yell your head off for 'er!"

Corey started down and the other cadets fell silent.

Each boy bowed beneath the appalling weight of being so small, so alone and so subject to a deranged old harpy's cruel caprice as to be completely helpless. Whenever she pleased Miss Bite might call the wrath of the major down on any of their innocent heads. The boys were caught in this world's finest military academy's heartless meat grinder of domination and submission.

But they had no time for introspection:

"You hounds what was in here fir help with yore multiplication tables, GIT yore worthless hind-ends back here t' practice 'em!!!" boomed the dragon from her awful lair.

And they all scampered back to her parlor.

Miss Bite's tiny sacrifice to Eris, her patron-goddess of envy and discord, kept right on marching, outwardly calm and erect, downstairs and outdoors.

The whipping he surely faced was going to be hard, but he feared it less than ostracism. He trembled beneath the Sword of Damocles. Exile from the major's patronage was the looming specter he feared most. That would have meant denial of access to his loving Donnybrooks.

His visible aspect was that of a letter perfect model cadet. Complete composure must be his hallmark on his march toward destiny, but inside he was mad with dread apprehension.

Yes, Corey would cheerfully bear the strop (chiefly because he didn't know what it felt like), but he could never countenance yet another exile.

His eyes were fixed upon his unrealized dream of a distant someday it seemed would never materialize -- his day.

But he knew all too well this wasn't his day as he reached the commandant's office and knocked at the door.

"Enter," the great man responded.

The boy entered and saluted his magnificently decorated idol, towering majestically over his feverishly affrighted mini protégé.

Glad to see his tiny protégé, the great man smiled and returned his salute.

"CADET BRECKEN REPORTING AS ORDERED, SIR!!!" struggled the fear frozen boy.

"And what are your orders, sir?" the man smiled fondly down upon his favorite little soldier.

"Sir, the c-cadet's orders are to deliver this note from his housemother into the major's hands," the boy answered, trying his best not to waiver from this most difficult task of his short life.

The man accepted the note and read it over. A serious expression darkened his brow. It was not a look of anger, but one of deep concern.

The commandant was not a mean man, nor was he natively cruel a la Bite, but he was required to bring order from that pell-mell chaos which reigns supreme in the minds of untutored little boys. And at military school the quickest way introduce a junior school cadet to the calm, cool reason of military discipline was through a series of red hot, awe inspiring lightning bolts to the cadet's posterior.

"Do you know what this note says, cadet?" he inquired in soft tones.

He had to make things hot enough for his little protégé without angry words.

"YES, SIR!!!" replied the cadet, "The, the cadet's housemother was k-kind enough to read it to h-him."

"Yes, that's her all right," the major mused, biting his lip to avoid smiling at his noxious old housemother's predictable perfidy. Breaking a little boy's spirit was a grim task. And breaking a delightful little protégé he loved was not a time for jocundity.

Another knotty consideration troubled the man. Corey's good health had only recently returned thanks to proper diet and love from the major and Leto post the boy's foolhardy hunger strike. Vigorous training and proper diet had set the boy on the right path. But, as Corey's true friend, his headmaster was concerned that he might be too weak to digest the kind of hard punishment his criminal housemother had prescribed. Mac's mentor was worried that might not gird him for such a hellish ordeal as The Beast demanded.

Major Donnybrook was unaware that Miss Bite had tried Mac in her own shower room blast furnace in the vain hope of breaking him herself. And he was ignorant of the fact that she had tenderized his poor little back like a cube steak before she had sent the tenderized tyke to him long before he had had enough time to heal.

Man and boy were caught up in the rigid protocols of military school etiquette, for the blistering strop had come down from its hook.

A cold blast of dread more terrifying than his shower room panic seized the boy.

In Corey's eyes the whole world had just tilted. Its entire insupportable mass had come to rest on this man and this boy and this small, sickeningly spinning office.

The boy was now more afraid than he had ever been in his life.

But, even in this horrible moment of truth, he knew he must somehow prove himself excellent. He must show himself to be worthy, even in the impossibility of the shame and degradation of being whipped.

He knew he must at least hide his fear.

A man and a boy stood before the awful altar of Eris.

The man was to be that pagan discord goddess's executioner, the boy her sacrifice.

Now two male entities must perform a mad puppet-dance of domination and submission to appease the lusts of the two ravening, maniacally envious, reptiles that were drooling hungrily for our Corey's dehumanization. They awaited breathless one boy's disgrace.

There was no way to prepare himself for what was to come, but our little sacrifice knew he must immediately invent one:

He did:

He must view this as a game.

He must never try to hold out on the major, an accomplished athlete in the prime of his majority. His Leto had advised her Mac never to hold out on the grownups, and no one in this world could or would expect it.

But bruised and aching he must at least put up a brave front. Our golden brat must somehow excel in this most terrifying of all sporting events. He must show his model his mettle by holding on for at least twenty lashes.

"Errol Flynn did it," he told himself, "Doug Fairbanks could do it.

"They, they do it in all their heroic movies -- and, and I've just GOTTA do it, too!"

But now his brave heart sank as his master commanded, "Cadet, I am going to take the strop to you. You are to stand directly behind this wooden chair, grip it firmly with both hands and stand up like a man for this. You will not release that chair until I have given you leave to do so.

"Are we clear?"

"Y-yes, sir!" whispered the breathless boy as he obediently prepared for the worst.

And the worst burned like fire!

The first lash across his already painfully blistered fundament hurt enough to wring a full throated scream from the fiercest Apache warrior ever to terrorize the Old South West.

But, with a superhuman effort, the boy kept silence -- and the whipping continued.

The heavy strokes of Zeus Alastor's withering firestorm fell harder and harder across Cadet Corey's tenderized and overstressed backside.

The pitiless flagellation went on and on and on until our pain-wracked little scamp wondered at his own determination not to be broken.

But, recently and grievously wounded by a deviant monster, he weakened as the hell of his present travail was increased exponentially. Afire, the tortured little captive of The Tower asked himself inside his stubborn little head, "Oh, GOD, H-How 'll I, I, I EVER-ever-ever m-make it ALL, all, all th' way, way to TWENTY?"

The man's searing strop blazed like fire as it branded the boy's cube steak backside.

"Tough kid," mused the major, "Let's turn up the heat and get this over with."

And he really poured it on.

As the flogging built to its deafening crescendo of capitulation and disgrace, a tenacious little gamecock knew he was going to lose. Between the seventh and eighth strokes a moaning, sweating, twitching little boy despaired, "I, I'm never, never g-gonna make, make, m-make it!!!! ... Oh, oh, oh GOD, God, God, help, help m-me hold-hold-hold on, on just, just, just a little longer, LONGER!!!!"

As the punishment continued its eternal march to our willful little superhero's rout, a dreadful thought came into his head:

If the terrific force he was exerting to keep from crying combined with the virulent force of the big man's all out assault on is britches, the two opposing forces must spark off an almighty bang of pure energy. That nuclear conflagration was sure to make Corey's intestines explode and fly all over the room. He knew it. His guts would unavoidably inundate the major's neat, clean office. He and the major would be buried beneath a sickening ocean of blood and offal.

He was driven mad by the dread realization that he might actually expire beneath the lash.

Insupportably hard blows continued to rain down on his tenderized backside.

Cadet Brecken could not imagine how he had weathered strokes one through thirteen. But, between thirteen and fourteen, a sweating, sweltering, suffering sacrifice to lust and envy capitulated.

Defeated and disgraced at last, Cadet Brecken evoked a stentorian catharsis of precisely the kind screams The Beast and her crony, Deepfreeze Donnybrook, wanted. Desperate, high pitched and ashamed Cadet Brecken's full throated protestations of slavish fealty rang out to the twin gorgons' delight and roused their vile and twisted libidos.

It had been just as they had dreamed and schemed:

Zeus on high had made his poor little boy scream like a little girl.

Dear old Miss Bite heard our broken-to-the-whip superhero's abandoned howls of shameful capitulation. Oh, yes, my dear, the boy's pitiful screams reverberated in all their desperate urgency through Heeler Hall's parlor window. There the bloated old poison toad was comfortably seated for his pain aria's optimal acoustic value.

The major's pet's pitiful cries for surcease were the catalytic agents that excited The Beast and The Deepfreeze to a state of purest rapture.

Luckily for Corey his almighty commandant also viewed the extreme blood rite they practiced as a sport.

Both fellows admired bravery in the face of insuperable strength and insupportable punishment as a prime test of manhood. Their mindsets agreed to recognize resistance in the face of insupportable travail as the embodiment of manly virtue. The boy had been correct to conduct himself in manly fashion beneath the firestorm of the man's furious strop.

This culture's males, an endless procession of poor little pups trailing back to the dawn of time, had been fated to bear up bravely under the awful punishments of their severe superiors. Brave little boys have always come to see this blood-rite as a sport.

The rules of the game:

121

The taskmaster must deliver more punishment to a coward than to a hero, for a weakling must be toughened up to transform him into a man.

The master must not cease from the flogging directly after his subject's submission. The punisher must continue the chastisement yet a bit, for he must not only impose his status as dominator, he must cement it in place.

Ergo, a coward gets ten to fifteen additional cuts, while the hero must endure only five more.

A lustily bawling Cadet Brecken only had to stand still for the hero's five. The major made sure those strokes fell more softly than the rest, but Mac couldn't feel any difference by then.

Oh, yes, my dear, that same proud and stiff-necked Brecken brat, the boy who'd had the cheek to defy her, was now groveling like a whipped dog at the feet of his earthly taskmaster.

Miss Bite had beaten the infuriating whelp until he couldn't stand up, but he had nonetheless refused to yield his lovely screams to her. But now a man who loved him had chopped him down for that very deviant's diversion:

"Brecken, Becken, BRECKEN is broken, broken, BROKEN!!!" gloated the reeking hellion.

But now an even greater fear than an early death beneath the lash galled our half-pint hero. What if his kind benefactor had abandoned him because of a rancid old hag's filthy lies?

What if he should be proscribed from further intercourse with his breathtaking dream girl?

What if he had lost the only open and loving hearts beating at the major's table -- or at the whole academy?

Had he lost everything?

"Alright, Mac," the man's kindly voice momentarily brought an apprehensive waif out of his hellish vortex of self-doubt, "It's over now. I want you to go into the bathroom and wash your face with cold water, comb your hair, calm down and then come back to my desk for a little talk."

"YE-YES, S-SIR!!!" bawled a sobbing pup -- red-cheeked at both ends.

"He's been through a lot," the commandant reflected as the boy disappeared into the bath and the man hung his razor strop back on its hook, "Poor kid."

To reiterate, the major was not an evil man, simply a soldier-robot. Punishment didn't get him off as it had done for The Beast and The Deepfreeze. It was simply a dandy shortcut to bring a gang of willful little rowdies into marshal conformity.

This severe day's work would be worthwhile if it got his nagging wife off his back. It must, for now she could crow over poor little Mac's downfall. But how long would it be before that crawling cobra wanted another pain-laced blood feast?

Alone in the bathroom, Corey stared disconsolately into the looking glass. He hated the defeated wretch reflected in it. He mourned the untimely death of Corey The Superhero, the wonder boy who could boldly withstand the barbarities of the cruelest torturer at the academy -- and had done so. Where was the hero who had scoffed in the face of that stinking Beast?

All that was left of the superhero was this lackluster ghost reflected in the glass.

He'd been sucked into a vortex of unbearable pain where he had surrendered to an implacable taskmaster. He had screamed like a girl for the amusement of his vilest, most deadly enemies.

Corey didn't realize that that no animal, hero or no hero, could stand up to the methodical application of unchecked and indefinite torture. Our boy had no idea that Douglas Fairbanks and Errol Flynn were not heroes at all but film stars reciting from a movie script. Our innocent was heartbroken to have tumbled down from the pedestal of his imagined invincibility. He was ashamed of failing his heroes of myth and legend.

The fear that he might lose his place in an even more celestial temple than his fancied Pantheon of Heroes troubled him, "What if the major forbids me to enter the temple of my beautiful love goddess, Leto?"

It would not have surprised him. The puffy red face staring out of the mirror was nothing short of frightful. Disgrace was written across the burning red, tear-streaked features of the strange, broken little boy reflected there.

But he was expected pull himself together and return to his commander-in-chief to hear and accept his headmaster's verdict.

"Cadet Brecken reporting as ordered, sir!" a washed, combed and hopefully less red and puffy cadet saluted his commanding officer.

"Have a seat, son," the major returned his protégé's salute.

It hurt him so very badly to sit on a hardwood chair!

He winced with pain as a backside freshly flailed into a throbbing mass of pulp perched precariously on that seat of fire. But he thought this might be some further test of unquestioning obedience, or another test of his manhood -- and so he perched.

"Well, that's as bad as it gets around here, Mac, and I'm proud of you for facing up to it courageously.

"You may correctly assume that I'd have to give a coward ten times ten of the stropping I dished to you.

"A cowardly boy has to learn the value of manly fortitude; but you are no coward, son. I'm proud to say you are pretty close to the top in the courage department."

"Thank you very much, Major Donnybrook!" beamed the major's protégé, doing his best not to squirm on his hot, hot seat.

"This little business is an everyday occurrence around here, so you should not worry that this would have an effect on our friendship.

"Miss Bite's adverse report will not alter your place with me and my family, son. You may rest assured you will always find a welcome with us, Mac."

"Thank you VERY much, SIR!!!"

Angels sang hosannas of celestial joy arose and reigned in Mac's relieved little head. The good news had not only elated him, it had delivered him from his seemingly eternal damnation into the hell of a painfully lonely and friendless childhood. And that wasn't all, for now the lovely Leto must surely to be his.

But this was as formal an occasion as any at The Tower, an academy where formality was the rule.

Observing his ebullient protégé's excitement, a serious minded commander raised and extended his palm for silence.

"Young man, this is a serious matter:

"I want you to try your very best to please Miss Bite from now on.

"Our experience today hasn't been pleasant for either one of us, and I'm sure neither is anxious to have it repeated, are we?"

"NO, SIR!!!" piped his squirming cub.

"Correct," the commandant nodded, "I realize that you are too young to fully appreciate this, Mac, but Miss Bite is sick. And it is her ill health that makes her so cross. She has a painful and terminal disease, and that is why she's so hard on you and the other boys.

"Now, I feel that you have what it takes to make it at the academy -- and in the army. I'm confident you have the ability to lead. Therefore, I expect to see some leadership from you in this matter.

"You are to make allowances for her illness and set a good example for the other boys to follow. You are to set an example of kindness and forbearance in the sad case of your poor old housemother's rather obvious shortcomings.

"It is vital that a leader set an example, but being a leader is never easy."

"Yes, SIR, I will do just as you say," responded Corey, "I begged you not to kill me when you broke me; and I promised unerring obedience in return; and I wasn't lying, major!"

Our newly compliant Corey (schooled at the end of the strop) happily declared his fealty. Cadet Brecken was bound and determined to pick up the cadence and fit right in to the often painful, ever grinding machinery of the academy's heartless juggernaut.

His spirit of compliance pleased a commandant whose job it was to beat just that quality into his toy soldiers.

In fact, our little cadet's boss was so pleased with his half-pint Napoleon's progress he immediately decided to let the engaging scamp in on one of the military's most closely guarded secrets for success:

"I know things seem terribly difficult for you right now, son. They are, and it's because you're just a fledgling cadet schoolboy. You're just beginning your first year of junior school training, and you're fighting hard to get accustomed to the rigors of a military life.

"Right now you have take the orders, but one day (with any kind of brains and luck), you'll be an officer. And when you're an officer you'll be the one who's giving the orders.

"Do you take my meaning, young sir?"

"Yes, SIR!!!" Corey brightened at the prospect, "NOW I've gotta TAKE it, but someday I'll be able to DISH IT OUT!"

"Smart boy!" smiled his amused mentor, "Dismissed."

"Thank you, SIR!!!" Mac rose and snapped to attention, and cadet and officer went into their saluting and hand shaking routine.

A happy little fledgling officer with a helium-inflated head full of lofty dreams of dishing it out and not having to take it anymore, ran out to attend classes, sports, parades, etc. Corey was walking on air. Though he had been and must continue to be the frequently scourged and rebuked captive of this campus dungeon, he was still his patron's resilient protégé. The regenerating gifts of stewardship and acceptance from Major Daddy coupled with the healing balm of his lovely Leto's honey sweet love were well worth any hardships he must endure to access them.

His elevated state of grace and his beautiful Love Queen Leto's hypnotic eyes would always lift him high above the hellish cruelties of his harsh new martial existence.

At lunch that day the lovers were reunited in the pastel bliss of their regenerating concupiscence.

In between Leto's mandatory dirty jokes, his May Queen interjected a serious note:

"You know, Mac, ol' lady Bite really IS more t' be pitied than anything else --"

"She's awful cruel t' us, Leto," he insisted, "I, I can't tell y' just how, how really bad it was -- you'd barf."

"Oh, believe me, Mac, I KNOW, 'n' Daddy knows, too. We both realize just how mean these darn ol' housemothers are t' you kids.

"Only it's just so hard t' get good help way up here in th' Tennessee boondocks:

"Th' real ol' time Southern ladies 're all educated, so THEY get jobs as classroom teachers in town 'n' here at The Tower. But these rude ol' housemothers 're just run o' the-mill hill trash from th' countryside hereabouts.

"Ol' lady Crop's got that riding crop she very seldom uses on her boys; Dame Forester over at Booker Hall has a martinet she scares her delinquents with; but mostly, they're jus' talk. They send th' kids they really think deserve it t' DADDY, an' you KNOW how he can tear y' up!

"You had 'o go through it just TODAY, my poor, brave li' l' soldier boy.

"Mac, Li' l' Leto knows JUST what's goin' on around here, 'n' she knows y' mus' really be SORE right now!

"But Miss Bite doesn't threaten. That mean ol' hag's got THE SILVER STREAK 'n' she jus' loves t' hurt li' l' boys just as BAD as she can. It gets 'er off to hear you scream.

"But that's just how it is, my poor, poor li' l' lover boy.

"Believe me, there's nothing WE can do about it 'cause you 'n' me're jus' little kids with no say in anything. THEY -- th' grownups -- call th' shots, not us, never us.

"Now Daddy wants you 'n' me both t' be especially nice t' ol' lady Bite 'cause she's sick 'n' gonna die (Not soon enough, I know, but she IS gonna die a lot sooner than us.).

"Those other two old biddies aren't even sick -- just old 'n' mean as hell. But ol' lady Bite IS in a lot o' pain 'cause she's dyin' of leukemia.

"DADDY says we gotta feel sorry for that dirty ol' sow, so I guess we gotta look like we do, no matter HOW sore we really are.

"You're at military school now, Cadet Mac, and at military school corporal punishment's a big part of the plan o' th' day.

"In my book you're my big strong superhero -- the only lover I want or will accept, my soldier boy! I want y' t' please Miss Bite to please me, won't you?

"Scream your head off for that sick ol' bag, 'cause YOU 'n' ME both know you're tougher than her."

"I'll do anything for th' beautiful queen of my heart, Leto!" Corey dove obligingly into her big hypnotic eyes.

"Good boy!" laughed she, pleased that she had wrapped him around her little finger so easily. Leto had her very own, very special and intimate plans for this particular towhead rowdy. The Beast and The Deepfreeze had had their gory fun, but our golden brats were going to have their own fun soon enough.

"Don't buck th' system at military school, boyfriend, it bucks back!"

"I know you must be right, girlfriend!"

And the golden brats got right straight back into some serious footsie-playing and dirty- joking (Albeit quietly and carefully in the ominous presence of the deadly cobra and her prying spies, of course.).

Cadet Corey could swallow anything for the sake of his lady love, even such unbelievably thorny crowns as the merciless Tower and its unrelenting Saint Nemesis Bite habitually forced down upon his bleeding brow. If our ex-human ex-superhero must live with the fact that he was a cog spinning in a heartlessly destructive military academy's eternal juggernaut, at least he was Leto's favorite cog.

Miss Bite was not up to her usual devil's dance that night. The skulking old hag was all used up behind all the rapture she had so recently and copiously enjoyed in her recent torture of Corey's fat pal, easy-scream McMoon in the shower the previous day.

And today the unparalleled paroxysm of Hard Case Corey's pitiful screams of shame and submission through her parlor window had delighted and drained her beyond description. That proud young gamecock's peals of disgraced surrender had heralded her black victory over our distressed towhead. And it had been a victory sweetened by the knowledge that her filthy lies and wily traps had delivered him up to be so humiliated. These hearty celebrations of decay and envy over love and youth had taken their toll and the sick old wretch must recuperate.

But the very next evening The Bite Beast made her sortie into the shower room torture pit to enjoy the floorshow of her putrid dreams:

Bite beat them all at once with her blistering flail and her naked little boys screamed and danced to her favorite caper, her flagellation fandango. She so doted on hearing these healthy little hounds scream out their paeans of urgent desperation, for they were hymns of capitulation to her own evil ego, and to the glorification of her snaky-headed idol, Eris.

To please the pretty little queen of his fancy, Leto's dutiful Cadet Brecken was willing to scream for mercy longer and louder than all the rest of his brothers in bondage to brighten the dark night of their hag housemother's lost and blighted soul. Brecken screamed for Bite long and loudly, and Bite basked in the glow of the slavish fate she had prescribed for her defeated captive, Brecken, Brecken, BRECKEN.

"APPLE CORE!"

"Here we stand like birds in the wilderness,
  "Birds in the wilderness,
  "Birds in the wilderness!
"Here we stand like birds in the wilderness
Waiting for something to eat!" sang the assembled junior school cadets, promptly gathered for their ten hundred hours morning break outside the back door of the McAdam Hall kitchen, each and every day.

The boys had gathered here for a treat every morning as they always had at the same time ever since the school's existence. The Tower boys were gathered like birds in the wilderness to observe a junior school tradition:

The distribution of daily morning snacks for active and hungry little schoolboys was de rigueur.

They sang their song and, as if called forth by some magic incantation, an overstuffed and affable black lady from the kitchen staff appeared to hand out fruit, cookies or candy for the boys' good old reliable morning ten hundred hours snack.

At the Tower these treats were usually fruit because the academy's millionaire founder had made his fortune as an expert scientist in the field of health and diet. The meals and snacks provided here were and had always been nothing short of exemplary.

This snack time tradition had been introduced in the far distant and long forgotten past by the powers that be. But, of course, when the establishment introduces one tradition, the rowdies must invariably bring forth their own innovation. And in this case cadet tradition had raced right up behind the midmorning feast tradition to steal the show:

"APPLE CORE!" bawled Supersonic Saber (an accomplished bully, doughty leader of the brawling blue devils gang and naturally a folk hero universally admired and respected throughout the school).

"BALTIMORE!" answered Big Milan (Little Milan's older brother who had been lucky enough to be permitted to stay at McAdam Hall after his poor little kid brother's expulsion into Heeler Hell).

"WHO'S YOUR FRIEND?" continued Supe in the cadence of the tired and true incantation.

"BUSTLE!!!" howled Big Milan.

Poor, heavyset Cadet Bustle let out an apprehensive yelp and bolted for the quad.

But the fleeing fat boy didn't get very far, for everyone else cut loose with a barrage of apple cores aimed directly at Cadet Bustle's comically wobbling posterior. No, portly little Cadet Bustle could never hope to escape the messy deluge of apple cores on his clumsy little sausage- legs.

Everyone laughed and loosed a sea of messy apple pulp, and it found and inundated the harried fat boy in full flight to escape his fate. Volley after volley rained down on Cadet Bustle's chubby flanks. The boys' hurricane of apple cores slopping and running inexorably all over him from every corner of the field of play distressed their mark.

Every morning (with the rare exception of a few and far between candy bar mornings) Baltimore's friend was in for a shower of apple cores, peach pits or banana peels.

The butt of the jest must invariably follow up his sloppy inundation with a quick and thorough wash and change before he might dare to report to any military school class. If any cadet had ever had the effrontery to show up for a class looking unmilitary in any detail he would not escape his instructors' righteous wrath.

But no cadet had ever been so obtuse as to brave the probable immediate whipping and the certainty of a slew of demerits attendant on such a sin.

It wasn't always Bustle in the barrel with the apple core bear. No, that would have been too unfair to please even the bullying little rowdies gathered in The Tower's schoolyard. Even Supe would not have countenanced such a vile injustice; but fat, slow moving cadets were favorite targets of such spirited cadet comedians as those who came out to play Baltimore-apple core in the time honored tradition of the game.

Corey had always thought the game was great fun during his carefree first year at The Tower.

But, just you wait, Corey Brecken, just you wait. The very sport which so amused him in his first year was to return to sting him in his much too eventful second term.

Cadet Brecken was a history and literature know it all. But it had caused envy in the unquiet ganglion of one Cadet Peters.

Peters erroneously regarded himself as the ultimate history buff. But, sadly, in every contest of wit and acumen he had to yield the history crown to Brecken.

A covetous Cadet Peters had always wanted to be the smartest cadet in history class, but he just didn't pack the gear.

Now Peters 's smoldering resentment he held against his rival superior enraged him and drove him to outright hatred of the schoolboy who'd bested him at every turn.

This second best schoolboy, haunted by his inferior status yearned for revenge.

And, one fine day, Corey bounced into the history classroom early and plunked himself down at his hardwood desk. He had positioned the calf of his leg below a fundament still aching from a recent nocturnal session with THE SILVER STREAK.

When he did so a nail placed there by an unknown enemy pierced his calf and penetrated his calf very close to the bone. It was painful, but Peters was deprived of his revenge, for his big moment was to have come when he heard his victorious rival yowl with pain and astonishment.

Obviously, he did not know Corey. Our boy's silent stoicism robbed Peters of his trophy, just as the superhero had defeated The Beast on their first encounter.

Fortunately for all concerned their teacher was not yet present; but Corey was having some trouble in removing the stubbornly lodged nail.

Brecken got some much needed help from one of his Heeler Hall confreres attending the class. And, even as Corey's little friend extracted the nail, he fingered the guilty party.

Brazen, defiant and caught out, Peters was left with no avenue of escape from Brecken's righteous ire. Ergo the denounced trickster rose and discovered himself as the culprit.

"YEAH, I did it!" bellowed the second best student, "What're YOU gonna do about it, Brecken?"

"See y' on th' quad at free play time, pissy-butt!

"Just make SURE y' meet me far enough from Heeler Hall that old lady Bite can't see what I'm gonna do to you, laughing boy!" grimaced our veteran schoolyard champion confidently.

Soon the teacher entered and the cadets snapped to attention.

"At ease" was called and history class was conducted without event.

In the fullness of time the history class was dismissed, formation was held, close order drill was completed and lunch with Leto was heaven on earth.

Then, at long, long last, free play time and Peters 's moment of truth came to pass:

Corey met his creampuff adversary on the field of honor, swung him around and around and dashed him down onto the hard ground repeatedly.

The great warrior sat astride the confessed and punished prankster.

East Tennessee was not the tropics and there were no sandspurs available, so our victor must improvise and stuff the dirt and wild onions native to the quad into his bawling culprit's nose and mouth.

Brecken forced handfuls of dirt into every one of his squirming victim's cranial orifices.

"YOU were a BAD, BAD putty tat, Peter-punk!" the champion aped The Tweety Bird of Loony Tunes fame to mock his squirming quarry, "Are y' gonna do it again, piss ant?"

"Y-Y-YES, I, I, I am, am, am, AM, you, you, you, YOU d-d-dirty B-B-BASTARD!!!!" bawled his vanquished, but still defiant prey.

"WRONG answer as usual, DUMDUM," smiled his delighted tormentor, eager to punish this drubbed dross again and again.

Corey snatched his blubbering game to its wobbly feet, gut-punched Peters repeatedly (just to laugh at his pain-distorted face and listen to his distressed wails).

Then the champ returned to his original routine of repeated bone-rattling trips into the hard, hard ground. After that punishment our towhead scrapper forced more dirt, weeds and filth into his mark's ears, mouth and eyes twice and thrice again. That second and third trip to the cold, hard earth coupled with its attendant diet of grass, dirt and wild onions finally brought a piercing howl of heartfelt contrition from the cowardly essence of a pathetic little sneak.

"N-NOOOO-NO-NO-NOOOOOOO, I aint, aint, AINT never, NEVER, I aint never, NEVER gonna do it no, no, no MORE!!!" bawled the thoroughly humiliated instigator and victim of Corey's rough justice, "LE' ME GO, B-B-B-Brecken, PLEASE, please, please, PLEASE le' me GO!!!!!"

"Le' me go WHO?" his master and conqueror demanded.

"Huh?" queried the confused dimwit, failing to comprehend the high and mighty conqueror's meaning.

"Le' me go, SIR!!!!" Corey enlightened him, "Thou shalt thenceforth address me as 'SIR,' thou naughty knave!"

"Y-Y-YES, S-S-SIRRR!!!" wailed the vanquished trickster in his chagrin and total defeat.

"That's right, dopey," gloated the victor, "From now on YOU had BETTER be th' nice, LADYLIKE little man we all know you are, 'n' call ME 'sir,' little miss pissy pants!"

Every cadet in Corey's history class and many others who'd heard of an impending fight ran as fast as they could to see it. They would cheer the victor and jeer the loser as schoolboys always have. Their intertwined bodies hid the fighters to evade the horrible punishments attendant upon discovery of such outlawed skylarking. The boys felt that the scrappers had provided them with the diversion of a good fight, and they deserved any protection they might proffer.

Life at the academy marched on from day to day, surprisingly without even one fatality.

On Saturdays the hike into town provided a rewarding jaunt. Our little cadets "stood off" their accrued demerits (five minutes per) and then bolted for town, and liberty. They all had more demerits than they thought they deserved.

Two movie theaters and a charming little down south screen door grocery store packed to the rafters with Moon Pies and other such down-home confections, both on Jubilation T. Cornpone Square, never failed to delight the boys.

The goobers' candy store gorge was immediately followed by a stampede into one of the movie houses' double feature shoot 'em up westerns (replete with CARTOONS, cliff-hanger serials and newsreels).

Having stood off his demerits one Saturday, Cadet Brecken was ambling the easy one mile over the two hills that led to Honeysuckle when he came upon a sight which gave him pause to reflect about that precarious balance between life and death in this crazy old world. The mystery of life and death is a subject seldom studied by the very young, but early erections were not our Corey's sole claim to precocity. He fell pensive when he encountered this small tragedy:

A little dog had run afoul of some speeding motorist. Now he lay dead by the roadside. Confronted with the scene of sudden and violent death, he wondered at the random nature of events in this life.

An elderly inhabitant of the district happened by on foot. Puzzled, the oldster stopped to inquire of a bemused cadet, "That yore dog, son?"

"Oh, no, sir," sighed Leto's polite little soldier, "We're not allowed t' have pets at the academy. I just happened along, 'n' I thought it was kind of a shame the poor little thing's dead out here on th' road."

Joe Delta

"WELL!" snorted the local, indignant at the academy's callousness, "If that don't jus' beat ALL I don' know whut DO!

"NOT allowin' a BOY t' have no DOG?

"Why, son, yew shore got a TOUGH row t' hoe down at that-there high flown mil'tary a-cademy o' yourn if THAT'S how they do ye!

"Not allowin' a BOY t' have no DOG, whut in tarnation's NEX'?"

The simple old countryman trudged on without the first idea in his head of the beastly excesses Corey and his cadet brothers daily endured at The Tower.

But, to Corey and his brothers, said beastly excesses were merely the plan of the day.

Youth is resilient and Corey pressed on over the two hills separating the smalltime, rural life of Honeysuckle from the urbane and cosmopolitan upper class hell on earth which was the finest military academy in all the world.

Soon he was standing beneath the statue of General Cornpone and embarking on a junior school goober's weekend candy store and double feature gorge.

The magic of the movies was an especial escape for our harried little cadets. Here they were lifted up above the cruel realities of their base enslavement by a sadomasochistic hierarchy of deviant and misanthropic housemothers whose daily delight in seeing and hearing the boys whipped and humiliated had ground them down.

Such living nightmares, coupled with the little cadets' extreme efforts to excel in both scholastics and sports for the honor of their families and school, required a much needed weekend release.

Privileged, but luckless, these little boys were eager to escape their tortured reality and escape into the comfortable stratosphere of their Hollywood make believe Saturdays:

Rocket Man, Batman and Superman made Corey and his cadet brothers float aloft on their wistful dream clouds of choice.

But Corey alone was to reap the most ecstatic of all rewards imagined and unimaginable, a reward he had never dreamt in all his little boy's dreams. His good fortune has placed him in the way of intoxicating, hot, sweet extracurricular amour.

136

He was to experience an unheard of event at this highly conservative military school, for Leto has smiled upon him and Major Daddy was now the father he had always been denied.

But on this present Saturday he had the good old double feature and his classmates' camaraderie for an escape valve.

Meanwhile, the academy's reality dictated that a boy must join a gang to survive.

The academy's gangs were not engaged in criminal activities other than that of being rabidly committed to the practice of never ending warfare against their rival gangs (and anyone stupid enough to think he could survive without a gang to back him up).

A series of blood-and-guts rumbles had winnowed the junior school gangs' number down to two survivors of those wars. The blue devils and the red devils reigned supreme. Their power over the entire goober population was both absolute and terrifying.

At first Corey gravitated toward the red devils because their leader was his drill master, Cadet Staff Sergeant Polio.

Polio was a gigantic bruiser from some cockamamie Caribbean island where he and his family worshipped the skulls of their dead ancestors rather than Christ. Cadet Polio had a skull in his dorm room at Booker Hall -- where else would they have placed such a goon?

Polio was especially spooky to Corey and the rest because he was a sexual pervert, a la old lady Bite with one difference. Bite was a sadist and Polio was a sodomite; and the menacing Polio regarded cute little Corey as a sex object as did Leto.

The difference here was that Corey loved Leto and not Polio, nor did he cotton to the profane invasion the big kid had proposed as our little hero's initiation into the red devils. Polio would take Corey into his merry band only after he had performed that shameful practice for which so many private schools have become notorious on him.

But Corey definitely preferred Leto to Polio, and, being a hero, the tadpole had the sand to refuse.

"NO!" Corey spoke up boldly on behalf of his poor, battered little body, a body already beaten black by a different variety of deviant,

"AND if y' beat me up 'n' MAKE me do it I'll tell th' MAJOR what y' did, and he'll take your STRIPES and march you off t' JAIL, too. So stand off!"

Our little bully had stood up to the big one with just the right words. The invocation of their almighty commandant's name was the most bone chilling form of extortion in all the academy. The magic of Corey's boastful words delivered him from an even more degrading insult at the hands of this latest leviathan than he had suffered already. Brecken's brass (and high connections) had handily spared him from outright sexual abuse.

But the all pervasive gang rule sword of Damocles still hung ominously over him to press its demand that all schoolboys join a gang. If he didn't he faced eternal hazing from the school's better organized savages.

To evade such a fate he celeritously hooked up with Supersonic Saber's gang.

To join the blue devils he didn't have to grin and bare it for a drooling pervert, for the chief of the blues was very conservative, not debauched.

All Corey had to do to prove he had the guts to be a blue devil was fight the gang leader, so a gutsy little challenger engaged the top dog on the field of honor the very next day.

Cadet Saber was not called Super Sonic for nothing. Supe was bigger, older, faster and stronger than our tiny contender, and he easily beat our plucky bantam.

"Don' worry about it, kid," laughed Supe, "You're a BLUE DEVIL now, 'n' can't NOBODY mess with a blue devil!

"Far as th' fight goes, y' did OKAY:

"Y' win a few, y' lose a few 'n' some get rained out."

Supe smiled amiably and the boys' friendship was cemented when the boss scrapper helped his junior up and shook his hand.

Corey was relieved to have been accepted into a top gang. Now he needn't fear being caught out alone and pummeled by every schoolboy in gangland.

Further, he was to discover one of the major perks of being a gang banger:

A tall, gangly upperclassman had made it his business to goad Corey pre blue devil conscription. The upperclassman was whiter than the driven snow, but he was every bit as tall as a Watusi.

The impudent daddy longlegs gloried in making fun of Corey for having prominent ears.

"Dumbo" was the offensive epithet his rangy tormentor tossed in poor little Corey's face when their paths crossed.

This particular annoyance was too big for little Corey to tackle solo. But one day Supe caught daddy longlegs' Dumbo act, and without a split second's hesitation the whole gang mobbed the jokester and made him wail his loud and tearful paeans of remorse for picking on a blue devil. The whole gang piled on to give him a beating that taught daddy longlegs the lesson that calling one blue devil names brought the whole gang down on him like an anvil to administer a heaping helping of corporal punishment.

A traditional All American saw is chicken every Sunday. That was good enough for The Tower's powers, and each and every Sunday chicken was faithfully served in the cavernous dining hall.

Our lovey-dovey Golden Brats always heralded the event with peals of (carefully repressed) merriment. But chicken is good and they were happy to take part in the festivities all the same.

Sunday chicken tradition was accompanied by one more revered and time honored Tower Sunday enclave:

The junior school cadets' dress uniform parade and pass in review.

This agonizingly formal ceremony was weekly performed on that big field between the junior and senior schools:

The Tower's ramrod-straight little goobers, tricked out smartly in gray and white dress uniforms, paraded at proud attention (with toy rifles issued especially for these events) onto and around the academy's huge field. The little boy soldiers marched, stiff and upright, to show off for The Brass around and around the huge expanse of green.

This magnificent spectacle of the junior school parade and pass in review was made complete by its enthusiastically loud musical accompaniment from the academy's marching band as it banged out Sousa hits.

On a raised dais, the august Donnybrook Clan (accompanied by the major's honored guests) looked down. The Tower's gods reviewed their troops from that Mount Olympus.

All protagonists breathlessly awaited the crucial moment during the march past when the headmaster would return his boy lieutenants' salutes. This was the splendid climax of the ceremony.

Meanwhile, a comely young princess looked down proudly (and quite cautiously) from her high perch to find her very own cadet lover.

And her lover (very, very carefully) raised his adoring eyes to meet those of his beloved enchantress.

On all of those occasions our enraptured lovers were spied on, suspected but never detected by The Deepfreeze and her ever watchful preschool Argus.

All this went along smoothly until the boy directly behind Cadet Brecken missed his step and dug his foot into Corey's heel with enough force to make his shoe come off during his contingent's final march off at the end of the parade.

A rattled Corey's first reflex was to try to recover it. But it was his good luck that McNichol spoke up in furtive, carefully whispered tones to become Corey's guardian angel.

"NO, honey!" stage-whispered Cadet McNichol, detecting Corey's intent, "Just leave that silly old shoe be. Continue the march, 'n' don't you worry, Corey baby, The Brass will LOVE you for it!"

In a flash Corey, reminded of the martial mindset, knew the good fairy marching beside him was right. A good soldier must be impervious to all distractions from his objective. And today the success of this parade was the toy soldiers' prime objective.

As they marched back to the quad to be dismissed, demons of doubt and fear pursued Corey. Paranoid images born of a constantly abused little boy's deepest fears seethed and fermented in him.

A cadet had no way of knowing what the heavies in the driver's seat would do next in their explosive, sadomasochistic world. Each cadet was issued one pair of shoes to be kept scrupulously shined and accounted for at all times. If he were braced by an officer or his malevolent housemother how could he ever explain the loss of a shoe?

Ghosts of the officially sanctioned cruelties imposed on his black and blue pelt daily haunted him, and he must perforce stew. He could be whipped for anything.

One fearful question galled Corey, why was I so careless, and what will they do to me?"

And that was a question scary enough to make a young shoe loser's blood run cold.

But an answer was ready and waiting for him:

Just as old lady Bite's hardy hounds trooped noisily into the hall to change back into fatigue uniform (while one painfully embarrassed little sprat hid from her to conceal the fact that he was minus a shoe), Bite called said sprat into her awful lair.

She indicated a long legged cadet captain towering heads above everyone and everything:

"Cadet Brecken, this young cadet captain has come to escort you to our esteemed commandant's office AT ONCE.

"WHAT have you been up to NOW, you filthy little WHELP?"

"NOTHING, MISS BITE!!!" howled the fleeing whelp.

"Come with me, cadet," instructed the officer, completely devoid of any expression.

"Yes, SIR!!!" barked his junior, relieved to escape his fire breathing housemother.

As he marched downstairs and down the sidewalk on one shoe, to the left and abreast and in step of his senior, Corey's mind was a madly whirling vortex of doubts and fears.

But a Tower cadet must remain outwardly stoical in the face of a highly probable dais ire, and so he did.

The cadet officer saluted his superior and reported as ordered.

He was saluted and dismissed by his commander.

"CADET BRECKEN REPORTING AS ORDERED, SIR!!!" barked the boy boldly, trying to hide an ever sinking heart.

The major's seat of judgment wads omnipotent. No excuse or explanation would ever be good enough to spare him the ordeal of all consuming strop-fire should the swinging balance judge him guilty.

An ashen faced boy awaited his master's commendation if McNichol was right or the hottest strop jig he'd ever danced if he was wrong. The littlest culprit spotted his missing footgear on his commander's desk. His hopes faded with each tick of the major's wall clock, hanging neatly next to the strop.

The man Corey had mistaken for a grim judge smiled a proud father's smile as he returned Corey's salute:

"Well, well, Cadet Brecken, I do believe I have a few things here that belong to you."

The beaming headmaster elucidated and enumerated, "This is the shoe you so gallantly left behind rather than disrupt a military operation in progress.

"Well done, Mac!

"You did the right thing, and I could not be prouder of you if you were my own son.

"Now, due to your quick thinking and decisive action, I'm promoting you to cadet corporal.

"Here are your corporal's stripes. I'm sure your housemother will be proud and happy to sew them on for you. Miss Bite should be glad to have such a credit to our academy as you in residence at her hall.

"Congratulations, Mac!"

"THANK YOU, SIR!!!!" our half-pint superhero stammered, overwhelmed.

"We all have to start someplace, Mac, and from this day forward you're on your way up in my outfit!" the major grinned, "See y' at dinner, son.

"Oh, by the way, I think it might just be chicken today. Must be Sunday, huh, corp?"

"YES, SIR!!!" shouted an overflowing heart, "And THANK you, SIR!!!"

Good Fairy McNichol had been right!

A flabbergasted new cadet corporal shook his commander's outstretched hand, shocked and elated at such a welcome up-tick in his fortunes.

Man and boy went into their saluting routine as the boy celeritously pulled on the lost-and-found shoe, pocketed his corporal's stripes and ran back to Heeler.

There he jumped into fatigues and bragged to his house brothers who'd also been wondering what his fate might be, for all their fates were eternally dangling in the balance.

Corey reported as ordered to his Golem housemother. He gave her the good news and his brand new corporal's stripes to sew onto his uniforms.

Miss Bite was not amused:

"He's our commandant, and we must all obey him, BOY, but I, for one, will never know what he sees in a blue-eyed, lollygagging, daydreaming little halfwit like YOU!" hissed the dragon, sweltering in the unquenchable fires of her own envy, "Oh, I'll sew the blamed stripes on your shirts and jackets all right, ye sad-eyed, long-faced little mongrel. But FIRST I'm a-gonna sew a few o' my OWN stripes into yore FILTHY hide:

"Strip buck naked 'n' git yore worthless carcass into that shower, cadet corporal STUPID!!!

"Mind ye turn that water up hot, hot, HOT a-cause yore lovin' ol' housemother's a-gonna teach ye JUST how CORPORAL a dose o' corporal punishment can get, you, you cocky, BRAINLESS li' l' pretty boy!!!!

"I mean I'm gonna BASTE ye BLACK, Blondie!!! I'm about t' give you TH' BEST WHIPPIN' O' YORE LIFE, Leto's DARLIN,' BLUE EYES, BLONDIE, you, you CUTSIE-POOTSIE little BLANKET-BABY, you, you, you NOBODY, you NOTHING!!!!"

"Let th' stupid ol' loony rave," thought Corey as he stripped off for yet another hard whipping from that same old mean spirited sad sack, "She's jus' jealous anyways."

The bloated old toad's poisonous hyperbole was nothing more than an easy algebraic equation for Schoolboy Corey now. He had her number. He knew exactly what The Bite wanted.

Following his quick witted girlfriend's sound advise, he had not the slightest trouble giving the perverted old monstrosity what she craved.

The same old sadistic child abuser who tried and failed to break him, the self same old anomalous and amorphous glob of stinking protoplasm now gloried in her nasty triumph. She drooled as she ogled her naked, helpless little doll-baby while he danced beneath her sled board of extreme vengeance.

But her victim was still the winner, and the toad was still a loser.

The Bite would have her fun while she was able. His twisted housemother cackled in her salacious glee as Corey jumped and screamed before her contemptuous porcine gaze.

Our little hero had been stripped of the last shred of what civilians call human dignity. He counted it no loss, for Leto had wished it and Corey was simply playing a part.

Corey skipped and wailed obscenely and obediently for the amusement of a spiritually and morally bankrupt abuser. Bite's formerly stubborn little hard case was keening and begging with the injured urgency of her most obedient slave.

It was just what she had wanted from the very first. The lowlife old crone was rapturous to see Leto's gallant put on such a lively show to delight her damned deviant soul

But a hero never performs for the sake of a toad. He pretended fealty to the dragon to keep his promise to Leto. It was the pert young queen of Corey's heart that commanded these performances, and her lover willingly complied:

As Corey screamed for Miss Bite, as he crawled and fawned ashamed like the cur this putrid, stinking hag had named him, the celestial Leto's bright face was ever before him and he endured.

He yielded up his degraded pleas to a revolting and misshapen behemoth who habitually beat him to glut her loathsome lust.

But he was determined this gross monster that cursed and beat him violently and without cause should never know why he did as she wished. This sacrifice which bought him Leto's favor, had elevated him high above a fetid old hag's stinking den of sin and corruption.

He was assured he was to be rewarded by his lady love.

Brecken had won the day. Bite was angry because he had won and she had lost. He could take it and The Bite Beast couldn't. The only thing the old sore loser was fit for was to dish it out.

The Beast had appeased her hunger on a small boy's bruised and throbbing flesh without cause, but Corey Brecken had won the day.

After his ordeal a hardy young corporal laughed and joked with house brothers gathered to congratulate him (sub rosa so the still smoking dragon couldn't hear them).

As his confreres offered their congratulations a reeking old lowlife was sewing on Corey's stripes (major's orders) as she cursed the little pest.

Cadet Corporal Corey had been richly blessed this fine day:

His cheeks of fire were set ablaze by this used up deviant who hated him, not by the highly placed and universally admired benefactor who loved him.

No cunning traps?

No apocryphal notes to denigrate him in the major's eyes?

Old lady Bite was obviously slipping.

Corey had won compliments and good cheer from his omnipotent chief. The man who loved him like a father, and whom he loved as a father was still in his corner.

"Eat your heart out, ol' lady Bite, y' filthy ol' bag-o-shite!" ruminated our bounce-back-kid as he drifted away from the wicked world of the academy into a welcome void after taps.

Hypnos obligingly unlocked Corey's dream world heaven with Leto and his dreams were sweet.

McMoon's Nightmare

After lunch the following day a fresh slice of dragon meat was thrown to Miss Bite.

All of The Beast's resident sufferers attending classes or drills or gang rumbles clearly heard the old pervert's latest chew-toy report to her.

"CADET CLAIRE REPORTING AS ORDERED, MA'AM!!!" piped a strange new voice.

A strange new boy had been condemned to Dear Old Granny Bite's private hell. But at this stage of the game none of this new stranger's bunkmates could ever have guessed, even in a thousand years, just how strange the new arrival was to be.

It need not be reiterated what cuddly old Housemother Bite's instructions for her brand new shower room pal were. By this time the reader must surely know that the confirmed deviant rattled off her usual set of commands.

Her introductory directives were the same for all The Beast's sad eyed novitiates. Nonetheless, here's a hint:

The death sow's instructions included a colorful allusion to filthy hounds; she ordered up of a piping hot shower; and a precipitous and vigorous introduction to THE SILVER STREAK followed. And all of this was standard operational procedure at Heeler Hall.

The new boy had been trapped in her sweltering torture chamber with The Tower Thing.

All her black and blue cadets snooped curiously just outside the dragon's garden of pain to listen to this poor little soul's agonizing initiation into the dark practices of Heeler Hell.

The listeners heard the tumult and felt great sympathy for the subject of the toad's vicious amusement, coupled with a blessed relief that none of them were in the barrel with The Bite this day.

The flagellation commenced, heated up and continued and the newbie amused his darling housemother with his abandoned cries for surcease.

But a surprise was in store for everyone concerned, and it was to be a terrible and disquieting departure from The Bite's habitual mode of vile self gratification. There was a shock in store for the demoniac old house-monster, and one which none of them might ever imagine:

Yes, a naked boy had darted obediently into the rising fog of The Beast's personal Tantalus.

Yes, her tiny victim had turned the shower up to its highest heat for his tormentor's insane enjoyment.

All of these elements were Heeler Hall regulation issue.

Yes, The Bite had given his neurons time to awaken to her hot, hot water's highest enhancement of her hapless quarry's tender sensibilities.

The misshapen sport had allowed her boy a little extra time to stew about her not yet known but scarcely uncertain intent, her tantalizing prelude to his coming torture.

Then the most dreadful apparition imaginable had made her bone chilling entrance, revealed and brandished her awful weapon. Immediately this eternally lost hell hag had begun her revolting feed on yet another shamefaced schoolboy.

"Let's hear him scream, old STREAK!!!" trumped the dragon.

It was as it had always been. The new cadet's pain was there, it was real, and the piercing cries of this innocent's awful extremity erupted out of the very essence of a soul in torment.

All these elements had been The Beast's fodder in days past. And today they should assuredly have sated the putrid old crone's lust.

But now they gave her no joy!

Her climax should be at its zenith now, as it had been when she had made all her other cadets cry.

But it was not!

She had dreamt of enjoying her distressed newbie's unabashed outcries of surrender to his slavish fate.

But she could not!

This otherwise cooperative little whelp wasn't fulfilling her.

Why?

Cadet Claire was not a normal little boy. He was a masochist who loved being tortured even more than Bite loved thrashing him to distraction.

Her inexplicably exotic, terribly strange micro newbie had suddenly assumed the effrontery to affect a phony Oriental dialect in an attempt to goad the ferocious old scourge to an even more virulent assault on his person.

The pain lover's goal was to spur the furious leviathan into an even hotter ravishment of his black and blue instrument. This novitiate nut flake was haranguing her into beating him harder than she was able to do and in so doing assuage his own perversion.

"Oh, PREASE, Missy Blight," screamed a happily orgasmic wild child beneath The Bite's most unutterable inferno of criminal abuse, "Whipee me until the BLOOD stleam DOWN!!!!

"WHIPPIE coolie, Cladet Craire, harder, harder, HARDER!!!"

But she could never whip him hard enough to sate his lust. And, because she had failed to punish him adequately, Cadet Claire flew into an immediate and desperate fury.

Sadist and masochist alike had been driven into a frenzy by their common frustration.

Suddenly the nut case newbie dropped his affected Oriental jabber and demanded hotter and hotter hell fire with the imperative air of an impatient superior:

"HARDER, I said, whip me HARDER, you, you PUNY old BITCH!!!

"WHIP ME RIGHT, Y' UGLY OL' HAG!!!!

"I said whip me RIGHT, y' slimy ol' scab!"

After a protracted period of just such errant nonsense dear old Housemother Bite finally had finally recognized that this was getting neither of them anywhere:

Her underage sex object's gratification had been dulled by her inability to whip him hard enough. At the same time she feared that she might accidentally be at the point of getting him off, and that would never do.

This impudent little poof had deprived her of the reward she viewed as her due. The fulfillment she'd wrung from her other bad little boys was conspicuously missing this fine day. Normal little boys' protestations of shame and capitulation were her meat and drink. These dearest trophies of her foul excesses had never failed to rouse the stinking old thug to elation.

Oh, no, my dear, surge of victory she'd experienced with those curs who hated torture was sadly absent now.

Cadet Claire's own venal disease had defeated her. The micro loony's reaction to her villainous practices had been the diametric opposite to those she had coerced out of her normal cadets:

She was rewarding him and depriving herself. All the dragon's exhausting efforts to make her perversion a paying concern for herself had failed her and she'd come up empty this time.

Now this small devil the lumbering devil had been flailing away at was so audacious as to give her orders and curse her and within the hearing of the others she had broken and prostituted.

It finally dawned on this dreaded Horror of Heeler Hall:

The only way to hurt this unbreakable hound was not to hurt him. And she broke off her frenzied tirade abruptly, and very much to his disappointment.

Their premier encounter had ended in stalemate, a frustrating fiasco for both unclean souls that had long since been condemned to burn forever in the personal hells of their own design.

Bite and Claire had metamorphosed into the tired but true old masochist vs. sadist wheeze in which masochist begs, "Whip me!"

And sadist says, "No."

Corporal Corey Brecken enjoyed a well deserved reputation as one of the hardest hitting little bullies in the celebrated Supersonic Saber's dreaded blue devil gang. It had long been established as grapevine word of mouth truth. No cadet with a faint hint of good sense would ever dare to rile our half-pint superhero.

But today it was Brecken's bad luck that Bite's old pal, the masochist, had a terribly different variety of sense, and it had not even a nodding acquaintance with anything in the vicinity of good.

Pursuant to his own twisted needs, Heeler's tormented newbie set about egging Bully Brecken into a fight he devoutly hoped to lose. His prurient need for chastisement had driven Claire to devise a way to instigate our towhead bully to rain down a storm of angry blows against his abuse hungry body to sate his twisted carnal lust. And we shall soon see this was not his only motive.

Corey had exercised scrupulous care to take no notice of Claire. By this time everyone knew this strange new house brother was battier than McNichol and Curley put together. And, for that reason, Corey had determined that it must be wise to ignore this boy and his incessant nagging to be whipped.

Brecken had resolved to follow a plan of peaceful resistance.

Sadly, there was never to be a moment's peace for any of the little exiles at The Tower.

Our boy had made an Herculean effort to maintain amiable relations with the balance of humanity, for he had been placed under strict orders from two irresistible women so to do:

He had made a well intentioned compact with his fervently burning love goddess not to get himself into any trouble. And he had his standing orders from his dear Grandmamma to keep the peace at all costs.

In The Tower's perpetually warring precincts, such an oath had often proved impossible to keep:

Our upright cadet hero was continually being set upon by churls, and honor required that he must prevail against them.

On his way to morning formation Bully Brecken found himself suddenly put upon by a persistent gadfly.

The masochist knew this was to be the glorious morning he would finally whine and wheedle his way past Corey's most formidable defenses --and trap him.

"Hey, Brecken," shouted Corey's cute little, big-eyed, plump-cheeked, totally loony house brother, "wait up!"

"Hi, Claire," smiled Corey good naturedly, "What's up?"

"Let's play Whip Wilson, master!"

A vapid, wet-dreamy, decidedly dewy-eyed expression had suffused Claire's features with an eager and expectant excitement. And a warm glow of unaccustomed color came into Claire's normally pallid cheeks as he daydreamed of his rough-and-tumble cowboy movie whip wielder.

"No time, for play," Corey was uncomfortable, but he was determined to laugh, "Assembly's about t' blow 'n' we gotta get in ranks on th' double!

"'Sides, th' movies I really go in for 're the swashbucklers with Doug Fairbanks 'n' Errol Flynn!"

Rebuffed but undeterred, a dewy-eyed Claire launched into his irritating ersatz Far Eastern dialect to unleash a tirade designed to nag Bully Brecken to action:

"Ah, so, Mastah Corlee Blecken, you no wannna WHIP me till the blood stleam down?

"Maybe now you tellee me tluth, oh gleat beeg bully:

"Pletty rittle Missy Reto Donnyblook call you her pletty rittle MAC now, huh?

"Ho, hyes, you GOT gleat beeg LOVE fo' pletty rittle Missy RETO, huh, mastah big shot ruver boy -- HUH?"

"Don't you DARE ever to say HER name again, y' slimy gob o' snot!!!" stormed Corey, "A creepy li' l' piss ant like YOU isn't fit to repeat the name of Miss Leto Donnybrook; 'n,' if y' know what's good for y,' you'll shut up!

"And NEVER again will you call ME pretty and live, got me?

"Are you NUTS, Claire?"

Claire knew he was playing with fire, but what he desperately wanted now was to be consumed in it.

He saw Corey had lost his notoriously hot temper and was walking right into the ensnarement he'd set.

"Ho, HYES," was Claire's impudent retort, "humble Cladet Craire want hew WHIP heem till the BLOOD stleam down:

"WHIP me, baby, WHIP me, WHIP me, WHIP me, WHIP ME!!!!!"

"You ARE nuts!" Brecken retreated from the nut, shocked and repulsed by this intoxicated basket case's inexplicable demand.

"WHIP ME, BULLY, WHIP me right NOW!!!!" choked Claire, aflame with the fond hope of gaining fulfillment his most insane and intimate driver's lust.

Puzzled and frightened, Corey took a step back. His inflamed house brother's unaccountable conduct had scared the wits out of him. But at the same time he was manfully struggling to come up with some flippant dismissal:

"Y' want 'o get whipped, huh, dopey?" Corey gasped, fighting for air, "Well, well d-don't you worry, son, th' BRASS 'll load y' up with more whippings than anybody could ever digest, so, so just leave, leave me out of it, will you?

"Listen, Claire, they're blowin' assembly right now, 'n' WE gotta get in ranks!"

Corey had heard the bugle's call, but Claire was in his dream world:

Lusting, needy, highly aroused and knowing the consequences of his act, the mini nut flake hugged Bully Brecken with the superhuman force of madness. He gripped Corey tightly and hugged him close to his body in a paroxysm of psychotic demand.

Our disgusted cadet superhero gut-punched his assailant with lightning immediacy and enough force to extricate himself from an offbeat sexual aggressor's unwelcome embrace.

A nearly orgasmic masochist staggered back with the wind knocked out of him beneath the authority of our junior hooligan's blow.

Brecken was about to attack, but Cadet McMoon ran up to rescue our poor, rage-blinded dupe from the calculated machinations of a clever predator's complex snare.

"COREY," the excited fat boy sounded the alarm, "cut it OUT!!!

"We're right under OLD LADY BITE'S window 'n' you KNOW she's jus' ITCHIN' for an excuse t' send y' RIGHT back t' th' MAJOR for another hiding!

"THIS is jus' what she's waitin' for, Brecks, so, so let Claire be before she sees what you're doin' 'n' fries y' up crisp for her breakfast!"

But the devious deviant fired a fresh salvo of invective against the monumental arrogance of his easily irritated mark:

"OOOOHHH, Mistah MACKEE-MAC, pletty Missy RETO wait fo' YOU:

"DOWN BY DE LAILLOAD TLACK WHERE NOBODY GO, THERE SI RITTLE RETO LITHOUT ANY CLOTHES!!!!"

"WHAT?" thundered a Brecken infuriate.

McMoon had been right about Bite and he knew it, but this graphically depictive salvo against his true love's perfection was too much to bear. Brecken's unquenchable wrath snatched him up like a rag doll and threw him into the churning vortex of this wily deviate's intricate head game.

He could not let such a gross insult to his beautiful Leto pass unpunished. Considerations of self preservation were now swept away in the raging tide of his most egregious ire. Not if The Beast had immediately dispatched him to the major's office to be whipped to death could his suicidal and arrogant wroth be restrained.

Little Baron Masoch had skidded one slur too many at the honor of Little Marquis De Sade's perfect love queen to escape and titter about it in this lunatic asylum's locker room.

Brecken tore off in hot pursuit of a fleeing instigator with murder in his heart.

But the sneaky little villain of this rancid piece had finally had the presence of mind to heed the bugle's clarion call. Claire knew it was time to break off his horseplay, and he was agile enough to dive into ranks before it was too late, for the frolicking cadet spotted outside formation when the last strains of the bugle died away was instant strop fodder.

Corey was overpowered by the eruption of his rage. Our half-pint hero, tempest tossed in his towering fury must punish the haranguer.

But he knew the rules and, though he was loath to break off the hunt, Brecken came to his senses just in time to jump into formation in time to avoid the notice of the big, bad Brass.

And that was lucky for him, for this morning two of the school's most senior, all grown up and serious field grade officers were present to observe the morning formation and roll call. These seasoned, sober-faced war veterans were professionally seasoned in the art of whipping stray cadets into shape, and this morning they were vigilant.

This made it a blood-chilling fact of life that woe would assuredly betide any boy taken in the act of skylarking on this fine day.

Alas, Claire's plot to get Brecken caught and flayed alive had failed, but the morning's events had delivered the scaly little devil a surprise victim:

Poor little Cadet McMoon.

While the others in this morning's chase had both been slick and spry enough to hop into ranks fast enough to escape the war gods' doleful stare, Corey's clumsy and obese roomie had been caught out of ranks when the bugle had trailed off into the mists of dawn.

Our kindhearted fat boy had been tearing after Corey to save him from Claire's trap, and been ensnared in it. He had only wanted to prevent his hot tempered roomie from throttling Claire in the sight of both The Brass and The Beast. And now it was the innocent fat boy who would pay for his house brothers' folly.

McMoon had pressed his pursuit with such assiduity that he had been unable to dive into ranks by the time the roll call had begun.

This poor soul was the hero of the day for trying to save his friend, but his fatal hero's flaw had been that he wasn't as agile as his confreres.

The eagle-eyed Major Hooten spied a fat little cadet skylarking out of ranks and immediately pointed out that discrepancy out to the scowling commandant.

Major Donnybrook had been taken aback by the misconduct of this chubby jackanapes at the very formal, very serious, event of morning formation.

The all-powerful Zeus Alastor motioned to the suspected miscreant to call him into his fearful presence to parlay. The great man wanted to hear the boy's explanation, and he would hear it.

McMoon saw the severity in his chief's aquiline gaze and nearly fainted. He stood momentarily frozen in his tracks, like a rabbit in the crosshairs. And then, momentarily bereft of reason, he proceeded to make the worst mistake a military school cadet could possibly have made:

He ran.

Terrified past distraction, our fat boy made a mad and senseless dash to elude his fate.

If he had but obeyed his headmaster's beckoning he might have saved himself a whipping. But his fear of the stropping and his hatred of physical pain had robbed him of his reason.

McMoon's hopeless bolt into nowhere sealed his fate, for he'd been lost the moment he disobeyed his wise and wonderful commander.

Disobedience?

"Such a thing was unthinkable here!" opined Major Hooten.

"Disobedience?" concurred the almighty Major Donnybrook, "This sort of thing is NOT done at The Tower."

Now the implacable strop must and should track the luckless Cadet McMoon across time and space. Though he flee to the end of the universe, the strop should certainly make him cry.

When he had run away he'd abandoned all hope of talking his way out of this already volatile fix. And, at the finest military academy in all the world, such an error must invariably be paid for in currency of shame and disgrace.

The Brass watched him with mild amusement.

"I suppose he's guilty, Lynwood," opined Major Hooten disinterestedly.

"Decidedly, Paul. Otherwise he would surely would have stayed to explain himself," sighed the commandant, unhappy but resigned to his fate of having to skin this little boy, a physical coward and a hopeless crybaby.

McMoon was trying to scale a particularly steep slope. He was puffing away in an all out effort to run past Booker Hall and reach the hill which led to the senior school, but to what end?

There had never been, and nor would there ever be, a successful escape from the disciplinarians in command here.

The politely chuckling majors watched the fugitive pant his way up the hill for a brief moment. Then the commandant dispatched two of his longest legged cadet captains to retrieve him.

With four of the school's longest legs chasing him, the benighted prey never made it to the end of Booker Hall before they'd outstripped and taken him.

The two big boys marched their little prisoner, bawling and babbling incoherently, back to face the terrible wrath of the mighty Zeus.

The captains saluted and reported as ordered, proud of themselves for a speedy retrieval of their squirming game.

The major saluted his officers, proud of his lanky captains' physical prowess.

And Cadet McMoon wailed a red-faced and discordant jumble of unintelligible blather.

No one was proud of McMoon.

But Corey was very sorry for his poor little pal and grateful to him for his timely intervention.

The commandant's little group trooped expeditiously into his office with a lamenting Cadet McMoon under close arrest, weeping and protesting his innocence at the top of his lungs:

"M-major, major, MAJOR, sir, sir, sir, SIR, d-d-don't, don't, DON'T w-whip, don't whip, whip M-ME!!!!!

"I, I, I'm a, I'm a, I'm a G, GOOD boy, a GOOD-GOOD b-boy, MAJOR, SIR!!!

"It, it, it, it, it WASN'T, WASN'T my, my, my, my fault!!!!!"

"Oh, Mac!" reflected Corey, haunted by regret and ashamed not to be able to speak up for his savior.

But, as the doomed boy's piteous protestations filled the air, the dutiful Cadet Brecken must answer roll call, "You're only making it worse on yourself carryin' on so, 'case th' major HATES cowards!"

"It-it-it wasn't, WASN'T, WASN'T never, never, never me, S-S-SIR!!!!!" howled the winnowing strop's living and breathing sacrifice, "It-it-it was all, all, all th' fault o' B, Brecken, Brecken 'n,' 'n' CLAIRE, m-major, MAJOR, S, S, SIR!!!

"I, it, it was THEM not ME!!!!

"I, I, I, I'M A GOOD BOY, GOOD B-BOY, A GOO-

"No, NO, don't, don't, don't whip me, sir-

"OWWWW!!!!"

"Oh, th' poor li' l' bastard!" Corey was really worried about his poor friend in the hot seat, "Now he's ratted out his comrades:

"Th' major's not gonna like THAT.

"Aw, poor li' l' ol' McMoon, he's really catchin' it!"

Corey was tarred with the shameful stain of his guilt. He hadn't confessed his part in this morning's debacle, but how could he?

He was at attention and answering roll call, and he had not received permission to speak from his superiors:

"I, I guess it mus' be like Leto said, we're just th' little kids here." thought he, "There's nothing WE can do when th' grownups make up their minds t' do anything."

All of the cadets assembled to answer roll call in the courtyard outside the major's office shuddered with nervous apprehension as they heard the sharp and oft-repeated report of leather on nethers sustain the melody, and the frenzied screams of their hard pressed comrade in distress take up the counterpoint in today's symphony of shame.

McMoon suffered even as they had done in their turns, but even more so.

Being a coward, the major put the fat boy through an ordeal far worse than Corey's.

Two lanky cadet captain heroes were constrained to hold a wiggling and wailing mini culprit face down across a desktop while an angry commandant put him through hell. Otherwise our allergic to corporal punishment McMoon would surely have made another run for it.

Woefully, the major did hate cowards, ergo McMoon's sufferings were nothing short of insupportable.

His pathetically ineffectual howls for mercy and clemency moved Corey, for he already felt terribly guilty for having lost his temper and causing this mess.

At the very same moment Cadet Brecken had heard the tumult of his poor friend's pitiless punishment and felt contrition and remorse, Cadet Claire had heard the very same cries and felt a wicked joy.

Claire's only regret was that he wasn't being basted himself. The mini nut flake daydreamed wistfully of experiencing deep humiliation in a like manner. And vicarious waves of orgasm had overtaken and delighted his little body and brought solace to his scabby little lost mind.

The balance of the cadets in the morning formation had various responses to their fallen comrade's chagrin:

Some felt sorry for him.

Others laughed at him for the rash ingenuousness that had gotten him into this thorny pickle.

The wild cacophony of despair rising out of the major's office had also reached the listening ears of Miss Bite and gladdened her black heart. The idea that her overtaxed little boys' slavish degradation was an event not confined to her hall of horrors was felicitous to such a heartless old toad as she.

Stretched across a desk and held firmly in place two gigantic cadet captains, Corey's wailing roomie was enduring the flaming culmination of every one of his worst nightmares -- a hiding.

Brecken's loving Leto had said the academy's protocols must be so rigid as to forbid him to speak without leave in ranks, even to deliver his suffering buddy from evil.

And if he had discovered himself as one of the key skylarks it would have been military school cadet suicide, for it would have meant facing his patron's censure.

He tried to speak:

"Sir, Cadet Brecken re-"

But his platoon leader snapped angrily:

"Shut up, rookie!

"Formation's no time t' shoot th' shit!"

He could have taken a whipping, but what if he lost his place as protégé?

If he did so he must surely have lost Leto!

While it is true that heroes are brave, not smart, this particular cadet superhero wasn't sufficiently dumb or brave to commit suicide -- yet.

No, my dear friends, masochists are not the innocent victims of their sadistic counterparts they might seem. Sadists and Masochists alike are the uncaring, salacious and malicious slaves of their mortally dangerous and leprously depraved driver, the impetus toward twisted sex. This heartless driver is a pitiless and implacable destroyer which both varieties of deviates covet in common. Both are mad and both are equally destructive. Masochist and sadist alike stand poised to bring ruin and humiliation to as many helpless mortals more innocent than themselves as they are able.

Today Bite and Claire had found a dupe in Cadet Brecken. But, when that cheezy little plot fizzled, they had been quick to snatch up and torture yet another screaming, struggling and, worst of all, innocent little child.

Formation was dismissed, classes, drills and heaven sent glimpses into the paradise in his little love queen's all compelling eyes ensued to fill up Schoolboy Corey's bustling duty day.

The events of the day flitted fleetly by our toy soldiers on Father Time's frantically flapping wings until Corey and his weary house brothers returned to the dragon's dungeon. Though a restful eventide was a real outside bet at Heeler a boy without hope is a boy who must needs welcome at least the sweet dream of such a rarity. And such a boy must grasp his long shot, since that's the only shot he's got. But was there to be such a blessing as rest for Cadet Brecken this eve?

Of course not:

"Damn that traitor Brecken!" obsessed McMoon to Milan as he lay in wait for our towhead suspect, "He left me, his roomie, flatfooted t' take a larruping' HE deserved his self!"

Poor Little Milan was at a loss for words. Both boys were his friends and the fat boy's wroth was hot and fearful in his eyes.

Burning, throbbing, and furious. McMoon had been whipped unjustly because he'd tried to help a wayward house brother out of trouble, and that brother had deserted him.

"Now them two bastards, Claire 'n' Brecken 're gonna have t' face him up t' th' WRONG they done me."

It was our injured little fat kid's devout hope that he could guilt-nag the house brothers he considered the authors of his misery into a contrite confession of their perfidy. The fuming fat boy was all primed up to shame the scapegraces into an admission of their guilt.

McMoon's pain and anguish told him that they alone were accountable for his still smoldering cheeks of fire.

In his mind McMoon had found his more agile delinquent bunk buddy guilty in absentia to this blackest of all treasons, desertion in the face of the strop. He'd found his Heeler fellows at fault for his panic, his loss of reason and the mad confusion that misled him into the cardinal error of running from the inescapable Zeus Alastor. In his simple mind his highly subjective case for the prosecution was airtight.

It had been he who was splayed athwart an office desktop facedown and had mincemeat made of his nethers.

And that wasn't the end of his woes, for he'd been forced to brook the further insult of mockery from his brother cadets all day:

McMoon had exposed his shame and declared his plight to a world that had simply laughed at him for his ingenuousness.

Awaiting Brecken, he'd become more and more furious.

"YOU, you, you son-of-a-bitchin' BASTARD, Brecken!" bawled the injured party in lieu of welcome home for his remiss pal.

Our melodramatic fat boy bared his bruised and blackened buttocks to both of his roommates and cried, "Just LOOK what th' old man DID t' me, boys; and, and it, it, it's all YOUR fault, Brecken,

you, you dirty BASTARD -- YOU, you 'n' that, that son-of-a-bitchin'
SISSY, Claire!

"Y-YOU, you, both did this to ME, just as, as like YOU swung that
damn razor strop yourselves, you, you, you JASAXES!!!!"

He'd meant to revile them as jackasses. But he was too flustered
behind his rigorous trial -- and what he perceived as his friends'
insouciance -- to verbalize anything but "JASAXES."

Little Milan whistled as he had when he'd seen those big, black
bruises The Beast had burned into Brecken's back when she'd
christened him into her Heeler Hell fraternity of enslavement. To be
sure poor McMoon's ravaged fundament had verily been blackened
to much the same hue as had Brecken's on the morning after the
shower room ego wars. The chief difference between the two was
that the major had flailed away only at McMoon's butt. The fat boy's
shoulders and legs had been spared while Miss Bite had savaged the
whole of Corey's back.

Corey was deeply sorry for his friend's pain but, to his way of
thinking, the event was at an end.

"I keep tellin' y', Mac," he sighed wearily, "Discipline 's why our
folks sent us here. We're all gonna get whipped sooner 'r later, like it
or not."

Despite his feelings of guilt and regret for having lost his temper
Brecken was forced to smile at his pal's shocked surprise for having
been tortured in an institution which was a monument to the practice
and glorification of just such legalized child abuse.

"What d' y' want ME to do about it, roomie?" our mini superhero
grimaced apologetically, "You got a hidin' for runnin' away from Th'
Brass, but it's over 'n' done with now. Believe me, th' best thing t'
do is just t' let it go. You know they whip me a lot, but that's what I
always do."

But McMoon was a crybaby by nature. He could never have dreamt
of assuming Corey's mantle of manly prowess. No, our boy hero's fat
little friend couldn't take it like a man. He'd always been quite content
to leave the amateur heroics to the likes of Bully Brecken.

Burning for revenge against those base traitors whom he held accountable for his strop-branding, the aggrieved party bellowed aggressively:

"Go tell th' major that I didn' do NOTHIN' wrong -- it, it was all YOUR fault, you, you two JAS, JASAXES.

"I, I, I'm a GOOD boy 'n' YOU AINT, 'n' YOU know good 'n' well you're th' ones that should 'a' got a whippin'!"

Then the poor soul dissolved into a very waterfall of inconsolable tears.

McMoon wept loud, long and pathetically, but Brecken defended himself:

"Think, Mac!" he abjured his injured pal, "If I do that we both end up with black asses. Even worse, the major might turn 'is back on me!

"You're m' roomie 'n' all, but I just can't take that kind o' chance with th' major. There's just TOO much at stake for me here:

"'Sides it wasn't ALL my fault, was it?" Corey reminded his steaming bud, "Who instigated this whole great big mess in th' first place?"

"It, it was CLAIRE, GAWDAMN 'IM!" our sore-stropped mini sorehead raged as he burned with pain and resentment.

"Well?" reasoned Corey, "Why don't you ask that li' l' flip out t' turn himself in?

"That calf eyed li' l' lamebrain 'll do it 'cause he WANTS t' get a whippin'."

"I already DID ask 'im, MISTER SMARTY PANTS!" wailed the exasperated human tear duct disconsolately.

"And?" Corey pressed for an answer, "What'd he say?"

"That FILTHY S. O. B. wanted t' CARESS my burnin' BACKSIDE!!!!" bellowed a fat boy in an even more extreme state of dismay, "I had to RUN for my LIFE t' get out o' his room and escape HIM 'n' his frou-frou ROOMIE, McNichol, both!

"Them two pervs wanted t' play with my poor burnin' butt -- and they even SAID so!"

Our three little roommates in the shadow of a deviant leviathan shared a common exile into this same dangerously leaky little canoe, the finest military academy in all the world. They were all here to do penitence for their innocent little home town sins.

McMoon's roommates were both sad to see his plight but they weren't able to repress their laughter at this latest tragicomic twist in McMoon's ironically convoluted tale of outrageous folly.

Their bellyaching house brother's topsy-turvy tale of woe was just too hilarious for the other boys to contain their mirth in the face of the juxtaposition of their poor little corn-fed mama's boy against two such urbane and perverted moderns as Claire and McNichol. No, it was just too rich, and Brecken and Little Milan cracked up.

Their laughter was so contagious the fat boy couldn't help but join in the social contagion and laugh.

But our three convulsed roommates' already precariously leaky canoe was about to be sunk.

"I could hear you three HOUNDS a-bayin' ALL th' way in my parlor," an enraged dragon had ominously blotted out the light from their doorway to scold, "Now GIT them FILTHY carcasses o' yourn in that shower a-cause I mean t' make you three CLOWNS laugh till it HURTS!!!"

"It wasn't them, ma'am," our mini superhero implored. Anxious to redeem himself for his error, he wanted to deliver both his roommates from evil, "It, it was all my fault, Miss Bite!"

The Bite might abuse him as she loved to do, but he must save his friends.

No such luck.

"SHORE it wuz all yore fault, ye crawlin' little WHELP!

"Oh, don't worry none, BLONDIE, I'm a-gonna baste ye RIGHT, but I done heered three o' ye laughin,' an' NOW all of us is gonna laugh TOGETHER!!!!"

They stripped obediently, padded naked into the shower of shame, turned up the water and prepared for the worst.

And the worst came slithering in to make them pay for all those gifts nature had given them, and denied to her.

Bold Corey had long been inured to The Beast's vile practices. The Tower Thing hurt him and he screamed, as per orders from his beautiful Leto. For him it was but one more in a long line of his deadly enemy's demoniac floorshows.

But Bite knew he was faking it and made the tenderfeet she could reach pay dearly for it. The boys our mini hero 'd tried his best to spare the shame of her steaming torture pit brought the bloated anomaly to orgasm with their frenzied scream-dancing.

The Bite had never been one to entertain considerations of a basic human decency unknown to her.

The ravishment THE SILVER STREAK brought to her tenderfoot and pre tenderized victim gave great pleasure to this wizened vampire as she flayed a baby and an already wounded fat boy alive.

All three dancing puppets wailed beneath the strident thunderclaps of THE SILVER STREAK.

The Beast feasted with a characteristically vicious enthusiasm on the bare flesh of her three wildly convulsed little bodies lost in the wild frenzy of her scream dance.

How she hated those bright-eyed young scamps with their healthy young bodies, but now they must delight her with the extremity of their awful torment.

This nightmare had at length stroked their living, suffering, bawling flesh until her perverted bloodlust was at length slaked. And following her crime this lost and damned reptile had slithered off exhausted to her lair to rest.

"Thank God the old loony's sick!" sighed the weeping Corey, "Come on, boys, we gotta get some rest 'n' somehow recover for reveille."

And they did.

Though he'd howled long and loud for the delight of his horrid housemistress, Cadet McMoon had found contentment because he'd scored a Pyrrhic victory over his major's pet roommate.

While it'd been true that Brecken hadn't confessed his sin to the all powerful Zeus and taken a pound of flesh hiding, his flawed mini hero was still getting his slippery little backsde SILVER STREAKED for less than nothing right beside him, the buddy he'd abandoned earlier.

Yes, McMoon's reticent roomie must scream his pain and outrage right beside the pal he'd betrayed now. Both boys shared the shock and misery of being flayed alive.

A deranged monstrosity had reduced them both to a living mass of howling, quivering jelly together.

In the terrible depths of The Beast's tantalizing torture trial, Corey's roommate brother-in-torment had forgiven him for the fault of refusing to confess to the major.

McMoon didn't know what was going on between Leto and Corey because he was a ten year old and ten year olds didn't know much in those days.

Ingenuous as he was, the fat boy did know that Brecken's major's pet status was vital to him:

That had been the only consideration which kept old lady Bite from out-and-out murdering the hated Brecken, Brecken, BRECKEN. Everyone in Heeler Hell knew that sick old hag had hated and persecuted the lively golden brat more painfully than all others from the very beginning.

Our fat boy had heard The Bite, in the grip of her passion, curse and taunt his roommate as she tortured him:

"BLONDIE, PRETTY BOY, LETO'S LITTLE PET, BLUE EYES!!!!!"

She bawled her deadly hatred for this most despised of all her filthy cur cadets because "BLONDIE" got a double dose of the perverted toad's vitriol.

Our good hearted fat boy's grudge had been deleted, for unspeakable Miss Bite's flaming flail had called up a hell hot enough to expiate all of Brecken's blackest sins.

Hearing the noisy contention in the showers, Cadet Claire's lust for degradation had awakened with a vengeance. He cried out from his room and in his noxious quasi oriental dialect:

"Oh, PREASE, dlear ol' Missy Brite, WHIPEE ME TOO!!!"

"Not TONGHT, Josephine!" Bite grinned complacently.

Now The Beast's twisted Elysium-for-Tantalus, was at its zenith:

While she was basting the steaming quarters of her normal boys, she'd also been privileged to glut all her basest delights by denying her despised masochist pest access to her torture palace.

Atop the world in her perverse victory over all of her troubling boys, the squalid old sport was enjoying a paroxysm of impure ecstasy.

For now Claire must be content with vicarious dreams. Ergo, the sick boy drank deep of THE SILVER STREAK against the bare wet flesh of her shower room victims. In this way Claire shared The Beast's vile repast with the pleasure of a famished gourmet enjoying the rarest of foods and the finest of wines. His lost and blighted heart had been warmed by the heartbreaking screams echoing stridently through the twilight peace of a tranquil East Tennessee evening, disrupted only by his dear old housemother's savage application of THE SILVER STREAK. Both Bite and Claire had awakened to thrill to their satanic joy.

"Mercy?" Miss Bite reprised her signature motto, "Not on your life, dear boy!"

Bite and Claire, interfacing flip-side slaves of the same perversion, were forever at loggerheads:

Claire wanted Bite to skin him alive.

Bite refused.

The big monster knew extreme pain and the shame of being dehumanized to the state of a lash-branded slave, prostituted to her every deviant whims. She also knew this was precisely the what would send her little monster's libido over the rainbow.

"What a nerve!" fumed the big monster indignantly.

That bloated old toad didn't whip her boy-toys for their pleasure, she did so exclusively for her own delight.

That excruciating night in a darkened, foggy shower an insatiable dragon was awash in waves of orgasmic intoxication impelling her deranged libido into the black, black, blackest vortex of hellish delight. While she outraged our poor, innocent Little Milan, the lusty and not-quite-so-innocent Brecken, and her easy scream McMoon, abuser Bite was torturing her normal boys:

They'd cringed at the shame of being herded into their sordid old enemy's slaughterhouse like animals to be transformed from healthy pink to bruised black. They hated the insane taskmistress who'd then scourged them. They hated THE SILVER STREAK as it turned their flesh to fire. Finally, they hated the disgrace of being held so low in The Tower's chain of command as to be obliged to endure such an insufferable insult passively and without complaint or recourse.

Miss Bite and her normal boys recognized these things as torture, but they were the things the masochist craved. In The Bite's view, the only way she might punish this needy little loony was not to punish him at all, an infuriating and frustrating turn of events for her.

But the passage of time and the keen observation which was native to such a seasoned sadist had finally discovered a cause for celebration. She'd discovered that her innocent-eyed toy conniver lived in deathly fear of being sent to the major's office. Miss Bite had ventured a tentative experiment and evaluated the effect of the heavyweight strop experience on Claire:

She'd handed him his note and dispatched him down that narrow walkway to doom on the off chance of having some fun, And sure enough her fun had been forthcoming.

The redoubtable arm of our beloved major had delivered far too hot a fire to be digested even by little mister whip-me-harder's abuse hungry libido.

On that lovely day Claire's had not been the screams of elation, but his most urgent and heartfelt wails of contrition and remorse.

Now she had him right where she wanted him.

The scurrilous old Bite was heated with rapture when she noted the pathos scribbled all over little Baron Masoch Junior's woebegone mug. And when she'd handed him his walking orders and seen his diminutive shoulders slump despondently as he saluted, about-faced and drifted down to walk the condemned cadets' Bridge of Sighs she was in her world.

Cadet Claire's aversion to this peculiar facet of his Heeler Hall captivity had awakened a new joie de vivre in his morbid housemother. Kindly old Miss Bite had been overjoyed to listen to Claire's ineffectual screams, for they were trophies of outrage from the core of her knotty little difficulty's being. The squalid Beast sat by her window and bathed in the hellish delight of his strident howls.

Every Heeler Hall boy, especially Corey, had known the dispiriting threat of the razor strop trail. All her boys had marched to the major's office and fallen directly into the bond fire of pain that awaited them here. Fear, like a living predator lay crouched and ready to devour all Tower schoolboys alive, just as it had deflated Claire.

"Fear done come up from Hades 'n' et that aggravatin' li'l' pest whole," gloated their cuddly old housemother, "Unholy Eris be praised!"

9

A PRICELESS HOLIDAY PRESENT

"Christmas comes but once a year, but when it comes it brings great cheer!"

But not for Corey:

McMoon had forgiven Brecken the night they were scourged together. The Beast's stinging, scalding whip dance had made his fat friend relent and recant his thirst for vengeance.

The major and Leto had forgiven our mini superhero (and theirs) for having been such a dope as to make waves and cause himself probable harm (and embarrassment to their school) through his early, ill advised hunger strike. Corey's powerful friends genuinely loved their wayward boy with every beat of their generous and loving hearts (a lusty young woman's heart in our pretty little Leto's case).

The darling Miss Bite had facilely fainted at forgiving Brecken his robust health and comely looks. She'd only donned the sham mask of beneficence toward him for appearances' sake. And she had done so merely to stand in well with the headmaster and his little princess.

Oh, no, my dear, this corrupt old tyrant would never forgive the little boy's unpardonable offence of being so generously blessed.

Would the darling Miss Bite ever forgive any little boy his good health and good fortune?

Would The Beast ever forgive him his cardinal sin of being loved by the high and mighty Donnybrooks?

"Not on your life, my dear, dear little blue eyes!"

Corey's teachers, his house and gang brothers all liked him. They had never forgiven him, for he'd never wronged them. He was their friend and they were his.

But his Grandpapa and Grandmamma were a terribly different matter:

Old Grandpa Joe's and Grandmamma Mad Carlotta had decreed that their loose filly's failed sociological experiment bad boy must suffer Christmas in exile.

Corey was due a harder lesson for embarrassing the highland chief at his highly entitled business connections' holy of holies, the bath and tennis club.

To impress the urgency of letting a sleeping Dinker lie on Corey he was not allowed home for the Yule.

His ever so sanctimonious grandparents' ukase was that he should not only be dispatched to distant and hurtful exile but he must spend Christmas at their cold, hard finest military academy in the world.

As if that snub hadn't been enough, it wasn't the only blow he had to countenance:

Leto and Daddy, both his high ranking Donnybrook sponsors were also leaving for the Yuletide. The Donnybrooks had hit the road for some out of state high jinks with their family in the north. The loving hearts who'd given their Mac the warmth and support that had sustained him in this icy desert had left.

Most of the cadets, even some of those pathetic souls eternally damned to Heeler Hell, were asked back into the holiday warmth of their far flung homes to celebrate the winter holiday. Those lucky ones had followed the major's lead to leave The Tower's lacerations, contusions, concussions and heartbreaks to go home and open their gaily beribboned gifts beneath the shimmering bough.

To make the situation of the lonely boys left behind completely untenable, the junior school's kitchen was shut for the holiday season.

Ergo, our scant minority of deserted schoolboys left to endure a forlorn Christmas had to climb sorrowfully up that steep old hill and eat at the senior school's mess.

Sadly, our Christmas-displaced-persons' normally tasty fare consumed in their lavish dining hall had spoiled the boys and they were terribly sad to be deprived of it.

Alas, cold scrambled eggs, cold oatmeal and limp bacon served at the senior school's cheerless breakfasts were not the worst of the boys' hilltop calamity. No, for dinner and supper our refugees had to force themselves to choke down cold salmon cakes every day:

Salmon cakes, salmon cakes everywhere, the boys did moan and bleat.

Salmon cakes, salmon cakes everywhere, but not one fit to eat.

In a word, the senior school mess was nothing short of criminal.

As if this cornucopia of anti-blessings hadn't been enough to break the schoolboys, THE SILVER SREAK could be relied upon to fill Bite's shower theatre of ballet with her pink little holiday leftovers' urgent Christmas carols. The darling Miss Bite had her holiday fun while they permeated the festive air with their outcries to liven her celebration of darkness.

Corey's cheerless holiday hell dragged on and on and on -- until his glorious day of liberation:

Our little boy had never been so grateful for anything he was in his moment of wild elation the day he and his ragtag crew of castaways were providentially permitted to reenter the junior school's drafty dining hall. And his joy built and increased exponentially when he saw the heartwarming smiles of welcome beaming out of his Leto's and her Daddy's adoring eyes when his beloved patrons welcomed their Mac back into their family.

But their loving Mac had failed to remark the resentful, unforgiving scowls which distorted the ghostly features of those three Donnybrooks languishing in the shadow of his benefactors' godlike brilliance. What time had he to note the envy of the twisted wraiths.

Why worry about what he hadn't noticed?

Too soon he would learn the answer to that query, but now he was content to ignore the unseen peril of those three carrion jackals that were intent upon his love goddess's shameful downfall, and his.

Leto's Mac had no time for the bitter Donnybrooks when he was enjoying the blessings of the sweet:

No more cold oatmeal and no more hard, dried out salmon cakes, only the comfort of the heavenly bliss in the loving eyes of his beautiful goddess.

A blessed anodyne was his sojourn with Leto; and the speedy return to what passes for normalcy at a military school.

The boys invited home for Christmas were all recaptured, rounded up and returned to Heeler Hell screaming and kicking. Thereunto, more victims to absorb some of their loving housemother's kind attentions had taken some of the heat off of our poor little castaways.

Classes and drills kept our cadet schoolboy busy, and meals with Leto gladdened Mac's heart:

Hurray!

Then Cadet Brecken's birthday came along in early January:

Arroo!

The elder Breckens were still disposed to rub salt into their unhappy grandson's wounds, and they had elected to stay ON Palm Beach for his commemoration.

The cold folks had dispatched their glum surrogates, the Burners, to give their towhead his annual feast.

But a faint silver lining presented itself, for Corey's present was picked out, purchased, wrapped and dispatched with her couriers direct from grandmamma:

It was a set of Fabrique Francais lead soldiers. And they were a toy his Gra' ma knew to be her "Bill's" favorite.

The Burners had materialized on the early afternoon of our bad boy's birthday. They took him to town and showed him a fine night out:

Their party dined at the best restaurant in Honeysuckle. Corey blew out his candles and they had ice cream and cake. And then they took in a movie.

It was an early Marylyn Monroe effort and, though it might seem tame today when compared to the same sizzling luminary's later and more revealing spectaculars of the same genre, this Technicolor wide screen vehicle's thrust toward lust was assuredly implicit -- and just as explicit as the 1949 traffic would allow.

Then grandpa's surrogates dropped our boy off and headed south with great dispatch, leaving Boss Joe's little problem child to the tender mercies of the scurvy deviant in residence there.

To Corey's relief it was late enough for all the denizens of Heeler Hell to be fast asleep, including The Horror. He'd been spared his sizzling shower room welcome.

But our poor little ten year old 's dreams post such an eventful night out had driven him several degrees past wild:

His terrible embarrassment, the one pretty little Leto 'd so enthusiastically admired when they'd met now reawakened to ensure that the meaty gist of the film would drive him mad.

He was eaten alive by thousands of questions which had perplexed his preteen mind:

"Why do I feel such an earthshaking need for something when I don't know WHAT it is?" he wondered, "Maybe it's a strange disease -- or maybe it's some kind o' need that's got 'o be fulfilled?"

He tossed on the stormy seas of his fitful nightmare dreaming. Frenzied questions of how and why had lashed him through this horrendous night.

The next day he could no longer abide the pang of those unanswered questions, for now he must find answers. He must be released from his torments, or be driven mad. He'd reached his sexual breaking point. Now -- and not one nanosecond later -- he must perforce learn the answers. If he didn't, both his mind and body would explode.

At breakfast he asked his best friend in all the world to help him unravel puzzling and painful rebus, "Leto's smart, she'll know jus' what t' do!"

Leto was far more experienced in the worldly contrivances of the grownup estate than he. She could certainly explain the origins of these horrible dreams which had nightly evoked their relentless attacks against his growing mind and body. And all this was happening at the same time cruel Fate was forcing him to countenance the savage Miss Bite and her dark inferno.

"Leto, I, I just had m' tenth birthday yesterday; an' my granddad's stooges came up t' take me out:

"Well, we, we went t' this kind o' grownup movie, 'n,' 'n' I, I got HARD.

"Girlfriend, what's WRONG with me?"

"Well, happy birthday, Mac! You're a whole year older now, my cute li' l' lover boy," beamed his sweetheart, treating him to a full blast of the love-fire from her magnificent eyes.

She'd passed his dilemma off with a merry smile. But she continued her intelligence with misty-eyed sympathy, "I think it's time big sister Leto gave little Mac th' very BEST birthday present a ten year old boy ever got:

"I love you, my darling, so I'm gonna teach you what life's all about. I, I'm happy t' help YOU with your problem -- 'cause you're gonna help ME with mine!" she giggled, "Now, you just listen to ME, Corey-boy, 'cause I'm about t' tell you th' most IMPORTANT thing I have EVER told you in all our lives:

"IF you do exactly what I tell you to do we'll both live happily ever after; but, if you DON'T do just exactly that, we're both DEAD!

"You 'n' me 're gonna meet 'n' play this Saturday; BUT it's got 'o be our secret.

"NEVER tell anybody that we meet or what we do outside th' dining hall because no one in this whole entire world can ever know anything about us:

"Understand?"

"Yes, Leto," she'd become was so very that grave he could see this was a time to be serious.

"NOBODY can ever know WHAT we do, or WHERE we do it!" she whispered breathlessly, "No kidding, IF anybody ever finds out 'n' tells on us, Daddy 'll KILL us both!"

Her hypnotic eyes flashed imperiously as she breathed, "I know you love me, Mac, and, if you swear on our eternal love you'll never blab about this to a living soul, I know you won't. Swear to me you'll never tell what we do 'n' where we go and I, I'll know it's th' truth.

"Only then will we be safe from my stuffy ol' Deepfreeze mom 'n' her spyin' cradle-creeps, my Mac!"

Corey took Leto's hand in his under the table and, ever so secretly, ever so gently, he swore, "I swear that I'll never tell where we go, what we do or that we ever even met anywhere but th' dining hall, and I swear it on our eternal love."

Now she could relax and dish, "Now, Corporal Brecken, you're gonna have t' keep your demerit count down real, REAL low from here on out.

"It's gettin' chilly nowadays 'n' I do not propose t' wait around all day for you stand off a hundred years worth o' demerits while I catch pneumonia!"

"YES, MA'AM!!!" he snapped to.

"How many y' got so far this week, boyfriend?"

"Five, girlfriend."

"Great, that's less 'n half an hour," she laughed, "Now you just make sure y' don't get any more, li'l' soldier!"

"NO, MA'AM!!!"

"Get this, blue eyes," she pinched him playfully, "Know th' parade field where you show off for me Sundays, 'n' I laugh while y' goof up 'n' leave your shoes all over th' field?"

"Sure, golden girl!" he smirked.

"Okay, listen carefully:

"To your left as you face th' reviewing stand from th' field, there's a little gate. It leads to a woodlot between th' academy 'n' town, 'n' beyond that gate there's a break in th' woods. Go through th' gate, through th' break in th' trees and into th' woods.

"When you're in th' woods, you're gonna follow a little pathway which leads to a clearing in th' woods. It's a shortcut to town that none o' th' goobers 'cept you know about. And, oh, my own wonderful, special Mac, when you come to me there, I'll have my super-special birthday present waiting only for you!"

The golden brats had never been quite so happy as they were now at this top secret breakfast of shared conspiracy.

"What's that dumb name that that mean ol' monstrosity calls y' with when she's cussin' y' out 'n' whippin' y',' my poor, poor li'l' lover boy?" our sly little Leto ribbed him.

He shuffled his feet and blushed to have to admit, "Blondie?"

"That's it!" she bubbled, "Well, Blondie, do y' want 'o meet Cookie on your way t' town this Saturday and collect her special birthday present for you?"

"Only if you're Cookie!"

"What?" she gibed, "I'm not sweet enough t' be Cookie?"

"You, you're sweeter than th' sweetest great big hot fudge sundae ever, my beautiful, beautiful Leto!" gushed her ardent gallant.

He spoke in a childhood code they both picked up. Being children, they understood the simile and knew it meant the rapturous enjoyment of a royally scrumptious feast.

Corey's innocence was the prize his more experienced Leto was destined to take away this Saturday. His pretty little teacher wanted his love just as urgently as he had longed for hers.

Cadet Brecken was about to learn love's sweetest lesson from Daddy's little darling. When the secret lovers met on their very own Saturday, Mac was to leave the magic of their trysting glade a wiser youth, and one that was walking on air.

"Yeah, SATURDAY!!!" piped his little princess, high of heart and titillated by the overwhelming thrill of her anticipation of their love's sweet fulfillment.

Today was a brand new day for Mistress Leto Donnybrook, for the horrendous memory of the shame and pain she'd felt that night her maidenhead had been brutally raped by a heartless predator last year no longer haunted our brave girl. No, not that worst of all memories, nor anything else could turn her away from her pathway to her happiness with a gentle lover of her own choosing. Not one more day would she waste in the dead past.

The pain she'd suffered then was a long dead memory on this happy day of a bold new life for her and her love.

Leto'd recovered her trials a fine, healthy little woman. Her robust and nubile young body had long since cast off the pain of her unhappy past. Today an adventurous little girl had come alive with a vibrant young woman's torrid desire. Enveloped in the warm glow of her perfect love for her Mac, she felt safe and confident that the selfless gentleness she'd read in her favorite's adoring eyes was to be her salvation from her ever more urgently growing fever.

With Mac's advent she'd been blessed with the strength and audacity to enter into the sweltering jungle of an adult woman's passion.

Today's loving schoolboy was no brutal and aggressive predator, but a devoted suitor who devoutly worshipped at her feet. And she'd seen and felt firsthand the hard evidence of his ability to satisfy a woman. With Mac she'd found the fortitude to venture fearlessly into the Great Adventure that only they must share.

Together, Mac and Leto were to watch their love blossom, bloom and flower beneath the summer sun of their resilient youth. What a miraculous flower that love must have been to take root and spring to life beneath the frozen snows of The Tower Military Academy's nuclear winter. Had this not always been the grim Fortress of Duress where little children such as they were scrupulously monitored, held strictly to account and painfully punished for the smallest of infractions?

It had.

Nonetheless, Love Goddess Leto Donnybrook wasn't about to let a little thing like The Tower scare her off her goal. Particularly when her goal was to give her most intimate present in all the world to her very most favorite cadet in all the world.

Precocious rather than wise, Mac's breathtaking child heroine was on the cusp of the realization of love's young dream -- and breaking one of society's most terribly forbidden taboos.

But Mac's breathtaking heroine regarded this titillating outlaw adventure as her due:

Waiting around forever to grow up was not for the exalted Mistress Leto Donnybrook when she knew what she wanted and precisely what to do to get it, and what she wanted was Cadet Corey "Mac" Brecken, and get out of her way.

"Oh, It's going to be just WONDERFUL!" was her fondly expectant sigh.

Lovely Leto just knew their love had to be more beautiful, more rewarding, more perfect right here, right now and with her perfect little cadet, than it could ever be again through all the vastness of infinite eternity. Our lovely knew it because she'd dreamed it a thousand, thousand times -- and so had her Mac.

They'd both said so over and over at every meal.

"Remember, Mac, tell no one, trust no one!" she'd warned, with grave urgency.

"I trust only you, my beautiful, beautiful Leto!" he'd panted.

Leto knew his heart was hers alone, and knowing that she felt warm and safe.

"Okay, junior, we're gonna meet," she said, "But it's really important that no one EVER knows a single thing about it!

"Get this:

"WE'RE Daddy's favorites, everyone knows it but, jus' because we are, mom and her rug-rats 're watchin' 'n' waitin' for us t' slip up. That ol' iceberg 'd just love t' get th' goods on us 'n' CATCH us in 'etr trap

"And, oh, my sweet, sweet lover boy, if she ever DOES, she can and will bring us DOWN!

"And, oh, my darling, from where we're sittin' right now, down is a long, long, long, hard fall!

"We, we can NEVER let THAT happen to US, my own soldier boy 'cause I don't even want 'o even THINK about what Daddy 'd do t' us to PUNISH us for all th' fun we're gonna be havin' on our own Saturdays!

"I trust YOU 'cause we're in love with each other; AND because you have almost as much to lose in this as I do.

"I love you, my own true-blue Mac, 'n' I'm NOT gonna chicken out," she whispered passionately, "I'll be in that clearing waiting for you Saturday, my own true Blondie!

"Come where I told y' to come, 'n' when you get there your Li' l' Schoolmarm Leto's gonna feed her Schoolboy Mac th' SWEETEST cookie he's ever had in all his life ... Oh, Mac, I'm gonna teach you so much, much more 'n you could EVER learn in all th' books 'n' in all th' classrooms in this great big whole wide world!"

"I can't wait, my goddess!" he panted expectantly. And they played "footsies" furiously (furtively, of course) under the table, just as his inspiring underage heartthrob had taught him.

Our taboo lovers were circumspect and scrupulously careful never to let their elders (and certainly not those ornery little cradle-creeps) detect the faintest hint of their semi-carefree mealtime kiddy-play. The youngest of all Donnybrook conspirators were eternally on the prowl to divine the meaning of the golden brats' covert whispers and muffled giggles. But so far luck had been with our two too young lovers. The Deepfreeze's irritating gnats had been unable to scrape together enough hard evidence to make even a halfway believable report of wrongdoing to the vengeance-hungry old misanthrope.

Our golden brats waited breathlessly for their Saturday to dawn. If you have never believed anything else in your life, believe this:

For Mac and Leto the days, hours and minutes of tedium separating them from Saturday dragged on and on and on until the bright sun of their Golden Day dawned at last.

On that beautiful day of days Corey ran eagerly to the great hall for breakfast with his blossoming beauty. Albeit he must be very, very careful in the presence of their fearsome elders and The Deepfreeze's dangerous mini finks.

Anxious and expectant, our lovers breakfasted together.

Mac and Leto did glance furtively at one another, but what was the matter with that?

It was usual that their senses soared when they'd been together; and mom's spies had no way to discover that our golden lovers had actually contrived a to plan to realize and attain their ecstasy.

Nevertheless, our heroes conversation gave no hint of what the staid grownups would surely have termed improper, sinful and salacious misbehavior had they but known. If the terrible Deepfreeze or her watching cradle-Argus had sniffed out the scent of sex in the offing, the lovers were lost.

But their airtight security had won the day, for now.

Directly after that tense breakfast, Cadet Brecken ran as fast as his feet would carry him to report to the study hall officer in charge.

Our boy bravely stood off his demerits like a good little robot. This was young Corey's big day, but standing off those pesky five demerits had proven the most exquisite torture The Tower had ever thrown at him:

The dire humiliations of the major's strop and The Beast's SILVER STREAK were dwarfed in comparison with the unbearable stress of this endless waiting. Though it was early January, copious, beads of sweat bedewed our hero's brow as those everlastingly tantalizing seconds tick, tick, ticked slowly by.

But, his eternal Tantalus ended at last when he saluted the duty officer and requested permission to be excused.

The officer returned this antsy little goober's stiff salute to bark, "Dismissed, corporal."

Leto's favorite hot dog shot out of that study hall like a bolt of lightning. Corey was bound for the break in the hedge that led to Leto's mysterious birthday present in her promised garden of earthly delights. Nothing might deter him as he dashed headlong onto the parade field, and into paradise.

He found himself on the woodland path. With some initial trepidation in venturing into the unknown (there are rattlers and water moccasins in Tennessee) he advanced down an unclear, overgrown path.

The foliage got deeper and deeper as he peered cautiously through what was rapidly becoming a much denser forest in the far-flung woodlot between their elite academy and the rustic outside world of Honeysuckle.

The stillness of the woods gave no hint that another living soul dwelt on earth.

Corey pressed on but he'd begun to worry that hip chick Leto might be playing a joke on her credulous beau.

"No!" he braced himself resolutely, "She said she'd be here, and she will."

He quickly dismissed doubt from his already roiling, feverishly agitated mind.

He must concentrate on the matter at hand. And he must be mindful that his girl has to be secretive and circumspect in approaching their forbidden tryst. Her high position in The Tower's spit-and-polish pecking order demanded it. She was the queen of the castle here and, though good luck had advanced her Mac to the rank of corporal by the grace of Daddy, Leto and God, he was still a dirty vassal in the school's elitist hierarchy.

The density and darkness of the deep woods had begun to clear and brighten.

Suddenly little Mac entered into The Promised Glade:

And its ambiance was revealed as celestial in its own right. The sunlight filtered through the foliage from the blue dome of the open sky illuminating the deep green conifers and the kaleidoscopic flame of the deciduous trees.

Birdsong lilted melodiously on the breeze serenading the ears of this gloriously natural tableau's entranced beholder.

And now this place of wonder and magic had been metamorphosed into a paradise beyond paradise:

Their own enchanted glen had been made beautiful beyond belief by his goddess's most desired and desirable presence. Leto stood before him, silent and bathed in their multicolored woodland panorama. Her magical presence at once had dimmed all the other the beauties of Mother Nature's organic treasures on display.

The girl he had so long loved, the beauty he'd so ravenously desired, had kept her word and waited for him.

His pretty May Queen, irresistible in a charming red and white checked cotton frock, bright red ribbons binding her loosely braided auburn curls, opened her arms in generous welcome to her ardent lover.

He'd admired the flamboyant leaves' kaleidoscopic hues before he'd looked into his glowing Leto's moved and moving eyes. But all his attention from now on was hers, for, in the field of kaleidoscopic wonderment, his girl had bested Ma Nature.

"Hi!" smiled she, breathlessly expectant.

"Hi!!!" gasped he, completely overcome.

Her boy dashed madly into his girl's welcoming arms.

As they came together, the powerful electricity of two searching, restless young animals drew them ever closer.

In this heavenly ambrosia moment they'd realized at once they were meant to be together for ever and ever.

No power in this universe had the force to part them on this, their very own day. Not mom's miniscule spies who'd hounded them relentlessly; not his inamorata's wicked and envious mother, the unloved and unloving woman who still pined to topple and punish them for their love; and not even Daddy's thrashing strop and Zeus's lightning flashing bolts together might have sundered their loving embraces on their day of days.

Their time to love was now!

They knew their love must be holy, for it burned within them with the power of a thousand, thousand, thousand suns.

There was a decided nip in the crisp air of this early January afternoon. But, as our precocious lovers melted fervently into love's first volcanic embrace, their radiant energies had combined to create a hot, hot Fourth Of July In January's Winter Fireworks. The summer-heat of their all consuming love had transmogrified the nip of January into the resplendent tropic scene of their mad passion's sweltering abandon.

Corey's fever burned Helios-bright as he dashed impetuously into his beautiful May Queen's arms.

Yes, our beautiful children both knew, and had known far too well, what they were doing was anathema in the eyes of their world's severely judgmental and outrageously punishing elders. They'd long realized that meeting in secret without discussing all of the pros and cons of the serious business of the marriage compact was explicitly taboo. The tribal elders should have insisted that these crazy kids meet with them while everyone concerned counted up each and every bean in both their family fortunes before anything quite so frivolous as love might have been proper.

This bold adventure, this taboo deeper, darker and direr than all of society's other taboos put together, was far more dangerous for them than anything they had ever done in their pretty, thoughtless little lives. Leto'd warned Corey that they risked everything they had or would ever have to be together.

So they had.

But our beautiful children must have their own true love NOW!

The impossibility of their obsessed situation and the awe-inspiring knowledge of what total devastation their capture could bring and the dreaded inevitability of their elders' unconscionably heavy punishments did not deter them. Rather it impelled our panting young lovers into the inescapable vortex of their mad love.

The stark realization of these terrifying possibilities coupled with the release of their unchained emotions had combined to make their forbidden tryst a totally inescapable explosion of raw passion.

There was no looking back now for her Mac and his Leto:

Their inescapable longing burned ever hotter, ever brighter with their insane intensity of purpose in the knowledge that they were making love beneath the dour shadow of the grim Tower, and in the awful proximity of its pitiless torturers.

The dizzying paroxysm of their outlawed congress now overwhelmed our lovers as all of their practical worldly considerations burst into flame and vanished into smoke in the inevitable conflagration of their own beautiful congress. Their first flaming embrace had commanded them into the arms of The Great Unknown, and that was and is a call which can be answered only by the brave.

Lost to reason, consumed in the all consuming heat of their inescapable passion, our beautiful children had flown celeritously into the eye of love's hurricane and been blown away to frolic in their indescribably sweet love nectar in Elysium's bright fields.

Sadly, theirs was a passion destined to deliver them into the coils of Aphrodite's golden net.

Mac and Leto had been called into the magic garden of earthly beauties by Nature's inescapable love song and bound to revel in the euphoria of their very own sweet summer wine. Too long had their young lives been darkened, overshadowed, watched and scolded lives. Young children too often cursed and beaten, our heroes have now entered into the realm of ecstasy.

Our summer lovers met in winter had melded together, tempest-tossed on this most unforgettable, terribly frightening, overpowering moment of abandoned amour.

Our golden kids had embraced the stormy ocean of their wild obsession's sweet summer honey. Our more-or-less innocent girl and boy had found themselves inundated in the pure joy of their unconquerable love as they met in a soul-searching union:

Now he is hers.

Now she is his.

Our beautiful children cast off the fetters of convention and adventured into the forbidden realm of license. They'd knowingly risked all and known that a love that knew no constraints was a prize worth any price. They'd breached the cold, grey walls of propriety, and, for her Mac and his Leto there had never been a past.

And, sadly for the lovers, there could never be a future.

No, our beautiful children must grab for their amour's shining star NOW.

Our golden kids must catch and hold on to the brass ring of their world of ineffable enchantment NOW.

They must have this most precious and beautiful living dream, sweeter, more irresistible, more powerful than any dream our beat-up, lonely little boy and his brutally abused little girl had ever been permitted to dream in their now suddenly detached and distant workaday desert-world of whippings, curses and insults. Here in their magic glen of erotic enchantment, that other world of cold, hard facts and figures had darted by and was now light years away from them.

Here and now paradise was theirs. Beneath the celestial arc of heaven and in the comforting cradle of Nature, Mac and Leto had rushed madly together and taken the brimming cup of pleasure they knew had been forbidden them in the dark world of The Tower, now galaxies removed from them.

Never in the caged confinement of a repressive society and decidedly never within the forbidding confines of the finest military academy in all the world would this sort of thing have been permitted, so they had taken it.

No, any joy this boy and this girl will ever be allowed they must take NOW.

Love was forbidden them, yet these two beautiful children had reached out for each other and captured love NOW!

"Oh, my cute li' l' lover-boy! ... You, you're a quick little bunny-rabbit!" his dream girl giggled, lovingly, restlessly, knowingly and gasping for air as she signaled for quarter, "Here I am, busy teaching you about all three bases, 'n' you're gettin' ready t' slide into home, y' li' l' rookie of th' year rascal!"

"Who's on first?" quipped her ardent swain.

"Can th' Abbot 'n' Costello corn, junior!" she bridled, "Love can be FUN all right, but love's not ONE bit funny, sonny:

"Love's dead serious, and don't you EVER forget it!"

"Whatever you say, Leto," gasped he, eager both to please and continue.

His embarrassment had quickly arisen to haunt him, and a disturbed and confused little boy quickly assured a more lucid little girl, "I, I promise I'll get a doctor 'n' get it cured-"

But his experienced girlfriend just giggled knowingly:

"All YOU need is li' l' ol' Nurse Leto, y' cute li' 'l soldier-boy. Nurse Leto's gonna cure that bad ol' 'disease' o' yours for y' right here 'n' now.

"And, oh. my darling boy, you are gonna LOVE th' cure!"

Foxy Leto had known more about grownup relationships than virgin Corey might ever have guessed in a million years of troubled postulation. And his girl love teacher enjoyed the warm glow that came with the knowledge that she was about to school her loving boy in the secret passage of life's most beautiful journey on their special day, and in this very glen.

Dizzy, light-headed with excitement, fighting for air, Mac could not tear his fixated gaze from the beautiful girl he'd loved from the very first moment they'd met, she who stood before him in her beauty and his every dream made flesh. Her body called him into her and her glowing eyes burned with the bright fires of passion as they were lifted high above this sad world of dark tragedy and into their bright world of daylight dreaming. The golden brats now soared high above this warring world, this lying, cheating sphere of conflicts and betrayals as the imperative of nature spurred our lovers into paradise, over the stormy seas of need and emotion and into the very core of earth's purest delight.

Corey's heart was exploding with his unbridled joy.

"Bring me to life!!!!" whispered she.

She was ready for him and patiently, gently showed him what to do.

Their love erupted into a raging bond fire and together the lovers burst spontaneously into an eruption of unquenchable fulfillment and wonder. Together they were transmogrified into the seismic crescendo of a resonating earthquake of raw passion.

His love goddess had been quick to instruct her pupil in the use of his wonderful and beautiful birthday present.

Her life lesson had stoked their ardor higher and higher until Corey's mind exploded into the ether.

"OH, my LOVE, it, it's so, so RIGHT!!!" cried Leto from the unfathomable depths of her pure delight.

Our beautiful children had streaked through the cosmos like a meteor of unleashed passion.

Our enchanted young initiate had found himself climbing skyward into an all-compelling whirlwind of wonderment as he traveled ever deeper into the jungles of life's most commanding mystery.

Our ecstatic taboo children were lost in a transport of the most ineffable rapture imaginable as they dared enter into and rocket through their giddy inner world of mystic enchantment. The beautiful lovers had dared to adventure into the steaming, uncharted regions of Destiny. They had dared to race into and attain this joy beyond ecstasy that they knew must be theirs.

These were wonders the boy had never even conceptualized before this day, and these wonders were nothing short of miraculous. And he was correct, for love is truly a miracle. The ecstatic union our fledgling fliers treasured on their first Saturday tryst had been a golden treasure they should never forget. Our taboo lovers' bliss was an atman beyond nirvana.

Our ardent boy had accepted the sweetest reward his lady love could ever have offered as they'd spiraled higher and deeper, caught in the powerful updraft of their forbidden and all-consuming passion. Our little lovers had climbed relentlessly on, wondering at their own stamina, in search of love's ultimate promise.

Our enraptured children had discovered the answer to life's convoluted rebus as their combined energies exploded into a life-altering detonation of overwhelming energy.

That chimera, illusive and hidden from the knowledge of all earthly creatures in existence present, past and future was now theirs.

Leto's was a wondrous gift, inescapable, unbound and without constraint. Her present had given Mac insuperable energy in the majesty of its raw power.

Both golden brats had reaped the rewards of unparalleled extremity, the ultimate earthly delight.

Suddenly, serendipitously, miraculously the young lovers' united bliss metamorphosed into their ultimate dream, their dearest attainment, the ultimate extrapolation, the culmination of each and every treasure this world has to offer was magically and immediately theirs.

Like a lightning bolt from the heavens the ultimate crescendo of love's inescapable power had catapulted our taboo tots into an atomic blast which had blown them away:

The event had melded and transposed the two mortals, Leto and Mac, into a divine celestial constellation. The golden brats had written their bliss across the sky in a meteor shower of transcendent release.

The ultimate beatitude of this physical world was theirs. The ultimate explosion of every energy that one ebullient soul can give to and take from another had encircled and elevated them above everyone and everything else on earth.

It was overpowering, it was beautiful and it was theirs.

Corey and Leto had joined and shared in the epitome of adoration and the most intimate offering Nature can provide:

Every dream they had dreamed was theirs. Every goal they'd ever worked to achieve and every treasure they'd ever coveted was theirs in this ineffable moment.

This was their day of perfect entwinement and rapturous connection. Two loving souls have known the rarest of all delights.

Their love was theirs alone and no dark power could ever hope to steal it from them on this magic day.

Nurse Leto had sought out, found and healed her perfect mate. Her gentle schoolboy had erased all her fearful memories of that heartless scoundrel's criminal act of assault once forced upon her yielding flesh. Her loving Mac had expurgated the violence and pain of that rape from her mind. The care, adoration and pleasure her lover has showered on her on their special day made her heart sing again.

Corey had at long last learned the whys and wherefores of his torment. And, as his pretty nurse Leto had promised, he'd just loved the cure. He'd learned the blissful art of loving from his own very gentle and attentive schoolteacher, and he was bursting with ecstasy:

Corey the exile, Corey the outcast, Corey The Beast's accursed, abused throw-away chew-toy and despised doll-baby, Corey, Grandpapa 's naughty little embarrassment fit only for exile to a far country was a thing of the past:

Cadet Brecken had this blessed day at last been able to cast off all those mistreated and forgotten waifs he had formerly been because he'd been promoted to Mac, Leto's lover boy!

Our beat-up little hero had never in his life felt so accepted, so loved and welcomed by anyone as he'd been in the arms of his adored and adoring May Queen. No, never in his overlooked, kicked-out, beat-up, SILVER STREAKED, razor stropped life had he felt so comfortably, so intimately, at home. Never had Cadet Brecken felt so secure.

But what of Mistress Leto Donnybrook, Mac's Divine Schoolmarm?

Our charming Miss Donnybrook had never known such a transcendent transport of elation in all her young life. Our Little Princess Of The Tower was never so happy as she'd been in her Corey's loving arms in this day of their wonder-woven tryst.

On this day of perfect delight she'd liberated herself and dared to taste the intoxicating nectar of womanly fulfillment. She'd sampled the sweet summer wine of love's celebration of life. She'd given herself completely to her schoolboy, and she'd been glad of it.

Our radiant Queen Leto, the austere old Tower's reigning beauty, was ever so pleased with herself as she'd been this sunny day. She was greatly satisfied that she'd chosen wisely in favoring her hardy little Mac over the other boys in the academy's diverse assortment of junior cadets available for a beautiful May Queen's perusal and selection. Mac was hers now and she was his, and it was all just so wonderful!

Our love-struck toys lay, gratefully enraptured and rewarded for a rest.

Our golden kids lay locked in fond embrace for a long moment.

(Their moment would have lasted a lot longer had January not been so nippy.)

But, too soon to suit them, even two enraptured lovers, lost in the concordance of their own private heaven, had realized the only warmth in this heaven was glowing deep inside their fast cooling hot little bodies. Outside, and they were outside, they were freezing.

When that shockingly uncomfortable eureka moment had struck, they rose from their reverie to don warm clothes -- and to do so as precipitously as possible. But they stayed yet a while in this verdant spot to hug and kiss.

"It's killin' me t' have t' leave you, my beautiful Leto," lamented her Lothario Junior.

His lover girl smiled and blushed at the compliment, but, more practical than sentimental, she advised, "It's all part o' th' game, lover-boy.

"Y' don't want your best girl t' catch cold, do y'?"

"Never!"

They lingered in the holy temple of their young love's mad fruition for a time, clothed in the hypnotically intoxicating study of one another's beloved features.

But finally she recalled:

"We both got things t' do," piped his busy little queen bee, after consulting her watch and suddenly remembering an already missed and perhaps hard to explain piano lesson, "Come on, cadet cutie, eat some o' th' picnic basket I packed before it's completely ruined:

"This chicken's GOTTA be ice cold by now, but th' baked beans 're in a crock pot, so they're still nice 'n' warm, 'n' this fruit Jello 's okay 'cause it's supposed t' be cold."

"This is great!" enthused her ardent swain, digging in and wolfing down chicken and beans alike with the appetite of a starving scavenger,

"You just took me all th' way t' heaven, 'n' NOW I find out you're a GREAT cook too?"

She smiled down on him so lovingly:

"So this is that poor little mutt th' grand 'n' glorious major felt so sorry for 'cause he wouldn't eat?

"THIS is th' stubborn li' l' dope Daddy was scared was gonna STARVE himself to death?

"Well, you're sure doin' okay for yourself TODAY, little soldier!"

"Good?" he corrected, "I'm doin' GREAT!!!

"Oh, my beautiful Leto, you, you've brought me to life. And not just once but more than once!" her grateful lover boy laughed, "And I thought I was sick!"

"Sick like a fox, you rascal!" lilted she merrily, "Well, you're all cured now, m' lovin' boyfriend!"

Our lovers ate and laughed about his mysterious malady and her miraculous cure.

Our becalmed and sated children then embraced and stood smiling dreamily into one another's love-glazed eyes as they dreamt of their perfect forevermore.

The cruel trials of their harrowed pasts had faded facilely away in the shifting mists of this bright new dawn in their lives as our love-struck kids reveled, deliciously consoled, in the arms of Aphrodite. They'd been truly recompensed in the golden present of this holy and priceless Saturday.

"Now, you remember, Mac," she cautioned him as they kissed goodbye, "This is the most beautiful thing we've ever done in our whole lives, 'n' WE did it together, blue eyes, jus' YOU 'n' ME!

"But NEVER forget that it is also the most DANGEROUS thing we could ever have done!

"You're a boy, so you'll want 'o brag about this. But don't you ever DARE! You can NEVER tell ANYONE what we did, or where we did it, OR when -- never!

"This is no joke, dear boy, 'case I'LL -- WE'LL -- lose everything we have, had or could ever hope to have if this EVER leaks:

"Mean ol' mom 'n' her jealous little cradle-creeps will WIN 'n' We'll LOSE, 'n' I mean we lose everything, my Mac, EVERYTHING!!!

"We can't afford to lose, y' hear me?

"Oh, Mac, they'll tell on us t' DADDY, an' when he gets mad he might, might jus' kill us both!

"I, I'm tellin' you, Mac, we, we can't ever get HIM mad!"

"I swear no one will ever know our secret but you 'n' me, Leto!" he promised faithfully, "And, as for Daddy, he gave me the beating of my life when he WASN'T mad at me and I don't ever want 'o see him when he is!"

He was hers.

She could count on his bond of silence, and she'd drawn great comfort from that.

Our thrice blessed lovers departed their sacred glen with melancholy regret, but greatly solaced and spectacularly fulfilled.

Nothing was ever going to be as it had been before our golden lovers' sun-drenched maiden tryst.

Nor did our half-pint hero wish it so. No, our boy wanted everything to be different, for, if it could be so, there should be many, many more sequestered sunlit Saturday love trysts. He'd eagerly welcomed this colossal change, embraced it and made it his sustenance.

On that first Saturday Corey easily found and followed the path out of the woods, onto the highway and thence to town. Our happy Leto's hero loped as easily over the two hills separating the academy from Honeysuckle as if they weren't there.

The informally assembled schoolboys bought and devoured huge quantities of Moon Pies, Sugar Daddies and Mary Jane confections at the village's screen door grocery store.

They then adjourned to one of the two local motion picture theatres to watch and enjoy the shoot-'em-up exploits of Gene Autry and Roy Rogers (or, in Cadet Claire's unique case, Whip Wilson and The Durango Kid, for both his heroes were accomplished in both the six-gun AND the bullwhip).

With the kid-oriented films of the era came the attendant animated cartoons. And the Nyoka, The Jungle Girl, Jungle Jim, Batman, Superman or Rocket Man serial adventures. In these cliff-hangers the heroine was eternally tied to the railroad tracks with a locomotive bearing down on her, or she was hanging precariously from a cliff, or at the point of being beheaded by one menacing African witch doctor or another. But the next week she was always swept away to safety in the powerful arms of the stalwart hero of the piece.

Saturday matinees provided a needful breath of the fresh air of home for our lonely little cadets. Kicked out of their families, locked up and cruelly used by uncaring strangers, our cadets' kiddy matinees were a blessed release.

Such escapes were uniform throughout the United States in The Forties. All across the country grownups had been desperate to get the brats out of the house for a few hours of weekend privacy (and a rare glimpse of what peace of mind used to look like before the kids had come along). Yes, the Saturday cowboy matinees had made America's harried parents a whole lot happier, and her theatre owners a lot richer from sea to shining sea in that bygone era.

But, for Corey/Mac," Leto's newly precocious, lovingly schooled lover boy, the thrill of playing in the Confederate general's square, tasting the sweetness of Moon Pies and Sugar Babies (even the rootin' tootin' shoot-'em-up double features) had only made him realize that nothing might aspire to compare to the indescribable delights of Leto's love tryst.

Honeysuckle' wonders were not nearly so scintillating as they'd been before he'd tasted the ineffable sweetness of a real live princess's passion.

The chilling realization that one breath of their taboo breaking delights must assuredly bring down a killing firestorm of retribution from the terrifying Brass. The knowledge that, should The Sword of Damocles ever fall, it would separate the pining lovers for life, cast a black pall of ill omen over him.

Corey had to bear the dreadful weight of this silence alone. Never must he speak of their glorious trysts. The intoxicating wonderment which had momentarily lit up his poor little life must never be revealed.

Still, he must bear this burden of silence for his beauty's sake. Leto, and only Leto, had eclipsed all of the other joys in his life, so her protection was paramount.

His dreams were still a boy's dreams, only now life's mysteries before this glorious initiation were mysteries no more. The nightmares which had formerly tormented him were now but a series of Technicolor nocturnal delights staring Leading Lady Leto and her Superhero Mac.

Life at the academy continued as before, without a hint from our half-pint hero that The Garden of Eden is in full bloom.

For Cadet Brecken Saturdays with his love goddess made the worst of The Mean Old Tower's beatings and curses a snap.

Our juvenile stars frolicked, unfettered and carefree in the sanctuary of their hallowed woodland glen. Here the thorny vicissitudes of their daily lives were forgotten in the forbidden fun of Saturdays together.

The extreme beatings and curses which stung, cut, bruised and degraded our boy were an ever present constant at Heeler Hell, as were the eternal petty fits of vitriol-spewed animosity flung in the pretty face of Daddy's-little-princess by her sickly and malicious Black Witch Mom.

All of the pricks and barbs thrown at our little heroes by the damned souls Fate had left in charge of them had always vanished in the wonder of the golden kids' woodland glade sanctuary. The solace of their weekly communions proved more than ample healing for our underage luminaries. They left their glen sufficiently revivified to continue with their bruised, sometimes bent, but ever resilient lives. Both children had remained scathed but unconquerable by their dour and vengeful persecutors.

Their Saturdays of Love were ever a soothing balm and a grateful vacation for our blue eyed boy's embattled nerves and beaten body and our bright and cunning girl's battered psyche, under siege from the spiteful mother and spying siblings who had long hated her for having won her Daddy's love.

Our principals' healing meetings had been going strong for several intoxicating months. It had given two sorely pressed golden kids a supreme happiness which was to comfort them through the longest days of their lives.

Our lovely, star-crossed targets of an ominously inescapable gathering thunderhead lived and loved on through the short grace period cruel Fate had allotted to them. Our golden kids continued their happy relationship, blissfully ignorant of that pitch-black storm cloud looming above their comely heads, poised to block the path to their beautiful dream of peace and happiness forevermore.

Patiently, ruthlessly, relentlessly our happy children's doom circled ever closer, hungrier, more intent on tearing and devouring two living, loving, taboo-defying hearts to sate the black bloodlusts of their self-righteous earthly enemies.

Just above their thoughtless, pretty heads, Fate, a hideous carnal vulture, waits upon her murderous feast, the bloodletting of their undoing.

The innocent-in-their-own-way lovers' heavenly days of summer love in the midst of nuclear winter were now tick, tick ticking away.

The golden brats' terrible descent from the alabaster celestial halls of Olympus into deep, black torture pits of the flaming bowels of Tantalus draws daily nearer.

"A LONG, LONG, LONG WAY DOWN!"

Corey had taken wise little Leto's advice and played ball by screaming his head off for the pervert in charge of Heeler Hell.

And, surprisingly, The Horror had been considerably less horrible.

Just as his girl had predicted, old lady Bite had loosened up some on her formerly truculent tough little nut. Cadet Corey 'd screamed regularly and loudly for the dragon in her torture pit of choice and she had reciprocated by no longer regarding him as a challenge to her suzerain.

Even better for both protagonists, Bite no longer had to wear herself out beating the little hard case's throbbing hide throughout the Tower nights.

Since the advent of Cadet Claire, Bite had begun to find alternate forms of punishment for her more difficult cases. She'd learned and practiced a few new twists and turns to the sadist's trade by using her iniquitous imagination. These new twists and turns of a twisted mind had enabled her to inflict non-corporal punishment on her boy victims.

She'd concocted methods of psychological torture to devil the masochistic Cadet Claire.

One of her favorite tricks was this:

Miss Bite's informants had only to single out and falsely accuse one of her boys of slouching around campus with his hands in his pockets and The Bite would bite. No evidence was required to convict the accused.

Miss Bite had only to call him into her sanctum sanctorum, fill all of his fatigue pants pockets with sand, sew them shut and command the "culprit" to leave the sand in his pockets for a full week of discomfort for his punishment.

The charges had never been true. The Beast's boys knew only too well they were under constant watch. But her word was law and her boys knew better than to gainsay it:

The shower room torture chamber stood eternally ready to claim a victim at the slightest hint of insubordination.

Ergo, the punishment proceeded, the accused 's pockets were filled with heavy sand, sewn shut, and he was issued specific orders not to let that sand out for a solid week of the pronounced discomfort pockets full of sand invariably occasioned him.

The alternative should be a steamy shower communion with THE SILVER STREAK.

Corey was singled out for the sand pocket torture once. And he'd endured his week without protest.

A pleasant aspect of Miss Bite's thaw was that of her newly laid out choreography for the in house birthday parties for some of her boys.

These events were conducted in the parlor for the behemoth's forlorn captives who'd found themselves constrained to celebrate their annual holiday at Heeler Hall, without the attendance of one single relative. Sad to relate, several of the lost boys moaning beneath the dragon's heavy yoke were being habitually abandoned by their insouciant elders to celebrate their birthdays apart.

Those undutiful elders who never bothered to attend had condemned their progeny to party with the charming Miss Bite. The offending parental flops had always mailed the housemother sufficient funds to cover the big cake, candles and ice cream blowout, then they'd blown it off.

Miss Bite's favorite ice cream was fudge ripple.

Do you need three guesses to guess which flavor of ice cream was invariably served at all Heeler birthdays?

In his pre-scream mode, Corey 'd never been invited to a single one of these festive dos. But scream mode had skyrocketed him into the position of welcome guest for all of them.

(Seeming to be nice to the major's pet protégé must be a first rate way for old lady Bite to stay "in" with the powerful Donnybrooks. And one she had been quick to employ.)

If The Bite was in a particularly festive mood post one of these parties, she would gather her boys around her comfy chair in that dark parlor cavern of hers to tell them ghost stories. A horror story wrapped up in the real life horror story of Heeler Hell's stark reality?

As one might surmise, Miss Bite was a past mistress at horror. Never did the skulking old brute miss a chance to stoke her boys' fires of doubt and wake up the demons lurking in the darkest recesses of their psyches to kindle the emotion of fear in her prey.

One evening the dragon's doleful tale was an old Tennessee hill legend:

"You boys know about th' CHICKEN FOOT LADY?"

"NO, MA'AM!!!"

"Wall, oncet, a long, long time ago, thar was this ol' Tinnessee hill woman that lived a-way, way up here in th' highest, mos' remote part o' all these here sky-high Smoky Mountains.

"That ol' hill woman done lived right near HERE -- right near th' academy!

"Whut chew boys think that there hill woman wuz?"

"What was she, ma'am?"

"She was a GIANTESS -- big as all-git-out!!!

"But that big ol' giant hill woman got 'er a MAN; an' that man give 'er a BABY.

"Now, boys, th' hill woman's old man went an' died on 'er.

"He lef' that ol' hill woman all alone wif only 'er darlin' little baby boy.

"Wall, that didn' make much never-mind t' her a-cause that ol' woman LOVED that newborn baby o' hern to distraction. And I say the truth when I tell ye all th' love that poor ol' hill woman had to give t' ANYONE, she give it to her beautiful little boy.

"But, way, way up in them high hills, just a mile or so away frum this here academy where we're at now, thar's MONSTERS 'n' WILD BEASTS th' like o' which you boys aint never seen nor heered of:

"Why, boys, you aint never, ever even dreamt o' setch critters as lives up in them high hills in th' wildest nightmares of all yore born days -- but them monsters be right near HERE!

"One dark, dark night the mos' HORRIBLE one o' them wild beasts crept up into that poor ol' hill woman's cabin and STOLT HER LITTLE BABY!!!

"Now, boys, I done already tolt ye this-here hill woman was a giantess, and she was -- 'n' hill women hereabouts shore aint NO pushovers:

"She fit that wild devil-monster wif all her might 'n' main t' save her baby. Them two done fit an' fit fir hours 'n' hours on end t' git a holt o' that baby!

"Why, boys, they down-right destroyed th' hill woman's cabin, 'n' ALL th' whole countryside around it were laid to waste!

"Finally, that gawdamn devil-beast went 'n' tore that pore ol' hill woman's LEG right off its stump 'n' she fainted dead away frum mortal pain 'n' blood-loss.

"When she come to, th' beast had done took her baby 'n' gone!

"She caught 'er a great big chicken out o' whut wuz lef' o' her barnyard, kilt it 'n' sewed its leg onto her own leg-stump so 's she could go after that thievin' devil beast 'n' git 'er baby back frum it.

"Oh, land, boys, that pore ole woman done hunted and hunted all through these hills, but she never could find 'er precious baby.

"And to THIS day that chicken-foot lady's still out thar a-lookin' fir her sweet, long-lost baby boy!

"Now, that baby 'd prob'ly be jest about YOUR AGE by this time, my dirty hounds.

"WAIT, listen at THAT!

"If ye listen on nights hereabouts y' kin hear that ol' chicken foot lady a-draggin' that chicken-foot behint 'er, just a-searchin' 'n' searchin' ever where fir 'er long lost baby boy:

"Her giant foot goes BOOM, an' her dead CHICKEN-foot jus' drag along scratchin' th' dirt goes SCRATTTTCCCHHH,

BOOM-SCRATTTCHHH,   BOOM-SCRATTTCCCHHH,
BOOM-SCRATTTCCCHHHH-"

At this point in the scary old Miss Bite's scary to little boys' story, every light in Heeler Hell had been extinguished by her favorite little cadet spies and confederates.

The Beast then produced a flashlight from her sewing basket and covertly clutched it, ready for the climax of her gory tale.

Out of the dark, out of the hush, out of the chill silence of the little boys' nightmares, was heard the booms and scratches of the chicken foot lady as she came closer and ever closer:

"That chicken foot lady's still out thar right clost t' whar WE be now," The Bite's hushed whisper warned, "and she's still a-lookin' fir that darlin' li' l' baby she done lost all them years ago.

"Now, when that chicken foot lady comes up on a pretty li' l' boy -- like YOU -- one she thinks might be her baby, she yells out, 'WHAR'S MAH BABY, OH, WHAR'S MAH BABY, AIR YOU MAH BABY?'

"Don' chew try t' git away 'cause she's done kotched ye now!

"She's GOT ye 'n' thar AINT no way fir ye to git away frum HER:

"IF ye say you AINT 'er baby, she'll dash yore BRAINS out 'n' KILL ye, right then 'n' thar!

"Y' see, whut happent to that pore ol' hill woman drove 'er plumb out o' her MIND 'n' she don' care WHUT she do now.

"She's already done KILT 'er a many a li' l' boy JEST LAK YEW!

"She's STILL mad, she's STILL a-lookin' 'n' she dern well MIGHT jus' kill YEW!"

As the booming and scratching got louder and louder and closer and closer, all the lights had gone out.

Now the dragon's helpers grabbed her cadets as yet uninitiated to this ghastly old sociopath 's dirty trick from behind to scare them at the climax of her psychodrama.

Their deranged housemother then switched on her flashlight and held it directly beneath that same hideous face all the Heeler Hall boys feared and hated most.

The Beast grabbed one of her novitiates from the front -- her one boy -- held him up to her doleful mug and shrieked, "AIR YEW MAH BABY, AIR YEW MAH BABY???!!!!"

The dragon's graphic illustration of the random nature of our universe in general and the capricious nature of her unchecked child abuse in particular had crashed with a deafening roar into her one captive boy's consciousness:

It was no surprise that her one boy, Cadet Brecken, was the chicken foot lady's baby of choice that night.

The poor old hill woman in the dragon's tale had had no control over her wretched existence, nor could she have guarded herself against the monster's random raid.

The monster itself was a predator that had stolen and killed to eat.

The boys were sent to The Tower to be broken to the whip with no say in the matter.

Miss Bite and her fellow abusers at The Tower were propelled by their own monster-natures to wreck their beastly excesses daily on the helpless children unlucky enough to be consigned to them. Those evil old hags were driven, as was the predator in the wicked crone's tale to assuage the insane appetites of their own child abusing, child destroying beast natures.

Bite now clutched Brecken just as she had done in the shower that first night, her flashlight highlighting those ghoulish features which had so revolted him, her foul mouth emitted her rotten signature stink.

"Oh, GOD!" Corey's troubled mind screamed, "No! Not that face, not, not AGAIN, NO!"

He tried to escape but Miss Bite of the illuminated and accentuated gruesome face held him, lifted him to her and held him closer and closer, struggling but helpless.

She was reprising her first torture night with him. The Bite now squeezed the air out of his lungs and pulled him closer to the face he hated in her vice-like grip as she had then.

When she'd remarked the pain and horror she could no more hide her pleasure in it than he might hide his pain. She pulled her prey up close to that luminous, flash-lit map of hell, brim-full of her hatred for this one boy.

The same mask of malice and perversion that had savaged Brecken, Brecken, BRECKEN when he'd danced for her at his first grueling torture trial here. He saw that hate-twisted face once again, leering down on him with bad intent, dripping with the sweat and shower water of his unforgettable night of pain and horror. Paralyzed with fear and panting for air, Corey had been caught up in a freak-out flashback. The shock of that vile face had flung him back to that night when this hell hag had introduced him, her little initiate, into the exquisite agonies of Heeler Hell and THE SILVER STREAK. Her cancer-fetid breath smothered him tonight as it had then and he quailed at whatever vile purpose his painful imprisonment might portend.

Suddenly, he'd been cornered, pinned like a butterfly in this randy, evil smelling old monster's scrapbook again.

The monster had trapped him into a reprise of that steaming nightmare.

In this shocking memory's riveting lightning strike he felt he must again be fated to endure another frenzied savaging in the insane clutches of this accursed monstrosity. In the unreason of panic he was at the point of enduring the behemoth's torture trial by SILVER STREAK again.

Miss Bite dropped him at last, but Corey could never escape the dreadful, constrictive feeling of having been trapped in the long ago night of torment of a hated past. He could never shake the feeling that he'd been trapped, imprisoned and had the indelible image of his maiden savaging branded deep into his psyche. The trauma he'd experienced when she'd made him pay dearly for his bold defiance in an ocean of the pain the old deviant had written in bruises across his naked body had never been forgotten.

The whole night of The Bite's chicken foot lady yarn he'd been unable to lose the picture of her ghoulish mask of malice:

The darkened shower room, the incessant drumming of the cascading water, its billows of fog sent aloft, the indescribable cruelty of his unspeakable ordeal. Hell had unleashed this amoral monster against a little boy's bare and vulnerable body to do its master's will that night. And tonight Hecate's handmaiden had regenerated her power over him because her memory yet haunted him.

Those unbearable memories had come crowding in on him. And the sight of that ghastly flash-lit face now opened the floodgates of terror to shock and put him on notice that Miss Bite was still at liberty to savage him at will.

And was this to be an idle night for any of The Beast's Heeler Hall cadets?

It was not.

The evening's activities included a very important event for them. Their beloved commandant's Deepfreeze had specific instructions from his nibs to entertain the poor little boys under the awful domination of the infamous Bite. The Beast's same merry inventions which had brought The Heeler Hall Horror such fearful notoriety had also awakened the headmaster's pity for those condemned to suffer them. Ergo, the major's frostbitten missus, abetted by her eldest daughter and younger offspring, were under strict orders to regale the Heeler cadets with hot cocoa, cookies, and card and board games this evening.

All this was to occur at the major's home while the Master of The Tower enjoyed one of his frequent club nights out, of course.

It need hardly be noted that Missus Donnybrook resented the imposition:

She resented it passionately, in much the same way she'd resented each and every thing she'd had to do accommodate anyone in all the world (with the lone exception of her darling confidante, Miss Bite).

It also may go without saying that the lovely Mistress Leto Donnybrook had been very pleased she to learn that she was to see her own cadet lover boy again. Our amorous heroine looked forward to seeing her amorous student.

But two things made her apprehensive about this gathering. One was the nagging doubt that they might not be safe, for, in this iffy venue, the propinquity of The Black Witch and her spy babies was a decided and mortal danger.

Her pushover Daddy was absent, but her mean old Deepfreeze mom and her cradle creep apparatchiki would be.

That brings us to our little princess's second worry: What if a careless word, an overly amorous glance, on clumsy Corey's part, might tip their hand and deliver them into the waiting jaws of their deadly enemy? Of course, the ravishingly beautiful, fastidiously self-contained school beauty queen would never make such a blunder herself.

Leto 'd always known, if the strictly taboo, esthetically beautiful, breathtakingly intimate things our top-secret lovers had been doing, ever came to the all seeing eye of Black Witch Medusa, then the world outside their magic glen would know -- and the lovers would be lost. That would have unleashed a catastrophe worse than all the horrors this world had previously known.

It would certainly have precipitated her fall from Daddy's grace and unleash a world of nightmarish punishments far beyond all human endurance to wound and scar her poor little lover boy -- and, most importantly, her!

"Oh, well!" she blithely dismissed her paranoid image of a hell beyond hell as just too awful ever to come true for pretty little Leto, "Shoot, nothin' as bad as that ever happens anyhow, not to ME."

Another reason Leto was looking forward to this evening's do was that, on this same game party night, her best girlfriend, Suzy Slats, was coming to a sleep over at the Donnybrook house.

Suzy was a bona fide Major Donnybrook approved girlfriend for the great man's beloved princess. This folksy young town girl was Leto's own age, and after careful examination she'd been granted the august major's permission for a sleep over after the cookies, cards and cadets were cleared away.

With her confidante present, Corey's lover felt a lot more relaxed, for Suzy had always been a big help to her and would certainly come in handy tonight:

Our adventuresome Aphrodite had been pining for a long overdue heart to heart catharsis about her favorite lover boy. Mac's Love goddess had been itching to relate her sizzling adventures to someone safe. The untold tale of her taboo woodland assignations had long weighed heavily on our lively young May Queen.

Our bodacious beauty had longed to be unburdened of her ineffable woodland frolics to a true friend, a friend who'd be sure to keep her secrets. And she knew Suzy to be just such a safe repository for her arcane adventures because Suzy and Leto had always shared all their naughtiest secrets in common. Corey's dream girl was perishing to tell someone. And it must specifically be a true friend like Suz who understood how important it was never to rat out the details of her best friend's love affair with her adoring blue-eyed boy.

Suzy would never blab. The two close chums had already shared their deepest, darkest secrets together. They shared a secret, one which, if brought to light, would have opened the floodgates of perdition to spew forth hell's most unbearable punishments over both girls, had either set of parents caught wind of what their "good-little-girls" had been up to in their absence.

Meantime, while the major's lady (with the two older girls doing all the work) was making preparations for the game party, the Heeler Hall boys cautiously picked their way through the darkness of a pitch-black, moonless night.

The boys picked their way carefully down the very same sidewalk along the margin of the big parade field where there was a break in the trees. And that break led to our beautiful lovers' trysting ground where kind trees had always hidden Mac and Leto while their passions consumed them every Saturday.

The cadets were bound for the major's house as per their housemother's orders, "Git yore mangy tails over thar and play some kine o' games with th' headmaster's kids, or I'll skin ye alive."

But Corey was not thinking of The Beast and her blow just now, for he could feel the nearness of their beloved break in the trees and his trysts with his girl. No living soul could penetrate the impenetrable darkness of this moonless night. But he could dream wistfully of his beauty queen and recall to his great comfort the revivifying updraft of their weekend adventures in paradise.

"If The Bite Beast only knew!" he reflected in the secret recesses of an extremely apprehensive mind, "But I sure am GLAD she doesn't!"

"D' you believe there's a REAL chicken foot lady?" queried a wan and querulous McMoon, lost in his native state of fright, his whey face discernable even through the ebon shroud of this moonless night.

"Don't be such a DOPE, Mac!" mocked Worrywart Crabtree, the gang's levelheaded science buff, "That's just an ol' hillbilly fairytale t' scare dumb little kids -- like YOU, moon face."

"'More things in heaven and earth, Horatio,'" an erudite McNichol quoted The Bard.

"There aint NO Horatio HERE, y' ol' sissy-pants goof-ball," bridled his hardboiled roomie, angry as usual at his lacy bunkmate's poetic whimsy.

The boys were ten years and under, so not one understood the fruitcake's Shakespearian allusion. McNichol dropped it instanter rather than stirring up a wasp's nest of such violence-prone yahoos.

But The Beast's ghost story was the last thing Corey'd wanted to reference. That grizzly allusion forced him back into the indelible memory of Bite's ghastly flash-lit visage in the old fiend's dark and spooky parlor. And the shower room savaging it had evoked quickly turned our hero's face as milk white as McMoon's.

The mention of that gory old hag's disgusting hill legend burned that satanic ghoul's revolting face into his brain to cast a tinge of terror over the evening.

Normally, Corey enjoyed a hike outside in the brisk night air enormously.

But normalcy was a scarce commodity at this academy. And normalcy was nowhere to be found at the Donnybrook's doorstep on this accursed night out.

Darkness and wintry country chill had never bothered our half-pint hero before. But tonight he felt stalked by the curse of some unknown and unnamable fiend.

Corey was still haunted by that fearful countenance by the time the boys were knocking on their esteemed commander's door.

Like our mini-heroine, our mini-hero was overjoyed at the chance to see his beautiful May Queen once again. But, like Leto, he was terribly afraid something might just go disastrously awry at an event featuring Leto's Deepfreeze mom (and her dreaded Argus eyes).

Trepidation or no trepidation, ruddy or pallid, orders are orders and Cadet Brecken was under orders to attend this do, or "git skint alive."

The major's sub zero harpy and her diverse brood greeted our gang of cadet schoolboys with as much faked civility as the cobra felt appropriate.

When the deadly reptile invited the Heeler boys in to endure her frozen game party, she had remarked upon young Corey's pallor and apprehensive state as soon as her black cobra stare had burned directly into her one boy's clear blue eyes.

For Corey the dragon had always been scathing and revolting, but The Black Witch was tonight especially terrifying, stupefying and completely unmanning.

"Why, my goodness!" rose a cobra ready to strike, "What makes you so pale, dear little Cadet Brecken? Oh, yes, my dear, you look as if you've seen a ghost!"

Her victim stood dumbstruck for a tick or two as the gorgon caustically put him to the question in her terse, spur of the moment Inquisition:

"I, I'm terribly sorry, ma'am," stammered a frightened little boy on the spot, "I didn't know I was s, so pale and, and I beg your forgiveness, Mrs. Donnybrook."

Leto shot him a quizzical glance. It was as if she was saying he'd done something wrong, something that would make things even worse. But was just plain impossible, for both lovers knew full well her mom already hated them both as much as she possibly could hate anything or anyone on earth. No, nothing he might ever say or do could make this unnatural old sow hate either of them one iota more.

But that glance of disapprobation had added exponentially to his May Queen's antsy little lover boy's already dire discomfort. Oh, yes, my dear, a gorgon knows just how to give a party:

She knows exactly how to initiate a fun evening by pricking our two guilty little innocents to a state of fearful confusion. The Black Witch had baited her fortunate beauty's already frightened little lover and observing the reaction of his nervous and upset little inamorata.

The Heeler Hell cadets were ushered into the living room following poor Corey's verbal chastisement (and its chilling effect on both of our golden brats).

In short order our toy cadets' permafrost proprietress curtly excused herself, dumped her guests on Leto and Suzy and retired to her private chambers to peruse her ladies' fashion periodicals.

Most of them were relieved to have the headmaster's crabby old lady out of the way. And they relaxed and concentrated on the games at hand as successfully as any military school cadet in his commandant's home has ever been able to relax and concentrate on anything.

Not so for our hot blooded romantic leads. Our unnerved lovebirds were still quite uncomfortable:

This painfully formal gathering was much worse than their amorous bouts in the sweltering ambiance of no holds barred woodland fun. Even dirty joking in their mealtime's formal but more familiar venue was more convivial than this icebound down home Donnybrook hot seat.

Leto and her Mac just knew this must be some kind of trap. Especially since The Black Witch's spies were still watching, still listening -- still dangerous.

The chatter and clatter of the dining hall to drown out some of their conversation was missing here. Ergo, they were unable to converse or socialize.

In the dour presence of Lin and Annie our haunted lovers daren't even risk an amorous glance at each other.

Pretty Leto had never been so trepid in her plucky life, for she believed her Black Witch upbraided lover-dope must have already made some fatal faux pas:

He'd been so flabbergasted at The Deepfreeze's first loaded question of this evening's inquisition his girl was terribly frightened of what he may have betrayed: "Oh, golly! Poor Mac must have given us away," she fretted.

The Black Witch's spy apparatus was busily tracking the golden brats' every move, listening for whatever stray guilty word they might add to their woefully sketchy sin dossier.

The darling Mrs. Donnybrook, epitome of what a warm and welcoming hostess for these sorely oppressed cadets should be, had already won two short term goals:

She'd handily eviscerated the despised Brecken, Brecken, BRECKEN. And she'd driven her hated, just-too-perfect daughter to distraction in so doing.

Now the cobra reclined, snug and smug, in her boudoir to leaf through her favorite ladies' gazettes. She was resting comfortably in the sweet-and-sour knowledge that she had handily trashed that snotty little Brecken whelp and summarily condemned both of those sickeningly sweet, revoltingly precious golden brats to a thorny purgatory of doubt and discomfort.

Such victories had been black-soul satisfying to this satanic devotee to Hecate's corrupting arts.

A heartless and unforgivably unnatural mother and a pitiless destroyer of her eldest child's most cherished hopes and dreams, The Black Witch had as yet no inkling of just how very close she was to discovering the lovers' fatal secret. The cobra knew not she was standing at the threshold of breaking the lovers' bond, exposing them to her husband, punishing them beyond endurance and devastating their entire lives.

Even so, she was so proud of her apt put-down of the annoying Leto's hardy little beast, the old reprobate telephoned her fellow gorgon to crow over our beautiful children.

They savored a good old fashioned evil gloat together:

"My dear Miss Bite!"

"My precious Mrs. Donnybrook! Are my filthy hounds behaving themselves over there?"

"Within reason, my darling," grinned the serpent, "That ghastly little Brecken brat showed up as pale as a ghost; and, when I braced him about it, the male brute fell apart completely.

"I know those two hot little ANIMALS are up to something; and I'll have them, my dear, I'll have them. Lin and Annie haven't been able to pin anything on them yet, but they WILL, my dear, they will!"

Both harpies enjoyed a good old homespun cackle over Corey's embarrassment.

"Good fir you, hon!" Miss Bite bragged up her pal, "I'll skin that little Brecken bug alive fir ye when 'e gits back here tonight a-cause I really HATE that imp!"

"YOU hate him?" shouted The Witch, "Darling, be assured that I LOATHE that disgusting little male THING.

"Do you realize that creature has co-opted both my husband and my eldest girl's affections?

"I can't even get a look-in with my Lynnwood the way those two accursed and completely unworthy golden brats monopolize him."

"I'll SKIN 'im ALIVE, my dearie!" bawled the dragon.

"You may whip him to your heart's content, my dear, and I dearly hope you do!" The Witch admonished her friend, "But never will you destroy that one with THE SILVER STREAK

"No, beat him black and bloody but you shan't conquer him. Not as long as he has HIS Leto and HIS Daddy to crawl back to. They'll pick him up, dust him off, and the little monster will heal -- and survive! With THEM on his side he'll always mend.

"Oh, no, my dear, the only way to destroy their darling little Cadet 'Mac' is for me to sort out some way to DIVIDE those three hopeless romantics, Leto, Daddy and their precious Mac:

"We must somehow separate these impediments to Brecken's destruction, and Leto's. But for us to accomplish this the magnificent major must turn on BOTH his darling golden brats, for, when he does, all THREE of them will come under MY power. And then what I do to them will be ever so delicious!

"Patience, dear Miss Bite, for in the fullness of time I shall find the cleverest way to break up their oh, so comfortable, oh, so revoltingly smarmy little love trio.

"Employing stealth and patience I shall one day find our opening, and, when I do, I will BREAK all their soppy, stupid, sentimental loving hearts."

"If you insist, dear lady," concurred The Beast, "But I'm still a-gonna smoke that damn li' l' Brecken's haunches TONIGHT!"

"Have your fun by all means, my dear," smiled The Black Witch complacently, for any misery these scrofulous hags were able to inflict on poor little Corey Brecken tickled their ebon fancy.

Both gorgons laughed in anticipation of young loves' downfall.

Malicious mom didn't yet realize how soon her tinker toy spies should provide the breakthrough to open the gates of hell for her pretty little rival-daughter and doom her gallant cadet hero to fulfill her ugliest dream: Leto was but a hair's breadth from falling prey to The Black Witch of The Tower. That monster of perdition lay poised to excoriate her own flesh and blood and forever end a pretty little girl's sweet, sweet dreams of love eternal. The Deepfreeze lurked on the very cusp of ending her pretty daughter's joie de vivre forevermore.

The warm and yielding flesh of our fortunate, until tonight, Daddy's little precious should soon be torn asunder by her vile and unnatural enemy.

That infuriating girl, that alluring little Jezebel The Black Witch mom never forgave for winning her dad's heart might soon be cast out of the heady stratosphere of love she'd always taken for granted as her birthright, denied the sunshine of the great man's favor and consigned to the dark and thorny abyss of her angry father's egregious chastisement. All our beautiful Leto's brightest successes shall too soon end on this darkest of all dark nights, for it is to be the night of our little heroine's shameful defeat:

Our proud young fairytale princess, our laughing coquette, the beauty who's always regarded the gorgon and her imps with the lofty scorn of a ravishing love star looking down on this group of those pitiable Donnybrook grotesques beneath her must soon be disabused as to what torments such grotesques have long held in store for her.

The grim game party ended at last and the guests had been dispatched back into their own comfortless ambiance, Heeler Hell. On returning to that warm and friendly place they were immediately commanded to write syrupy thank you notes to the icebound Donnybrook matriarch for giving them such a fun time in such a cozy atmosphere.

But one boy hadn't been dismissed to pen his thank you note directly upon his return.

"Oh, no, my dear," gloated the leviathan, "Cadet Corey Brecken must be immediately stripped naked and marched into the shower for a blistering date with his loving ol' housemother's SILVER STREAK."

Only after being skinned alive was Corey allowed to write his thank you note to the wretched hag who had designated him for his whipping.

At the major's house the deadly serpent who'd informed on him had deigned to exit her boudoir to see her only friend's hardy, red cheeked little charges out. But the cobra had quickly slithered back into her bedroom fastness, leaving Leto and Suzy to do all the work of cleaning up.

Those two good natured and energetic young ladies had never shrunk from distaff work. They'd long since become inured to housework through daily practice.

What Leto especially minded was that the viper had issued instructions that she allow the Deepfreeze espionage apparatchiks to stay up for an indefinite period, explicitly to continue to play board games, but implicitly to monitor the big girls conversation in the hope of discovering those closely kept secrets dear to Leto's heart.

Leto and Suzy gossiped with extreme caution as they put the house in order to insure that her sibling snitches learned naught. The big girls finished their work, but they were careful not to let the toddling spies catch even one word of what they were saying.

"WE are going to bed like SENSIBLE people," announced the pygmy snitches' pretty big sister after she and Suzy had finished, "YOU shrimps can stay up just as late as you're crazy enough to, like mom says:

"But I would advise YOU to hit th' hay 'n' get some beauty sleep. Lord knows YOU need more beauty sleep than you'll ever be able to get in ONE lifetime!"

"Aw, dry up, Leto!" yapped Annie.

"YEAH!" barked Lin.

Blowback from the harpy's espionage community was anticipated, and just as easily dismissed by their dominant big sis.

"Well, WE'RE goin' t' bed, and we're th' BIG girls!" announced Suzy in support of her girlfriend.

Outside the viper's door Leto shouted, "We're all done cleanin' up after th' party, mom.

"Okay if we go t' bed now?"

"This house had better be SPOTLESS when I get up in the morning, YOUNG LADY!" came the serpent's hiss within.

"It IS, ma!" countered Daddy's best girl, "How 'bout it?"

"Very well," sighed The Deepfreeze, anxious to return to her journals.

"How 'bout these li' l' rug rats, ma?" groused Leto, "THEY wan' 'o stay up ALL NIGHT!"

"Lynnwood Junior and Antoinette, you may stay up for ONE HALF HOUR more, and no longer, before they retire!" was the brusque rejoinder from behind a door shut against the world in general.

"You heard it, y' li' l DO-DOS!" Leto stuck out her very mature tongue at her difficult siblings.

"O-kay, okay," Lin and Annie harmonized discordantly, malcontents opposed to mom's verdict.

But those two were determined to disobey. They couldn't break off their investigation until they had the goods on their too perfect big sis.

That said, all five Donnybrook household pugilists retired to their respective corners.

The snoops were the lone exception. They'd feigned bedtime preparations; but as soon as the big girls had gone into Leto's bedchamber, they set up camp outside her door.

"That ought 'o take care o' those li' l' drips, Suz," smiled Corey's love goddess closing her bedroom door, totally deceiving herself, "But we better talk about somethin' besides BOYS for about half an hour or so, 'cause when we DO talk about 'em, GIRL, I've got a hot news flash for YOU that's gonna knock y' for a loop!"

"Oh, tell me what, Lee?" her pal insisted, "Tell me, tell me, c' m' oooonnnn!"

"Not now!" giggled Daddy's star.

But the truth was that she'd been bursting to speak of the pleasures she had experienced with her lover boy for ages, "BUT, when I do tell, OH, BOY!!!"

"Me too!" enthused Suzy, anxious to dish the dirt, "One o' th' town-boys - "

"NO, Suz!" Leto put a cautionary finger to her lips, "Little pitchers got BIG ears, so no secrets yet!"

But it was already too late.

The Deepfreeze's hungry little jackals had heard every word the big girls had said, and they'd already said too much.

Leto's sibling enemies would never rest until big sis had been brought down and boiled alive.

"Okay, bunk-buddy," smiled Suzy, "I guess we can gab about school, or piano lessons, OR th' time I sneaked th' key t' m' dad's liquor cabinet 'n' we were all alone at my house, all afternoon?"

"What a GAS!" Leto warmed to their top-secret liquor cabinet sin, "We got SO tipsy on your ol' dad's crème de menthe, 'n' I was SO scared we'd get caught!"

"Me too!" Suzy giggled in her guilt-tinged remembrance as they recalled the forbidden secrets they'd shared that day, "Lucky we got that Listerine out o' th' medicine cabinet t' hide th' smell of booze; AND we acted real straight-laced th' whole rest o' th' day so 's our stuffy ol' grownups would never know."

Then the girls proceeded to delve deep into the boozy details of the liquor cabinet caper. They belabored the topic endlessly, for they had to wait out the toddlers' half hour curfew.

At last the half hour came and went. But what the girls didn't know was that mom's sneaks were still on their case.

"Okay, Suzy-q," smirked Leto, "You first: What about you an' th' town-boy?"

"Oh, Lee!" gasped a blushing Suzy, indicating her newly budding, slightly protruding breast, "We were making out and I, I got so hot 'n' bothered I actually let him TOUCH me here!

"Oh, God, it, it was just, just so, SO EXCITING!!!"

"YOU think THAT'S exciting?" cried Leto, rushing into the spotlight to take a bow.

At this point, Lin's little eye was peeping into her keyhole and Annie had pressed a water glass against her door to amplify the sound of what the big girls were saying.

Leto didn't know it, but she was talking herself into the abyss.

"Sister, that aint nothin'!" Cadet Brecken's bold seductress opened up on her pal with her full array of heavy artillery, "Did you see that little Cadet Brecken t' night, th' cute li' l' blond kid?"

"Yeah, he IS cute but he's also kind o' small," her chum began.

Wrong move, Suzy:

"NO, missy, you TALK but y' don't KNOW what you're talkin' about!" Leto refused to sit still for any derision of her prize stud, "DYNAMITE comes in small packages, dopey, BUT it'll blow you 'n' me 'n' this whole darn house clean off th' face of the earth in a split second, y' green tomato:

"Corey, but Daddy 'n' me always call 'im 'Mac,' 'cause he's our very most favorite cadet in this whole academy; and he's my BOYFRIEND, too, Suzy-girl:

"I stand out in those cold ol' woods on th' way to town 'n' just wait 'n' wait for that boy EVERY Saturday, honey. And, oh, girl, it's WORTH every single minute of all that long, long wait when he comes to me. An 'it seems like I wait a million years to ME. But he comes to me 'n' it's alright!"

"OH, LEE!!!" gasped Suzy, "What ARE you saying?"

"I LOVE my Mac, 'n,' 'n' I want him with me all my life -- FOREVER, that's what I'm saying!" evoked our heroine forcefully, "Oh, girlfriend, I wait for him, my, my own special schoolboy in th' woods between th' parade field 'n' town 'n' when he comes we fly to heaven.

"Oh, sure, I know I'm royalty at th' academy, Daddy's li' l' princess, but I still gotta wait for my sweet li' l' corporal for what seems like FOREVER. Oh, Suz, I, I wait for my golden schoolboy just like a common tramp, and when he comes 'n' takes me in his arms it's all worthwhile 'cause he REALLY loves me!

"My, my beautiful blue eyed baby, Mac, runs into my arms, and, oh, Suz, we HUG, we, we KISS - "

Now our pretty little spellbinder paused to allow Suzy's curiosity to build until her desire for her friend's earth shaking news had built to an earth-shaking crescendo:

"And then WE DO IT!!!"

"Oh, LEE, you DON'T!!!!" gasped Suzy in dismay.

"Oh, yes, we DO!!!" moaned a woman child in love, "We DO IT and we love it!!!"

But Leto's wee enemies' time had come:

"Annie!" whispered Lin urgently, "RUN GET MOM!!!

"THIS IS IT!!!!"

"NUH-UHHH!!!" protested Annie, "I don' want 'o miss NONE o' THIS!!!"

"YEAH-HUHHHH!!!!" he argued with toddler logic, "Ya GOTTA!!!"

But he saw that it was no use.

Annie was hypnotized by this mysterious delight Leto had found and wanted to learn more about a thing she'd never before even imagined.

No, Lin knew he must fly as fast as his little feet could into the mischief of telling The Black Witch on his big sis. He was a baby and a baby has no way of knowing that he was about to tear his family apart by telling, he knew only that mom wanted him to tell.

He cried out in frustration as he darted off, "Oh, ANNIE, YOU are just IMPOSSIBLE!!!!"

He returned in seconds with a very interested Deepfreeze in tow.

They pushed tiny Annie aside to peep into the keyhole.

But, as the prying eyes and sharp ears of the conspirators watched and listened, what was heard?

"Yes, Suzy, we DO IT!" whispered Leto, hoarse and breathless, in the intoxication of her passion, "We KISS, we touch each other ALL OVER until, until we, we just can't, we can't STAND it ONE MORE SECOND, and, and then, then WE DO IT, WE DO IT. Oh believe me when I tell you it, it's just plain HEAVEN!"

"And you even let him - "

"Oh, yes, Suzy, YES, I let him and I, I WANT him to! Oh, honey, I want him to do it SO BAD that, that, I, I'm just BURSTING!!!

"I, I even showed him HOW t' do it our first time; and, Oh, Suzy, Suzy, that FIRST time was just so, SO WONDERFUL 'cause, 'cause it was the very first time EVER for Mac, the first time he'd EVER done it:

"It was his first time EVER, and I taught him how!"

"Oh, my God, Lee, that's, that's just so BIG, that's just so, I, I don' know. But, oh, girl, how COULD you?" gasped Suzy, agape with wonderment.

"I, I know, I know," sighed Corey's beloved sex schoolmarm, lost in her rosy afterglow recollection of their first magic Saturday, "I, I know it, it seems so, so BAD, like -- you know -- like SUCH a big SIN just talking about it like this. I know, I know it seems so, so AWFUL.

"Oh but, Suz, it's, it's JUST SO BEAUTIFUL when we DO IT it's not BAD, it, it's HEAVEN ON EARTH!!!!

"We DO IT, Suzy, 'n' we LOVE it, 'n' HE loves ME 'n' I LOVE HIM:

"That way it's NO sin. It's NEVER a sin when you're really. REALLY in LOVE with each other!

"I LOVE MAC, SUZY, 'n' he LOVES ME; and, and, OH LORD, I know it sounds crazy, Sue, but, but when we're together LIKE THAT, it's, it's just THE biggest thing that's EVER happened to either of us in our whole, entire LIVES!"

"Oh, gosh, Lee!" exclaimed her friend, impelled into our heroine's powerful romantic vortex.

Leto's magical eyes widened and began to tear with the heartfelt fervor of her passion, "Oh, girl, I LOVE COREY BRECKEN!!! I, I'm SO in LOVE with that boy, girlfriend, it, it's HEAVEN!!!!

"Oh, Suzy, LOVE'S the most important thing a woman can EVER have, and it's just th' ONLY thing that can ever make THIS woman happy!"

"Well, then I just I have t' be happy FOR y', Lee. It's my job as your best friend to -"

"Oh, THANKS, Suz!!!" emoted Corey's priceless prize, "I jus' KNEW you'd understand!"

But love and understanding were all over and done with that very moment:

The gorgon had found the key to her door and burst in on our secret sharers and a private conversation, now shockingly public.

Young Mistress Leto Donnybrook's happiness ends forevermore here in this split second.

Here and now the pleasant kingdom of Leto and Mac was smashed into a shower of irreparably shattered shards, shards which were but yesterday the hopeful, loving hearts of two more-or-less-innocent young children.

"Now that you have had your heaven, my pretty lovebirds," gloated a Black Witch, triumphant, "Here comes hell, YOU FILTHY LITTLE WHORE!!!!"

A punishing fury unleashed slapped, slappped, SLAPPPED her shocked and amazed daughter as her pain-wracked head jerked sharply around and around like that of a violently shaken rag doll. Corey's heavenly love goddess was being brutalized by a hell borne fury's gnarly claws of vengeance, again, AGAIN, AGAIN, harder and harder and HARDER.

The Black Witch was now ecstatically at liberty to do the same things The Beast had done to Leto's favorite cadet in the rising fog of her steaming torture chamber.

This time Leto was the helpless chew-toy of a raving horror. Now both of our heroic lovers then know to their sorrow what an aroused adult's naked fury can steal from an isolated and friendless child. This diabolically strong and determined adult abuser's tortures had, swiftly and mercilessly, intruded upon the intimacy of our formerly happy woman-child's love life to invade it, to wound it and to end it.

"Oh, how can this be happening to ME?" wondered Mac's tender lover girl's viciously assaulted, panic stricken mind inside the relentless battery delivered by her Deepfreeze mother's icy talons, talons which strike, and strike, and strike home again and again with all the debilitating shock of a hard, cruel, hate-crazed woman.

How could this horribly ugly creature be doing such painful, ugly things to pretty Princess Leto?

She was far too charming, much too captivating, too impeccable, too adorable, for this to be happening to her. But it was, and she was suffering a merciless (and unaccustomed) beating at the hands of an infuriated hell fury.

The girl's shock and confusion at the loss of her imagined privacy, the brutalizing acts which transmogrified her own private bedroom from an oasis where secrets might be shared with the security of the confessional into this strange and fearful nightmare clime of pain had appalled her. Leto was being savaged in what had, brief moments ago, been her sanctum sanctorum.

Leto was tortured by The Witch as Corey had been savaged by The Beast. Our poor little heroes' love bond was now eternal, for they were both being horribly abused to glut the deranged appetites of The Tower's two worst deviants.

Corey's sweet lover girl's rout was complete. Her raving mother slapped her pretty daughter here and there and everywhere, around and around the room. The crazed fury chased her hapless prey down implacably to thrash her pitilessly. A Deepfreeze Infuriate swore at our abused beauty as if she were the lowliest of hill trash and beat her daughter like a wild animal.

The loyal Suzy Slats celeritously acquired the uncommon good sense to grab her clothes, take to her heels and run for her life from the scene of this terrific, ongoing and unabated crime of passion. Leto's terrified preteen confidante ran for her life from the horrors she'd witnessed, nor did she hesitate or slow down until she was well away from The Tower's dangerous precincts.

"NOW, my dear little Miss Leto Donnybrook," her grim executioner paused in her abuse to take a breather and proudly survey the damage she'd inflicted on her battered child, "Oh, yes, my dear, I am going to call your DARLING daddy and INFORM him JUST exactly what kind of a FILTHY little two-bit WHORE his PRECIOUS little FAVORITE is!!!"

"Ooooh, nooo. M, m, mama!!!!" begged the unredeemable wretch's sore, cut, bruised and weeping victim, "No, no, not Daddy!

"Pleassse, mama, please mama, please mama -- pllleeeaaasse!!!!

"D, don't, d, d, don't tell, tell Daddy on me, PLEASSSE!!!!"

The gorgon's infuriatingly pretty eldest daughter was at her reptile mom's feet begging for mercy, bleeding from the rough working over that unconscionable vengeance machine had given her.

This was precisely where The Deepfreeze had long dreamed of having her pretty, imperious, over confident daughter.

Our poor heroine had repeatedly predicted this worst of all possible outcomes to her lover that she might be assured of his silence. But disaster had tracked them down, not because of anything Mac said but through her own failing.

She knew what she'd known then. There would be no mercy for them. Their slavish fate was to be only the awful shame of this unthinkable discovery, followed by the heartless infliction of incredibly cruel punishments against their two healthy, rapidly developing young bodies, and more-or-less innocent minds.

It was too late to beg. It was impossible to do so in the midst of the unendurable shame of Deepfreeze's extreme punishment, and Corey's savvy little Leto, of all people, knew full well the futility of begging mercy of the merciless.

But the primal imperative of self preservation had kicked in to force her to put by her pride and beg, "Please, ma, I, I'll do anything, ANYTHING!!!

"PLEASE, MA, PLEASE DON'T TELL DADDY, PLEASE!!!!"

"Oh, no, my dear!" spat The Black Witch contemptuously.

How long has this lost High Priestess of Hecate awaited her ebon moment and how she was savoring the shame of her proud, imprudent, beautiful rival's humbling hour of defeat and degradation.

Poor Leto's lithe, captivating young body, the same desirable form which had attracted and invited her Mac to use her with so much tenderness, was now paying a terrible price for their dalliance at the hands of their common enemy.

Gorgon-mom was grimacing with wicked satisfaction because she'd stripped Daddy's favorite of every shred of her proud pretence and was at liberty to brand the adored and adoring Leto a trollop in the great man's eyes.

Oh, yes, my dear, the major was about to provide yet another delectable caper in The Black Witch's destructive kermis:

The crushing news that both of his delightful little favorites had basely deceived him was sure to break his loving heart and make this vicious fury's joy complete.

Hell borne furies and their imps have hearts of stone, ergo they do not love. Their premier joy is to tear out and devour the living, loving hearts of flesh around them.

Oh, yes, my dear, that maddeningly beautiful little pushover, Leto, must be displayed, naked and fallible, before her angry father, a father hoodwinked into believing his daughter has always been an evil little girl by her truly evil mother. Mrs. Donnybrook, heartless engine of vengeance, was in a position to break the hearts of all three of these poor, misguided fools, these dupes so stupidly ingenuous as to allow love to enter and move their lives. Her perverse pleasure was to be in witnessing the destruction of those three fools' foolhardy happiness, and the sundering of their silly love-bond.

While the merciless Deepfreeze throttled our fallen angel, the poor girl's heartless siblings, those cold hearted engineers of her undoing, laughed and scornfully mocked her in her misery. Schooled in hatred the imps even snuck in some punches and kicks of their own as their mom beat their beautiful sister.

"Not so lofty now, my high-headed young beauty?" the witch spat at her own offspring whom she'd hated and envied so long, "Not nearly so arrogant as when YOU were your high-and-mighty-Daddy's best beloved little pet, are you, you cheap little tramp?

"No, you're NOT the proud and fair Miss Leto Donnybrook anymore!

"What are you now, WHAT ARE YOU NOW, you, you DISGRACEFUL little FLOOZY?

"Not proud now, miss, not by a long shot!

"I OWN you now, MISS, and I mean to teach you SHAME!!!"

The heartless wretch then grabbed our poor girl by the throat:

"Now, you listen to me, MISS! ... I have called YOUR major, and HE is coming home now, AND I told him to bring the STROP!

"Do you know what that means, do you KNOW WHAT IT MEANS?

"It means that YOU, my pretty little BIMBO, you, my lovely, lively sweet-singing siren, are going to get just a LITTLE taste of what that, that, filthy little criminal, your DYNAMITE DELINQUENT LOVER is going to get quite, quite a LOT of in the very near future!"

"Oh-oh, mama!" begged her pitiful prey, "P, please, please NOT, NOT THAT!!!!"

"Oh, YES, my dear!" declared the monster in charge, "YOU are in for a good old fashioned STROPPING, my pretty!

"Now, YOU settle down and LISTEN to ME, you, you LOOSE filly:

"You had BETTER blame this WHOLE filthy-dirty, revolting little mess on HIM if you want to save even ONE teensy little SCRAP of your OWN precious hide for posterity-

"POSTERITY?" raged the gorgon, "Speaking of posterity, my darling daughter, God only knows WHAT manner of posterity biology might soon be forcing upon YOU -- and a lot sooner than you want!

"YOU, you didn't even think of THAT! Not for one MINUTE, one half of a SECOND, did you think when you let that criminal little animal have your body, did you, you SALT BITCH?

"But YOU never think at all. All YOU ever do is FEEL! It felt SO good to let that little hotshot dump his dirty laundry in your hot little pot, DIDN'T IT?

"Don't you realize your father and I might have to pay out GOOD MONEY to send you to Puerto Rico to get rid of your --unwanted cargo?"

"Don't make me blame it all on Mac please, mama?" the battered beauty wept, "Don't, don't m, make m, me do THAT to my poor, poor li' l baby, please?

"It, it wasn't really HIS fault, mom, I, I taught him how. And, and Daddy, Daddy might jus' get mad enough at 'im t' KILL th' poor li' l soul!!!"

But such pleas are unheard by a heart of stone.

"Oh, YES, my dear, you WILL!" hissed a serpent triumphant, "You WILL name your dear, sweet little lover boy the CULPRIT, you will brand him the INSTIGATOR ... You will tell your Daddy that your MAC is the snake who led you into such dirty, DIRTY, criminal behavior. That, that he's a DEPRAVED LITTLE MONSTER and CRIMINAL. And I sincerely hope your father DOES kill that innocent-eyed little hellion, your doting Daddy's precious little pet cadet, that, that SMARMY little cutie pie, Brecken, Brecken, BRECKEN!!!"

The Black Witch's hatred of poor Leto never abated.

The roughing-up persisted in a steady, devastating barrage against her sore and beaten body and mind until the poor, tormented soul could resist no longer. Hammered and battered into compliance, our little heroine at last surrendered all, her pride, her free will, her everything to The Black Witch's sinister design for her beloved little lover boy's long and fatal fall from The Brass's grace:

"Y-yes, m-mama!" a broken fawn sobbed from the depths of her sorrow in awful capitulation, "You, you're r-right, ma, I, I'll betray him. He, he's nothin' t' ME anyhow, j-just, just a-a-another scruffy li' l' c-cadet. He, he IS a m-monster, 'n' it, it's all, all j-just-just-just l-like. like you tol' m-me t' SAY it was. Only p, pl, please, please, PLEASE DON' HIT ME no more, ma!!! ... I, I, I CAN'T, CAN'T TAKE NO MORE, MA, PLEASE NO MORE, NO MORE, NO MORE!!!"

The eternal flame of love that had nurtured and brought warmth and joy to Cadet Corey Brecken in his difficult life at the academy had been snuffed out by a cruel avenger's heartless abuse of his beloved girl to be lost in the shifting quicksand of brokenhearted memories. The Deepfreeze's brutality had broken his lover girl and forced her to desert him, and their love.

The Deepfreeze's long unslaked thirst for revenge, a thing she'd harbored deep in her stony heart ever since the day her soft hearted man and his favorite little girl had brought that disgustingly cute Brecken brat into their inner circle, was at last to be glutted:

"This poor little boy has been cast adrift here," the commandant had told her that first day.

"Has he, major?" the vengeful monster recalled her master's rationale for honoring that revoltingly cute little scamp with a place at the family board. But this night The Black Witch was set free to spitefully mock her sentimental spouse's argument for Corey's introduction into the family.

"The boy is all alone and adrift here at the academy. What he needs now is a family life, friends and a little kindness," Corey's patron had said.

"Well, so what?" a stony cobra fumed in the bitterness of her worst memory.

"He feels so all alone, so lost here," The major had said.

"NONSENSE, you sentimental FOOL," ranted the witch in her silent retrospective rebuttal, "YOU let that DIRTY little SNAKE into your precious Leto's life, now it's BITTEN her!

"LOST is he?

"I'll LOOSE him in the BOWELS OF HELL, I'll loose him all right, my dear, and I'LL lose him where no one will EVER find him!"

How long has Mrs. Donnybrook pined to see that blond, blue eyed love-poaching rogue cast into the outer darkness.

That Palm Beach stray, his nibs' pet protégé had been the object of the cobra's lethal and poisonous contempt.

Oh, yes, my dear, too long had she thirsted for the blood of Brecken, Brecken, BRECKEN, and tonight his blood was to be hers for the taking.

"Well, well, well, that cuddly little stray whelp was just SO perfect for your darling little salt-bitch, wasn't he, major?

"And, oh, YES, my dear, our nitwit commandant's 'promising little protégé,' was just so, so perfect for you, you soft-hearted, soft-headed old booby, you, you grand and glorious Major Lynnwood Donnybrook!"

The Black Witch was smug, for she alone had hated that randy little cur from the start. A cold orgasm now welled up from the bowels of hell to console this vile monster in the anticipation of Brecken's discovery to his patron as the sneaking seducer of his beloved Leto.

Even better in her sight, the charming little light of both her adoring Mac's and her doting Daddy's lives was the key witness for the prosecution:

Who should arise to denounce the headmaster's perfect protégé to his patron as her seducer and, in so doing, forfeit forever her lofty seat as Daddy's favorite?

"Oh, yes, my dear, Leto, Leto, LETO will bring down their silly house of cards," gloated the cobra, "Today Brecken SHALL be delivered up unto ME, and my sharp, long-patient talons will SHRED HIM TO BITS, for my long-suffering patience has prevailed!"

"It was all quite predictable, really:

"Those two disgustingly adorable babes in the woods had run as fast as their libidos could take them into mischief; they'd enjoyed their brainless fun -- their SIN; and now their big fling had flung them straight into my trap.

"Now those love happy little ANIMALS are assured a quick trial and a harsh judgment. And then, my dear, I shall thrill to the cries and supplications I've long awaited from those two disgustingly 'perfect' golden brats as they suffer the exquisite punishments we've planned for them. SATAN BE PRAISED, ERIS BE GLORIFIED!"

Miss Bite, had done a thorough job of softening up Brecken, but such kiddy play should never be enough to quench the all-consuming fires of this ravenous witch's eternal bloodlust.

No, never while that hated, too cute little outsider and her maddeningly beautiful young rival were free to enjoy the flagrant liberty of the headmaster's favor would The Black Witch and her behemoth ally know contentment.

Sadly, such abandoned wretches can know no peace throughout eternity, for insatiability was the root cause of The Black Witch's damnation from the beginning of the beginning.

For the nonce, our lovely Leto's discovery and pain, followed by her shocking revelations to her gullible hubby was a big payday even for such a relentless spirit of evil. It cannot satiate her, for nothing ever will.

But the lovers' fall and her satanic victory over beauty and love was her palliative.

A motivating lust for vengeance and destruction had forever spurred this damned soul to the most unspeakable acts of malice and mischief. No power can ever sate the crouching, drooling, famished ghoul Mrs. Donnybrook has been and ever shall be until the ultimate Day of Wrath consigns her to the eternal flame.

But tonight's victory was hers:

The major was certain to punish both her trapped and helpless little victims.

"Oh, yes, my dear," gloated the cobra, "my proper and prideful field grade officer knows precisely how to wreak vengeance on two bad kids who've masqueraded as perfect angels and then run to the woods to sin like, like rutting animals. Our mighty commandant will never show mercy to the thoughtless, unmilitary children who've dared to insult our family's honor and slake their forbidden lusts in the very shadow of his pristine Tower."

"Oh, YES, my dear, that revolting Brecken brat will lose everything his bright-eyed eagerness to learn and altogether sickening cuteness have won him!" smirked The Beast.

"Oh, yes, dear girl!" purred The Witch, "The major's DARLING little protégé, his beloved Mac, is to be cast down, down, down into the fiery inferno by his BELOVED master, his DARLING major!

"That, that revolting little male animal, that disgusting bug, will be forever ANATHEMA, and I shall see to it personally!

"And what's more the major's special little darling -- the entrancing Mistress Leto -- that, that FILTHY little dime store chippie is fallen! The little tramp will forever remain a broken toy beneath my heel and the casualty of her own mindless dalliance!

"Oh, YES, my dear, those two excessively lovable little golden brats have debauched one another for the very LAST time; and their outdoor paradise is a naught but a lost dream of the dead, dead past!"

That specious old hag was correct in that respect: Our beautiful children were from this night the slaves of this vile, calculating and relentless monster.

The Black Witch's three heartbroken marionettes must dance in this black hearted cobra's puppet show of reciprocity, heavily laced with her personal brand of a satanic deviant's hypocrisy. To glut her morbid lust, her hawk-faced husband was to be the third and punishing puppet to caper in The Black Witch's theatre of the macabre while the lost Donnybrook wailed her victory screed, "Haspid be thanked, Eris be praised, Satan be reverenced!"

They danced for her, bereft of all they had held dear. Their all-consuming passions they have now surrendered to provide her with the rarest of delicacies at her sickening banquet of the damned. She'd suborned, subverted, vilified and stolen their love that had formerly solaced, guided and comforted them through their harsh lives.

In all her misbegotten existence she'd never had any use for love but to steal it.

She had sniffed out, discovered and used their weaknesses to defeat three loving, living and giving hearts. She'd played all three marionettes for fools, broken their hearts and was now using the big doll to punish the little ones for their cardinal sin of loving.

She had cause indeed to exalt her dark and filthy gods of discord, sedition, destruction and perversion on this, the blackest of all black nights in all those three loving hearts' lives. Fate had abandoned our three unfortunates to the living hell of a self-righteous and thoroughly puritanical society matriarch's Bacchanal of deception, blame, accusation and, above all, the punishment, punishment, PUNISHMENT of Brecken, Brecken, BRECKEN!

When the major returned to what had once been his happy home, Leto's love for her Mac had been beaten out of her. The heavenly joy of her Beautiful Love Adventure was put to flight in the roiling sea of the pitiless torments of an expert criminal in the art of child abuse. Our pretty heroine's love was lost in the endless nightmare of guilt and pain an unnatural fury had forced upon her.

She'd surrendered all and been left, bereft of friends and solace, to weep the bitter tears of a woman-child drowned in the angry sea of her jealous mother's vengeance.

The Black Witch's virulent physical and psychological insult had so overwhelmed and dimmed poor Leto's keen wisdom that her storied wits which had long guided our lovers through enemy territory had snapped beneath the avalanche of that vengeful enemy's rampant fury.

The only thing our battered beauty knew any longer was that ugly things like this were not supposed to happen to pretty little girls:

"Maybe it WAS all Mac's fault?" she questioned her own better judgment in her pain and weakness. Her heart knew it a dirty lie, but was it not a lie she must repeat to survive?

She was still sharp enough to know it was.

"I, I love him so," she mourned in her agony, "Oh, how can I do this to him?"

But torture had steamrolled her resistance flat, ripped what had used to be her pride to shreds and reduced her to a puppet.

In the shame and shock of losing everything she'd cherished, our heroine had been suborned; and stark survival dictated that she had to evade further abuse at any cost.

"Maybe my stuffy old drip of a mom's right?" a beaten, pathetic waif wept, "How d' I know?

"It, it's jus' like I told Mac when I had 'o tell 'im t' scream for 'er to keep ol' lady Bite from KILLIN' 'im:

"We, we're jus' th' little kids, 'n' WE can't do n-nothin' about what th' grownups want 'o do. So, so be smart 'n' play ball."

Maybe it was time to take her own advice.

"Maybe I should play ball with The Deepfreeze. Maybe, maybe I gotta throw my, my poor, lost little lover boy to those howlin' wolves."

She wept for him, but she must.

"I, I gotta give up!" she hung her head in shame, "I've GOTTA tell on Mac before that crazy ol' bitch kills me.

"Oh, God forgive me, it, it's nothin' but a big, fat LIE!

"What a lousy trick to play on my poor, poor li' l baby boy.

"But, but that gawdamn Deepfreeze HATES 'im 'n' she'll tell on 'im anyhow. Oh, but my precious little baby's cooked either way; 'n' this, this is th' ONLY way out for ME!"

She was correct, For her to countenance more pain at this point was unthinkable.

Daddy heard the gorgon's account of the children's "scandalously incorrect affair," and he grieved for them.

"The unpardonable crimes of those two wayward and promiscuous underage delinquents," the cobra's fangs struck deep, "require the sternest measures at your command, Major Donnybrook."

The great man had listened to the worst in stony silence. But The Black Witch had seen the sorrow in his loving eyes and rejoiced in the knowledge that her bad news had broken him. Her denunciation of our taboo-breaking golden brats to their lord and master had completely unmanned the mighty headmaster (and she was loving it), for the heavy blow has drawn him into her seismic vortex of destruction.

And now, to serve their worst enemy's monstrous ends, a heartbroken man has taken his jewel, his flower, his favorite, the dearest and best little girl in all the world aside for a dose of corporal discipline she was never to forget, or forgive.

A wayward, taboo flouting little girl had sinned against propriety's most explicit proscription. The very severest of all punishments was to be applied.

A father and a daughter who should never again live as they had lived or love as they had loved disappeared into dread silence of the major's den.

Leto was more terrified this moment than she'd been in her life.

And she had every right to be so:

Her dad, the warm and caring dad she'd known for years, had metamorphosed into a grim and heartless executioner. Remote, estranged from a guilty little girl's love, a monolith of doom cast a black shadow over her.

"Oh, merciful heaven," her terrified mind cried out in the fearful silence of this calm, cool withdrawing room torture chamber, "this grim faced stranger cannot be th' same Daddy I've known and loved all my life.

"He, he scares me more than anything!"

She labored hard to catch her breath, but could not; and in this familiar yet suddenly strange place poor little Leto knew the cold grip of mortal fright.

Her whole world had turned suddenly ominous and eerie as she was led to the den for the whipping of her life.

"Oh, Daddy," she gasped as he'd closed the door behind them.

But The Black Witch's spell had been cast and there was nothing more to say. Nothing would ever be the same for any of the Donnybrooks again, for tonight a loving father and a hero-worshiping daughter's bond of love and trust would lie forever sundered.

Oh, yes, my dear, this night Leto and Daddy had been conscripted to dance for the vile diversion of a soul that's been damned since the day of our world's Creation.

The Deepfreeze was witnessing the fruition of the bumper crop of discord, a seed she'd sown herself:

In our proud major's pain-blind eyes, his own little darling must have duped and betrayed him. His best brightest and girl had blithely betrayed him, his academy's good name and his family honor.

She'd renounced her high place as his princess to chase after a randy, rutting little male animal and an outcast from the boy's own hearth and home. Daddy's bright-eyed little treasure had pursued the worst sin imaginable, a thing he could never have imagined her capable of doing, for his divine angel had run into the slough of sin -- and after a younger boy.

Without any consideration of the dire consequences of her illegal, immoral, utterly forbidden and thoroughly scandalous behavior, she'd set sail on a madcap spree to satisfy her own selfish appetites -- and HIS!

HIS?

"Wait till I get my hands on HIM!" the great man's rage erupted to torment him.

His storm clouds only darkened further in the heartbroken anguish of a loving father's desolation:

"My little girl!" he grieved silently, "Her only consideration was for herself -- and that infuriating, fair haired ANIMAL!

"This is NOT the good sense and level-headed responsibility I've tried to instill in my eldest daughter, and by my sterling example."

No, she must never again be his special girl. Never must he hold her so dear post her apocalyptic revelation.

"Love me, Daddy!" Leto had demanded as her right as the fairest and wisest.

"Love me, SIR!!!" Mac had begged, not verbally but with those disarmingly irresistible sky blue eyes. The poor boy had been so lost and alone the mighty man had succumbed to his charm (as had his pretty Leto).

"Well, such sentimental frivolities are all over and done with tonight," the major now concluded, for tonight it was to be an upright father's prime imperative to punish his wayward and capricious wood nymph, his beloved who quailed before him, for her crime.

Yes, he must beat the animal lust out of his devious and sinful little girl.

Good luck with that one, major:

An headstrong, attractive and affectionate woman-child had tasted the intoxicating sweetness of young love's inescapably heavenly honey. And after tonight's firestorm of abuse has ended she'll be bound to crave much, much more of just such earthy consolation to assuage and sustain her after this direst of tragedies.

No, dear commander, you'll not command her in this, for her shocking discovery and the extreme punishments which had quickly followed it must be solaced just as soon as her comely body heals.

Now a desperately frightened little girl gripped the back of an office chair as per her executioner's order.

She was mercilessly whipped by her angry papa until she'd screamed uncontrollably beneath the red-hot flames of the strop.

The man made sure he drove his haughty little princess well beyond the point of surrendering her pride, her will, her everything to the stinging, burning, insatiably demanding pain.

The great man broke his own precious little girl like a cadet.

He made her forfeit her humanity to grovel at her master's feet like a whipped animal as had all the boys before her.

A fuming, self-righteous major had humiliated his daughter so grievously she was determined never to forgive him for forcing her to lose control and debase herself at his feet like a crawling, cringing brute. He had shamed her intolerably. He'd knocked her off her pedestal, methodically denuded her of every shred of her self worth and broken her spirit in the same way he'd broken his cadets.

In this unbearable moment, in their once comfortable home turned torture chamber, Leto's undoing was complete, and The Black Witch's triumph realized, for the two most prideful of all Donnybrook peacocks should never be reconciled.

Listening to her just-too-perfect daughter's disgrace outside the den, the gorgon rode triumphantly above the world in a black cloud of orgasmic release. The great man's unforgiving strop outraged poor Leto's soft and yielding flesh and left the mark of its burning brand across her helpless, dancing quarters until she keened piteously in her awful extremity; and The Black Witch and her spies celebrated our beloved heroine's shameful downfall.

Her envious family had proven her most implacable enemies.

A repentant supplicant had then bawled her tear-drenched confession to Daddy. Trembling and lost in the deep shock of separation from her Mac and her Daddy, Corey's beloved sex-schoolmarm regurgitated her beautiful love story. But beneath her wrathful father's withering stare the beauty of Mac's love goddess's fairytale romance evaporated. Capture and punishment have contaminated their love story and turned our two beautiful children into ugly sinners. For parental consumption Leto must transmute their classic romance into a contrite tale of two naughty kids who'd flaunted legality and convention to hide in the woods and do those deliciously forbidden things they were forbidden.

Thoroughly and painfully chastised, Mac's beauty queen tearfully admitted she and her own true love had secretly courted, fallen in love, kissed passionately, touched tenderly, lusted voraciously and yielded themselves up to the flames of their sinful and severely proscribed passion.

With eyes lowered tearful she described how the overwhelmingly inescapable joys had inundated them. In the humiliation of capture, defeat and submission Corey's broken blossom confessed how they had attained love's earthly paradise in an explosion of pure passion.

And, most importantly of all, her elder's suborned supplicant confessed that it had all been Mac's fault, all that bad, bad little boy's idea; and that she'd merely been his dupe, his victim of circumstance and an innocent bystander:

"Oh, yes, yes, yes Dad, dad, daddy, it, it, it was, was all, all, ALL Corey, Corey B, b, bracken's do, doing -- all, all that, that dirty, DIRTY MAC'S IDEA!!!" screamed a poor little animal begging for release from pain, "He, he had, had us ALL fooled, DAD, 'n' I know, know he mus' be, be th' DEVIL!!!!

"NO, NO, NOT ME:

"WHIP MAC, DAD, DAD, DADDY, WHIP HIM, HIM, HIM, HIM!!!"

Here was the out for which the commandant had been searching.

It was all he needed to hear.

It was the only thing he wanted to hear, and it was the only thing he would allow himself to hear. It had been The Black Witch's lie and poor Leto had been coerced into selling her lover to her grownups.

Now our grand and glorious Major Donnybrook had all the evidence he needed to comfortably blame this whole thing on an impudent upstart, a pushy little non-Donnybrook culprit and, quite conveniently, his minor subaltern.

Most importantly, in her now skewed perception, it was the lie of convenience that had ended her unbearable torture.

But at what price?

It was a perfidy hateful to her because she knew she had sent her own true Mac to a hell worse than the deepest, darkest, hottest fires of perdition.

She so longed to tell the truth now that her torment had abated; but to what end should she?

The torture would have continued and never ended until she told exactly the same lie once more.

Poor Leto hung her head in shame.

Her heavenly trysts with her ardent hardy pony had brought them just as low as her horrifying prediction to Mac had said, and now even lower than she could ever have imagined in those bygone abstract thoughts, for her grownups had already hurt her so -- and nor was it over.

She still loved her beau, even in her unbearable fall. Her tears burned like fire, for she knew her beloved little sex pupil was fated to face her father's terrifyingly over the top punishments her angry father's wroth should wreck on the more-or-less-innocent body of the boy she'd named her seducer.

"Oh, but Corey will still love me, I know he will. He, he'll understand I jus' had 'o do it, I. I know he will," she hoped and prayed in her faith in him.

She knew him and she knew he'd gladly bear all the horrible torments her father would surely have visited on her without Mac's suffering body to shield hers. She knew her hero would brave it all a thousand, thousand, thousand times over before he would betray her, as she had betrayed him.

"Oh, Lord!" she panicked, "Daddy must NEVER even suspect that I was his sex-teacher!"

The killing avalanche of societal condemnation and persecution bourgeois society reserves for its cheeky little sex pioneers must be escaped at all costs. With the realization she did not have the strength to face being put on public exhibition as Sex Schoolmarm Leto, impudent taboo-breaker and woodland nymph, Mac's celestial sex teacher's courage fled her.

No, not her but her healthy, lucky-till-now little Shetland pony must face the howling wolves in the cold, hard world of discovery, condemnation and exposure; and he must bear it all alone. She'd left it to him to face and accept a fate so horrible she'd run away and hidden her dimpled cheeks and pretty face at the very thought of it. The carrion furies of societal judgment were to lick and gnaw at the broken, dismembered corpse of her lover boy surrogate, while lucky Leto's perfect beauty should remain intact.

She knew him and she knew she might rely on his silence:

He had sworn a terrible oath on their eternal love never to reveal any part of what they had done together, nor where they had done it, nor even that they'd met in secret outside the big, drafty dining hall.

Leto knew her Mac would remain constant to his word, even unto death.

She knew he would never break, not even under the cruelest of tortures.

Leto knew her Daddy, too: She realized the major would punish her lover boy horribly for all of those enlivening and invigorating things they'd done and been to one another in the sunlit glen of their own dear trysting glade.

She knew Daddy would tear Mac up. But she also knew she could never hope to save him without sacrificing herself, and she could never dare do that.

"Well, uh, Mac, Mac's a boy, isn't he?" her head persuaded her heart, "And, uh, boys 're supposed t' be used to the rough stuff 'n' able t' take it, aren't they?"

She could never have borne the icy desert of her elders' endless condemnation and flagellation for another instant. Our adorable Leto had been made a pawn in The Black Witch's ugly game:

"WHIP M-MAC, DADDY, NOT ME!!!" the demoniac cobra's talking doll wailed in the punishing nightmare of the great commander's lash.

Pictures of their rosy love trysts raced madly across her tortured consciousness as the headmaster had beaten her. Her love for Mac, his love for her and the ineffably intoxicating beauty of their earthly paradise with her love in her arms flew fleetly past like Technicolor pictures on a movie screen.

But now all her cute, luckless, baby-kitten dreams must be drowned in the merciless horror of her parents' unleashed fury:

"Oh, Lord!" she sorrowed, "It was all just too perfect, jus' too, too beautiful t' last after all."

Where was the regenerating glow that had lifted our beautiful too young lovers heavenward in the ecstatic flight of their electric union?

Forever lost.

Where was the vital regenerating lightning bolt that had jolted two beautiful children in love to awaken to pure elation when they'd come together in the heavenly paroxysm of their heaven-sent release only yesterday?

Proscribed as contraband by order of the grand and glorious commandant.

The ecstasies of yesterday had passed today into the long lost realm of forlorn remembrances.

Why?

Because torture turns true love false. Because eternal love is lost when eternity is slowly, tantalizingly ticked off in the everlastingly painful seconds of a truly loving girlfriend's agony.

"Oh, Lord, how could all those heavenly things we said and did in our love have been so wrong?" she moaned, "I was so sure our love was so right, so very, very right."

But the grownups had declared it wrong, and they control everything, don't they?

Yes, Leto's angry, cruel, terrible and inescapable grownups were free to employ any method of persuasion at their disposal. And, when they'd brought their ghastly tortures to bear, she'd handed over everything to them, even the ardent schoolboy she still loved so dearly.

Her grownups had overtaxed her outraged body until she'd begged for their mercy, their grace, their condescension, their kind permission to say and do exactly what they wanted her to say and do.

A repentant sinner had recanted each and every one of her "shamelessly inappropriate" acts against her noble family's honor,

And only then was the physical torture withdrawn.

But now the conversation turned unpleasant:

The grave topic of tonight's family meeting was to be her parents' plan for little Miss Leto 's upcoming prim, proper and highly disciplined education within the very tight constriction of an out of state parochial academy.

Suddenly, our sly little adventuress found it hard to choose between this latest psychological torture and the grueling inferno of Daddy's burning, stinging, bruising physical abuse.

A tediously boring, gloomy and frightful universe of talk, talk, talk about a most difficult future for our little heroine hung dismally in the calm, cool night air.

Leto must sit uncomfortably through a protracted and humdrum mapping out of a procession of confining, puritan-monitored tomorrows our frisky little coquette should never be able to stomach.

"Young lady," her father intoned with his finest aquiline severity, tinged with just the correct degree of icebound sanctimony, "for some time now, your mother has advocated an out of state parochial boarding school for you:

"Now, this school is miles away from our present home and completely removed from our lives here.

"There your strict, parochial education will be undertaken at an all girls boarding school."

"Oh, GROSS!"

Only this morning she should have been at liberty to shout it. But on this dark night of discovery and exile Daddy's little disgrace could only think it.

"It is located in the Northern Midwest, "the great man continued, "Heretofore, I've said no. I'd always preferred to keep my favorite little girl safe at home.

"But it seems that line of reasoning has been rendered obsolete by your reprehensible conduct, miss.

"You've shown open contempt for our way of life and you have failed to honor the wonderful home and family life I have so generously provided for you here.

"Obviously, you care nothing for our family, or its good name. Very much to the contrary, you have graphically demonstrated that you are no longer the lovely little girl I'd cherished and held dear:

"No, miss, you are now a scandalously delinquent young coquette whose uncontrollable urges have caused you to run amok. And you've done so at MY academy -- my place of work where I can ill afford to have your flagrantly scandalous misbehavior blacken our good name.

"I find myself with no recourse but to concur with your mother and stand behind her evaluation of this problem.

"Henceforth, you are to be educated, regimented and disciplined in a faraway Midwestern all girls' boarding school. No boys whatsoever are allowed on campus. The only males there are a few elderly professors and some common, strictly segregated, kitchen lawn, and laundry help.

"It is our opinion that you'll be a lot safer matriculating completely free of such distracting temptations as seem to possess your confused mind here. Such temptations have driven you to practice deception and commit the most scandalous and forbidden of all acts imaginable, to engage in what can most charitably be described as your ... indiscriminate folly.

"You cannot be trusted at a school full of rowdy young male animals like, like this, this MAC:

"I, I must say I am nothing short of DUMBFOUNDED to learn of that, that boy's unpardonable treachery!

"I'd never have suspected it of a boy I, I've always thought to be a model cadet, an excellent boy, and, and a boy I've shown special favor.

"I, I am at a loss to know how he DARES to show ME such blatant, such, such inexcusable, such barefaced INSUBORDINATION!"

"Oh, golly!" Leto gasped inside, "Daddy's REALLY gonna to give my poor, poor li' l baby the heat!"

Maybe this would be the last chance she'd ever get to own up and save her lover boy, "Leto, girl, you got just a tiny little hint of what he's gonna get, and that was way too much for you, so you, you know what's he's up against," she tried to talk herself into being brave enough to come clean, "But can I tell Daddy the truth he doesn't want 'o hear when I KNOW he'll whip me for it?"

No, pretty Leto had had every last scintilla of courage beaten out of her.

Her sad eyes were full of tears for him, but fear had frozen her, gagged her and rendered her mute.

"That FILTHY CUR has most certainly shown his stripe, Lynwood Senior. BRECKEN has shown you he was NEVER worthy of your patronage," urged the victoriously vicious Black Witch reverently, emphatically and hypocritically.

Leto's red hot passion for Mac versus her overpowering self-interest were locked in a tug of war. But to survive this long night of The Black Witch she must suppress her feelings and play along.

She was tempted to think it might even have been better never to have known love than to go through the flaming hell she was suffering. She knew she was wrong, she realized it was cowardly, but she must save herself. She must let her pitiless grownups eat her more-or-less innocent little lover boy alive.

"Oh, I love him so," she wept, "He, he gave me such joy.

"How, how can I?"

To save herself she must let them put him through their churning, crushing, killing meat grinder. If she dared defy them they wouldn't hesitate to tear her apart in his stead.

"I'm sad to say your words have been proven correct, dear," sighed a deflated commandant, sadly resigned to the prospect of punishing the non-Donnybrook sinner in his two little favorites' taboo and ill advised comedy of errors love story, "I shall proceed against my fledgling protégé, a boy in whom I once saw such promise-

"But that, that's all over now:

"Cadet Brecken stands revealed as a treasonous sneak who's poisoned this silly girl's credulous mind. He's been the author of her undoing, a blight on her existence and now he's turned her into a lewd delinquent.

"Not one of you is to give this, this Cadet Brecken a sign that there's ought amiss at suppertime tomorrow.

"Brecken is not to have a single clue that I know of his perfidy until I am ready to act.

"THAT is an order which pertains directly and specifically to YOU, Miss Leto Donnybrook!"

"Oh, poor Mac!" Leto's broken spirit cried out within her, "What have I let him in for?"

(The horror of this thing they were forcing her to do stabbed through and through our poor, weak heroine's heart like a dozen razor-sharp cavalry sabers. Her hot blood ran ice-cold at the specter of that unbearable array of trials her little lost lover must endure for her sake.)

"Attend to your father's words, you whoring DISGRACE!" stormed an infuriate harpy, affecting moral injury.

Their eldest daughter was a bawling, crawling mess, yet her elders-and-betters were unmoved.

"You have heard my words, daughter," the major's eyes flashed, boring a hole straight through his erring daughter's resolve, "I have given you an ORDER, miss:

"You no longer have a secret romance. You've confessed everything, you silly little wench. It's all out in the open now, miss. You can no longer pretend innocence!

"I am ASHAMED of you for being fool enough to have been deceived and, even worse, duplicitous! You went right along with that little lowlife's sweet words, his stolen kisses and the, the damnable caresses of that, that seducer!

"You've deceived your loving father and mother. YOU have hidden yourself -- and him -- away from us in the woods because you KNEW what you did was wrong, wrong, WRONG!

"At supper tomorrow YOU, my flighty, filthy young flirt, will carry on in your accustomed loose filly tradition.

"Yes, miss, you will flaunt your charms in the face of your partner in crime. You will desecrate the propriety of our table one last time. You will carry on in the same way you've done when the two of you were sneaking around under our noses and telling dirty jokes at MY table. You'll carry on as you did when you made forbidden dates in the dining hall ... AND carried them out in the woods.

"Tomorrow at supper you'll continue the same unladylike behavior your sly little seducer expects:

"You will do all this TOMORROW EVENING, miss!"

Broken, insulted and injured beyond endurance or even sanity, she must comply.

But she tried one last ploy:

She hung her comely head and wept to elicit Doting Daddy's pity. It had always worked before this dark night of startling revelations and cruel punishments.

Post discovery, Daddy was no longer doting and our poor little soul's ruse fell flat.

"Your tears no longer move me, Mac's salty bit o' fluff!" the great man braced her, unruffled, "You, my charming little baggage, SHALL toss your carefree curls and tell that beloved little viper of yours one of your nastiest dirty jokes. And, when that filthy, godless, Communist pygmy laughs, I shall lower the boom!"

The image of being forced to set her lover boy up for his inescapable tribulation of pain and banishment gave our beauty no peace.

She could no longer hold back her tears.

"You will STOP that unladylike sniveling at ONCE, Miss Donnybrook!" was her fierce chief's command.

After two or three tries in the certain knowledge that she would be beaten severely if she failed, she staunched her tears of remorse.

How she missed her loving Mac's soft and tender caresses to solace her pain.

She'd been torn apart. She must cry but, forbidden the luxury of human release, she must do so deep in her wounded psyche. Her wicked and intractable judges must never suspect she was mourning the loss of her Mac.

The commandant mapped out his campaign strategy against his outcast protégé:

"Are we clear on this?" the major demanded an immediate answer from his errant hussy, "Do you know what you are to do, Miss Leto Donnybrook?"

Poor Leto was grieving for the loss of the two males she'd loved so completely before tonight's debacle. Stripped of everything except survival instinct, she must quell even her tears. To escape her enemies' extreme reprisals she'd retreated to a hiding place in the most inaccessible regions of her soul.

Mac was surely to be a casualty in a campaign she was powerless to resist but had been dragooned into abetting.

Her close-knit bond with Daddy was forever sundered. She was her Daddy's favorite no more. And, after the merciless way he'd humiliated her, her love for him was a thing of the past.

Both of the men she loved best had been taken from her.

But what of Daddy?
The major was heartbroken.

Now he must eschew the adoration of his best beloved child and kick his best beloved cadet-protégé out of the family. He must strictly forbid all future intercourse between Cadet Brecken and any Donnybrook for all eternity. The great man had loved his golden brats, but he could no longer afford such a liability as love.

He must no longer give his love or accept it from the two children he loved so dearly. He must not love them, tainted as they were.

Now the great man stood menacingly over his daughter and awaited her answer.

Pure terror evoked the abject compliance of a beaten dog. His severity demanded but one answer.

"Well, girl?" barked the dour commander curtly.

"Yes, Daddy."

It was the only thing she'd ever dare say beneath her father's smoldering, furious and domineering presence ever again.

She grieved for the boy she'd offered up to the leveling typhoon of her father's self-righteous fury. She bemoaned the blindness of her brokenhearted father, a loving patron turned vengeful juggernaut ready to flay his human half's pet protégé alive to satisfy the feigned propriety of his robot side's Deepfreeze hypocrite.

Our mourning heroine knew this mess was all her fault:

She'd been the one so anxious to brag up her amorous woodland adventures in the ostensible privacy of her own bedchamber. But her careless words had betrayed both pretty lovers into the anxiously waiting jaws of her unnatural mother's trap and propelled them into the hell of shame, punishment and the freezing cold of banishment.

Her poor heart was desolate when she recalled that it had been she who'd brought this inescapable flaming tower of puritanical wroth down upon them.

Was there no place in all this world that was hers?

Leto was learning the lesson Mac had learned when he'd cried his heart out on a tropical cold front porch that was not his in a town that was not his in a world that was not his. He'd learned then that he was nothing but a pet to The Mad Carlotta. His grandmamma had adopted him as a replacement for her deceased Toy Pekinese, Buddy. The difference between dog and boy was that the Buddy had never been packed off to such a nightmarish obedience school as The Tower Military Academy.

Were none of our poor Leto's secrets safe from the prying eyes and ears of the envious spies surrounding her?

They were not.

Sadly, in this Grownup World children were (and are) mere chattels and pets, kept merely for the amusement of their gigantic, boorish and bullyragging elders.

The one place she had dared to think herself secure, her home, was revealed as a vipers' nest in her awful waking nightmare tonight. Our poor, benighted miss had failed to realize there could never be a secure place for Daddy's Precious Little Pet. Decidedly not when evil siblings and a vengeful mother envy Daddy's pet that distinction.

Those misfits had an ax to grind. And they were grinding it to behead their heretofore fortunate and beautiful rival.

She had allowed herself to be caught in the very trap she'd warned Mac their enemies were baiting for them before the first of their honey-sweet woodland trysts. Tonight that trap had slammed shut and her dread enemies had stripped her of pretense, tortured her and made her surrender Mac to them.

And then they'd forbidden her to cry for him:

As a devilish climax to their cruelty they'd used the man who'd been her loving Daddy only that morning to punish her and then issue their frightful commandments against the lovers.

She'd given her adoring Mac up for devastation. She'd been co-opted into their ruthless quicksand of torturous inquisition. They'd made her say their words, doom her lover and now they were exiling her.

They'd coerced her into blaming everything on her more-or-less innocent love pupil. She'd surrendered him to a cobra who had from the first day of their love's awakening tracked them to ground. The Deepfreeze had known the golden brats were in love the day Leto had brought Mac to Daddy's august table. From that first day the cobra had hated them, plotted their fall and, finally, coerced a confession from Mac's love goddess.

Powerless in the face of her reptilian mother's evil, she could divine no way to escape it:

She'd never be free to come clean with Daddy. Doing so would have made things so much worse for her -- and no better for her poor Mac.

"No, Daddy can never know the truth!" she reflected, "the truth's just too expensive a luxury for me."

Nor must the cold and unforgiving world around the kids ever know what had passed between her Schoolboy Mac and his loving Schoolmarm Leto. Their woodland paradise that had shielded our taboo lovers' delight in their heavenly embraces must remain forever untold.

Leto, who had been Mac's brave, kind, gentle guide through the essence of life's sweetest mysteries yesterday was reduced to the vile rank of her scheming hypocrite mother's broken toy confederate tonight.

A physically perfect young beauty, Mac's girl was scarcely the dauntless heroine of the flowery classic romances of literature.

But Mac's sweet, flowery, darling, gutless Leto was his very own beloved heroine, and she is ours.

Leto is not to be confused with anyone the least bit dauntless.

Mac's little darling was engaging, compelling, intriguing, enchanting, exciting and enticing, but never dauntless.

Such singular qualities belong to other heroines perhaps, but never to Corey's fetching love goddess:

Leto was born into a pampered life of ease. When hotly pursued and painfully coerced by implacable tormentors she lacked the self-sacrificing spirit of those unflinching heroines from the flaming pages of classic romance:

She would never be prepared to leap from the highest parapet of a menacing Norman knight's castle with the fair Rowena. Mac's cuddly little lover girl could never have braved the sanctimonious scorn of her peers a la Madame Bovary, Heloise or Hester Prynne.

No, Leto's trials and the awful pain that had impelled her to surrender were not the stuff of romantic fiction. Her pain was far too compelling, for it had been real and no idle dream of yesteryear's fiction.

Our young lovers' enemies were just as bad, wrong and reprehensible as the old villains of storybook romance. Their villains were amoral sneaks, liars, cheats and two-faced hypocrites. In storybooks, they surely would have been defeated by the overwhelming force of good:

It was too bad for our golden brats that their enemies were real. And it was tragic that the only stalwart champion they might have looked to for succor, a decorated war hero, had been facilely subverted to act as The Black Witch's executioner.

Yes, it was too bad for our two little heroes that real life bad guys win when they're adults, and kids lose because they're only kids.

You who have never been tortured will never know what his Leto and her Mac suffered at the hands of the unfeeling brutes in command of The Tower and our helpless children's destinies.

Pretty Leto was then and would forever be our star towhead's beloved. She who had been his first, most fervent and most intimate lover he would love unto the last day of his life. Never should he turn his back on his beloved, nor shall we.

Torturers have had their way with Mac's proud young beauty. And, if you are in the hands of torturers long enough, they shall have their way with you.

She'd fallen in with her hideous mother's deceitful game under The Witch's most sickeningly extreme methods of persuasion.

This unnatural mother's (until tonight) insuperable rival was now to be exiled into the snows of a Midwestern exile and to face further humiliations in some ice-bound parochial girls' prison.

Her doting Daddy was lost to her. Her adoring Mac was never again to be seen or even spoken of as long as they lived:

Oh, but Corey's lady love had her kindly parent's carte blanche to speak to him and give him the kiss of death at his last supper tomorrow night:

"Oh, yes, my cringing little slave girl, I grant you free rein to tell the dirty joke that will doom Becken, Brecken, BRECKEN into my waiting hands," gloated the bloodthirsty Deepfreeze, "Into the hands of one who has so long and anxiously anticipated his precipitous fall ... and PUNISHMENT."

Leto realized Mac was to be her surrogate sacrifice to be given into her elders' cold and inescapable wrath to save herself and her heart wept for her love.

Oh, but her father's hot hellfire must burn her lover boy to save her. Yesterday the headmaster was Mac's kindest and most powerful supporter. Tomorrow his revered chief was to be his executioner. Now his powerful arm must brand the writhing quarters of the protégé he'd so loved. And all for Leto's sweet sake.

The fiction of impeccable Donnybrook rectitude must be supported by her half-pint superhero's silence. Mac must forever remain the Donnybrooks' unswerving pillar by admitting nothing of what had passed between them in their glen.

Leto's faithful lover must forgive her lack of courage and face her father's wrathful onslaught by himself. She knew he could and would do so. Corey's pretty little seductress knew him right down through to his skin, and who better than she to know?

Her assumption that her Mac would accept the pain as his hard lot in their awful crisis was correct.

Brecken, Brecken, BRECKEN was at last helpless, friendless and loveless at the foot of the altar of Eris and it had been the perfidious practices of The Witch, The Beast and the rug-rats that had brought him there. Their sneaking, their spying and their criminal torture of a helpless young girl to extract a specious indictment against her lover had doomed Leto's lover to the academy's earthly hellfire.

The disturbing little boy they had hated so long was their helpless quarry. He should be doubly punished while they sat on the sidelines to mock him with the intelligence that his torment was coming to him compliments of his own true love's naming him her seducer.

Cadet Brecken was friendless, naked and deserted by his ex-patrons. And his diseased enemies itched to grind him fine by applying the unendurable shame and loss to him that only a total outcast can know.

They meant to bow him lower than low beneath the fury of his dear old headmaster, for the commandant's was a fury carefully engineered and set in motion by their own ghastly tricks.

Brecken, Brecken, BRECKEN shall cry out in the endless perdition they'd contrived for him.

He must pay them back ten thousand, thousand, thousand fold in the currency of his unheeded tears for all the pent-up bitterness and envy they hoarded up against him for being lovable.

The cobra, that unforgivable priestess of Hecate, that devotee to the rampant confusion streaming from the snaky head of Eris, had made her own pretty daughter, our adoring schoolboy's hot love goddess, scream in a storm of protracted agonies she'd suffered at The Deepfreeze's thorny hands until Leto had offered up her beloved to feed her enemies' ghastly and perfidious hunger.

The major believed his faithful little protégé to be guilty of deception and predatory practices against his best beloved.

That great man, so easily duped and suborned to their common enemy's cause, was a devastating machine of destruction now set in motion to punish a helpless little boy with the unfettered fury of his mighty hand.

"Better," gloated the dark conspirators, "that annoying little cock-hound, Brecken, Brecken, BRECKEN'S, dear old headmaster shall turn his back on that disgustingly cute protégé after he's thrashed him. His loving foster father will cast him into the outer darkness for us."

"Now this much, much too adorable, little annoyance is to be thrown out of our lives at last!" gloated The Deepfreeze, "Is this not a deliciously diabolical twist to my victory over life and love?

"Corey the culprit, those credulous fools' 'good old Mac,' stands accused by the guileful words spoken through his pretty little girlfriend's pouting red lips."

Corey was adjudicated guilty in absentia by his hoodwinked patron. He was "responsible" for leading the major's easily deceived little darling astray by their common enemy's testimony from the those same ruby lips that had welcomed him into her forested love nest. The Witch's lie had cast a poor, weak little girl's more-or-less-innocent lover down to burn in the hottest fires of The Tower's too real hell.

That lie had not only delivered Mac up to them for humiliation, it also hounded The Black Witch's pretty rival with remorse.

Discussion was at an end and the house retired,

Destiny too often sends us defeats, and failure is no stranger to us. Innumerable stumbling blocks bar our paths to lives of comfort and ease. Reverses slow what halting progress we do make to follow those maddeningly illusory dreams of success.

But we have some triumphs. And these lend us the fortitude to carry on in our uphill struggle to reach that transitory dream: The Happy Ending.

The Great Balance tips and tips again. Ultimately, our successes regenerate us and we continue to strive ever upward through that thorny pathway of trial and error we call life.

We've just read of our beautiful children's errors.

Herein lie their trials:

The morning after the shocking discovery of our underage lovers' adventurous dalliance the elder Donnybrooks sat at their kitchen table enjoying an early cup of coffee.

"Leave Leto home with me today, Lynnwood Senior," suggested the major's unforgivably unforgiving spouse, "I do not believe she's been properly subordinated to your plan re her seducer as yet and feel that she may require further persuasion to convince her to act in concert with your wishes in the little matter of bringing down that, that jumped-up little FRAUD, that, that salacious little MALE ANIMAL."

"You may well be correct, dear," agreed the great man, "I did detect some reticence in her. And her seducer seems to have the power to command her --"

"Yes, he had us ALL fooled," lied The Black Witch, a born hater who'd always loathed our Corey, "I do believe the frisky little trollop is planning to warn her corrupter of your plan for his rightful punishment."

Our poor outnumbered heroine's heart sunk lower.

Her own dear Daddy was about to turn her over to this withering vengeance machine for another day's extremely unfriendly persuasion. The mighty Zeus was turning Mac's little Aphrodite over to her punishing enemy without turning a hair:

"Leto, you are to remain here to be home-schooled by your mother today," the almighty commandant passed sentence on his cringing waif in disfavor, "Tonight at supper YOU will be the one to signal young Corporal Brecken's downfall.

"I shall wait patiently throughout the day for your mother's instruction to take optimal effect on you. Your exemplary mother will stiffen you up for our upcoming field problem.

"Yes, I expect you to be the one who denounces this penny-ante traitor, this snake-in-the-grass Lothario!

"You will show him up in front of everyone, and then I shall proceed against him:

"I am going to TAN YOUR LITTLE BOYFRIEND'S HIDE for him, my darling little CHIPPY!"

"Oh, DADDY!!!!"

But Daddy had left.

And a terrified little girl burst into tears and flew terrified for the imagined protection of her bedroom.

But that refuge proved to be no more a sanctuary this morning than it had last night.

"You are MINE now, my pretty TROLLOP," howled the banshee of vengeance, "Prepare yourself for PAIN!!!!"

Leto screamed in the throes of her abuser's torture, but her screams went unheeded.

Her pitiless tormentor entered, punished her rival for the great man's affections savagely and kept it up all day long to drive home her point (and delight in her beautiful rival's awful shame).

Meantime, our ingenuous Cadet Brecken wondered that day why his kind master hadn't spoken to him either at breakfast or at lunch.

He was also puzzled by the conspicuous absence of his adored inamorata.

But it's not a junior cadet's place to question his highly placed and munificent benefactor's motives.

At suppertime Cadet Corey waited anxiously in the cool of the cavernous junior school dining hall for the stately arrival of his beloved headmaster's family.

He stood at attention behind his chair anticipating the grand entry of his devoutly reverenced patron -- the tsar and autocrat of the Tower Academy.

But uppermost in his mind was the even greater expectation of an even more glorious advent:

The triumphant entry of his own lovely May Queen.

Our half-pint hero fidgeted, his heart brimming with joyous anticipation.

"ATTENTION!" was at last called by the cadet officer of the day.

The great man breezed smartly in and took his place.

Our reverent headmaster tapped his fork against his water glass.

Total silence ensued and the reverent major invoked his blessing on the meal.

"SEATS!" was called.

And little Corey's Brecken's Last Supper had begun.

Outwardly things were very much as they had always been.

But Corey could see that things were nowhere in the neighborhood of what they should be.

The joy of anticipation he'd felt soon turned to the bitter ashes of disappointment as this meal commenced:

Then his heavenly Leto, slunk in, hiding her fair face away. And it was a face heavily made up to conceal her sore cuts and bruises. She was ashamed of the beauty marks with which her thoughtful old mother had decorated her this long hard day of cruel subordination into the enemy camp.

A forlorn Leto slid silently into the seat next to her Mac, a place where they had yesterday been so happy.

He wondered why his pampered lover girl, the princess royal of the junior school, had showed up on time for this meal. His stylish Leto had never been on time for one meal he could remember.

Where was her cheery greeting for him?

Where was her warm smile of welcome?

There was none.

It seemed to him a wax dummy was seated stiffly and uncomfortably beside him.

Was there a sly pinch for her favorite's fanny today?

No.

She dared not speak a word, for she knew her Mac was forever lost to her. Her mind was numbed with pain, fear, loss and confusion.

In place of her accustomed merry greeting, his graceful beauty winced with pain when her arm had accidentally scraped against the back of her chair as she sat.

Corey caught sight of a dark, wide bruise on that adorable arm when her sleeve had been brushed momentarily aside to reveal the mark. His congenial and loquacious little dinner companion of a young boy's soon to be broken dreams moved haltingly, sat stiffly and spoke never a word to him or anyone.

She was sitting right next to him, but she seemed so far away.

The beauty who'd dreamed of being Missus Corey Brecken was alive no more.

She'd been replaced by what seemed to be an inexplicably corpselike effigy.

"HI, Leto!" her lover piped in hope.

But she remained silent and impassive.

Hope, his final torture, now faded into the past along with all of those happy memories of their former dining hall jocundity.

His love sat lost in the guilt and heartbreak engendered by her part in his coming avalanche of horrors. Those horrors she must call forth to destroy her unsuspecting lover.

She knew it was inevitable, but she hid her face from it -- and from him.

She was under strictest of constraints never to give the boy she loved a hint of his fast-approaching day of reckoning:

"I, I must never let my poor Mac see the dread in my eyes. I jus' better keep 'em lowered or, or he'll KNOW!"

Those wondrous orbs he'd adored for so long no longer dared release the pent-up oceans of sorrow -- her tears.

Never must she disobey her egregious father.

No, Corey, things were not as they should be and they never would be more.

Never when your high spirited Leto had hung her proud head so low were they as they should be.

But she would not raise her eyes to her beloved's.

She looked not right or left. She kept those kaleidoscope orbs hidden from all the world.

How could things be right when his girl stared so fixedly and despondently at her plate, and only there.

It was all too evident that this beautiful little girl's happiness had been driven out of her by some inhuman and unknown means.

But how could that be?

Was she not the beauty queen of the junior school?

Was she not Daddy's little darling?

What could have changed everything in just one day?

The answer hit him with the world-changing force of a thunderbolt: "They've BROKEN her!"

No one could ever have recognized the look of a fellow human being whose spirit has been broken to the whip better than a little boy who had been so broken. He'd seen that same whipped dog look in his mirror image that frightful day his headmaster had broken him. He'd seen it in his own red, shamefaced reflection when The Tower's breaker, a merciless tamer of bad little boys, had taken such great pains to break his own high-flying little spirit and bring a lively spark to heel.

But to do it to her was unthinkable. How could his patron, an officer and a gentleman, have brought himself to practice such an unconscionable act of torture on such a helpless fawn, his own best beloved daughter?

How could he have brought himself to break her like an animal?

But he had.

The Top Brass had broken Mac's adored Leto.

"How could he hurt her like that when, when all she wanted was to love me, and, and be adored by me?" raged the soul of a cadet infuriate.

Corey knew he was powerless to avenge her in this nightmare world of punishing titans, but he burned with an unquenchable thirst for revenge against the academy's most powerful adult for this inexcusable brutality against the body of his precious little love queen.

As junior cadet he was in no position even to question the will of The Brass and Mac knew it. The vile abuser who had practiced this sickening cruelty on the lissome form of his beloved (and fairly innocent) little leading lady must be inviolate.

Now hatred smoldered hot inside him.

Both his fiery introduction to her Daddy's strop and Leto's own wise words of instruction had warned him never to buck the system, it bucks back.

And tonight he was to find out just how hard it bucked.

This little boy was powerless before the naked might of his elders and betters. A cadet should never think for a minute he might question The Will of The Brass as they frowned down on the entire thoroughly intimidated cadet corps from the lofty perch of their unassailable Power.

But tonight one little cadet hated The Brass!

One little cadet wanted to kill his strongest taskmaster!

One little cadet despised himself for being so small and weak he couldn't take a stand against The Great Man. He hated himself for being powerless to fight for his beautiful love goddess. Careful schooling and frequent beatings had taught him well that he must never stand up for himself, but did chivalry not demand that he stand up for his girl?

Was that not worth the whipping he was certain to get?

God, how he hated their accursed, well-oiled abuse machine. He hated that The Tower had never been brought to book, much less pronounced guilty of its unspeakable excesses and innumerable crimes simply because that Great Dispenser of Punishments was "always right."

Tonight Corey Brecken hated himself and the whole world for allowing these wrongs to go on and on and on, unquestioned and unchecked.

Yes, grandpapa, yes, grandmamma, military school "made a man" of your ten year old.

From feudal times, the emperor, or the mafia don, or the lord of the manor, has taught his first son how to balance the ledgers to administer his estate in perpetuity; the second son was sent to the priesthood; and the third son was trained to kill for the state and advance the system's fortunes -- and the family's.

Empires have pushed aggressively out into the world to prey on the wealth and resources of others weaker and less well organized.

Soldiers were required for this and the soldiery has been composed of boys who have been kicked and beaten enough to build up such a head of angry steam, such hatred of those who punish them that they have always been delighted to get out there and kill their punishers' rivals.

Unchecked avarice has predictably spawned endless wars, and now little Corey Brecken had been all pumped up to get out there and be sucker enough to fight the next war against whatever manufactured foreign foe the actual domestic enemy-in-charge sells to him.

Seething with anger and crippled by the crushing weight of his low rank and adverse circumstance, Corey glanced across the dinner table and saw hatred, spite and hungry expectancy looking back at him from the faces of our beautiful lovers' avowed enemies.

He was frozen at the sight of a victorious Black Witch about to strike. Her attendant spying, smirking, plotting hellions were obviously watching, waiting and panting for his blood.

Six malicious eyes were trained on him, for he had long been the hated and haunted prey of their ceaseless hunt. Three revenge driven jackals were about to taste the sweet blood of one Cadet Brecken. Corey's fall, his extreme whipping and casting down from their father's grace were to be their blood feast.

Three sweating, starving carrion beasts grinned at their quarry maliciously in their hideous moment of triumph. The shocking sight of his and Leto's smug worst enemies, breathlessly awaiting her lover's doom and the moment they could mob him to lick his vanquished bones clean, froze the blood in his veins.

These once trivial small bores had never been able to make him feel like a hunted animal before, but tonight their hour had come. They knew it and so did he.

Suddenly, a lethal epiphany panicked our half-pint hero:

"They KNOW, they, they know EVERYTHING, EVERYTHING we did, everything we've lived for, everything we took such pains to hide from THEM!"

Corey saw his sworn foes eye his succulent little body with the keen, excited hunger of a pack of famished hyenas.

His merciless natural enemies were sizing him up and totaling the life expectancy of crippled elk calf Corey Brecken as he lay exposed on the endless plain of a sun-scorched African veldt.

They were contemptible in their new found power.

They obviously regarded him as the butt of some lethal. hilarious cosmic jest while they leered down upon their towhead quarry voraciously, coldly and eager to possess and rend him.

They made no bones about showing their trembling prey the saliva dripping down their hungry jaws and their vicious, bared fangs. Theirs was the glare of a pack of hungry-for-blood scavengers inspecting their helpless prey at their leisure while they measured up every inch of our succulent little cadet's meaty body for their orgy of gore. They'd counted up every ounce of flesh they longed to devour and each drop of blood they could sip from the prostrate form of their delicious kill.

These Deadly Donnybrooks, these waiting, watching beasts of prey, the unprincipled wretches he knew had always been his and Leto's most implacable enemies from the very beginning were boldly measuring him and inspecting him with bad intent.

They openly displayed their carnivore's thirst to shred every inch of his fallen carcass and drink every drop of his spilt blood.

These vengeance-famished hyenas meant business.

He saw the secret schemers, those sneaks and plotters he'd always known to be his and Leto's avowed enemies, for what they were and what they had been from the first: Bloodthirsty monsters that had stalked him and his ravishing Leto from the first.

Bold in their triumph, these wily sneaks now felt confident to reveal themselves for the ghouls and bloodsuckers they were. Insatiable rabid beasts that had devoured his love goddess, they now couched in wait to lick his bones clean as well. They were ecstatic in this hour of his imminent, unconditional and unendurable surrender to the all consuming fires of disgrace, punishment and an exile lonelier than any he could ever have imagined.

In their provident past his fair and overconfident Leto had always assured her gallant that, while they must exercise top-secret care to avoid detection, she was in complete control of the situation. The canny Leto had always been able to lord it over the restive mom and her drippy spies. Our young lovers were then so certain their enemies would never gain the upper hand.

Alas, fair Leto had made her faux pas and their reptilian enemies had broken Corey's adorable little general.

And tonight these unspeakable enemies of life and love sat in domination of the dinner table battlefield. Our golden brats must bow down before them, feel the shame of their forbidden love's discovery, feel the branding of the lash against their flesh and then be driven into exile.

These hungry monsters were scant moments from the realization of their savage goal. The dogged hell-beasts were biding their time. They were waiting at the ready for the mighty lion to choose his moment of the kill.

When our leonine major has mauled his wounded elk calf protégé, these ravenous hyenas should descend upon his bloodied and broken corpse en masse and tear his bleeding, broken body limb from limb.

Corey saw his deserted castaway's future written across the tightly drawn lines of his hateful enemies' over-expectant, tense faces.

It was evident that not one Donnybrook had ever won a poker hand: The famine in the scavengers' jaws and flashing fangs, the relentless yearning in their burnt-red vampires' eyes had telegraphed their knockout punch to the doomed little boy.

Helpless to resist, drawn into their cleverly contrived, ever-tightening noose, their quarry sat motionless before them. He fidgeted uncomfortably, for he knew he was about to be punished beyond his endurance. His foes had this lone and deserted boy right where they wanted him.

They enjoyed seeing him squirm. They knew they were soon to thrill to the sound of his pain-wracked screams from the fierce lion's office.

A little lost cadet, he was completely at the mercy of his implacable adversaries, enemies at once ruthless and disinclined to forgive his past bright successes when they had sat glumly in the shadow of his brilliance and watched him win the prize. But tonight he was a friendless stranger, a lost soul hopelessly entangled in their diabolically clever network of intricate schemes and vile contrivances.

Our lost half-pint hero was struggling for egress to no avail from their austere, authoritarian net of unforgiving judgment and torture.

"Oh, yes, my dear, this very night we are to have our deliciously horrible fun with you, Brecken, Brecken, BRECKEN!!!" The Deepfreeze's cold, dead cobra stare of unadulterated hatred told him.

Tonight he was The Black Witch's squirming voodoo doll. He was destined to be hurt again and again and again by The Tower's strong, vengeful and merciless breakers.

His slavish fate had been decreed by Eris's handmaiden:

He was to be scathed and vivisected to delight his bestial, drooling enemies' mad caprice. And he must countenance whatever torments the soulless keepers of this madhouse academy might deign to visit upon a helpless boy's trembling, writhing flesh.

The great man was no exception to the Donnybrook anti-poker face:

When the mighty lion had caught sight of his "good old Mac's" admiring eyes in entering the dining hall, he quickly turned his face away from his ex-protégé to find a reason to chat with the grotesque cobra by his side.

There was an ominous chill in the great hall on this unhallowed eve.

A massive storm front hovered over the almighty major's normally congenial board.

The threat of impending tragedy was palpable in the tense air as Leto's august father fixed his little girl with an inescapable lightning-bolt of demand. A killing shaft from those piercing eyes sent his broken fawn the mute command:

"Tell your dirty joke, girl, and open the floodgates of my fury against your little seducer."

Her eyes begged for mercy, but found none in his.

She must signal the onset of her implacable grownups' vengeance games. She must tell her lover boy the joke that would wholly disenfranchise and destroy him.

Suborned, broken to the whip, a submissive little slave girl obeyed her lord and master.

Our comely broken blossom, only yesterday her gallant Corey's very own true love, but tonight The Black Witch's conspiratorial chattel, was close to tears. But she was proscribed from showing emotion by her almighty lord and master, a dangerously angry heartbroken man.

Tonight the commandant was nothing other than The Black Witch's engine of vengeance, forged in the blast furnace of disappointment and disillusionment -- a destructive weapon.

The revulsion she felt for the vile thing she must do made her shudder in the freezing chill of her family's cold hearted purpose.

But The Lord and Master of The Terrible Tower and the overpowering hegemony he held over all those there present, had dictated that she jump through his hateful hoop to betray her lost love quickly or face a fate unthinkable.

To serve the putrid ends of their reptilian enemy, Mac's cruelly conscripted lady in red must promptly hand him over to his punisher with a joke, for orders are orders.

(But our clever Leto had hid a clue inside her jest that she knew both golden kids would pick up on. It was her tip-off to Mac of his imminent danger, and the intelligence that he must face it all alone.)

"Get this, Mac:

"Th' Lone Ranger says to Tonto, 'We're surrounded by Indians, kemosabe.'

"An' Tonto says to th' Lone Ranger, 'What you mean WE, white eyes?' "

She'd relayed her bad news in secret kid's code:

"Corey-boy, you, you 're in for it, 'n' I, I can't help y' anymore. I can't, can't even LOVE y' anymore; 'n,' 'n' you, you gotta take your medicine ALL ALONE!

Her eyes begged her lover's for forgiveness. He loved her and forgiveness for any fault was and should always be her carte blanc. He'd already seen the effects of the extreme cruelty they'd forced her to bear, and he understood.

Before the glowering grownups could catch on to her slick tip-off, Mac's love goddess scampered across to the Indian side of the table to unsheathe her scalp-knife:

Mac's own true love spoke up for all to hear, "Okay, Mac, now it's YOUR turn t' tell ME a dirty joke, 'n' make sure y' tell me a REAL DIRTY ONE, lover boy!"

"Why does it have to be now?" his frantic mind wondered as his alarmingly accurate understanding of what was to come gripped him like the cold hand of Death.

If only he could find some halfway sane answer to the convoluted maze of this much too worldly for a ten year old disaster.

He called on his Eternal Spirit:

"Oh, God, why do I have to be me?

"Why can't I be someone else, ANYBODY else!

"Why can't I be someplace else, ANYPLACE in the world -- just, just so it's not HERE, not NOW?

"Oh, GOD, I'm REALLY gonna get it!

"Please, PLEASE don't make me be me -- not, not TONIGHT!

"Oh, please take me away from HERE and NOW -- PLEASE!!!!"

Questions, questions and more questions cascaded through his desperate brain.

He cried out from the fearful darkness of this horrifying moment of truth, this unthinkable moment, this moment when his precious lady love had thrown him to the dogs across the table like a chewed up, spat out scrap of meat.

"Can't I just die right now -- PLEASE?"

No dice, Corey. It is to be you and it is to be now, and it is going to be, as you've surmised, a lot more than you'll ever be able to stomach.

Your enemies have you, boy, and you're going to dance and sweat and cry for their disgusting entertainment.

Our little castaway must once again face the crippling injustice of a legion of more unendurable punishments and humiliations than he's weathered in the past.

Ten thousand times ten thousand, thousand, thousand nightmares of the flesh the powers that be were sure to pour over him like a river of molten metal await our half-pint superhero, and he must take it like a man.

Escape? Impossible: Runaways had always been methodically brought back, whipped and sent to walk the everlasting bullpen.

"Why can't I even faint t' postpone what's coming? Even, even just for a few minutes?"

But Corey had never passed out in his life:

How he'd wished he could have blacked out to end the pain when another boy had accidentally dropped a hammer out of a tree house on his head during their boyhood construction of that haven.

No such luck.

At this ridiculously out of context moment, he recalled yet another anti-blackout when a violently angry Katie Robertson had swung an iron-bound swing at his head on the Coconut Row Elementary School playground and connected. It had been two years ago when the enraged schoolgirl struck him on the temple with her murderous tool -- and her bad intent. He remembered the blinding pain of that deadly blow. The agony had been unbearable.

In that hour of ineffable stress, he begged The Almighty for the release of unconsciousness:

No dice, kid.

Snapped back into the horror of the here and now, young Corey was dumbstruck.

Tell a joke?

In shock he was unable to utter a single syllable.

Tell a joke?

To compound this agony of embarrassment he'd begun to laugh involuntarily, hysterically and for no reason.

This was the almighty lion's opening, and it was exactly the event for which his majesty had awaited, his signal to press on and bring this saucy crippled elk calf down.

The commandant of beasts sprang nobly forth to fell his hapless prey:

"You WILL control yourself when you've been privileged to sit at MY table in MY presence, Cadet Corporal Brecken!" the enraged headmaster reprimanded his jangled junior in nervous prostration.

"You know the rules here, my fine young friend; and I am SURE you realize that raucous laughter in this orderly dining hall is STRICTLY forbidden."

A terrified Corey wished with all his heart that he could obey, but he was too far gone with fright. He'd lost control of himself and laughed on.

"You are to STOP that ridiculous laughter at ONCE, cadet," came the even sterner command, "Do you UNDERSTAND ME, young sir?

"You SHALL put an end to this insubordinate frippery AT ONCE!"

"The, the c, cadet re, re, requests per, per, permission to, to to be ex, ex, excused, sir, sir!" Corey managed to blurt out between uncontrollable guffaws.

The prelude to a little lost protégé's brat-fry has been concluded and Cadet Brecken's symphony of shame was now to begin in earnest:

"NO, my fine young sir, you may NOT be excused.

"I, I am not inclined to pardon YOU, my viciously precocious little blue jay -- for ANYTHING."

"The, the, c-cadet-"

"NO, my fine young game cock, I do NOT excuse ANYTHING you have ever done -- and nor will I EVER!!!" snapped a trapped and isolated little boy's enraged overlord.

The man expeditiously pressed on to pronounce our boy's sentence:

"Cadet Brecken, you will stand up and accompany me to my office IMMEDIATELY."

Our fear-frozen little boy stood straight-upright at attention and obeyed his commander's order without delay.

At this evening's festive board all three of the golden brats' vengeance-hungry enemies were ecstatic. The joy of their signal victory over our defeated young lovers flared up furiously in their unspoken hatred from the raging fires in their monstrously cruel gaze:

Our beaten and broken Leto to a puritan all girls' school up north, and her thoroughly whipped and suffering Mac back to Heeler Hall and The Beast. And this time without the protection of his kind master.

Black Witch Mom watched in delight as her two helpless little captive animals endured the stinging whips of her destructive vengeance spree.

Corey's ruthlessly suborned ex-sweetheart breathed a fervent prayer:

"Oh, God in heaven, please, please don't, oh, please don't let Daddy KILL him!"

The remainder of the sheep in the big, calm dining hall grazed on unconcerned:

Better that Brecken be marched off into the shambles than they.

Our condemned boy marched briskly beside the stiff-jawed man, to the left, abreast and in step.

They posted directly into his place of execution.

Corey knew his "fast friends" of yesterday's convenience had deserted him and that pain and hopelessness were to be his sole companions at The Tower from this day forward.

If he could only black out!

"Sorry, Corey," Destiny laughed in his face, "Heroes are not for fainting, little soldier: Heroes have to stand up and take their medicine like men."

The major began:

"My, my SORRY excuse for a daughter has confessed to me all of your carnal and CRIMINAL dalliances in that accursed woodlot on the way to town. She has confessed it to both her mother and to me.

"I have been given to understand that you, my strutting little gamecock, led that, that goofy little dupe off into the lewdest and most inappropriate behavior imaginable. And, and that you IMMORAL, DELINQUENT children have been up to some extremely criminal nastiness there every Saturday afternoon since January.

"I am now about to PUNISH you for that, my fine little Mister Brecken; and now I want YOUR confession -- and I want it NOW."

The man has demanded an admission of the boy's part in what his true love's grownups viewed as our beautiful children's crime.

"Now I am going to hear YOUR confession, my fine feathered bird:

"Did you meet and, and err secretly and with such shameless boldness and, and SCANDALOUS frequency?

"Is it true that, that you've been, been laying your filthy dirty pipe in MY daughter, boy?"

The shock of those crude words his headmaster had chosen to tar their holy love made Corey recoil. The insult was like a jolting slap cross his face and the boy dearly wished with all his heart the man had hit him rather than baiting him with such an insult to the taboo lovers' childlike try for their own true love's bliss.

But our tough towhead immediately rallied to his lady's defense. A small, defenseless elk calf in the deadly paws of a gigantic lion, a frightened little animal about to be slashed, mauled, torn and eviscerated by a big one, struggled up through the black clouds of his dread to speak up for Leto's honor.

He had no idea where he found the guts to do so, but he poked out his brave bantam's chest to declare:

"Sir, no matter who has told my commandant such a rank falsehood, I must stand up against such a slander against Miss Leto Donnybrook's good name!

"Major, I have to speak up for the lily-white honor of your fine young daughter. I, I could NEVER support such a falsehood!

"If, if any, anyone has, has offended my commander, it, it, it's MY fault and, and no one else's!"

262

The great man's was a rage beyond rage then. He scowled blackly down over the boy captive trembling before him.

Mac knew he was about to pay for his ineffectual defense of his headmaster's most beautiful daughter in disgrace.

"High-sounding words, you bold-faced little LIAR," rumbled a volcano about to erupt.

The man spoke softy, but he was furious with this impudent little boy's audacious pluck.

The man proceeded immediately to prosecute the boy's punishment:

The lion made a manly effort to hide his rage as he calmly directed his tiny elk kill to assume its pose of shame.

"Now, cadet, you will get hold of the back of that chair and hold on to it until I've finished with you.

"Leto's little lover boy, are you?

"Well, Leto's toy soldier, you are going to pay for a father's shame and his daughter's disgrace and heartbreak. You're going to pay dearly for your misdeeds -- AND your confounded IMPUDENCE, my boy.

"You have been denounced for your, your treason against us by your very own partner in crime!

"For that bare-faced LIE that you have DARED to tell me to my face you shall pay a price, a price that will make you wish you had never heard the name Leto Donnybrook in all your LIFE."

Corey gripped his whipping-post chair hard and hung on for dear life while his enraged commandant made mincemeat of him. The man drove the boy through the worst of all the stinging, burning, sweltering, wailing, begging, screaming infernos he'd ever experienced in all his hard, hard life at the academy -- and therefore the hardest in all the world.

Our little hero stood up bravely for his bitter medicine while an infuriate father laid his infernal strop across his burning, stinging hindquarters with insane force.

Corey wailed to assuage his brokenhearted headmaster's loss. A brutally abused little boy had been caught in the vengeful snare of The Deepfreeze, a misanthropic deviant who'd hoodwinked her too credulous husband into the unenviable position of her executioner.

The commander has this night been wheedled and suborned into prosecuting his two especial favorites' extremity.

The great man branded this epic travesty into the heaving pelt of his more-or-less-innocent ex-foster son's throbbing, twitching, suffering flesh while as the outraged screams of a soul in torment permeated the entire building.

Corey was that little lost soul enduring the flames of this unbearable Tantalus and he sent his loud lamentations heavenward. The boy howled out his supplications even as this man he'd so respected and admired, he who'd only that morning been his kindliest mentor and most powerful friend, exacted his unendurable toll for those "high-sounding words" of a "bold-faced little liar."

This boy the man had loved from the start, this boy the man had so enjoyed teaching and guiding into officer-hood, this boy was on this dark night of young love's discovery and punishment anathema to his patron.

A brokenhearted man flaying a brokenhearted boy had lost his protégé. He's already lost the heart of his beloved and delightfully cunning little girl as well, for now he has broken her heart, her body and her spirit:

The great man's best beloved had left him for good on this tragic night of discovery, torture. confession and falsehood.

These were losses none of our three sorely afflicted lovers and losers would ever be able to reclaim. Their open hearted innocence has been raped and murdered by a high priestess of evil. Their hopes for love and happiness were at an end.

But now our great man has someone to blame. To that end, he whipped his screaming protégé-scapegoat mercilessly, furiously, thoroughly -- and for everything: Someone had to pay for three lives in ruins and the major's screaming non-Donnybrook subaltern was paying the tab for all.

The entire plethora of this wicked old world's sins were coming out of Corey's hide. The complete catalog had been placed (comfortably for all save one) and squarely on one little boy's frail shoulders, and he was screaming his little lungs out for their expiation.

Well, isn't that what scapegoats are all about?

Scapegoat Corey must pay for aiming so high as to woo and win the fairest. He was paying for accepting her love, the most breathtaking of all prizes.

He was paying for lying to his commander-in-chief, though he could scarcely do otherwise. He was bound to keep a solemn oath sworn on their eternal love. He was constrained by an oath of honor to persist in a lie so crucial it was the only protection of his May Queen's honorable reputation. Tattling on Leto was a thing he would never do.

But that was just a fraction of all the reasons his master was making him suffer the unbearable humiliations of his day of wrath:

Our towhead superhero was paying an unholy tax for worshiping a decidedly beautiful and supremely vain little girl. His breathtaking woman-child had welcomed his reverence and invited his hot and heavy adoration. Adoration from a devotee to affirm her status as a superbly ravishing love goddess was what she'd always desired, and what she'd perceived as her due.

And Leto's beloved was enduring his wrathful master's blistering trial for worshiping a commandant so full of himself that he knew he must be none other than God's commanding officer.

Cadet Brecken was paying for his ingenuous loyalty to a military school that saw no problem in chewing up and spitting out a cheeky little cadet-upstart who'd so impudently overstepped his bounds as to love his superior's favorite child. In the eyes of the almighty academy Cadet Brecken was just another insignificant, highly expendable schoolboy cadet of the hundreds it had already torn to bits, standard operational procedure.

But his fatal mistake was that of being exiled to this far country. This bad boy had come to an array of spit-and-polish child abusers for discipline. Their personable Mac had been accepted and loved by the elite, tasted forbidden fruit and been denounced as her seducer by his suborned inamorata:

Let the young scoundrel be punished.

This most contemptible cog in his frosty grandparents' best military school in all the world was, therefore, a cog to be eliminated. A megalomaniacal autocrat with a cadre of adult sycophant-martinets with license to decide his fate were marching him through the flames of hell barefoot. Corey Brecken, the helpless toy of abusers and lunatics, was paying for a considerable catalog of sins. He was caught up in the pain of redeeming every trespass in his beloved major's own personal currency: shame, pain and outrage.

Protracted agony will always make a poor little animal in its throes wail, beg and debase itself, and our Corey was such a creature. But never would he acknowledge Leto's schoolmarm role in their tempestuously taboo affair of amour. Never would this boy confess there had even been a love tryst to the man who was torturing him for each and every heavenly moment her Mac and his Leto had experienced in the ineffable bliss of their celestial hideaway. He had sworn those intoxicating beauties should remain forever a secret.

Even as his enraged headmaster's bold faced little liar and fallen favorite screamed his shame and paid this awful debt he still admitted nothing.

The slightest affront to the almighty Major Donnybrook, that monolith to prideful arrogance, was an impudence to be avenged savagely and without a scintilla of mercy.

Corey'd been sucked into a decimating vortex of withering rage. The anguished object of his high and mighty chief's apotheosis of retribution reeled beneath the insupportable weight of this very epitome of child abuse.

Little Corey has long since paid for all his shortcomings a thousand, thousand, thousand times, over and over and over at the business end of the major's strop, yet a child's unbounded torment continued, long, hard and unabated. Never in this world -- or any other -- could the strongest monster ever called to battle extract a confession from a little boyfriend who's given his word to his little girlfriend in the name of love. Never in his life would one word against his beloved's supposed honor escape the wailing lips of our underaged Lothario.

Corey's love goddess has read her devotee aright, "My Mac 'll never tell, I just know it!"

Corey Brecken has prostrated himself, a willing sacrifice, at his girlfriend's feet. She has offered him up to her mother's stygian goddess perfidy, to Eris and her charnel altar of hatred and envy. For

Leto and from Leto her faithful Mac was to be burnt at the feet of The Black Witch's pagan goddess of discord.

Savage cruelty against both taboo lovers has been vigorously prosecuted by a committed executioner and dupe while those two spirits of evil who'd incited it hid their hideous and profane faces behind the pious mask of societal propriety. Those twisted gorgons have had the last laugh on the major's perfect Leto, her annoyingly cute (but now condemned) Brecken, Brecken, BRECKEN and their subordinated and brokenhearted executioner.

Our sagacious little Leto had known how vilely these inexcusable brutes should gloat if they could win this obscene victory over our two too young taboo lovers. Now the unthinkably ugly thought was fact. The lovers' scheming enemies had won because of her own ill-chosen words. Now they'd brutalized our tortured little heroine until she'd lost the will to save her hero.

As our golden brats' foes enjoyed her Mac's stentorian screams from his infuriate commander's office, chagrinned Leto hid her face in shame to pray for her embattled lover's life even as her triumphant enemies laughed at her.

But her Mac had held out, and he was her hero:

Beaten black-and-blue, yowling like the filthy hound his oh-so compassionate old housemother 'd never failed to name him, Corey'd begged and screamed beneath the nuclear firestorm of his wrathful headmaster's scathing rage. But never should he confess that our lucky boy had met his breathtaking girl in secret. Never should he confess they'd hungered so tenderly, loved so passionately and given themselves up to one another so completely in their hallowed glade. And he should never admit she was his loving teacher.

In the hottest hell of extreme travail, our brave Corey now escaped -- as he had in Bite's shower room sessions -- to behold and find comfort in the holy image of his Leto's face. Even in this raging, burning crucible of pain he heeded not the angry censures his manfully flailing headmaster's anger spewed over him. He heard only his love's urgent plea never to reveal their secret:

"No one can EVER know that we meet here, or what we do, or even where we do it!" she'd cajoled him and exacted his bond, "DADDY would KILL us!"

Our half-pint hero had sworn never to confess to breaking their elders' taboos. He'd sworn never to admit they'd loved so deliciously, so completely, when the law said they were too young to trespass upon adult love turf (but they had dared it, and found it heavenly). The blissful memories of their beautiful trysts must forever remain a closely kept secret because that solemn compact was essential to the continuation of their bold adventure.

Our little lovers' exciting adventure was one a repressive grownup society had been specifically proscribed by all adult laws and mores. Leto and Mac knew full well every adult in Christendom would charge out to condemn, castigate and punish them mercilessly for their "unpardonable sin" had they fallen into The Deepfreeze's unforgiving hands.

Their vital secret must be closely kept from the prying eyes and ears of snoopers, grownups and spies.

Why?

Because the grownups would employ torture to exact confessions from our "dirty little sinners."

He was just a little boy and the pain he was going through could make him cry and scream and beg as he suffered the insupportable tortures inflicted on his tiny person by an accomplished athlete in the majority of his years, and at the apex of his manly prowess.

But Cadet Corporal Corey Brecken would never admit he'd done anything "wrong" with Miss Leto Donnybrook no matter how corporal the punishment against our littlest corporal for the lie he must embrace to save poor Leto's good name.

Heroes are not smart, they are brave, and her Mac endured to honor his promise. Not only on their golden day of comfort and delight, but here and now in hell, tossed and battered in this jolting, seething, wrenching perdition of hard-driven pain, he kept his word.

The Almighty Major Donnybrook continued the all-out barrage against his disgraced ex protégé's impregnable fortress of stubbornness as long as he dared. But with the passage of time the great man's ire abated, his wisdom overruled his murderous passion and reason finally returned to overrule his rage.

He saw things for what they actually were once again:

Before him writhed a little boy in real danger of permanent injury and not the sneaking viper his frigid spouse had painted Mac to incite her dupe to destroy him. He was still only the engaging little Mac, the same protégé who'd reverenced the mighty man and obeyed his every wish. Only yesterday he'd loved the boy and watched over him as a concerned foster father should.

What had possessed him now?

While The Black Witch had reported, and he had accepted, the notion that Mac was a clever, crawling worm who'd stolen up his own dear Leto's skirt (two years her junior) to seduce the innocent, he couldn't really believe it. As it was with The Bite's note of accusation, he knew all the protagonists in this new shady scenario too well to accept it now.

Further, no cadet placed in his care must ever be returned to his parents damaged beyond repair.

Our rigid headmaster must never seem to forgive either of those bad kids. Their profane love's sneakiness, and the flagrant audacity of their delinquent transgressions must never be condoned. But their all too human error had been as inevitable as their love had been compelling, and mutual.

The great man, sufficiently recovered from his attack of temper, could at last see an injured little cadet for what he was:

"He, he's still our Mac."

Another consideration was the possibility of a black mark against the school's good name:

If the discovery of a dead or crippled cadet ever got out, his finest military academy in all the world might be closed down, and its irreproachable headmaster's pristine honor might well be held in question. And the very sobering probability of a litigation against the academy by the boy's grandparents, should he be returned home damaged or dead, was a real concern. The great man must bow to convention, forbear and loose his tiny miscreant from hell fire.

Major Donnybrook never would forgive the transgressions of this treasonous toy protégé -- the scamp, the perfidious despoiler of his pretty little wood nymph who'd actually seduced the boy.

And he'd never forgive that girl though she'd been his heart's delight, his enchanting favorite, his Leto. No, his heart's delight had metamorphosed into a sexually promiscuous delinquent. She must never be absolved from the lurid stigma of her scarlet sins, nor should she be forgiven for flaunting her feminine charms in the face of his perfect society's legalistic hodgepodge of archaic nonsense. Mac or no Mac, Leto or no Leto the culprits must never again know the loving comfort of their exalted father's absolution.

His terrible whipping was over at last. But now the man gripped the trembling, pain-convulsed waif's arms and held him up for inspection. As it had been that first night with his housemother, it hurt Corey so badly it took his breath away. The commandant scooped his disgraced ex-protégé up roughly and held him so frighteningly close to his hawk-face that the aquiline features terrified the boy. Panting and sobbing, he quailed beneath the thunderbolt-glare of his taskmaster's piercing eyes.

The man stared directly into his tear-streaked bright blue eyes -- the same eyes that had compelled his ex-darling daughter's love (and his own).

And, in the midst of a little boy's unendurable shame and outrage, Zeus Alastor pronounced his final sentence on his fallen protégé. And ths was to be a mark of censure that would hurt the boy far, far worse than any whipping ever could:

"Cadet Brecken, henceforth you will no longer be permitted to take your meals at my table. You know that it is because you have shown yourself untrustworthy and disloyal that I herewith judge you unworthy of my notice.

"From this night forward you will find yourself another place to take meals."

Corey was lost.

No outcast's cries for mercy would ever reach his major's ears now.

"Further, you will never again speak to any member of the Donnybrook family for the remainder of your tuition here.

"I specifically and most emphatically forbid you to speak to -- or even to look in the direction of -- Miss Leto Donnybrook."

"Whip me to death, sir, but don't do this to me!" Corey's eyes begged.

He knew he could never have repeated those words aloud, for the major would doubtless have killed him for them on the spot.

"No, cadet, be silent and face this bitterest of all medicines in all the world like a man," his headmaster's steely eyes commanded, "You will never again speak a single word to my eldest daughter, not for the rest of your life, you, you unworthy cadet. And, and, if, if EVER I see you disobey this order, I will personally BEAT the insubordination out of you! ... Are we clear, cadet?"

"Yes, yes, sir!" sobbed the brokenhearted kid watching his life drip, drip, drip down the drain and into the revolting open sewer we call Heeler Hell.

The man knew he'd just stripped the boy of the vital privileges he so sorely needed to survive at the academy; but this dark night he gleaned a perverse pleasure in exposing a boy he'd loved like a son only yesterday to the academy's most rapacious ravening vulture, The Bite. What would prevent the ex-protégé's degraded behemoth housemother from killing him now?

Not he.

The vision of Brecken at the mercy of Bite was rewarding to the headmaster in his present state of wrath. The contemplation of this particular randy little Casanova's continuing trials at the hands of a criminally insane freak pleased him now:

This is not justice, major, this is vengeance.

"Wash your face, comb your hair, make yourself presentable and return to the dining hall, cadet. And there you are to finish your last supper with us:

"You will NOT raise your eyes from your plate, nor will you say ONE solitary word to anyone at my table. Never are you to speak to any member of my family, Cadet Brecken, NEVER!

"And, if you speak one word to Miss Leto Donnybrook, we'll come right straight back here and pick up where we left off.

"Are we clear, cadet?"

"Y, yes, m, major."

Poor Corey's sorely aching body has been abused beyond all endurance. But the major's battery was now eclipsed in comparison to this new, horrible, psychological abuse. The transient pain of such an extreme whipping as his master had given him mends with time. But such corporal punishment paled in comparison to this awful edict of separation from the protection of the his all powerful patron and his cruel proscription from his beautiful May Queen's life giving love.

Such an unconscionable punishment would never heal.

He'd been condemned to the same oblivion he had feared the day the major first broke him to the whip; but this time there was to be no forgiveness, no acceptance from his two most vital sponsors. This leveling stroke of separation had reduced our little fighter's dynamic spirit to dust. His youthful resilience fled him, for he'd been abandoned by everyone who had ever loved him here, and his good old foster dad had stripped him of all. The man had cut the boy off from his only true and loving friends in this aloof place where the harshest of lives were regimented by the cruelest engines of reciprocity on earth.

In his short life he'd already faced the barren desert of lone exile once -- and now he must face exile again.

He had long since become inured to the angry curses and punishing blows of his adult enemies. Thrashings predictably and habitually rained down on his resilient hide, and he'd been able to recover overnight. He was young and healthy. He had always healed quickly.

Physical blows he could support, but not tonight's killing psychological blow.

The major's beloved Mac had been cast off the sunlit peaks of Olympus into the stygian smoke and eternal fires of Tantalus. Almighty Zeus has forbidden him the consolation of Aphrodite's needful solace.

After what he'd been through, his orders were to wash, comb, stiffen his pain-wracked backbone, return to supper and sit through it without breaking down completely?

The pain was far too much for any ten year old to bear.

Yet he must bear it.

He was as alone as he had been on the first day he'd been excoriated by Grandpa Joe and marked for transportation to the great unknown of this finest military academy in all the world. The bitter gall of loneliness burned his soul, for he was just as alone as he had been when he'd been plunked down into his frostbitten grandparents' big front porch lawn chair, now so long ago and far away.

He'd burst into tears and cried his heart out then, and he broke down and cried the same way tonight:

Cast into the outer darkness of Heeler Hell, cut off from Daddy and Leto and forbidden ever to speak to her or even to glance in her direction.

This was a punishment was too unspeakable, too unbearable to be supported by the strongest of men, let alone our forlorn little outcast.

Our majestic major saw the harm his hard words had inflicted on Leto's little Don Juan. He regarded that outburst of pure anguish he'd called forth from his broken protégé. The great man had noted fresh tears in this thoroughly chastised rascal's eyes, and our prideful war hero had found great satisfaction in them.

He'd hit and hurt a place in the boy so deep the strop could never have reached it, and he had broken the boy's heart.

This angry and unforgiving father still wanted those bad kids to suffer, and the great man smiled, quite pleased with himself.

He turned his back on an ex-protégé he'd stropped to bits, then cruelly rejected, and walked calmly out on a desolate little child he'd once loved.

He was in a hurry to rejoin the others at his table.

As the great man posted into the hallway, the inconsolable lamentations of an outraged and deserted protégé rang loudly from an abandoned exile's savaged soul and echoed through the entire building.

Marooned here to be beaten, broken, broken and broken again, our irreproachable commandant's castaway gave vent to his grief. A small sacrifice to the Donnybrook's propriety let his scalding tears pour forth undeterred. He no longer cared if anyone saw him as a hero.

He's known the prestige of being the headmaster's pet protégé, he's tasted the forbidden bliss of his beauteous May Queen's sweet, sweet love and he's always realized how vital were Leto and Daddy to his survival.

And now it was over.

After a while Corey somehow regained enough strength to limp to the bathroom, wash, comb and painfully hobble back to his assigned seat.

Then it was his misfortune to endure the saddest, most solitary and cheerless meal of his entire existence.

Life with the Donnybrooks had been nice while it lasted. But now it was over and he must now endure a threadbare and forlorn existence. Yesterday two pretty young lovers had sat together and laughed and loved together at this very same table. Tonight two forcibly estranged ex-lovers sat side by side, but both were miles apart and deep in misery. Yesterday's lovers sat together on this cold, dark tonight, prisoners and slaves of The Black Witch's frigid hypocrisy. They must bear the heavy weight of their last meal together separated, in physical pain and emotional turmoil. Such a cruel mockery was an additional toll their punishers had levied. They'd been cast down from the highest halls of honor into the lowliest torture pits of hell. Two pretty little children's tearful eyes bent low in our children's forced shame to sate the wroth of her hard father and bring pleasure to that lost priestess of Satan, her mother.

Disjointed ideas gushed out of Corey's troubled brain like the spurts of bright red blood rushing from the severed arteries of a dying man.

Our lovers were ashamed, but their secret shames were theirs alone. Their shame was not their grownups' brutally enforced feigned contrition.

Our golden brats had never bought into that grownups malarkey.

No, Corey's and Leto's sorrows were their own:

Leto knew she'd been a weakling unable to resist taking her Black Witch mom's rotten deal. Instead she was dragooned into throwing her loving Mac to her mother's hyena feeding-frenzy.

She was overcome with remorse.

And her Mac was powerless to shield the girl he loved from those intrusive imps who'd engineered her downfall. Ergo, she'd been exposed to the grownups' rage.

And she had to reveal their jealously guarded secret. Corey had no way of knowing what they'd done to make her tell, but he knew she was proud and high-spirited and that they must have really done a job on her to force her to forsake their holy love.

Was this the prideful beauty who'd pushed aside the borders of convention to glory in the sunlit pastures of their electrifying Elysium?

No.

Heartbreak was the only thing left for them to share. Memories of their evisceration, the loss of their heavenly woodland trysts, the cataclysm that had ended their heavenly life together were now to be their sad fate this dark night.

They'd lost the love of the kind and generous father they'd formerly shared, as lovers share all the things they hold dear in common.

Three broken hearts will never mend.

Deepfreeze and the rug rats were swollen with pride for the chaos they'd brought upon our beautiful lovers -- and their dear Daddy:

The great man would never recover from this heartrending schism. There will be no reconciliation between father and daughter. They were far too proud to brook the shame that had been thrust upon them by the plotters 'discovery of the lovers' adventure.

Our formerly blessed Donnybrooks, the two who had once been blessed with the ability to love, would never be able to piece their family back together.

And the gruesome trio of destroyers who'd never known what love was were not interested in mending a thing they'd taken such delicious relish in rending asunder.

Never again would there be another bright-eyed cadet protégé to gladden the magnificent man's arrogance with hero worship. No, never would he adopt another eager-to-learn little "Mac" to groom and guide down the difficult path to success in the military.

This mournful man who'd nursed such lofty dreams for his beautiful, brilliant and accomplished future debutante was desolate to know that perfect girl had led Mac into temptation.

Those hopes were now but fairytales.

But now the time for fairytales was forever past.

His beautiful children, his ideal boy and his perfect girl have transmogrified into two ungrateful, deceitful little monsters.

Three warm and yielding hearts have broken. Hearts once open to love and joy have sunk into the inescapable quicksand of disillusionment.

On this Black Witch's dark night three vanquished heroes sat disconsolately across the board from three rejoicing devotees of Eris, three stone-hard hearts that had never had the least interest in love.

The Deepfreeze and her snoops celebrated their triumph.

Three children of light and life faced three lost souls as the children of Hecate feasted perversely on their despair:

They'd robbed the high-and-mighty major and his beautiful golden brats of their soppy love. Torturing the two little cuties, watching them wriggle, hearing the sweet, sweet screams of their deep duress and knowing they'd caused it all had all been so delicious to the gorgon and her minions. It had brought their own twisted brand of heaven into the horrid depths of their own stygian corner of hell.

"WHEN I WAS YOUNG AND HAD NO SENSE ... "

Corey left the dining hall after his last supper of scorn and deprivation in a state of shock. His all powerful headmaster had abandoned him to a sea of covetous enemies, boys envious of his lofty place of honor -- and his place with Leto.

In the dark cool of the apple core courtyard Brecken rested secure in the illusion that the worst had passed over him, an error soon to be debunked.

For him the worst was yet to be.

Exhausted by the shameful showing up he'd had to face, sorely hurt and depleted by the merciless beating he'd taken, and then forced to sit through an everlasting last supper with his girl without so much as a word or glance in her direction, The Deepfreeze's victim had been left desolate.

In the cruel restraint of his commandant's marshal law never again to reveal a hint of his mad passion for his inamorata, our half-pint hero was far past spent.

The only thing he wanted to do now was slink back to Heeler Hall like a whipped dog, unnoticed. But suddenly he found his path barred by an ogre:

To add insult to this uninvited encounter's injury, the churlish intruder who'd made so bold as to bar his way was none other than his Leto's rapist, the football captain, the sociopath dog.

That towering sexual predator now morphed into a monument to his own hypocrisy.

Affecting the unfamiliar disguise of an archangelic accuser, the snarling cur sneered disdainfully down on the smaller, younger cadet to blather:

"Ca-det Brecken, YOU have sullied the honor of a high-born young gentlewoman you aint even fit to raise your unworthy eyes to. I ought 'o slap your face, boy, but I wouldn't dirty mah hands on you:

"Brecken, you are nothin' but a MONSTER an' a CRIMINAL!"

Beaten and broken, yesterday's superhero made no reply. Already shamed by the grownups -- and cruelly abused by them -- our little David was in no shape to face yet another gigantic Goliath.

Corey was a fighter by nature. He might well have taken this babbling rapist on and trashed him had the commandant not so recently ripped his guts out -- but he had. And our ex-protégé in the dog house hung his once proud head and walked passively by.

His girl too had excoriated her once adored, still ardent hero.

"Oh, yes, my dear, The Prideful And Powerful Donnybrooks have hollowed out their toothsome little Brecken, Brecken, BRECKEN," gloated The Deepfreeze, "Now he hasn't even got the fortitude to stand up to a bully on my lovely, lovely darkest of dark nights."

Mac had always hated this two-faced bastard now hectoring him for a less criminal sex act than he had committed two years past when he'd roughly robbed a little girl of her virginity.

"What Leto and I shared was never a crime," our hero knew in his heart, "Love made us do what we did."

But in the eyes of our repressive society the criminality in our golden brats' romance was hers as his elder. In Mac's view her love and generosity was never a crime. He'd always known the heaven on earth she'd blessed him with was worlds removed from crime. He realized the adult courts' Blind Justice would have punished her for their paradise. That's why he'd kept their secret never to admit they'd met and made secret love.

"Let the world punish me," he reasoned, "I'll never let 'em get their hands on her!"

He held the big tub of guts before him in the lowliest despite imaginable for the brutal crime the big boor had forced upon his lovely Leto.

But this evening's Corey Brecken has been demoted from protégé to whipping boy. Now he was only an empty husk of what this morning's swaggering mini-bully had been, a thoroughly butchered corpse:

The all-powerful Donnybrook chief and his breathtaking princess had taken him to their hearts, elevated him to the favored position of foster son, loved him and been his refuge. But this night the same Donnybrooks have condemned their erstwhile pet to outcast. Leto and Daddy made him into a faltering, tiny puff of ectoplasm. Now he is so small, so spent, so rejected he dares not try it on with this contemptible senior classman twice his size.

He knew The Brass were down on him. He thought this might just be one of their canned hunt setups. It was easy to smell a rat when the rat stood directly in front of one, gigantic and reeking to high heaven with its putrid corruption.

Henceforth The Brass had earmarked Brecken to take the blame for everything.

Corey, in deep shock, failed to appreciate the tragicomic irony explicit in the archangel-rapist-knight-champion's challenge. A deviant sex criminal in this clearly contrived mock-defense of the honor of the very girl whose honor he had stolen was tripe. How could this bullying lout who'd debauched his Leto and disguised himself in sheep's clothing be taken seriously?

"Sully the honor of a high-born young lady?"

This big baboon should know all about that, but this monkey was solid brass.

Nonetheless, Corey's showing up continued without respite: up stepped our hero-worshiping poof, Cadet McNichol. The same boy who'd once compared Corey to his screen idol, Alan Ladd, was present to bait his fallen superhero. McNichol echoed the cheesy jock's insult:

"Oh, you, you brute!" his frilly house brother emoted, "I, I just ought 'o slap your face for you, Mister Corey Brecken!"

Other cadets in the dim courtyard made it clear they regarded Cadet Brecken with repugnance. They'd all condemned him but no one else spoke. They merely grunted their tacit approval of his false witnesses' accusation of a major's pet turned away by his patron.

Suddenly an epiphany struck him like lightning: "They KNOW!" Everyone at school knew what Mac and Leto had been up to.

With this epiphany Corey realized this was only to be the beginning of his woes. He was in for a killing gauntlet run.

Just as his brutalized and tortured to compliance Leto had warned him in that cryptic joke, this was a trial he must face friendless, alone -- and without her love and support:

"Tonto says t' th' Lone ranger, 'What you mean WE, white eyes?'"

No more Tonto, kemosabe.

Dizzy and unsure of foot, our hero (and everyone else's cooked goose) somehow made his stumbling way back to Heeler Hall.

He climbed the stair, a considerable effort for such a thoroughly gutted goose as he.

"Thank God The Bite's asleep!" he breathed relieved in the darkness of the hall.

She'd worn herself out by picking on his house brothers, especially poor McMoon.

Corey slunk silently to his room.

McMoon and Little Milan then gathered round for an urgent meeting (and the last friendly conversation anyone would have with Cadet Brecken before his shunning obliterated him). His frightened roomies whispered low so no one could hear:

"Listen, Brecken," confided McMoon, "You're really in for it, but, but Li' l' Milan 'n' me, we're your friends 'n' always will be. Only NOW we can never, ever let on we are:

"Word's come down from upstairs that EVERY junior school cadet's gotta HATE you -"

"Damn, Brecken, I don' know what you ever could 'a' done t' get Th' Brass down on you THIS bad," broke in Little Milan, "But NO-BODY in th' whole junior school's allowed t' talk to you no more!"

"An' if, if we do, we can only talk in th' line o' duty," gasped McMoon, white faced with terror, "They, they already tol' us it's every cadet's DUTY t' tell you you're a MONSTER an' a CRIMINAL. That, that's all anyone's allowed t' say!

"WE, we know good 'n' well that THAT can't be true, so WE aint gonna say it!"

"We aint gonna call you that, bo!" put in the plucky Little Milan (in an extremely soft whisper), "So, after this, we jus' won't say nothin' at all. Sorry, big daddy, but we're jus' small fry, we can't buck Th' Brass. After what you been through t' night nobody knows that better 'n you!"

"You're right there, son," Corey replied, thunderstruck at the severity of The Brass' punishment, "I'm sunk, roomies, but I don' want 'o take either o' you down with me.

"It, it's not your problem, so you gotta do what they say. It, it's th' only thing you CAN do. It, it's okay, you guys -- I understand."

"What in th' blue-eyed world did you DO t' get 'em THIS stirred up, Brecks?" quizzed McMoon.

"I can't tell y' that, boys," sighed the outcast, "If I told anyone what really happened, nobody 'd believe it anyways, and it'd cause a lot o' trouble for a very dear someone I swore a blood oath to protect no matter what!

"Don't talk t' me, boys, don't let on you're my friends for anything, 'cause they'll come after YOU if y' do. Boys, I've made too much trouble for too many people already. I, I don' want 'o bring my mess down on you!"

His own true friends said goodnight, and it was the last thing they said.

Everyone knew Brecken was poison.

They knew it because someone had let the cat out of the bag.

But who would profit by telling such a scandalously scarlet tale?

Not his all powerful commandant and assuredly not the haughty May Queen, Leto. The loss of face this scandal would bring to the family name was unthinkable to both proud creatures. The shame of this awful revelation was far too catastrophic for either of those preening poseurs to countenance.

Corey concluded, "It was The Black Witch!"

This caper reeked of the calumny of one of that pagan's filthy connivances:

The perfidious Deepfreeze had dispatched her cradle-creeps to broadcast the sordid details of The Golden Brats' dalliance, capture and punishment to every corner of the school. It had been The Deepfreeze's ambrosia to herald the news of our delightful lovers' long, hard fall throughout the academy. The deadly cobra'd reveled in cataloguing the lurid details of her beaten daughter's confession. She'd gloated over her tiny enemies' dehumanizing punishments, the same outrages whose commission had so delighted her at their infliction.

The tale of the lovers' humiliation and the stern major's edict of excommunication against a little boy he'd loved, but had now marooned, was particularly delicious to her. Brecken, Brecken, BRECKEN was henceforth a leprous castaway. Corey was now to be alone in a crowd of boys who had been his friends but were proscribed from befriending him.

And The Deepfreeze was loving it:

"His ex-playmates will now be his executioners." mused the witch, "Oh, yes, my dear, the whole campus is abuzz with news of Brecken's damnation. Brecken, Brecken, BRECKEN anathema forever.

"Your pet's 'seduction' of your darling easily led loose filly is the subject of every single mouth's vicious gossip, major -- Eris be praised -- Satan be reverenced!"

The witch had sent her spies to tell the tragic tale of their holy love's comet ride into the fatal snare she'd set for them. And naturally their tales were tainted with the cobra's perfidious distortions.

But why had The Beast not joined the big pile-on?

Let's hear that bloated congenital anomaly's reasons from her:

"Oh, no, my dear, Brecken's neuron receptors 're already way, way too overtaxed fir 'im to feel anything' more. Th' mangy cur's neurons have already been tortured past their optimum levels, an' by his sweet ol' beloved patron, too," mused the pervert complacently, "Blue eyes can't never fully appreciate the pent-up pain storm his dear ol' nemesis- housemother's a-dyin' to unleash on Brecken, Brecken, BRECKEN'S naked body.

"No, poor dear Corey, yore darlin' housemother won't harass her toothsome little chew-toy tonight a-cause she's content to know you're all hers from now on, Donnybrooks' little lover boy.

"Yore darlin' ol' Miss Bite kin wait, a-cause yore a-gonna scream in 'er good ol' shower playroom soon enough."

She's ached to hear him sing his strident arias of pain ever since the Donnybrooks had adopted him, spoiled him and in so doing robbed her of her own perverse fun. Now his punishment should come when he'd recovered just enough to really feel the exquisite heat she'd painstakingly planned and prepared for him.

"Oh, yes, my dear, our major's li'l pet aint nothing' more 'n th' big boss's estranged castoff now.

"No, no, my dear, dear little blue eyes," gloated the smug behemoth, "I must never allow ye to heal completely, never, never entirely, but only jest enough t' appreciate the kind o' hellfire I done helt in store fir ye, you bad, bad little boy. And now yore highfalutin friends 've done run out on ye: They done give ye to ME, Blondie!

"Oh, unholy Eris, how I always done hated them li'l Golden Brats -- oh, Hecate, how I hate them now!

"But they've done been caught out now, separated, violated and, and all through the dissemblin' guile o' my best friend, my sister in Satan, my high placed cohort.

"Mrs. Donnybrook's got 'er ol' man's huntin' permit in hand, her open season on Brecken's precious little chippie 's mind. Little Miss Leto's angry 'n' envious mom's been given free rein by her stupid booby husband to regulate that li'l spoiled piece. Daddy's ex-precious is gonna be bossed by her ma now," cackled The Beast, "My formidable Mrs. Donnybrook 'll teach that fun-lovin' li'l tramp what it is t' be a first class LADY:

"She'll show 'er how 'er own underhanded ways, th' ways of the upper class homemaker, gits things done. She'll teach that hyper-libidinous sex kitten her failure t' hide from our cold, cruel world in the secret warmth o' th' arms of 'er tender little teddy bear cadet -- his granddaddy's little embarrassment, his grand mammy's failed pet lab rat, that, that INSUBORDINATE little TROUBLEMAKER!

"Oh, no, dear, dear Leto, your blue eyed toy soldier can't save ye from us now a-cause we've got ye bof, y' wet wench!

"Th' fling ye flung with yore sexy li' l Cadet Blondie was nothing' but futile, FUTILE!

"No more teddy bears for you, missy.

"It's like yore ma says:

"It is the function of the upper class 'lady' to seek out and seduce an officer of the highest rank. She must trap an Attila and wed him. He must have th' absolute power over the common clay beneath 'is feet to crush the life out of 'em. Then she can dupe that super-brute into herdin' 'em all into the shambles 'n' leadin' 'em t' rack and ruin. They're all MEN, and MEN deserve it!

"In short, it's her job to make a cold world one hell of a whole lot colder for everyone else. And that cannot be done by hidin' from its wickedness in the arms of a schoolboy sweetheart. Oh, NO, my dear, it must be done by embracing a cold-blooded king cobra like yore pappy, a killer with unlimited license to wreck havoc on all subordinates."

Poor Mac is lost, dragon-meat; and poor Leto's been suborned by a viper to learn how to be a viper:

Mac's golden heroine was presently being taught to embrace the savage ways of this scheming, warring jungle we call a world and make it even colder. Admittedly, she's always had the makings of a sweet-singing upper-caste siren -- beauty, brains, talent, ambition and guile. Now her scheming gorgon-mom was leading her lovely daughter down, down, down the heartless trail to espouse her own signature death-style, pure evil. Leto was already a proven seductress, she'd deserted and surrendered the boy she'd loved so well on command (after a heavy dose of unfriendly persuasion), and her reptile-mom was sure to turn her from deceitful coquette into bloodthirsty vampire soon enough. The Deepfreeze knew she'd be able to model Leto like clay the day Mac's girl had given up her ardent pet cadet to the waiting talons and fangs of Eris. The Witch had subverted Mac's bright young angel that dark, dark night -- and bound and subverted her beaten-docile slave girl to darkness. Miss Leto Donnybrook must perforce shed her daydreaming cinemascope-big-screen heroine skin for the gleaming scales of a venomous serpent. The Black Witch should soon teach her tractable coquette how to use her softness and charm to scheme, to deceive, to gain, to hurt -- to kill.

And what of the girl's formerly loved Brecken The Fortunate, Brecken The Major's Pet, BRECKEN The Protégé? Leto's long lost pet and love toy has been killed. His earthly remains have been conveniently consigned to The Beast. Surrendered to the leviathan by his own true love, our half-pint hero was naught but dragon meat.

Alone in his poor little room -- his brothers ordered to hate him and forbidden to speak to him -- a sorely battered little chunk of his elders' finest military school in all the world's slag crawled into his cheerless upper bunk.

Nightmares shall be his only dreams, for what else have coldhearted The Brass left him?

Once upon a time when he'd enjoyed his solicitous headmaster's favor, Corey had become familiarized with the doctrine of predestination due to his regular attendance at the church of his model's choice. He'd congratulated himself and been highly honored to accompany his exalted commander, his beautiful Leto (and what the lovers saw as an annoying but insignificant supporting cast) to their Sunday devotions.

It had been fun while it lasted:

Anglican Sunday schools of that day were far more exacting than those of most denominations. Ergo his Calvinist audience always stood amazed to note little Corey's acumen in the history of The Old Testament. They'd wondered how one so young could know so much about the adventures of such patriarchal OLD TESTAMENT luminaries as Moses, Joshua, Samson, Saul and David. (But every little sprat matriculating at Bethesda By The Sea's Sunday school was required to consume and digest just such weighty fare at an early age).

But, in our Corey's present pariah-state, predestination evoked terror in our fallen golden brat-angel:

Cast down from Zeus's alabaster Olympic halls and into the yawning abyss of Tantalus, Corey could find no solid ground in academy's extremely shifty shifting sands. They sifted him lower and lower from his superior's beatific favor into banishment and disgrace.

When they'd been his friends the same good church folk who'd found it so easy to deny him assured him that he was certainly one of the elect: The elect are predestined to enjoy eternal bliss, but the damned are predestined to suffer perdition's endless hellfire.

Beaten, denounced, judged and marooned by his beloved foster family, shunned and deserted by his friends, this seemed a whole lot like eternal damnation to this gregarious little boy condemned to eternal isolation.

The Almighty Donnybrooks had kicked Corey out of heaven on earth; and now he was desperately frightened about his iffy prospects in the matter of all eternity.

As a castaway, our boy's chances of being one of the elect anymore looked pretty dim.

Corey was only a little boy and he had no way of knowing that politics govern -- not men alone -- but their religious dogmas. Those prideful and exclusionary philosophies bespoken in such dictum were and are colored by the political expediency of the age.

Predestination was a convenience for a Scots protestant monarch who'd waged civil war against his elder sister, a la Lynnwood Junior and Antoinette versus Leto. His war won, he proceeded with an inquisition against those of his sister's rival faith and mounted a most shocking bloodbath throughout his domain.

That "good" king of the elect was at liberty to torture and execute just as many Roman Catholic opponents as he could catch, and still remain heaven-bound. Conversely, his foemen were damned, irregardless of what good or ill they'd done.

Our highly privileged Donnybrooks were as exalted as that Scots monarch had been, but their kingdom was within the confines of The Tower:

There Good King Lynnwood must be elect and predestination was surely his ally. Whatever excesses the major committed, that privileged scion had to be the omnipotent limb of Christian Justice:

The awesome firestorm of criminal abuse the elder Donnybrooks had loosed upon our taboo lovers had been their right, for our beautiful children were, politically and expediently, tarred with the brush of the damned.

When he'd basked in sunshine of Donnybrook favor, our hero et al (save the major's envious wife and her pygmy spies -- pagans to a man) had been convinced that their golden haired favorite must be elect. The major's protégé beamed so full of promise he must certainly have been divinely chosen to be that great king's protégé.

It had been "right" for James, Queen Mary's envious and lethal younger brother to usurp Scotland's throne away from her. It was meet that he burn Catholics, for the king could do no wrong -- and must ascend to paradise.

By the same measure, King Lynnwood of The Tower must be right to adopt, play with, discard and heartlessly abuse any poor little cadet he pleased, for a Donnybrook can do no wrong. And our lovely Leto, Queen of the Castle, must assuredly have license to use and discard any inconsequential Dirty Vassal she listeth.

The Donnybrooks were strong, aristocratic and in command of everything. The father was king, and a king does not mourn the loss of his fallen and exiled pet protégé forever.

Mac's irreplaceable Leto'd wept bitterly when her family had punished her and taken her beautiful blue-eyed toy away from her, but she was pretty and there would be armies of Macs marching to her gates of love for years to come. Sure, he was cute, but what's one more dirty vassal more or less when you're the May Queen? Only a passing fancy. A discarded tool. A thing to be used and thrown away whenever his fickle (if elect) tyrant king and his faithless (yet still elect) May Queen opt to forsake him.

Corey was hounded by many a black nightmare of his own ongoing inquisition throughout that troubled night, and a long succession of such nights.

His darling Donnybrooks had robbed him of everything, his fondest aspirations and his loftiest dreams of success. Those joys he'd so fondly had cherished, his dreams of the heavenly fulfillment he had in the soft, warm arms of his vibrant queen were now the ashes of his heartbreak and regret. He was haunted by the memories of success, now failure, and the ineffable heaven of their love turned to the ashen hell of their parting.

Cadet Brecken made formation early the next day. He attended morning classes, marched through close order drill period and muddled through classes and team sports. But it was as his prophetic roommates warned him: he was snubbed, ignored and left exclusively alone by every member of the junior school's cadet corps. Everyone had turned his face from this leper, this "criminal," this "monster," this ten-year-old schoolboy corruptor of savvy young twelve-year-old girls.

This shunning was the cruelest blow The Almighty Brass had ever struck against our little shutout. Isolation was far more destructive than dear old Miss Bite's SILVER STREAK, or even his burly commandant's flaming strop, or any of the many imaginative torments they'd taken pains to employ on the flesh of their little robot-cadet, once a real, live boy.

But Cadet Brecken was attending the academy to perform to optimum, and do his best to advance in order to get back to home. He must carry on in disfavor to face renewed punishment. He must come through this, the most trying day he'd ever faced in this hard academy's endless parade of days of frostbitten desolation:

Our Donnybrook-abandoned Corey's immediate and vital task must be to search out some sequestered nook where he could conceal himself from those patrons who'd loved, then deserted him. He must hide from the sight of his highhanded ex-patron and his pretty little ex-love schoolmarm, for both then despised him.

A powerful and relentless family that had once been his bulwark against The Beast, his highly placed friends, his fastness, were now as intent upon his ruin as they had been upon his promotion.

A hurt and lonely little boy sought and found his cloistered hiding place from an angry ex-patron, a brainwashed ex-lover and her unnatural mother.

He'd done well to ferret out a haven where they could never see him, a place so far from the Donnybrook table of honor he was invisible there.

He knew he must never again look longingly upon his love goddess's heavenly face but be sequestered from her sight, to be forgotten.

Fortunately for our outcast, there was a second, much smaller, dining hall across the corridor from the great hall. There he might hide his face from them. He'd found himself a haven where he might sit, eat, nurse his ever-present bruises and a discarded toy's broken heart.

What was even better, some upper classmen sat at his newfound table. And his older fellows had the rind to converse with their beat-up little junior. It was just as if he'd been magically transformed into an actual human being again. The older boys neither knew nor cared that this animated and amusing little goober had been excommunicated by The Brass. The big boys hadn't been coerced into joining in his shunning, so they interacted freely with our towhead leper (within the limits of distant upper-lower classman civility, of course).

Our outcast enjoyed a peaceful, convivial repast with friendly dining companions this blessed noontide.

But, once he stepped out of concealment and into the open courtyard, trouble was waiting. When Corey ventured outside McAdam Hall a runty little scrap of a junior school cadet had been posted there to harass this randy little monster criminal. The Brass's goob in waiting was a nondescript runt our hero didn't recall. But the scamp obviously knew all about Leto's lover boy and his precipitous fall from grace. The shrimp had been posted there to rub our towhead's nose deep into the stink of the scandal The Black Witch had telegraphed and everyone was babbling about. The impudent instigator cried out in a loud sing-song:

"WHEN I WAS YOUNG AND HAD NO SENSE
"I TOOK MY GIRL BEHIND THE FENCE
"I LIFTED UP HER SKIRT AT THE GARDEN GATE,
"AND THEN I BEGAN TO OPERATE!"

Several more junior classmen joined in his chorus of derision against Leto's outnumbered lover in disgrace.

His haranguers laughed uproariously while Brecken stood dumbfounded by their effrontery. He was definitely chagrinned by their ill-usage of him and his lady love. Their rude implication against his beloved May Queen's honor filled him with fury. It hurt our little bully shamefully to be constrained to allow their gross insult pass unpunished. Though he burned with shame at his enforced resignation to suffer himself and the fair Leto to be scandalously lampooned by a gang of baying lamebrains he might easily have beaten bloody -- if he were not presently and permanently in her all powerful father's disfavor. But he was. And he realized at once this was yet another snare to trip him into retaliating violently against this gaggle of weaklings and instigators.

The cowardly are bold when they know that reprisals against the strong by the even stronger omnipotent shall be swift and devastating. They might mock Bully Brecken with an ease they'd never before have dared. But now he must never allow himself to betray the slightest hint of emotion in his present state of isolation and disfavor.

Emotion was regarded as weakness in the austere clime of The Tower Military Academy. A Real Man remains impassive. He must never heed the rude jibes of cowardly haranguers such as these poor marksmen eager to shoot at an easy mark, severely proscribed from reacting.

"They are my inferiors," he told himself, and he was correct.

Corey was itching to beat his beautiful Leto's rude detractors to a bloody pulp. He longed to tear them limb from limb with his bare hands, but military protocol forbade it. Rather than let them see he cared he must laugh and pretend their heartless jeers were taken as being all in good fun.

A true hero must press stoically past such fools and mockers, and continue with the serious business of afternoon classes. That was what he did.

These Lilliputian enemies were chip, chip, chipping away at young Corey's pride and sense of self-worth because that was what they'd been specifically detailed to do by his bigger enemies. The bloodthirsty carrion who'd ragged him and the unconscionable adults who'd put them up to it were sanguine in the certainty of their eventual victory over this one isolated, insignificant little boy.

The Brass would ultimately bring their proud puerile prey down. No one knew better than they when you isolate one tiny schoolboy from his fellows, declare him a knave and exhibit him in the pillory of public disgrace, his fellow schoolboys will discover what delicious relish was to be found in an unleashed mob's bloodthirsty onset. When they saw it was allowed, his fellows were tripping over one another to degrade and humiliate one of their own who'd been caught out in what The Brass called "sin." Inch by inch Cadet Brecken was being winnowed and ground down into dust and swept away into nothingness, major's orders.

Corey, their credulous schoolboy, believed what his superiors chose to drum, drum, drum into his impressionable little head. Our freckle-faced golden brat in Coventry must accept his teachers' deadly conspiracy, their devil's dogma, into his captive mind, a mind they'd carefully prepared, a mind they'd sown and tilled to yield their own reckless and destructive crop -- their child-victim's early destruction.

Cut off from the balance of humanity, pilloried and mocked by jeering vigilantes (from the commandant to the most junior of all his goobers) their tiny martyr must soon surrender his own will to the tyranny of their majority. He fell prey to their murderous indoctrination. In time their dupe must finally believe he really was what they said he was, a blight on humanity to be speedily eliminated from the face of this earth.

The grownups had but to declare him a monster and a criminal, a felon who's wronged the very family all cadets were duty-bound to love and reverence, even as Corey himself had done faithfully. Tragically ironic as it may have been, those benefactors he had so devoutly loved and reverenced, the superior whose love he needed desperately for his continued existence, had thrown him to the dogs. His patrons' love was no longer a bright reality but a broken dream, a fabrication, a convenience and diversion which had tickled their fancy. The major and his princess, the vital protagonists who moved the family all cadets must revere had deserted one cadet. His loving patrons had exposed their disgraced ex-protégé naked to be torn apart by the sharp fangs and shredding talons of his worst enemies, and theirs.

The Donnybrooks had punished him and he'd survived. But he should never survive the jeers and taunts of the mob his May Queen's mom had set on him:

The voices of the many must soon suborn the will of the one to their fatal and erroneous idea that he'd outlived his usefulness, become an obsolete and useless relic, a puff of smoke -- like the love of the Donnybrooks.

No, The Brass had but to repeat their abominable falsehood ad infinitum, to dispatch their "inform him that he's a MONSTER and a CRIMINAL, for that is your duty" toadies in order to drive Brecken mad, and they did.

It should not be The Beast's savage and frequent outrages against his resilient young body that were to bring him to his untimely end.

Corey's finale was never to be the living hell he'd so often suffered at the business end of his headmaster's strop. His was to be an even crueler destiny:

"Oh, no, my dear," grimaced the victorious Black Witch, "being broken to the whip is far too lenient an end for Brecken, Brecken, BRECKEN."

His undoing was to be meticulously engineered by unrelenting psychological warfare, the torture of his little mind, an agony which drove our despairing cadet ever onward to his own destruction. He fled the invisible whips of these hell-borne furies surrounding him. He flew desperately before their cruel blows, but he was unable to run from the slavish destiny that his blind tribal elders, his pitiless betters -- always so convinced that they know best -- had set in play.

Our ravaged and ragged little boy was running the most ruinous gauntlet of all, for his new trials were all-consuming loneliness, friendlessness and betrayal. Damned to total isolation, he stumbled blindly into the yawning death-trap the grownups thought best for the erring boy who'd been so unlucky as to offend them. He sought, but never found, succor and, at the end of their gauntlet, madness and death awaited him.

But, of course, it had been all for his own good:

Was it not for his own good that the headmaster had adopted his fair-haired boy? Surely, it must have been for his own good that his beloved Leto had taken her pleasure from his robust body and then offered that same eager to please instrument up as a sacrifice to feed her unnatural mother's pagan goddess.

Corey was SILVER STREAKED in the gruesome old Beast's steaming torture chamber the night after his ex-patron had prosecuted his own chastisement. As she beat him his dear old housemother took great pains to assure her writhing chew-toy that his almighty Donnybrooks had indeed deserted him forever. His stinking housemother took perverse pleasure in informing him that the Donnybrooks saw him as non existent.

It was well that Corey had built up an immunity to the old viper's Bite by now. The vitriolic nonsense she spewed forth no longer bothered him. A seasoned young veteran of The Beast's floor show was inured to the hard curses and resounding blows of the behemoth.

He'd been The Beast's mortal enemy from their very first encounter and he hated the slimy old toad just as much as she despised him. To Corey Bite was less than nobody. The notion that he cared a whit for what such a baseborn piece of hill trash said or did to him was laughable. The Beast of Heeler Hall could no more penetrate our hero's defenses than she had on their first nightmare shower room duel of wills.

No, it was The Brass relentlessly chipping away at him and the shunning that were to grind him to dust.

"Oh, Leto!" came his brokenhearted cry from the endless wilderness of painful separation from everything and everyone he loved broke forth unheeded, "Please, please, come back to me!"

Psychological torture was his enemies' deadliest, most irresistible, of all the weaponry in their wide array of ordinance. Their diabolical propaganda warfare had finally pricked him to madness.

They had brought this highborn little buck to ground for the slaughter.

Two startling surprises awaited Corey one day in the midst of this darkest of all travails:

The first was modestly comforting, the second horrendous.

Time passed slowly and dreadfully. Days crept painfully on and on to become weeks, Weeks weighed our hero down like lead. Months crawled like ragged crippled vagrants after the weeks to drag mortally, drearily on and on and on.

The Brass's scourge of isolation had beaten Corey down. Our condemned boy had stumbled down, down, down through the avenging furies' death-gauntlet. His blood ran cold as he ran desperately through Tantalus. It had been a longer time than he could assess, contemplate or countenance.

Somewhere in the jumbled torture chamber of his mind there appeared a clump of trees, an oasis, a welcome sanctuary for all Heeler Hell's victim- cadets. It was a group of trees growing in between Heeler and Booker halls. The trees had sheltered those harried Heeler Hall cadets, for this hallowed place was hidden from Miss Bite's parlor window on the world. It was located on the far side of the building and obscured from the dragon's scrutiny.

Corey and his house brothers had usually visited their sanctuary at free play period to get a rest from The Horror.

Corey was there one free play hour during his shunning to hide himself away from his sorrows alone.

But, suddenly, he was not alone:

Cadet Curley rushed in to join him. Curley was looking for respite from The Beast, too, a rare commodity in Heeler Hell.

Corey smiled and waved as the rough and ready teddy-bear-hugger entered the grove and sat nearby. Brecken didn't speak, for power had forbidden him the comfort of all human contact. Such had been his lot for so long he'd become used to being ignored by his schoolmates and hall brothers. Further, he didn't want to make trouble for Curley.

"Guess it's pretty tough on y' these days, huh, Brecks?" Curley asked to our hero's astonishment.

"Curley!" was the outcast's urgent warning, "Don't get me wrong, but you're gonna get yourself to a whole lot o' trouble if y' talk t' ME -- except t' curse me as a criminal monster -"

"Oh, sure, sure," grinned the boy Corey'd never once seen crack a smile or be friendly to anyone before, "I know all that crap: Th' major's put his bad mark on y' -- like Th' Phantom in th' funnies -- 'n' now everybody's scared t' let on they're your friends. But most of 'em still are --they're just chicken t' 'let on.

"Well, I'M your friend. I always have been since y' took that God-awful whalin' off o' ol' lady Bite without a yelp!

"Tha's right, I'm your friend 'cause you got BALLS, Brecken!

"Don't let my tough guy front put you off, bo. A guy who won't let 'em take 'is teddy bear away from 'im at a military school's GOTTA be th' roughest, toughest guy goin', so that's what I am, 'n' that's WHY I am."

Brecken was amazed at such a revelation coming out of Hard Case Curley, a boy who seldom spoke, except to berate his effeminate roommates, McNichol and Claire.

Our hero looked nervously around to see if they were being watched. He feared for his house brother's safety should anyone see him talking to The Tower's Little Damned Soul.

"I think what they're doin' to y' STINKS, bo!" Curley continued to speak up boldly for his brother, "We ALL do -- 'cep' for McNichol, 'n' HE'S jus' jealous that Leto got what he couldn't have.

"I don' care what y' did t' th' major's spoiled li' l princess, they shouldn't rag anyone th' way they've been raggin' YOU. It just aint right, 'n' they -- all of 'em -- aint right t' be doin' this to anyone!"

"Thanks, bud," ventured Corey, "but you're really stickin' your neck out a mile by even talkin' t' ME!"

Curley was about to make some brave reply, but they were interrupted by the sudden appearance of Cadet Claire into their sheltering arbor.

Corey's bad luck still stalked him.

The innocent-eyed little conniver had yet dedicated himself to fomenting violent chaos. This confirmed masochist had never abandoned the hope of being beaten by the fabled Bully Brecken.

The irritating pain-nut started his harangue without a second's delay, and he employed that maddening pseudo-Oriental affectation he knew Corey could not abide:

"Ho, Meestah Cloley Blecken, Missy Reeto Dlonnyblook lover-boy-sweethawt, you wheep me now, Reeto's joy-boy?

"You wheep poor Cladet Craire till the blood stleam down now, YES?

"NO?

"WHIP MY ASS RIGHT NOW, GAWDAMN YOU! ... What's th' matter, you CHICKEN, Brecken?"

"Let Brecken be, y' sick puppy!" Curley stood up for him, "Don't you know what kind o' hell they're puttin' 'im through?

"He's your house brother, y' stupe!

"YOU know good 'n' well what THEY'LL do to 'im if they catch 'im whippin' YOUR worthless ass!

"Hell, YOU'D make dern sure they DID catch 'im, too, wouldn't y,' HUH?

"What kind o' creep are you, y' lousy little puke?" his pal demanded of the pitiless masochist, "Don't y' even HAVE a heart, y' creepy li' l sis?"

But our mini hero was determined to take no notice of the deviant's rude jibes.

But Claire did not have heart, "No, you no whipee humble Clade' Craire?

"Hookay, hew ask fo' dees:

"When I was young and had no sense

"I took MEESSY REETO behind da fence.

"Me takee down she PANTS behin'

de garden ga'

"An' then we begin to COPULATE -"

That was it!

Our hero lunged at the baiting loony to shut him up permanently.

"I'LL KILL YOU, CLAIRE!" he bellowed.

But it was Curley looking out for his brother this time and the teddy-hugger was a lot faster on his feet than poor old McMoon had ever dreamt of being:

Curley intercepted our enraged hero with lightning speed. The teddy-hugger pinned him with superhuman strength and refused to let him up to avenge his May Queen's almost pristine honor.

Brecken had never believed any of his house brothers' bravado could hope to match his own, but Cadet Curley now restrained him with ease. Corey's conceit had always assured him none of his confreres could possibly be so strong as he, but this one was even stronger. He was amazed.

"LE' ME AT 'IM!!!" raged Corey, but his struggles were to no avail, "I'LL TEACH 'IM T' MIND 'IS OWN -"

"Brecken, YOU stay put!" commanded the teddy-hugger with authority, "Claire, YOU light out o' here:

"LIGHT OUT, or 'll tell ol' lady Bite YOU been talkin' t' Brecken 'n' gettin' FRIENDLY with 'im!

"That ol' bitty will send you RIGHT-STRAIGHT to th' MAJOR!

"You want 'o go to TH' MAJOR with ol' lady Bite's note in your hot little hand, CHINEE BOY?"

"No, NO!!!" screamed the horrified Cadet Claire as he raced madly out of the arbor and across the quad.

Curley knew Claire's Achilles heel and had used it to defeat him. The masochist ran from the horrifying threat of a visit to the major's strop as fast as his legs would carry him.

"He's gone like a cool breeze," laughed Curley, "Now, IF you promise y' won't be dumb enough t' go after 'im I can let y' up now.

"How 'bout it, you okay now, Brecken?

"He's out on th' quad where ol' lady Bite can see th' show if y' splatter 'im now, and he WILL tell on y,' and she WILL send you to the MAJOR.

"C' m' ON, Corey-boy, TALK to me!

"You okay?

"Is it safe t' let y' up?"

"Yeah, yeah, I, I'm alright.

"Th, thanks, Curls. I, I'm over it now," Corey promised.

The brand new Heeler Hall champion strong man released our hero, and the two friends had a good laugh on the boy who wanted the whole world to whip him, with the exception of their commander.

For the first time in months Corey had made verbal contact with another person. And for this house brother's kindness he was to be eternally grateful.

"Listen, thanks, Curley!" said he.

"Aw, you'd do th' same for me," smiled the teddy-hugger as he rushed off to class, "You're okay, kid."

But Corey knew he was a long mile from being "okay."

Protracted isolation from human intercourse other than classes, and Miss Bite's frequent summonses to her shower room to be STREAKED and reviled had made our boy a lot more introspective than the average ten-year-old-going-on-eleven. the everlasting months of his cruelly enforced loneliness had done their dirty work. His isolation had skewed his mental perceptions and cognitive reasoning processes, not for a day but for all time. He now wondered if he'd ever done one right thing or set one true course in all his life. Slowly, methodically, inescapably his enemies had poisoned Corey's mind.

Supersonic Saber was a tough nut to crack. But even Supe couldn't buck the will of the headmaster. No cadet in his right mind would be so stupid, so poor Corey 'd been kicked out of the blue devils at the first hint of Donnybrook trouble.

As the shunning had continued to eat Corey alive, his strong young physique weakened and dissipated. And it was then his boxing, wrestling and swimming teams had dumped him as well.

As Brecken watched Curley dart off to his class, his mind skimmed back to that fateful day when poor old McMoon tried to save him from the deviant Claire's wily trap. His poor little roomie was whipped severely for trying to help his enraged friend.

"Maybe McMoon was right," a boy on his way to psychosis recalled regretfully, "Maybe I should 'a' gone to th' major 'n' confessed that it was ME 'n' CLAIRE who made 'im late for formation. BOTH of us would 'a' got a black ass; 'n' I could 'a' lost everything right then 'n' there.

"I, I was so scared o' that when th' ol' man broke me.

"I probably wouldn't 'a' lost it then, though, I'd 'a' just got a whippin' 'n been forgiven; but I've sure as hell lost everything now!

"Lose it then?

"Lose it now?

"What's th' difference WHEN y' lose everything if you're gonna lose everything anyhow?"

But Corey knew the answer before he'd posited the question. If he had been forbidden the major's table he and Leto would have been parted and he'd never have experienced the intoxicating beauty of their vital and regenerating taboo trysts. No, there would have been a difference and it would have been a killing difference. It would have been a catastrophe too terrible to contemplate. Even after he'd lost he knew he could not have done otherwise.

He regretted letting his poor little roomie down that dreary day. But Leto's lover boy should never regret having courted her and winning the intoxicating honey of her love. The golden brats had been criminally punished, but the wonder of her love had been worth all the pain he'd suffered for it, and the debilitating madness into which he'd sunk: Their magic woodland trysts was worth the living hell of this barren, killing desert The Brass had brought him.

Our underage lovers had been hardy and bold enough to taste the overwhelming reward of love. It might have seemed wrong to the others, but it had been the only right and gentle thing he could remember having done in all his roughshod bully boy life of blood, bruise, strife and victory.

Curley's saving him from Claire's snare and telling him he had other friends too cowed to declare themselves had been Corey's first surprise of this fine day.

But the second surprise was not to be nearly so pleasant:

"CADET BRECKEN, REPORT IMMEDIATELY TO YOUR HOUSEMOTHER IN HER PARLOR, YOU AWFUL MONSTER!" barked his ex-admirer McNichol officiously (and well within the line of his duty) from the hallway by Corey's door.

Cadet Brecken scooted directly into the dragon's reeking lair posthaste.

"CADET BRECKEN REPORTING AS ORDERED, MA'AM!!!!"

"Well, well, well, if it aint pretty little Leto's li' l' darlin' -- TH' BLUE-EYED WONDER," The Beast's thin, cruel lips curled in a contemptuous smile as she sneered her contempt down on him,

"Cadet Corporal Brecken, th' Donnybrooks' EX-golden boy -- with th' emphasis on th' EX -- reports t' his dear old housemother, do he?

"Well, it looks like th' Donnybrooks might jus' still have some use fir ye, CA-DET BLONDIE:

"My friend, Mrs. Donnybrook, is ailin' today, I'm sorry t' say.

"Th' pore soul's con-fined to 'er home unable t' git to the dinin' hall, so she needs ONE boy to pick 'er up a covered lunch 'n' de-liver it t' HER at 'er house.

"Don't ask me WHY, but she especially asked fir YOU! Guess they aint NO accountin' fir taste, huh. goofball?

"Jus' THINK, boy:

"Maybe she's a-gonna forgive ye?

"Why, I wouldn't be ONE bit surprised if they DID jus' go right on 'n' forgive ye fir yore horrible crime!

"Y' never know what THEM people 're gonna do, do ye?"

The hag studied the boy's haunted, hunted sky blue eyes to spy out the faintest glimmer of any hope she might have awakened in him -- and found it!

She commanded him:

"Ca-det Brecken, you will report to the kitchen at McAdam Hall. There you will obtain a covered carryout tray especially prepared for your headmaster's missus. You will then deliver that meal di-rectly to the home of your beloved commandant, you cur!"

"YES, MA'AM!!!"

Corey saluted, about-faced smartly and clambered noisily downstairs to McAdam, bent upon his top-drawer mission.

"Can it be true?" he wondered, "Will I be forgiven?"

A drowning boy will clutch at any hint of hope in his desperate fight to survive. And, though the whole thing seemed pretty fishy -- given the players, he had to try to save himself.

"Bite giving ME a chance?" he wondered,

"The Black Witch forgiving ANYONE for ANYTHING?

"Never!

"But, but maybe?"

A boy robbed of everything else lives for hope alone, and he must embrace it. Desperate and friendless, stripped of everything worth living for, the improbability of this vague last chance beckoned with its siren song.

Miss Bite watched amused from her window as her little target for abuse scurried precipitously to the McAdam kitchen.

Our toy soldier was walking blithely into their trap, the filthy ensnarement of his perverse enemies.

The kindly black lady in the kitchen gave Corey Mrs. Donnybrook's covered tray, our boy stepped out into the courtyard and their fun began:

"APPLE CORE!" bellowed Super Sonic, who'd been waiting in the courtyard for him as per orders.

"BALTIMORE!" responded Beasterling.

"WHO'S YOUR FRIEND?"

"BRECKEN!!!!"

Corey was pelted with a long ton of apple cores and inundated in dripping, juicy globules of fruit pulp. Nor had he the luxury of running from the premeditated assault, for he feared he might drop Mrs. Donnybrook's VIP lunch.

No, our cadet under fire must walk, very slowly, quite carefully, to his revered commandant's residence.

Worse, he must complete his chore without pausing to clean up, or the poison cobra's lunch might get cold.

He soldiered on, chagrinned and covered with fruit slop, while his ghoulish housemother cackled with ghastly delight at the sight of her shower room stripper-slave's humiliation.

He was constrained to deliver The Black Witch's food still hot, so he pressed on and knocked at the Donnybrooks' door.

The monster within quickly opened to him, she'd been waiting to gut him.

Smug in her knowledge of her complete power over this tiny ant, the vile Medusa leered down upon the doomed:

"Why, my dear, DEAR little Cadet Brecken, what an AWFUL mess you are!"

"CADET BRECKEN REPORTING WITH MRS. DONNY-BROOK'S COVERED LUNCH, MA'AM!!!"

"Goodness!" what a word for a Black Witch to prostitute, "You are certainly a sight to behold!

"Only THINK that my frisky little STREET CORNER WHORE'S golden Adonis has come to such an un-pretty pass!

"What DID that silly tart EVER see in YOU, Brecken, you awful little mess?

"Why ever would you ever DARE to appear at your commandant's home in such a disheveled state, young sir?

"Have you a reasonable excuse for this travesty, cadet?"

The very core of Corey's being was repulsed by the lethal threat of this gloating vampire. He was seething with a rage he must suppress at the vile harpy's insult against his adored love goddess.

The rancid hag keenly spotted his repressed storm of anger and hatred. She'd observed it in her victim's rapid breathing and his lowered eyes. The Deepfreeze gloried in the pain and confusion she awakens in Leto's blue eyed bauble.

Did the horrid vengeance machine demand an immediate answer to her absurd question?

He didn't know.

But he did know better than to make an excuse for failure, for it is axiomatic that the military has no time for failed subordinate's excuses:

"NO EXCUSE, MA'AM!!!!" he piped.

"I INSIST upon an IMMEDIATE explanation of this outrage, CADET!!!" the harpy pursued her flying prey, bent upon his slaughter.

"Since you insist, ma'am," he faltered, "a group of boys in the McAdam court --"

"A group of BOYS?" The Black Witch affected hauteur, "BOYS?

"So, my DARLING little Cadet BRECKEN, YOU have been skylarking with the BOYS at McAdam, have you?

"You dare tell me that while I've been sitting here PATIENTLY in MY diminished condition awaiting your sloppy and tardy luncheon delivery, have you?"

"It, it wasn't exact-" he began.

"SILENCE!" the cobra stormed, "Your HEADMASTER shall hear of THIS, my dirty little LOOSE FILLY'S PRETTY LITTLE BLOND LOVER BOY!

"NOW, you get back to Heeler Hall and report to your housemother to be cleaned up, you, YOU unmilitary little bollocks! THAT certainly is not MY job, and even if it were I'm far too ill to countenance such a horribly disgusting chore."

"YES, MA'AM!!!"

Not forgiveness but a STREAKING was to be Corey's reward for this errand of mercy to the merciless:

Hope and charity were cardinal sins in the hate-narrowed eyes of the avenging furies now in control. They would never miss a chance to punish such flagrant offences against their dark goddess with a vengeance far beyond any human understanding of the word.

"They're gonna have their fun with me," Corey kicked himself for having fallen for their rancid ruse.

He climbed Miss Bite's stairway stealthily in the vain hope of evading the dragon's radar.

No such luck:

"CADET BRECKEN," barked the horror's watchful toady-lookouts, lookouts posted in the hallway, "REPORT TO THE HOUSEMOTHER ON THE DOUBLE!"

Her quarry slunk quickly into the presence of the behemoth hoping to get it over with:

"CADET BRECKEN REPORTING AS ORDERED, MA'AM!!!!"

He was shocked to find the "afflicted" Mrs. Donnybrook seated with the dragon in her lair.

Oh, yes, my dear, The Deepfreeze had longed to witness her victim's punishment. She must have sprinted ahead of him so these twin demons might gloat together over their hapless prey's preplanned trial.

Our shaking hero found himself alone, desperately frightened and facing two gigantic, sex-hungry torturers.

"SHUT UP, YE DISGRACEFUL LITTLE WHELP!!!!" yowled his darling housemother.

Then The Beast abruptly instructed her attendants:

"YOU filthy hounds move that-there easy chair over t' the shower room door; and then I want ALL o' my boys t' CLEAR OUT an' STAY CLEAR o' this-here building fir at least a HOUR!

"Leave us alone, boys, a-cause WE have some IMPORTANT business t' clear up with our playful li' l pal, Corporal Brecken.

"Now do what I say and SCAT, rats!"

And they humped themselves to obey and exit.

"Brecken's in for it!"

"Better him than me!"

"You said it!" The Bite's toadies giggled as they ran downstairs.

"Mrs. Donnybrook's been a-makin' some mighty disturbin' complaints about YOU, young Mister Corey -- an' after I done GIVE you a chanct t' make things right with them Donnybrooks, too!" the dragon bared her fangs with a relish that chilled Corey to the marrow.

And, as if that hadn't been enough to scare a little boy to death, The Black Witch chimed in:

"This AWFUL little boy has completely disgraced himself, his hall and his lovely housemother today, my dear Miss Bite," Noting her quarry's helpless fear with pleasure, the cobra struck again, "He's admitted SKYLARKING with those delinquent McAdam Hall rowdies, and after you had entrusted him with the delivery of my lunch.

"But, due to his carelessness, my lunch arrived late, cold and in such a jumbled mess I was completely unable to stomach it!

"Why, my dear lady, I am at a loss to know what IS to be done with this INCORRIGIBLE boy."

Lies!

He burned with resentment, but a little cadet about to be flayed alive by two lumbering adult ogres was powerless in the face of their infamy. These morally bankrupt high ranking dignitaries in the academy's class conscious pecking order were warming up to peck him, rend him and tear him to shreds.

Lies on top of lies:

"Why, my dear Miss Bite, I stood ready to FORGIVE the benighted scamp; but how can I forgive it after such a gross insult?"

Poor little Corey saw it in their hungry eyes: They were psyching themselves up to have their extreme and deviant fun with him. These two abandoned women had no other means of sexual release at their call, were turning themselves on with this slow lead in to his impending physical ordeal by enjoying the effects of his psychological torture.

"Oh, my darling Mrs. Donnybrook, you ARE such a DELICATE and REFINED gentlewoman. Of course, you wouldn't be able t' guess how to deal with a hardened little gangster like this un, BUT I DO!"

"And, pray tell my lovely Miss Bite," inquired the headmaster's gentle creature, a creature every bit as gentle as the coldest python and as refined as a serial killer.

She thirsted to hear some of the gory details of her confederate's extreme punishments.

"PUNISHMENT, dear lady!" trumpeted The Beast in a transport of her vilest joy, "CORPORAL PUNISHMENT for our MESSY LITTLE CORPORAL!

"This, this RANDY little RUMPER who's despoiled yore PORE LEETLE GAL, this, this MONSTER, this CRIMINAL has got one hell of a dose o' CORPORAL PUNISHMENT a-comin' to 'im! What Brecken needs is PUNISHMENT and PLENTY of it!"

His tormentors then turned their baleful stare upon their chew-toy de jour:

"YOU git into yore room, BOY, roared the dragon, "You STRIP that filthy BODY o' yourn NAKED, you, you SKYLARKIN' SCRAP O' MEAT! Turn that shower up nice 'n' HOT!

"BUT don't go in there yet a-cause I want ye t' march yourself right back in here JAYBIRD NAKED with no towel, no clothes on. YOU come back in here t' us BUCK NAKED 'n' report back t' me JUS' like that -- HEAR me?"

"YES, MA'AM!!!" our little hero cried out, trying his best to hide his deep shame.

The monsters who were baiting him were delighted to see him tremble before them and run to wait upon their unspeakable pleasures. They took great joy from his confusion and embarrassment. The punishing furies laughed as he ran to fulfill their deviant preferences.

Until this moment he'd thought all the shame he could possibly have felt must long since have been stripped, kicked, beaten and slapped out of him as he'd been run through the emasculating meat grinder of the finest academy in all the world. But, returning to the stinking dragon's parlor stitch-less, and being ogled by two heinous, leering, drooling perverts, he had to blush with a chagrin reawakened.

The Black Witch was eager to abuse him verbally:

"Why, pretty little Cadet Brecken," simpered that delighted vampire, "where IS that KILLER WANG my silly little salt-bitch of a daughter fell so madly in love with?

"Is your darling Leto's pride and joy all shriveled up now?

"Why, so it is!"

Both demons laughed uproariously as The Deepfreeze warmed to her subject and our Corey felt the sting of a fury's lash.

Leto's ardent suitor realized they'd tortured all of their sweetest secrets out of his goddess. But when these rancid old dregs denigrated the golden brats' sacred love and spat their insults in his face, his sorrow was unbearable.

"Oh, dearie ME, I fear our antsy little WHORE'S dream boy's no longer HALF the man he was, my dear Miss Bite," gloried the witch, "Just SEE how his little RIBS poke out!

"Honestly, there doesn't seem to be enough meat left on his threadbare little bones to make a decent meal for a dog, does there?" smirked The Deepfreeze.

"No, ma'am, there is NOT!" came The Beast's gleeful response.

"And look at those deep, dark circles under his poor little bright-blue eyes, those selfsame eyes with which my dopey little slut fell so hopelessly in love.

"Is this not the ominous shadow which surely predicts this DARLING little boy's eminent DEATH?" quipped The Witch merrily.

"Indeed it IS, ma'am!" chuckled The Beast jovially.

"Whatever can we DO to restore this poor benighted creature's failing health, dear?" wondered a Black Witch, dripping with faux concern, a mask to hide her rabid hatred of the poor, benighted creature in question.

"GIVE 'IM A GOOD, HEALTHY LARUPIN,' DARLIN' LADY!" trumped the dragon merrily.

"Then, by all means, let us proceed, my dear," hissed a delighted cobra.

With that the prelude to their brat-fry was concluded.

Beast and Witch hastened to drop the compassionate act and bared their gleaming fangs and sharp talons to prosecute the monstrous passion of their malevolence and perversity.

"CADET CORPORAL DIRTY DOG BRECKEN, GIT INTA THAT SHOWER 'N' GET READY FIR SOME TALL CORPORAL PUNISHMENT, LETO'S FILTHY LITTLE STUD-PONY!" bellowed the leviathon.

"YES, MA'AM!!!" barked Corey, trying his best to hide the overwhelming revulsion and terror he felt in facing the sickening, twisted trial they were bound to inflict.

"If the witch could only be right!" hope flickered desperately through the frenzied circuits of our condemned boy's frenzied brain, "If only Death could take me out o' this hell RIGHT NOW I, I'd escape what, what they're gonna DO t' me.

"Dear God, WHY does this have t' happen to ME?

"Take me, Death!" his exhausted, fear-addled brain begged, "Please, please jus' take me NOW!"

No such luck, little Corey:

"Use the end shower in that first tier o' stalls, BOY!" commanded his punisher, "I had them boys SET that easy chair at th' door so 's Mrs. Donnybrook kin WATCH while I shellac yore worthless hide!"

"Oh, heaven!" a naked and ashamed little boy's mind cried out of the pitch blackness of that heartless Beast's torture pit.

This shameful exhibition had gone far beyond anything this one little boy could be expected to countenance.

Nonetheless, it proceeded:

The steam clouds rose and the burning, crushing, methodical rise and fall of THE SILVER STREAK made Corey cry and dance for the diversion of his enemies. The Black Witch's snide commentaries on his reduced and harrowed anatomy continued unabated. The laughter and jibes of his cold-blooded, merciless torturers continued ad infinitum as the scoundrels savored his awful disgrace.

Long after an abused boy was thrashed past the end of his tether and collapsed, the heavy blows of an outrageous behemoth continued to reverberate against his quivering flesh. And the gorgons' ceaseless mockery went on and on.

The Beast was putting on a show for The Witch.

Obscenely obese and insanely hate-powered, this raging giant lashed furiously away at Corey's exposed person while her sanguine playmate in their unforgivable palace of perversion sat in comfort and watched the entertainment from her easy chair.

Deepfreeze laughed aloud to witness the trial of this maddeningly cute golden brat, this annoying major's pet, this monster and criminal Lynnwood had coddled, and Leto had adored -- and enjoyed.

"Those FOOLS!" laughed a vengeful gorgon in the perverse joy of her horrid victory. "Leto welcomed that teddy bear wretch into her belly and the great major made a fool out of himself over him; but I'm made of sterner stuff:

"I hated him all along!"

She'd longed for her chance to impose her rough justice on Brecken, Brecken, BRECKEN for the high crime of robbing her and her spies of their birthright. This black hearted angel of vengeance had longed to tear this boy limb from limb from the moment she'd laid eyes on him.

And now she was overseeing his punishment and it was rousing her to orgasm. Her time had come. She was feasting delectably on the delicacy of this little boy's agony as her tub-of-lard playmate flayed the tortured little creature to abject misery at their matinee cabaret.

"Oh, yes, my dear, for me this is paradise."

Corey suffered the monsters' fete of unendurable outrage.

But The Deepfreeze was looking forward to his survival that he might suffer everlastingly in her thrall.

As it had begun with tantalizing leisure, the cowardly frolic of these deranged monsters, the monsters' fete of extreme child abuse now ended abruptly.

The lunatic strength of The Beast's malicious whip hand was spent and the ugly old torturers abruptly broke off their attack on youth, beauty, life and love. The sated furies exited, guffawing boisterously at the devastation their irresistible size and raw power had brought down against their toothsome little chew-toy.

Like the night The Heeler Hall Horror had first savaged an indomitably proud and stubborn Corey Brecken, he suddenly found himself alone and throbbing in a world of pain and steam. Again he'd been abandoned, naked, ashamed and black-and-blue.

But now, far, far worse for our castoff toy, this time he'd been forced to perform for an audience. Shame drowned him as the realization sunk in on him that he was now a dancing show animal for two accursed perverts' inexcusable, eviscerating and dehumanizing amusements. He'd been danced out and exhibited to an audience of his and Leto's insane worst enemies who'd always hated the lovers.

Now they had won.

Now they had the major's license to glut their deviant desires and enjoy the golden brats' tears.

He'd suffered their rankest abuse and cried as they'd assuaged their inexcusable lusts in a filthy old hell hag's steam-shrouded pornographic cabaret.

Proud little Corey had not only been tortured, he'd been put on shameful display for love's deadliest enemies, The Black Witch and The Beast.

One question nagged his shock-dazed brain as he lay on the floor waiting for time to return enough strength to his throbbing sinews to let him stand up and drag himself off to bed, "Where will it end?"

He could still hear them laughing and boasting about what they'd done to him as they took their comfort in The Beast's parlor.

And a second query entered his young mind, "Why should I keep on living?"

12

ONE ESCAPE

The humblest slave on the harshest, most dehumanizing Sold Down The River plantation in Mississippi or Louisiana on black slavery's darkest day might find consolation through the companionship of fellow sufferers. A condemned Jew headed for the gas chamber in the worst Final Solution Nazi death camp was still able to elicit a kind word from his brothers and sisters in like distress. The most forlorn of exiles in the cruelest house of the dead in the notorious frozen Siberian Gulag of the Stalinist Era might yet interface with his fellows. Every one of these most hard-pressed human beings in the waking nightmare we call the world's history has enjoyed the fellowship of his equally disenfranchised companions who've been trapped in the drear prisons of their common sorrow.

But not Cadet Corporal Corey Brecken. For him no such luxury was accessible. His master's ex-protégé, his May Queen's ex-pet, was totally friendless, alone and shunned by his fellows.

Corey was as much a maroon as Ben Gunn, the seaman loneliness drove mad in Stevenson's TREASURE ISLAND; and the lad was as much a castaway from his species as Enoch Arden, the title character of that celebrated poem. Enoch had been alone for so long he'd lost the gift of speech. And, as it had been with the tragic maroons before him, so it was with him:

Little Cadet Brecken faced every reveille call without a "good morning" from anyone. He was a lone figure in a barracks full of cadets specifically forbidden to acknowledge his existence. Every night he heard taps without a single "good night."

No Tower cadet was permitted to post a letter of complaint to his elders and betters -- as if any such an intelligence wouldn't have been spurned as nonsense from a whiney little black sheep who couldn't "take his medicine like a man."

Why?

Because the rule stated that all postal communications must be read and approved by the cadet's housemother before they were mailed. And, if the darling Miss Bite (or any other junior school housemother) had ever found evidence that one of her boys had complained about anything, she was duty-bound to escort his growing body to the shower and feed it more of what he'd complained of than the unlucky little culprit could have digested in ten lifetimes.

A letter of complaint would have been a terrible mistake. A cadet writing such should soon regret with all his heart, soul and welted, writhing body as clouds of steam rose from his embattled haunches.

How could our Corey ever have begun such a missive?

Cadet Brecken had been beaten black-and-blue ever since the seventh day after his arrival; and, for more months than he could calculate, there'd been no more wide-eyed admirers to revere him. He could no longer look for love from his high ranking champions. He had no major, no hope and, worst of all, no Leto.

How could he relate his travail to his grandsires? His thoroughly surrealistic sadomasochistic experiences had been so topsy-turvy no one in his right mind would ever have believed any part of it. His down-to-earth forebears would have laughed it off as flights of fancy concocted by a bad little boy desperate to get out of a stropping or two and get them to call him home.

No, a boy cannot cry wolf when he's being digested in the wolf's belly, and that's exactly where our mini hero was.

Sociologists speak of the twelve biogenetic drivers, our demons that must be placated to sustain animal life. We human animals are able to survive only so long as these insistent and intransigent demands are met with clockwork regularity. If the human organism is deprived of several of these life preservers it will not be long before it withers -- and dies.

Corey Brecken was on his way out via just such enforced neglect. In fairness to the academy not one of its schoolboys had ever been deprived of such drivers as temperature control, clothing, shoes, food, water, shelter from the elements or sleep. Such deprivation should have been unthinkable, even at such a mad tea party as The Tower Academy. Disclosure and revelation of such inhuman acts would certainly have opened the floodgates of scandal and ruin for that proud institution, heaven forefend.

But one human organism has been singled out to suffer the deprivation of several of his life-drivers' requirements:

Human companionship and intercourse had been withdrawn; and a little boy's own tribe's protection from his natural enemies has been methodically withheld. What protection from his natural enemies had the animals of his own tribe supplied when his tribe had transmogrified itself into his worst and most unnatural of all natural enemies?

The love, affection and sexual release he'd come to expect and needed so desperately had been clinically withheld for a protracted time period. The divine generosity of his breathtaking ex-love goddess's gift of divine solace was but a brokenhearted memory. The gift his Leto had bestowed on him so early in life had been brutally ripped from him, and with a abrupt cruelty so savage as to have been unthinkable.

The life-preserving things they'd withheld from our tiny Brecken organism were in the process of killing it. The entity known as Corey Brecken had begun to falter and fail. It had entered into a downward spiral which must ultimately culminate in shutdown and end life.

Dumped by its blue devils, dumped by its sports teams the Brecken organism was sinking into a bottomless slough from which it might never return. His musculature had lost both tone and vitality. His mind was under such a shock-barrage of severity from the endless attacks of those surrounding him, so he was nearly gone.

In this once happy early summer of his existence, Death was beginning to look extremely good to our embattled little boy. Ever since The Black Witch had ridiculed his wraithlike form and mocked his failing health, Corey had yearned for The Reaper's cold embrace. He pined for some escape, any escape, from the maddening currents of the whirling vortex of torment which has lashed him daily through this finest military school in all the world. Now he knew he must escape the academy. And the only way so to do was to die:

If he ran away he'd only be brought back by the local or state authorities, whipped and condemned to walk a bullpen of eternal disgrace. All the cadets who'd tried to escape The Tower's tortures via physical-geographical flight had been returned for continued torture.

No, death must be his egress, his only one.

But how?

The only firearms at school were no such thing. They were wooden toy rifles kept especially for Sunday parades and locked away in the armory to be issued to our little toy soldiers only for that purpose.

The parades which had once been their joy presently mocked our too young lovers. Corey had been censured and forbidden to raise his eyes to his lady love ever again. Leto has been summarily proscribed from the guilty secret joy of glimpsing her Mac, and their boss had forbidden these joys for all eternity. Our golden brats' happiness had been anathematized by the powers that be, and parades had become love's funeral marches.

Parade days, like life itself, held no joy for our underage trampled blossoms. True to his word, their implacable master had beaten the sweet love out of his best beloved child.

Our hero couldn't abide the thought of death by a blade. The prospect of sticking a knife into himself, or slitting his own throat or wrists repulsed him.

The yahoos at the Honeysuckle hardware store might have sold him a gun and enough ammo to get the job done. But Grandpa Joe, champion deer and pheasant hunter, had never taken his grandson on even one of his hunting trips, cold as he was toward the innocent child of his trollop and that commie. Corey didn't have an inkling as to how to use such a tool effectively, or at all.

He'd become obsessed with this driving impetus to end his misery, but as yet he had not the know-how. But then one of old lady Bite's hill saws suddenly popped up in his head to save him from this of unwanted existence. It had wound its eerie way through the chambers of his half-forgotten remembrances and entered his now completely insane, death-obsessed mind:

"If you drink from a wiggler stream, you will die," whispered the old saw into his receptive ear.

The age-old wisdom of the hill folk must have been correct. Hadn't they been the sole inhabitants of these Great Smoky Mountains since they'd killed off the last Creek and Cherokee inhabitants who'd been the original natives?

(When the hill folk said "wiggler stream" they meant a stagnant offshoot of an actual stream, a befouled and becalmed pool full of mosquito larvae, or "wigglers" in their rural argot.)

Corey hoped this divine inspiration would bring about his quick expiration.

Junior academy war games in the high mountains near the school were coming up soon. It was to be the first of such exercises scheduled since the current crop of Heeler Hall cadets had been billeted here, their first field problem!

The boys were excited at the prospect of a new and thrilling adventure.

I should say all the lads save one. Our lone exception was no longer excited by anything in this life. Presently death was his only interest. Cadet Brecken had made up his mind:

The day of the war games was to be his last. He was now completely insane, having been made so by the callous insouciance of his tribe.

The big day arrived. Heeler Hall was ablaze with the cadets' excitement at the big war games' eagerly awaited approach.

The boys rushed eagerly downstairs and into formation on this awe-inspiring dawn of the big field operation.

Corey raced fleetly down the steps to join them, so he could find his wiggler stream -- and Death.

He reached the foot of the stairs, stepped outside; and then he saw HER:

His poor broken heart -- and all the world around him -- stood stalk-still as a Cadet Brecken momentarily renewed beheld his adored goddess of beauty for the very first time in more months than he knew.

Was this really the girl he once had loved, the girl he'd missed for a thousand, thousand, thousand eternities in his barren desert of loneliness after her father had savagely whipped him and kicked him out?

Was this his May Queen, the girl who had electrified him at the ecstatic moment of their first lightning-bolt touch in a deserted McAdam barrack bathroom a thousand years ago?

It was she!

"Hi, Leto!" he blurted out seconds before the major's proscription had been remembered to squelch the ardor of his thundering heart.

He stood there, overcome by her nearness.

"Oh, just look at her!" daydreamed his fevered brain, "I'm not made of stone!"

"I cannot see her and not speak -"

His love goddess appeared to him so stylish and so adorable her Mac could only see the raw power of her nearness and feminine attraction.

His ex-schoolmarm was every bit as lovely as he remembered her in his dreams all the way through their long, dour days of cruelly enforced separation, and even better.

She wore a little fur cap perched jauntily on the back of those richly cascading auburn curls. She held a matching muff to keep her dainty hands from the chill.

Her dressy little outfit was picture-perfect, her regal pose, immaculate and Miss Leto Donnybrook appeared the very model of aristocratic young womanhood.

(Leto's girlfriend Suzy -- the pal who'd returned to her adventuresome confidante's side a few days after her fear of The Deepfreeze's orgy of destruction had worn off -- accompanied her more experienced girlfriend today.)

315

But the enchanted towhead saw no one other than his long lost Leto, the breathtaking inamorata he ingenuously believed had come back to him after their long, hard limbo of loneliness.

An entranced Corey searched his enigmatic Leto's kaleidoscopic orbs, those compelling eyes, the eyes which had demanded her lover's undivided attention, devotion and reverence, to make contact. He dove deep into the enchanted lake of his beloved's rainbow retinae to find himself. '

In the past she'd answered his love with her own. In the past she'd always welcomed him in to live beatifically there in the magical world of her wondrous eyes. She had always held him dear. She had cradled her beloved little schoolboy like a baby in the bliss of her divine love.

Corey now desperately needed the comfort he sought when the golden brats had gazed deeply into one another's souls -- and found magic, because our beautiful kids had believed in magic.

Corey searched in vain to find himself reflected in her loving gaze, but there was nothing there.

Leto's love for her Mac was gone.

In all their beautiful yesterdays he'd always seen his ardor reflected in her gaze. But on this cold day the girl who'd loved him with every fiber of her being had left him to face the music solo.

His Leto had been replaced by this stranger, this beautiful phantasm, presently and sightlessly starring right through him.

Once she'd been a living, loving girl, but now she was only the Donnybrooks' wind-up doll. She'd morphed into a clockwork girl. This strange thing standing before him in an inexplicable trancelike state was a thing that did not see, acknowledge or want to know him.

A bloodless robot had cut him dead and curtly excluded him. He'd been cast out again, and this time by his last hope.

The beatings, the shunning and the wanton torture sessions The Tower had put him through were but fluffy will 'o the wisps in comparison with this rebuff.

Formerly warm, giving and generous, today Leto's were the cold, unfeeling orbs of a scrupulously tutored heartbreaker. The Black Witch hadn't been idle during those heartless and excruciating months of their protracted separation. Today her pupil was the creation of her deviant mother's witchcraft. The robot that had once been his love goddess froze him with its carefully practiced exclusionary stare. This somnambulist -- once his lover girl -- had summarily ossified her lover boy.

Hope as he might, his real living girl was gone:

The Black Witch had cut out Leto's living, giving heart and taken it from her proud young breast, the breast that used to long for her adoring Mac's gentle touch when their fervently churning bodies had exploded in the release of their forbidden passion. Leto's cold and unnatural mom replaced her subordinated daughter's true, kind and giving heart with an ice cold heart of brass.

Both young ladies standing outside Heeler Hall today stared haughtily down on this brazen upstart -- with just the proper degree of disdain, of course.

At the academy all this was just as it should be. Such behavior in Donnybrooks, and the friends of Donnybrooks, had been and should always be quite proper, de rigueur and socially acceptable in the eyes of The Tower's rigid and class-conscious hierarchy.

"Cadet BRECKEN, everyone knows MY father has FORBIDDEN you ever to even LOOK at me!" condescended this tin robot icily, "YOU have been FORBIDDEN to speak to me -- or to anyone in my family -- for ANY reason.

"Pray do NOT embarrass ME, or yourself, by foolishly disobeying our exalted chief again. IF you do, I will be forced to REPORT your insubordinate misconduct to your superiors."

It was Leto's face, it was Leto's voice, but the brusque command had come straight from the major's mindset. Her beloved voice had spoken those cruel, cutting words, but those words were decidedly Donnybrook dogma.

Had his adored and adoring Leto actually scolded him as if he were a disobedient stray mongrel?

Never had such a fatal arrow flown through his beloved Aphrodite's mouth from the bow of Artemis to end her own true Mac's poor life.

The words that had come from those pouting lips were not the words of his love goddess, but the dismissive ukase of her angry father. And those words' cold, unfeeling delivery came directly from the scorpions and serpents crawling through The Black Witch's unclean brain. His lost love had recited the screed of a lost soul, designed to destroy all love and all lovers.

How could his love goddess have brought herself to this?

But she had.

And the awful truth hit him like a sledgehammer: Cut dead by a heartless, soulless automaton he was lost.

It was the shocking fact that the grownup monsters of The Tower had taken his passionate paramour's warmth and humanity, cut them out of her and replaced them with their own machinery. Our taboo lovers' enemies had turned a loving, living girl into a Donnybrook party line parroting puppet.

Corey was already determined his life must end. But now, as he stared into the dead eyes of their soulless machine as it continued its metallic jibber jabber, he was sure.

"My friend, Miss Slats, and I have come to Hooker Hall to call on my dear friend, Miss Bite. And since you are handy, BRECKEN, you may open the door for us, escort us upstairs, announce us and then be about your business. BUT you may NOT EVER speak to ME!"

"YES, MISS!!!" he acknowledged the order as he admitted them to Heeler Hell.

"NO, Brecken, you must not speak to me again -- NEVER!" the pretty little robot without a heart snubbed her desolate ex, "I hope that we are CLEAR on this; but I FORBID you to make reply to ME, cadet!"

"There's th' major again," thought he, even in his terrible pain.

He'd kept a stony silence in the presence of Miss Donnybrook and friend.

Silently, sullenly he did as he'd been so loftily commanded by this foreign machine, this appendage of the Donnybrooks' tyranny. Her grownups' will had been enunciated through the mouth of their little scrap-metal snob, and their poor little outcast must obey.

His ex-love, his flesh and blood little girl, the beauty he'd loved so passionately when she'd been alive -- and still loved.

Now his schoolmistress in love's enchanted classroom preceded her broken toy up the stairway.

He escorted the two dismissive damsels into The Bite's parlor and announced the arrival of the two silly little snips.

Then he rushed precipitously downstairs to answer the most crucial formation call he was ever to attend -- present on the count of four.

He stumbled blindly down the stairway and melted immediately into ranks, committed to the cause of ending his accursed caricature of a life that same day.

A talking doll is not a living entity but a dead shell, the walking ghost of a beauty which has passed away, so why stick around only to mourn their love's death?

If a little boy had been singled out, cut off from the herd, hunted, reviled, rejected, marooned, hounded and driven to desperation until he yearns for cold Death's unfeeling embrace, his path leads inexorably to life's physical end, so why wait for it passively?

Along came his love goddess, as beautiful and desirable to look upon ever she'd been, but she was dead. Anything and everything that ever has made our wounded and bleeding little boy's life livable here at The Proud Tower has been stolen. For him there was nothing to hope for, to dream of, or struggle for and he must make haste to leave this Academy of Satan behind. He must escape the twin gorgons' vile torture pit by the most precipitous means of dispatch available:

He must commit suicide.

He knew the grownups could find all kinds of stuff in their Bible and their silly old law books against suicide. They'd used all those when they had read the golden kids the riot act on their forbidden passion. But he knew they only wanted to trick him into staying here so that they might torture him again and again. He realized they got themselves off sexually like that. The only way they could get themselves excited about sex was by watching a naked and friendless waif wail and writhe wildly in the withering grasp of the abominable humiliations his perverted grownups lived to contrive and prosecute upon his frail young body.

No!

The endless torments they'd poured over his lamenting body and spirit must end, and they must end NOW.

Their deviant practices had roused the grownups to orgasm.

He'd seen it a thousand times in the lively glint of pleasure in their eyes while they'd been busily savaging him.

"Yeah, you cheesy grownups!" Corey reviled them silently, "You can't hide.

"I know you're getting yourselves off on my pain, sadistically, vicariously and by watching me in my sufferings.

"Leto 'n' me, we couldn't hide our love from you and you punished us and punished us and punished us. But now you can't hide your sick, sick love from me!

"I know you hate real sex. You even deny its existence. You've married your mournful, twisted love to the perverse thrill you get out o' sublimating th' sex act through your practice of the most extreme tortures you can on our more-or-less innocent little bodies.

"And you did it to HER!

"I, I can never, NEVER forgive you for that; and I'm taking your favorite play toy from you -- TODAY!"

Their sublimation of the real delight of our fond young lovers' surrender to the delight of sexual release for their middle aged deviance and sadistic thrills was the only thing that now rewarded the grownups in Corey's mind. It was the catalyst that they used to bring their blunted, waning libidos to life.

Had these selfsame adults not reviled and tortured Mac and Leto for having dared to love in the beauty of their trysting glade?

They had, for they were monsters dedicated to cruelty:

The time his poor Leto had made her fatal slip by bragging to her friend when she thought herself safe had awakened the powers that be to beat and demonize our beautiful underage heroes. These sorry excuses for responsible adults had taken our amorous little culprits to task. They had punished two beautiful children mercilessly behind the pious mask of propriety.

But sham had not hidden their true faces from their screaming little victims' sights. Theirs was the unforgiving and bloodthirsty mien of extreme vengeance, the horrid visage of their need to shift blame and punish the open natures, frail minds and vulnerable bodies of two smaller human beings far more innocent than they.

"I will beat the filth out of you!" his dour headmaster boasted as he beat the lovers with all the might of a powerful arm, suborned to witchcraft.

"Grow up!" the grownups had decreed, "Why can't you behave more like a grownup?"

Well, Leto was all grown up. She was nothing more than a tin robot conduit of her old folks' moldy party line.

But brave Corey had persisted in loving her. He'd resolved that no earthly power was going to beat the love for his vibrant goddess out of him.

He would never name her as his sex-schoolmarm because that would have sealed her undoing in the eyes of her father and his precious propriety.

The little maroon realized that all the Donnybrooks -- and everyone else -- knew that a more experienced twelve year old had to have been her ten year old boyfriend's teacher. But her faithful Mac would never confess it.

The ten year old they had abandoned still loved his twelve year old sex teacher (and her unbending Daddy) enough to take the blame for everything to maintain the fiction of Leto's innocence. His prideful ex-patron needed his vain illusion desperately, and so his protégé in disgrace had willingly surrendered his own honor that shame need never overtake and kill his patron.

They all knew it was a lie, but it shielded the two Donnybrooks their faithful but forsaken ex-favorite most loved.

And Mac's own personal arrogance was assuaged when he played the selfless sacrificial lamb.

Never would the soulless machine that had berated him love with the brightly burning fire of the passionate woman-child who'd dared hold him so close to her raging heart in the throes of their holy passion. Leto, Mac's pliant queen of beneficence and warmth, had been sucked into the maelstrom of her grownups' societal correctness. Now she was lost to him forever. Our poor little heroine's suffering had wrung all the tears she had from her when she'd cried for their lost paradise, and found that her elders were deaf, and her paradise was stolen.

Today, lover-boy Mac, your flawless beauty's a relic of the past.

Corey had been consigned by his betters and elders to suffer The Heeler Hall Horror's perverse delights in perpetuity.

Corey had so admired the way his Leto had used to stand up, so tall, so bravely, against the unfeeling iron maiden of puritanical convention.

But presently her robot-effigy was its mouthpiece, the arbiter of our once living Leto's vilest enemies.

His Leto was no more. Adventuring into the frightening, uncharted, irresistibly exhilarating wilds of adult sexuality to bathe in the delights of its unfolding mysteries was no more:

"BRECKEN! How dare you DISOBEY your HEADMASTER?" their windup toy demanded of her ex-lover boy, "How DARE you speak to ME?

"How DARE you, how dare you, how dare you how dare you howdareyouhowdareyouhowdare, how, dare, y, y, y-"

Their tin doll had bought into its forbears' web of lies and become one with this killing juggernaut that was The Tower. But it was winding down.

"Grow up, Corey?" he questioned angrily, "Grow up into a, a robot? "NO, thanks!"

As of today the grownups and their military school could swan dive to hell and they could damn well take their classes, drills, disciplines and worldly-wise sophistries with them. They'd labored long and hard to make life hell for all of those poor little kids who'd been dumb enough to get themselves kicked out and packed off to the finest military academy in all the world.

Corey Brecken was leaving it all behind today.

He was headed into an uncharted realm he knew nothing about -- save the metaphysical conjectures of his elders' grim old fairytales. What's more, he cared nothing for them, and he cared even less for their lies and myths.

The junior school cadet corps formed up on the quad for the big field problem:

"SIR, first squad all present or accounted for!"

"SIR, second squad all present or accounted for!"

"SIR, third squad all present or accounted for!"

And off they marched to the armory to get their toy rifles, packs and a few walkie-talkies.

Back to the quad they marched to divide into two opposing armies and proceed with the big war games.

Corey's platoon was part of the mighty major's invincible army of the elect, predestined to win over the pre-damned opposition army.

The two armies split up to march smartly off and deploy at prearranged positions in the hills. The boys proceeded to climb into the mountains for action.

Later in the games both armies would advance on enemy strongholds, mount offensives and take as many prisoners as they might. But at this opening stage of the conflict the protagonists simply occupied their own positions and prepared themselves for battle.

Corey's own private operation was also proceeding according to plan:

His army was way up in the wild and wooly boondocks. The kids were occupying the loftiest and least traversed levels of the Smoky Mountains, and our boy knew he was bound to find a wiggler stream somewhere way up here.

Then a little suicide's luck struck a vein of pure gold:

"Crabtree and Brecken!" barked their thunderbolt-god commandant.

"YES, SIR!!!!" yipped the two eager little puppy-soldiers in question.

"Do you see that tallest of all the peaks, soldiers?" queried Zeus almighty, indicating a towering spire which oversaw the entire terrain below with his commanding index finger.

"YES, SIR!!!!"

"You two soldiers will take these binoculars and this walkie-talkie up to the highest point of that peak. It will be a spot where you can -- and will -- scout the battlefield.

"When you have reached it, you will climb up to its loftiest vantage point. Thence you will observe all troop movements below and report what you see back to me.

"Soldiers, I want regular communiqués on the enemy's exact position and any sorties he might launch against us.

"Now, are we clear, soldiers?"

"YES, SIR!!!!"

"I'm depending on you two to make regular half hourly reports to my fire base with your walkie-talkie," the major intoned gravely, "The success or failure of our entire operation depends on the accuracy of your observations.

"Are we clear?"

"YES, SIR!!!!"

"Now take these snacks with you and get up there fast!" he said, "Good luck, soldiers!"

"YES, SIR -- and THANK YOU, major!!!"

Of course, it was all a lot of hooey to get rid of an unpopular and eternally carping worrywart (Crabtree) and a social leper whose (once beloved) presence their commandant now found obnoxious (Guess who?).

With his two nuisances out of the way, that high and mighty field commander and those boys who were still in the great man's good graces (at the moment) relaxed with hot cocoa and Smores to await the enemy commander's surrender, an event scheduled to occur a couple of hours thence.

As our two rejected boys mounted the face of the mountain range's most dominant spire, Corey remarked the higher they climbed the more luxuriant was the virgin overgrowth of wild foliage here. The higher our two scouts ascended, so much more beautiful was the verdant face of Nature.

The ascent would have been quite difficult for a grownup, but our preadolescent boys were as agile, energetic and resilient as mountain goats. And the difficulty in attaining their goal merely piqued the children's sense of adventure and it made this sortie all the sweeter.

Mindful of their purpose, our boys climbed upward and upward, hard and fast to win the mock war. And when they reached the loftiest vantage point on the high perch they checked the terrain for enemy troop movements.

Finding nothing to report, they sought out a glade where they might enjoy a break. Crabtree lay passively down to rest but Corey was searching feverishly for something of vital importance to his purpose, something he must find quickly before they were recalled, before this brief window of opportunity slammed shut in his face -- and before his courage failed him.

At that moment conditions were auspicious for his lethal plan's success. But there was not a moment to lose:

Crabtree, the suicide's only witness, was no fighter, but Corey was. Ergo his lone witness could never rat on him, for Crabtree could easily be browbeaten into keeping his mouth shut about what must transpire here.

Our hero must quickly to locate a stagnant mosquito pool and employ his fatal dram.

He was sickened by the prospect of possibly having to fling himself headlong from this high mountain to die. He feared the fall might not kill, but cripple him for life. And our juvenile suicide did not want to be an object of pity, he wanted to be a corpse. But, if Corey couldn't find his wiggler stream, he would have to jump and hope to escape life's unadulterated torment thus. It wasn't what he'd planned, and it was definitely not what he wanted.

Suddenly a bright new day dawned for The Tower's determined and demented sacrifice:

He'd found his wiggler stream and his joy was boundless.

A stream came bubbling merrily up through this forgotten mountain fastness.

"This is a start!" he triumphed.

The birds perched high above the boys sang warning songs against these rude intruders into their far retreat so sweetly in our little Corey's ears it was a joy for him to hear their angry complaints.

The bright sun of early morning filtered so dreamily, brilliantly, restfully, through the tall pines and oaks around them, winking gaily through the gloomy foliage of this thick virgin forest.

Here in this mountain paradise little Corey Becken sent up a fervent prayer of thanksgiving for Nature's bounty. Our mad boy was so grateful for the bliss of so beautiful a day. In his insane eyes it was the most beautiful day of his life, for it was to be his last.

"This is it!" he gloried.

The merry brook rushed headily downstream to feed into a sequestered mountain pond. Upstream lay the dead and decomposing corpse of a rattlesnake. Our suicide saw this as a good sign, an omen of The Reaper's presence.

Fortuitously, right in front of his feet and on the very spot on which he stood, there buzzed a teeming flight of agitated adult mosquitoes. Alarmed by his presence, the insect vampires circled up in a death-cloud from their stagnant offshoot hatchery.

"It's MY WIGGLER STREAM!!!!!"

Here was his death-vehicle, here was the bog of his heartfelt desire. Surely there must be enough disease, stagnation and poison in this rotten, polluted ditch to kill a horse, and Corey Brecken's hell-bent death quest was achieved.

"ALEA JACTA EST!"

Our suicide dropped down to his knees without a nanosecond's pause and rammed his face deep into that stinking, putrid hole and drank, drank, drank his fill of disease and death.

Brecken drank long and hard and with avid purpose, for his was a hero's toast to his own martyrdom and oblivion.

But prissy little Cadet Crabtree saw what he was doing and cried out his frenzied alarm:

"BRECKEN, cut that OUT!!! ... Don't y' know that if you drink from a wiggler stream you DIE?"

Corey knew Crabtree was a born runner-and-teller. To prevent the discovery of his dread purpose before the toxin had taken effect, our hero grasped his house brother's throat tightly. And the superhuman strength of an homicidal maniac terrified his pal:

"If y' tell ANYONE what I did, NOSEY POSEY, if you tell Th' Brass, I won't be th' FIRST one who dies today. YOU'RE gonna be th' first one who dies, Crabs! Get this 'n' get it straight: IF you tell on me I'll damn sure KILL YOU FIRST -- WE CLEAR?"

The stronger boy had the thoroughly confused Cadet Crabtree pinned down. There was no way he could get to the communicator to tattle on his house brother. Brecken's strength was the strength of madness and the poor little worrywart was no match for a lunatic adamantly committed to taking his own life. Crabtree must helplessly yield to his master in strength and determination:

"Okay, okay, I, I was jus' tryin' t' help!

"I did, didn' mean nothin' by it, Brecks!

"Don't, don't KILL me, buddy!

"Please, please don't, don't HURT me --please?"

Crabtree was frozen stiff with a panic engendered by the lunatic fire in the eyes of the maniac holding him prisoner. The little neat-freak was actually starting to cry, off-put by such an atomic explosion of sudden, violent and unexpected -- messiness.

Corey let his terrified house brother up and said some comforting words of clarification to his terrified victim:

"Haven't you SEEN what they do t' me EVERY DAY, Crabs?" our hell-bent suicide demanded (albeit his voice was more kindly now), "Don' tell me you don't know what they've BEEN doin' t' me ever since we got t' Heeler?

"Don't you realize what it DOES to a guy t' be a total outcast?

"Cadet Brecken's only job in this life is jus' t' be IGNORED by everyone, or t' be told off for what everyone THINKS I did wrong by all of 'em EVERY gawdamn day; 'n' then TORTURED by a couple o' lowdown old PERVERTS like our slimy dragon-housemother and that scabby old Donnybrook bitch.

"What if that was YOUR life, li' l bo?

"Would you want 'o live, if that was all there was t' live for?

"What if they made sure YOUR life was just pain, pain, PAIN and more pain?

"Well, how 'bout it, house brother, would YOU want 'o live th' life I've lived?"

"Well, I, I jus' never thought about it like that," was all Crabtree could say.

"Yeah, YOU never thought about it that way 'cause YOU never HAD to think about it that way!" railed Corey, the lucid loony, "An' y' never HAD 'o think about it THAT WAY 'cause THEY never DID t' you what they did t' me, did they, WELL, DID THEY?"

"Do, don't get mad at ME, Brecks, PLEASE, just, just don't get EXCITED!" the overwhelmed Crabtree begged urgently, "Jus, just don't, don't get riled up, Corey, PLEASE don't!"

"I don' want 'o scare y' 'n' I don' want 'o hurt you, Crabs," continued his deranged captor -- more calmly because he only wanted to scare the little sis enough to insure his silence, "I don' want 'o do ANYBODY harm on this, th' last day o' my life.

"I, I'm gonna die t-day, buddy, 'n' I'm gonna die because they DROVE me 'n' DROVE 'n' DROVE me till they finally made me to realize death's th' only way out o' the living hell they're puttin' me through.

"If, if I stay alive they'll just keep right on torturing, torturing TORTURING me EVERY DAY -- and, and I can't stand it anymore.

"Listen, IF you let it be 'n' SWEAR you won't tell on me, if you swear NEVER t' tell that I drank out o' that wiggler stream to get to the eternal peace I've been wantin' for such a long, long, long time, you, you'll be okay. But ONLY if y' don't tell 'em what I did before I'm dead, get it?

"If y' shut up you'll be okay 'cause I won't do a thing to y,' Crabs; BUT, if you tell 'em while I'm still ALIVE, I WILL kill you!"

"I SWEAR it, I swear it ON MY LIFE!" sobbed the frightened Crabtree, "I'll, I'll NEVER tell 'em, Brecks!

"They'll NEVER get NOTHIN' out o' me, Corey-boy, not EVER, not, not even when you're DEAD!"

"Okay, then," Corey relaxed his grip on poor Crabtree's throat, "That's all I want, Crabs. See how easy it was?"

Corey abruptly turned his attention back to the military maneuvers and asked, "See any enemy troop movements, Crabs?"

Crabtree studied the battlefield with the major's field glasses and reported, "No,"

"Okay," instructed his mad master, "report in then. But remember I'm WATCHIN' you:

"I don' want 'o hurt you, but IF you TELL, I WILL KILL YOU!"

Crabtree did precisely as was told, and then the boys relaxed as much as their dramatic situation allowed.

The major's little exile-scouts lay down to await recall from Corey's high killing ground.

Corey enjoyed the tranquility and loveliness of the beautiful locus of his execution, drinking in the peace and quiet and the abundant profusion of glorious plant life around him. It was all so verdant and voluptuous with the awakening of a myriad of tender new shoots sprouting from every aspect of their lush surroundings.

Our Styx-bound cadet found deep delight in the impressionist play of light and shadow dancing over the ground the boys presently occupied. A gay bird song then completed this mountain masterpiece of heavenly tranquility to make our Corey's last day on earth glorious.

But, of course, the edgy Crabtree fretted uncomfortably, as all restless worrywarts must.

After a while the officer commanding the enemy army surrendered to the major, as he'd been predestined to do.

With that formality out of the way, the boys were recalled from their mountaintop advantage to rejoin the troop.

The headmaster's victorious army fell in, mustered, its squad leaders reported to their chief and their triumphant troop marched smartly back main side. Basin trumpeted on his bugle and the cadet corps sang martial airs as they went.

They rested on the way back to enjoy the treats the major had packed for his boys at home (the accursed scene of poor little Leto's capture and torture).

They marched back to the quad and were dismissed by their godlike headmaster, with his thanks.

But one of his little soldiers was starting to get terribly nervous:

"It's been a while," worried Corey, "Wonder why I'm not dead yet?"

But the old hill legend spinners had regrettably neglected to mention that death-by-wiggler-stream came only after months long devastating siege of swamp fever, protracted and ruinously debilitating periods of burning temperatures, constant diarrhea and, finally, death due to the fatally depleted victim's total dehydration.

It's doubtful that a child of Corey's youth and inexperience would have understood what all that college vocabulary stuff meant, had anyone cared enough to explain it to a little lost castaway.

The Heeler boys thundered victoriously upstairs after the war games intent on getting cleaned up after their bout in the bush.

But their dear old housemother stopped them in their tracks with a sharp and vehement Banshee wail:

"I WANT CADET COREY BRECKEN IN THAT-THERE SHOWER ROOM, ALL ALONE AND ALL NAKED AND RIGHT NOW -- NOBODY ELSE -- JUS' BRECKEN!!!

"Th' rest o' you filthy hounds kin jes WAIT on me t' finish what I'm a-gonna do t' HIM!

"Steer clear o' th' shower a-cause I want that whelp -- ALONE!"

Miss Bite wrinkled her contemptuous snout, and easily found her one boy prey.

The furious Beast got hold of and brutally assaulted the one boy she'd singled out for outrage. She shook him like a rag doll and slapped his upturned face, savagely and repeatedly.

"YOU, Brecken, th' dirtiest dog in th' WORLD! YOU, Blondie, th' filthiest cur that THINKS he's STILL pretty Missy Leto's darlin' li' l blue-eyed lover boy?

"Wall, ye AINT!

"Leto Donnybrook don' care no more 'bout YOU than she do a PISS ANT:

"Her mama done opent 'er eyes to th' fac' that SHE'S a somebody 'n' you are a NOBODY!

"Hound, she's a-way too good fir a MANGY LITTLE MONGREL WHELP th' likes o' YOU!

"YOU, you jus' HAD 'o DISOBEY yore beloved ol' HEADMASTER, didn' ye, BOY?

"YES, you jus' HAD 'o have th' EF-FRONTERY t' speak t' a high born young woman that's a-way TOO GOOD fir th' FILTHY, DIRTY likes o' YOU, didn' ye, you DIS-GUSTIN' little MONSTER, you, you delinquent li' l CRIMINAL?"

The Beast slapped him across his bruised and bleeding face again and again to force a response:

"DIDN'T YE, BOY, DIDN'T YE?"

"Y-YES, M-M-MA'AM!!!" he wailed in his pain.

In her black fury a raging two ton sow-from-hell was much too excited to wait:

The Beast roughly cuffed and stripped a tiny, vulnerable child naked with her own bloodstained claws.

Then she dragged him through the hall to the showers. And all the while the hulking leviathan continued to slap, punch and revile her tasty little tidbit as she bullied him, dazed and giddy, into her pain garden.

"I WANT THIS CRAWLIN,' SNEAKIN' INSIGNIFICANT BUG, IN THERE -- NAKED AND NOW!"

The Heeler Hall boys stood transfixed with terror. The behemoth had never been quite so virulent in her mistreatment of any other boy ere now.

"Ol' lady Bite REALLY hates Brecken," they whispered, awestruck with wonder.

"I, I'M SCARED!" gasped one.

"It IS scary!" they all agreed.

Those of his confreres who'd opted for the ease and convenience of turning against him during his endlessly lonely long gauntlet of adversity smiled knowingly, "He's REALLY in for it now!"

"Better him than me!"

But Corey's real friends, primarily McMoon, Little Milan and Curley, bemoaned his deadly plight, though fear held them dumb and paralyzed prisoners.

Only two little boys knew the truth, one sworn by the most terrible blood oath never to speak out until the other was dead:

"Go on 'n' DIE, Brecken, y' crazy bastard!" thought Crabtree (the little sorehead was angry at Brecken for having cowed him -- and even angrier at himself for having knuckled under), "You wanted it so bad, you got it, buddy!"

It had been a long time since he'd drunk the toxin he thought would kill him instantly but it hadn't done the job, and Corey was beginning to wonder, "How many more larrupin's do I have t' take before Death comes 'n' saves me?"

But suddenly there was an immediate answer:

He wasn't feeling quite himself. At this point in time the old, familiar things he'd always taken for granted were beginning to look increasingly, swimmingly, twistingly, disjointedly out of focus. What Corey saw was alarmingly strange, wobbly and multicolored in the feverish perception of his incipient delirium.

Everything was revolving, faster and faster, like a crazy merry-go-round. It was all jumping up and down. It was all jumbled up and topsy-turvy like one of the crazier rides at an interstellar fun fair.

The hallucinations he viewed now were even freakier than those he'd seen in his trial at his major's office through the visual distortions of a little boy's fear on the day his headmaster had broken his rebellious spirit.

He was shaky on his feet, he, he was, was beginning to feel -- hard to find the right word -- hard to find any word?

"Funny?"

No.

"Strange?"

No.

He was faltering, stumbling, haunted and delusional, on a pair of inexplicably wobbly pins.

He was too woozy to think now.

A hungry Beast threw her battered chew-toy into her arena of shame and turned up her hot, hot water to its highest level. The Bite watched and drooled with anticipation as the shimmering waterfall cascaded over her waiting prey's naked, shining flesh. This dread tormentor of the innocents regarded her venue of release expectantly as her beloved steam-billows rose above the scene of this child's ordeal. A morbid and insane abuser of helpless minors marshaled all her strength for what she viewed as her quarry's well deserved and delicious hour of outrageous degradation.

But Corey no longer cared what happened to him -- or anyone else now --because old lady Bite's shower torture chamber looked so strange and wonderful, so otherworldly, so resplendently beautiful in his deranged perception.

Delusional, hallucinating and carried off by the rapid onset of advancing swamp fever, this ambiance was so agreeably and intriguingly foreign, so colorfully alien to anything he'd ever experienced he floated above reality, dizzy and drunk in his feverish delight.

The heretofore dreaded steam of her grim waterfall took on a colorfully dancing glow. The brilliance of The Bite's inescapable, brightly shimmering and magically beckoning invitation into some unknown and unknowable mystery intrigued him.

The deviant's hated torture pit of exquisite agony had metamorphosed into a Technicolor movie scene for Corey's diversion:

This was a quite lovely, otherworldly lyric.

The hideous dragon's prey has begun to drift into delirium. Corey was no longer there, but in his own netherworld, a place in which he was present and absent, simultaneously.

Our doomed little hero no longer knew fear. Fear existed somewhere far away. He was uncaring at this unthinkable moment of his imminent torture, the moment when The Beast was to drown his tiny body in the stygian gloom of her titanic shadow and lift her flail to strike him HARD.

He cared not.

Corey's spirit has now left his body and his mind has divorced itself from this awful reality, for it was a reality he no longer felt.

He felt the same powerful revulsion as always at this vile Thing's nearness as she stood behind his bare, vulnerable back, like she had the night of his savage initiation to Heeler Hell. But now he no longer cared about that because reality was no longer pertinent, for he was free.

That incongruity, that dread curse on all young children, towered over him, dark and silent for that long moment she needed to watch his terror to build-

But his terror was gone.

Then a hell-born fury launched her scathing firestorm, an all-out twisted volcano of vengeance against the naked back of this more-or-less innocent -- unaccountably insouciant -- man-child.

THE SILVER STREAK does its worst.

The Beast's feared vehicle's insane lashes reverberate hard and fast against its unfeeling victim's drenched and naked form.

But THE SILVER STREAK'S worst is no longer enough.

Its reeking mistress bawls out her vilest curses at her defenseless prey, but the battery is all in vain.

Today Corey Brecken is free. Today the hot and heavy blows of her dreaded brand fell fecklessly on a happy little boy's still living, yet now unfeeling flesh.

But all this beastly psychodrama was being played out someplace far beyond Corey's conscious being. His enemy and her awful weapon did exist -- but on a distant planet -- a place where they never could hurt him.

Cadet Brecken, her intended mark, no longer occupied his former body in this world. He larks, completely impervious to the perverse old wretch's fearful fire.

His spirit has flown.

He's escaped The Tower.

A whirling, drifting, spinning, sailing, fast-flying man-child's essence has been transported to nowhere. And his nowhere is not even close to his earthly corpus. He floated, galaxies above his deviant tormentor.

Corey was nowhere close to whatever solar system where his deadly foe was busily (and futilely) plying her cruel punishment on his disconnected form.

The boy was light years away from a frustrated old pervert essaying, to no avail, to assuage her shameful blood-feast.

He clearly hears the strokes of her desperately flailing weapon noisily reverberating against his wet, bare skin. He hears a sadistic monster yowling her towering insults against his fragile ego. But her vile abuses have no effect on his disembodied spirit. The blows of this scandalous scum of the earth, this revolting gutter-scraping, no longer affect him.

None of these things exist in Corey's brand new universe.

The pleasant, euphoric Empire of Delirium, countenance no loony old bats with crazy shower room torture chambers. Such phantasms whirl crazily around and around back on earth.

But Corey's essence is spinning down and down, faster and faster into an unknowable locus, millions and trillions of light years past The Milky Way.

With the rapid advance of his disease, the rants of The Beast, the resounding of THE SILVER STREAK on the naked back of a strange little boy somewhere in another time and place are silent here.

Nor does our battered child remember yet one among the endless catalogue of excruciating tortures he'd endured on unquiet Terra's Tower Academy at present.

The only sound he detects is a faint and distant ringing. A sound like the tolling of myriad church bells in a distant world galaxies removed from Terra's troubles.

The sound comes closer and closer.

It rings persistently louder and louder until it expunges all other sounds, until those all-intrusive chimes erase all elements which used to comprise our Corey's roiling, toiling world. The fast-exiting spirit of the living entity once called Corey Brecken has left the thing he'd called "reality."

Corey is falling out of what he used to think was the real universe.

But where is he bound?

Our free-floating boy drifts placidly outward and away from what we call life.

He swims, outward bound, away from everything he has been.

He drifts into the soft, sound sleep of eternal, ephemeral final darkness.

He is drifting down The River Styx toward the final moments of a castaway exile's life. Shame on his elders-and-betters for making his a life of shame, blame and pain, a life which has brought him here to seek the peace of endless repose.

Corey Brecken spins down, out and away into something he did not, could not ever have dreamed.

Now he stands before the terrible gates of The Grand Mystery, an enigma which must remain forever closed to any living creature.

Little Corey Brecken has stepped through the portal of nonbeing to behold the awe-inspiring Gateway To Eternity. His esoteric being beholds a gigantic, shining portal, a frightening thing no living human has ever passed through and returned to live again.

He is grateful. And, if he had been able to gather a single thought together or verbalize a single phrase it would have been:

"Thank you for letting me go!

"I, I know I've been -- done bad, bad things. Please, please forgive me-"

But all his bygone cognitive skills, his powers to think or speak are gone now. He doesn't need them. The core of his being has taken wing to speed onward into the oblivion which he so desperately sought.

The gates swing open and he passes through into eternity.

Corey's universe becomes dark, darker still until it resolves itself into an unfathomable pitch black void.

Our boy's soul has entered into its place of departure, a foreign yet strangely familiar place where the future does not exist.

This peaceful realm skims rapidly past the swirling confusion of what's passed before, and he hears a whisper of welcome into his new mystery, his new home.

There is no Tower Military Academy now.

There is no metallic-robotic, tattletale scold. There is no insulting burlesque of what once was the most exciting and gentle creature ever to welcome him to her arms and body. The Donnybrook party-line mechanical doll is gone. The witch's contrivance has long ago ticked-tock-ticked itself into nonbeing.

There are no more betters and elders to judge and exile him to a world of cruel disgraces and exquisite tortures. Their time had long since passed. There are no heartless abusers to punish him, not here.

All of these were but turbulent nightmares he'd dreamt in the long dead past, nightmares long forgotten in this newly tranquil state.

Here there are no fickle patrons, no inconstant lovers, no one to raise a boy's expectations to the highest palaces of heaven, then dash him into the dark oblivion of hell.

How intoxicatingly beautiful it had been for him when he'd basked in the sunshine of their furtive love. And how bitter was his heartbreak in losing the consolation of the earthly paradise they'd woven so skillfully with charming promises and dreamy deceptions. How excruciating was his pain when they'd abandoned a boy who'd loved them unreservedly.

Here bad dreams have no hold on his freed spirit.

Here these things no longer exist, ergo they cannot spark his now absent lustful hopes for earthly fulfillment, nor can they break his poor, lonely, loving heart.

Nevermore shall the Donnybrooks' passing fancies, vainglorious illusions of this passing world, bait his senses with the accursed illusion of their profane love.

In his nowhere world life's perplexing contradictions just don't exist. They do not enter the strange new realm stretching out before him.

Lost in wonderment, he crosses over the storied River Styx and into the heart of the living cosmos's Grand Mystery. Here there is only the soft, gentle, welcoming darkness. Nothing else exists, only the comfort of a silent void, a boundless ocean of eternal peace.

"I've escaped The Tower!" his grateful spirit soars.

Our little boy is transported. It is not a new plane of awareness, but a state of blissful non-awareness.

He is free to fly fleetly back, back, back through the memories of the heretofore forgotten and half-forgotten events in his past life, those flashbacks which precede the death of the living organism:

He is swinging in the front porch swan-glide of his infancy at his grandsire's spacious home in Kingwood in West Virginia. Baby Corey is singing joyfully on Old Grandpa Joe's rangy hunting preserve in the beautiful hills of his native home, forgotten till now.

Now he's merrily sledding down the snowbound hills of his toddler days.

Now he's building snowmen and igloos in the winter.

Now?

"Oh, heaven!" he comes, ever so gently, ever so lovingly to his beloved Queen Leto to possess her gracious, generously given love reward.

Now our two randy scamps glory in the fastness of their sunlit hiding place of forbidden love. Now our two ecstatic golden kids frolic anew in their hot woodlot oasis outside The Icebound Tower. They race together to experience the indescribable joy which calls them to experience love's enchantment. Deep in the black heartlessness of The Tower's nuclear winter our young lovers know the bliss of their Never Land as they race to love's all-compelling crescendo. Its pyrotechnic grandeur drives them into, through and past the fulfillment of nature's perfection. Their intoxication drives them directly into the ineffable ecstasy of their personal Elysium.

Now our lovers are propelled by Eros's commanding lightning bolt into one ecstatic entity in the now so far away, now too long ago dream of rapturous afternoons lost to envy and power.

Now, and finally, his high-flying, Cosmos-swimming spirit is gratefully released from its sorely beaten body's extreme trial in its direst hour of woe in The Beast's shower, dedicated to that perverse old monster's most excessive tortures and foulest perversions.

Now his spirit soars free of the locus of his mortal body's withering degradation. Corey is free of his countless demeaning humiliations.

Miss Bite's unfelt thrashing of his mortal shell which had once been Brecken is noisily proceeding somewhere back in the now eons distant Milky Way.

These dark deeds are no longer even memories to him now.

Corey's essence does not feel it, nor will he feel it more. No, this little cadet shall remain absent and unaccounted for in that lost and damned world of The Tower Military Academy, a place now blessedly remote from the true Corey.

What has freed our boy-slave from his earthly chains?

Now, at last, a more-or-less innocent little man-child swims outward and upward. Reaching heavenward he begs his kind Maker's forgiveness for his taboo-violating, iconoclastic (but fun) sex sins. And our liberated bad boy begs his heavenly Master's forgiveness for his long standing, prideful (but fun) practice of bullying his weaker schoolfellows.

And our free-floating little soul's benevolent Savior finds him to deliver him from eternal darkness. He is spared the everlasting torment of final exile into the outer darkness of endless renunciation.

At last Corey Brecken's epic journey is at an end and our guileless innocent has been so judged by his Eternal Judge. Thankfully The Only Judge fit to judge has bathed our ten year old sinner of sin.

What were a little boy's naughty pranks compared to the nightmarish cruelties visited upon this boy by grim, unprincipled adult judges?

Our towhead hero has found endless comfort in the assurance of the Eternal welcome which awaits him here in the sheltering arms of One whose constant and forgiving Nature has accepted our youthful more-or-less innocent into a Heart Whose Blood was shed to deliver him from his own childish errors.

It is our little outcast's bliss that he's found divine acceptance after the selfish and calculating mortal loves he has known in his short life have toyed with him, rejected him and punished him for the very qualities they'd found endearing in him. They'd had their fun with an open and trusting boy they viewed as a mere toy, a cute little pet, a chattel to be played with and cast aside when convenient.

He is flesh no more, ergo the hurtful memories of his hungry users, the guileful means they'd employed to enjoy and discard him are eradicated. His pricking thorns of the flesh are now replaced by the peace and happiness of his eternal repose.

The one gift he's yearned for and never had is at last his:

He is free.

AN AWAKENING

Records log, Tower Military Academy Medical
Infirmary:
1May, 1949 @ 1601hrs.
10 yr old white male emergency pt. admitted:
condition, critical.
Temp. 105, P. 180 Resp., 102,
BP 60/40
Objective symptoms:

Pt. comatose @ unresponsive to light, sound.
Pulse rapid @ resp. shallow; c dangerously elevated temp.
Abrasions and contusions to upper arms and scalp.
Ecchymosis general and pronounced to trapezii,
infraspinati, deltoids, latissimus dorsi, glutei
maximi, adductores maximi, biceps femoris and
semimembranosi

Pt. suspect battery victim.
Call doctor notified @ en route.

But Corey knew nothing of such things, for he was then blissfully
absent from this world. At present his newfound universe was
light years inside an all encompassing womb of sightless, soundless
nothingness.

But our half-pint hero's strong, young and decidedly stubborn young body had been even more determined to live than his troubled mind and spirit had been to die.

Whatever the outcome of that struggle, Cadet Brecken was presently in a state of suspended animation, his essence hurtling earthward in precipitous freefall down to his interior cosmos of the uncharted world of impenetrable darkness. Uninterrupted by a single sight or sound, the placid quietude of a soul already at peace and lost to this unquiet world of envy and strife was undisturbed.

But, with the passage of time, The Tower infirmary's comatose little critical case was amazed to be able to hear distant, disembodied sounds.

Some time later Corey began to feel the almost imperceptible touches of the eerie and forgotten outer world.

Once, he knew not when, he beheld a frightfully disconcerting incongruity:

A distant sliver of light had invaded the dark quietude of his lovely new non-existence. The unsettling and distant beam grew and shone forth brightly somewhere out there in his placid black night -- and that bothered him.

Gradually, the light became ever brighter and closer till the invasive phenomenon seemed to have settled in precisely the same space where he rested.

When his eyes began to focus he discovered he and the light had actually become companion occupants of his room -- wherever that room might be. And, watching over him in this unearthly place, it seemed there was -- and then there actually was -- a glowing, celestial figure solely comprised of white light.

It was his impression this enchanted entity displayed the primary characteristics of some sort of caretaker. He saw a guardian angel observing him, accessing his condition and even protecting him from any future harm. He concluded this bright being must be an angel of light dispatched from on high to this unlikely place to care for him.

"But, but you, you're an ANGEL!" he spoke to his celestial inhabitant of some inexplicable world of eternal light -- and his words were a child's words of wonder, reverence and love, "But they, they all told me I was headed the, the other way–"

"Coming back to us at last are you, young man?" his guardian angel smiled, calmly -- and professionally, "Well, you're a healthy little specimen and those brand new antibiotic wonder drugs we developed during The War seem to have done wonders for you.

"I can assure you I am no angel:

"I am a nurse employed at your military academy's medical infirmary; and you are my patient, Cadet Brecken.

"Yours has been a very difficult case indeed, my fine young fellow. You've frightened the life out of all of us. You've been completely unconscious and in a coma ever since you came to us two weeks ago. You have been running dangerously elevated temperatures, AND you've remained comatose and critical all that time."

He wasn't dead.

This wasn't heaven.

He's still trapped in the same hard, cruel world from which he'd attempted to escape -- even feet first.

But God had overruled His headstrong little creature to decree that he should stay. No one argues with his Creator, and Cadet Brecken must resign himself to the difficult fact of his rude awakening. The difficult reality that the school was assuredly set to inflict even more punishment against his poor, sore little bones was inescapable.

Further, in such a dangerous place as this, he must be strictly on his guard.

"Now, Cadet Brecken, this is a serious inquiry," his nurse leant forward, intent on to putting him to the question, "When you were unconscious you cried out for a 'Leto.'

"Did you mean Major Donnybrook's daughter, Leto?"

He could not, would not answer.

"At another point in your delirium you cried out to your headmaster for forgiveness. What made you say such a thing? And what did you mean just now when you just said 'they all' said you were headed 'the other way?' What were 'they all' talking about? Was it hell; and who, specifically, are 'they, 'ung man?"

"Watch out, she's no angel, she's a grownup -- THEY can NEVER be trusted!" his brain flashed, panic-stricken, "You can't tell HER what really happened!"

But protocol demanded that he reply, respectfully, quickly, quietly and politely.

"Oh, uh, did, did I say that, ma'am?" our dissembling Leto's apt love pupil lied with poise in the perfect disguise of childlike innocence, "I, I guess I must've, if YOU say so, ma'am, but, but, it's jus' like y' said:

"I, I've been so sick for so long -- I, I guess I was probably out o' my head with th' fever -- 'cause, 'cause I don' know what all that stuff means myself."

She rose abruptly, suddenly aloof and frighteningly severe:

"He's hiding something," she'd concluded, "He's just another junior school cadet!

"Those, those poor little ninnies come to us beat to a pulp, and immediately commence covering up for those criminally abusive housemothers -- and that brute of a headmaster -- at the foot of the hill. Why, the minute I asked this one the first question he just clammed right up!

"I can see I'm not going to get any evidence against those monsters out of HIM."

He was just another in a long, long line of maddeningly close-mouthed beaten and abused junior school cadets.

"Very well," she said coldly, "Cadet Brecken, we've fed you intravenously, then we had to spoon-feed you.

"We've been giving you sponge baths for two long weeks now.

"Do you think that you can at last manage to take a shower if I walk you there and wash your back?"

"Yes, ma'am," he wanted to appear co-operative to placate this terrifying adult, "I, I'll do my best for you, ma'am."

"MISS, not ma'am" she curtly corrected him, "I am MISS Charity.

"Yes, miss," he fell in line, "I'll do my very best for YOU, miss."

Not only did they try, they succeeded! Even better, it was the first shower in his remembrance that didn't include a blistering, courtesy of THE SILVER STREAK.

Life at the infirmary was easier than main side existence had been;

The radio played. "Baby Snooks" and "Bergen and McCarthy" joked and Frankie Lane sang "Cool, clear water" and "Mule train" for the boys' amusement.

Corey was placed with two roommates in his infirmary dorm. He'd never met either main side but they were both from the junior school cadet corps.

They didn't seem to know of his involvement with their commander's best beloved, and never did they speak of the golden brats' long, hard fall.

Ergo, they weren't afraid to talk.

They immediately advised him to do and not to do what he'd already done and not done:

"NEVER talk to the grownups here on th' top o' th' hill about anything that's goin' on we all came from," they warned with great urgency, "The doctors 'n' nurses 're tryin' t' get th' goods on th' major 'n' our cheesy ol' housemothers.

"Well, they can BURN all those ol' witches -- but never our major!"

His new roomies were hot to trot right out of the infirmary and get back to main side routine, for the food up here exuded from the senior school's unforgivably inept kitchen. The grub here wasn't one iota better then than it was during our unfortunate Cadet Brecken's cold and lonely Yule. Anxious to escape the awful senior school food, Corey's new buddies affected the habit of cooling their thermometers in their ice water glasses. They yearned to create a false illusion of wellness to get back down the hill. Only through their deception might the schemers escape the infirmary early.

Corey had his own ideas on fever. He carefully set his thermometer close to the radiator to create his own illusion of lingering illness.

He was trying to stay as far from the twin perverts he knew must be waiting with fetid breath to punish him on his return to them. Better bad food than those two hell-born furies' flaming scourges.

Our inquisitive nurse was no time waster. She was quick to roll out the heavy artillery and aim it directly between a frightened child's eyes. Ergo, an inquisitive nurse was replaced by a doctor-inquisitor.

"Well, now, son," a pleasant-faced medico smiled soothingly, "your nurse seems to think things mightn't be going along as smoothly as they should main side. Cadet Brecken, were you in some sort of trouble there?"

"Well, I, I was in, in a little trouble, sir," Cory admitted grudgingly, "But, but they, they all said it was all MY fault!"

"YOUR fault, cadet?" the man exclaimed in amazement, "The fault of a ten year old boy?

"Your entire existence is planned out and set in motion for you by those adult officers, teachers and housemothers in command of your situation. It's not even remotely possible for anything -- let alone everything -- to be all YOUR fault, little man.

"Now, who in the world was so ridiculous as to tell you such a monstrously cruel lie as that?

"I demand to know who said it, Corey!"

"Everyone, sir."

"Grownups as well, cadet?"

"Yes, sir."

"Exactly what did they say was all YOUR fault, son?"

"I, I cannot -- MUST not -- say more, sir," the boy gasped, desperately frightened, "I, I mean no insubordination, sir, but I, I've al, already said too much. I am unable to say more -- sir."

"You must," the man pursued him, "I insist!"

"I, I must say no more," the boy fled, "I must not sully the honor of, of one my heart holds most dear in all th' world."

"A girl, do you mean?" the man pursued.

"Sir, I, I've said too much," a fearfully upset boy implored, "I must not say more.

"I, I beg you, please, please to let me alone, doctor!"

"It's a girl alright," the kindly old doc concluded, "The cockamamie rumors from down the hill seem to have some validity.

"Well, well, those two kids must've been phenomenally precocious! Theirs is a case history that has the makings of an intriguing seminar on early sexual awakenings -- or a case history in the JAMA.

"But this poor little soul's done in and I must allow him to rest and recover."

The man helped the boy back to bed.

"Now, you listen to me, son," the physician concluded, "You are only a little boy. If the adult officers and housemothers erroneously put in charge of your wellbeing told you that everything is all your fault, they are liars -- blatant liars. And those so called adults should be ashamed of themselves for foisting the blame for their shortcomings and failures in guidance off on the shoulders of one poor, sick little boy."

"Th-thank you, sir!"

Corey had never viewed his lamentable situation in such a salutary light (never having been allowed). He was so grateful for such a welcome grain of sanity at this belated hour:

"Thank you, doctor!" said he, "But please, please don't ask me any more about what happened main side. It, it was far too shameful."

"All right, son," the man had observed the boy was exhausted and in a state of emotional upheaval bordering on shock.

He desperately needed rest, and the man let him.

Corey continued his thermometer-to-radiator trick until the nurses caught and scolded him. Those angels of mercy then watched him more closely, discovered his fever had abated and made the obvious determination that he was then fit for duty.

Even heroes get scared. That day our half-pint model was petrified.

He was on his way back the bloodthirsty Beast, Heeler Hell and a commandant oblivious to all his pain and tears, except that the major now welcomed them.

Haunted by his own hungry, howling demons of foreboding, Corey marched manfully downhill to face a cruel destiny.

"All right, Brecken," was all the dragon said when he reported in (and she spoke calmly and without rancor to his bewilderment).

"What?" he'd puzzled inwardly.

She'd neither cursed him nor run him into the shower to misuse and disgrace him.

In his room a joyful band of his house brothers rallied round their past and present hero. His friends were at last at liberty to converse congenially with him.

"Guess what, Brecks?" enthused the breathless, always frightened, McMoon, "Th' major took THE SILVER STREAK away from th' dragon!

"NOW th' ol' bat aint even allowed t' whip us AT ALL!"

"That big, fat slob's just damn well lucky th' ol' man let 'er keep 'er job!" rejoiced Little Milan.

"There was a big-stink inquiry," put in Curley, "Th' Bite is NEVER gonna be allowed t' parade us in t' that shower o' hers t' SKIN us no more!"

"It was all YOU, my big, strong HERO!" purred McNichol throatily, Corey's friend-aspiring-to-be-lover once more.

"What happened 'when I blacked out after th' war games, you guys?" Corey queried.

" Well," McNichol began.

"Shut up, sissy!" barked the teddy hugger. Curley took up the narrative.

Here's a synopsis of his tale:

The Beast had beaten and screamed at her unfeeling captive chew-toy until she'd finally realized he was unconscious.

Then she'd panicked.

Puzzled and infuriate, The Bite had demanded to know why her victim had fainted, "What th' hail's wrong with this sneakin,' philanderin' li' l' mongrel?

"Lissen at THIS, ye crawlin' curs:

"Speak up rat NOW or I'm a-gonna run ever' ONE o' you in here an' BASTE ye good until SOMEBODY own up!"

But only Crabtree knew. And, believing Corey was dead, the worrywart felt released from his oath never to reveal. He spoke up at once to save his own skin.

"Don't whip us, Miss Bite!" begged Heeler Hell's resident coward, "It, it was ALL Brecken's fault, ma'am:

"He, he MADE me swear not t' tell ANYONE he drank bad water out o' a dirty ol' wiggler hole up there on top o' th' whole world up there.

"Jus' us two knew, 'cause we were th' only ones sent t' scout:

"He, he said he wanted t' DIE so bad he was gonna KILL me if I told on him before he was dead.

"Well, well, he's dead now, 'n' I can tell!"

Mortally frightened, The Bite had called an ambulance.

The drivers had arrived, collected what was left of a feverish and demented Corey Brecken and rushed The Beast's comatose little tidbit off to be treated.

The major had discovered what happened and changed his mind about his precious little Mac, again: The commandant came down HARD on his harrowed ex-protégé's malicious tormentors (both at home and Heeler Hell). He'd taken The Bite's STREAK away from her, and he'd forbidden her to administer corporal discipline to any cadet until further notice. Further proscribing The Deepfreeze from torturing Cadet Brecken ever again.

From that day the newly hobbled housemothers had to send only their most refractory cases to the headmaster's office for correction. And their awful weapons of abuse were confiscated without exception.

Instigated by the infirmary staff, the headmaster and the founders had launched their own investigation,

The Brass had been put under terrific pressure to talk and talk fast, and none of those sadistic sycophants had come up smelling the least bit rosy.

"It's heaven around here now, compared t' the way it WAS," sighed Curley, "Y' know, brother, McNichol's right about this one -- for a CHANGE: You ARE our big, strong HERO, and it IS all on account o' you!"

"WOW!" wondered Corey, "I, I've finally done somethin' right with my life!"

But suddenly a residual force of evil interrupted the boys' celebration.

"Cadet Brecken," roared the dragon, "yore beloved commander wants t' see ye in 'is office -- ON TH' DOUBLE, BOY!"

Our ecstatic ex-protégé flew down the straight and narrow path to McAdam to report in to his sponsor turned executioner.

"Well, Mac, welcome back!" a little boy's ex-hero shook his hand, "I regret to say that things can never be as they were before your, your indiscretion."

"No, sir," a protégé in disgrace sighed sadly, "I, I understand how it must be, major."

"I cannot forgive either one of you two scatterbrains the crazy things you did," the beat-up kid's ex-model continued, "You can never sit with us at table, son, although I doubt that you'd want to presently: Leto's up north attending a strict parochial school there these days."

Their dour tribal elder had punished his far too young iconoclasts again.

He'd exiled the brightest light in their lives, the beauty Daddy and Mac still loved. Perhaps the great man might deceive himself with the fiction that his love was dead, but Corey was not so foolish. Mac knew from the beginning his love for his frisky little heroine should be eternal.

"But now I realize you couldn't have been exclusively responsible for that, that scandalously forbidden affair," sighed the sorrowful man, "You, you thoughtless kids both had your fun, her mother found out and, and then it was up to me to make you pay for it.

"The law is the law. And when you break the law, son, you must suffer. I am here to teach you (and Leto) obedience. And you found obedience is one of life's cardinal lessons.

"But, due to her own beastly excesses, your two-ton housemother is no longer at liberty to punish ANY cadet. I have given specific orders to that effect and, if she disobeys that order, I want to be informed of it immediately, cadet.

"Get it?"

"GOT IT, SIR!!!"

"She got away with her over the top rough stuff once, Mac; but, if and when I find out she's up to her old shenanigans, I will fire from this academy so fast the wig 'll fly off her head."

Man and boy grinned at the picture of so pleasant a prospect.

"But there's an even more important, and regrettably serious, reason I've called for you, Mac:

"I am very sorry to say that your grandfather has passed on, son.

"You will be rejoining your grandmother in Miami when the current semester ends here to carry on in civilian life."

"But we live in Palm Beach, sir," piped a confused cadet.

"Well, Mac, at present your grandmother is visiting with the Burners, in Miami," the headmaster corrected him, "The widow must require the comfort and companionship of her close friends to get her through this time of grief."

The Burners as gra' ma's close friends?

That didn't sound right.

Arrogant and aristocratic, Corey's grandmamma never regarded Harold and Pegeen as anything but lackeys.

Corey'd always surmised that the Palm Beachers in the old girl's bridge club were her closest friends.

"I will personally escort you to the airport when the time comes. You'll fly home and debark a couple of hours later at Miami International Airport. It'll be a breeze, Mac.

"At Miami International you will be greeted by the Burners and reunited with your grandma forthwith.

"She called me yesterday and we made the arrangements.

"I'm sorry about your granddad, Mac.

"That will be all, cadet. You are dismissed."

"YES, SIR!!!"

They shook hands and saluted.

Miss Bite had a letter for Corey as soon as he got back.

He took it directly to his room to read.

It was from Gra'ma:

"April 26, 1949

"My dear Bill,

"Grandpa Joe finally died last week, kiddo. The old fool's been hanging on and piling up debts to those money grubbing doctors and insatiable hospitals of his for I don't know how long."

"That's my sentimental Gra' ma alright!" smiled he.

She continued, "Well, he's kicked the bucket now; but he's gone and left everything we have left in the world in trust to that incredible numbskull, that slob, that idiot's idea of an idiot, Harold Burner, halfwit accountant.

350

"I protested, of course, but the judge said that I hadn't enough business experience to administer the estate myself.

"Can you beat that? I could never have imagined such gall out of that crooked courthouse gang hiding out across the bridge in West Palm!

"Do you remember how your grandpa always said that he could trust Harold with our money because he was too dumb to steal? That was a good joke maybe, but I never thought he was serious, and I still don't buy it:

"We have five properties scattered over Palm Beach and West Palm, but I've yet to see an accounting of the rents collected, and nor do I have an inkling where all that money's been deposited.

"Harold hasn't presented one accounting since Joe's death.

"Too dumb to steal, my foot! Why, back in Steubenville the law caught Harold and his no account old man stealing the trees and shrubs from the city parks. They sold them to the customers at his dad's two-bit landscape firm, and both bums cooled their heels in jail until they could scrape up the dough to buy their way out of trouble.

"Joe said he thought the experience taught Harold a lesson. But I know good and well Harold Burner's way too thick to learn a lesson about anything.

"I know he's stealing from us.

"Too bad Joe's dead. Harold was always terrified of him and now he's not here to scare the living hell out of the big lummox the way he did when he was alive -- even when your poor granddad was so sick, Bill.

"I've engaged Dim Nemetz to act as my attorney. He's got to make my suspicions known to the court and demand a strict accounting from that light-fingered accountant. Then we'll find out Harold's been up to no good all along. We'll drag him through court by the ears and I'll be appointed trustee -- as I should have been from the start.

"They've got me down here in Miami now. Our place up on Seabreeze and all the properties we own are going to have to stay rented out for a long time to pay off grandpa's debts, dear boy.

"I made Harold rent me my own little efficiency apartment. You'll like it. It's down on the Bay.

351

"You know me, Bill, I'd never live under the same roof with those two sneaks, not on a bet.

"But I can't afford your military school anymore, due to our own indebtedness and Harold's embezzling, so I'll be seeing you soon, kiddo.

"Love,

"Grandma."

Corey was escaping from Heeler Hell, both with ease and celerity.

But he could never guess what his life back home might presently be. He knew life was no longer to be so easy as it had formerly been. Nonetheless, he knew of no way a ten year old could extricate his family from this distressing pass.

Life at the academy was easier than it had ever been. Under the new order the days and weeks went dancing and skipping fleetly by for him and his carefree pals until his time of departure's arrival.

He said goodbye to his muzzled housemother and newly emancipated companions, boys who should be grateful to him because his highly intensified tortures had put an end to theirs.

A smiling Major Donnybrook helped his old buddy, Mac, downstairs and into the car with his baggage.

The man drove the boy across the Tennessee-North Carolina border and into the great big airport circus awaiting them there. Our intrigued boy's bustling, jostling place of departure delighted him with all of its cosmopolitan sights, sounds, odors and colors. It was just like being lost in the hubbub of a big city to him.

"Goodbye, my protégé, and lots of luck back home," beamed his old patron, dropping his stiff-necked commandant act and hugging his beloved little golden brat foster son close to his heart, "And, just for the record, Mac, I do forgive you two naughty little clowns.

"You were just a couple of good kids looking for a little bit of forbidden fun and it nearly got y' killed; but what did you know? Kids are always trying to sneak one over on the grownups; but sex makes life a little too serious for kids to handle.

"I'm going to bring my difficult little darling back home just as soon as I can make it look respectable to the board."

"Thanks, Daddy!" Corey enthused.

"He has forgiven us!" a half-pint hero rejoiced mentally, "Now I guess we'll have to work on forgiving him, too."

"I mean it when I wish you good luck, son," cautioned his nibs, "From what your grandma said of your situation it looks like you're really going to need it."

"YES, SIR!!!" piped his pet cadet, "I know it's not gonna be easy, major, but m' gra' ma 'n' me'll muddle through somehow."

"I know you will, Mac," concurred his rediscovered foster dad, "You've got more guts than most of the grown men I knew in The War.

"Leto will be sad never to see you again, kid, but all our prayers go with you."

"Thank you, SIR!!!"

Our two military school toy soldiers went into their saluting/handshaking routine for the last time.

Corey ascended the ramp to board the plane.

From his seat he waved goodbye to his beloved if flip-flop commandant foster dad.

On board the captain and his stewardesses issued their preflight instructions, the aircraft taxied and went aloft, the terrain's constituents below our little passenger of the air shrank miraculously into lesser and lesser unfamiliar shapes.

And our half-pint hero was on his way home.

Corey reflected as he dozed in his comfortable seat upon his rocky Tower adventure, A lot has happened to our boy in one short year (a sojourn which had seemed to last forever in its times of savagery, and a year he had barely survived).

He began his Tower adventure a friendless waif, an exile at the mercy of coldhearted superiors disinclined toward mercy.

Then he'd been rescued from such vultures and found favor in the loving and sheltering arms of The Tower's elite.

He'd experienced the wonder of knowing the headmaster's breathtaking Leto's love and giving his own true to her. He'd made a beautiful young woman happy and found his ultimate joy in the solace of her arms.

But the kids had ravenous enemies who'd cheerfully consigned them to a long, long fall into defeat and disfavor. The cruelty of those unforgiving conspirators had all but destroyed them and only their youthful resilience had spared their somewhat innocent lives.

He'd been ostracized, exposed to the fangs and claws of the ravenous monsters who finally drove him to suicide.

In making that awful sacrifice he'd finally become a true hero, the one boy whose grim commitment had saved his brothers from the evil that would surely have devoured them whole as it had him.

That was a lot of living for a ten year old -- going on eleven.

Oh well, today he was healthy once more, alive and on his way home -- but what and where was that home to be?

Printed in the United States
By Bookmasters